ONE DEADLY NIGHT

A British Murder Mystery

THE WILD FENS MURDER MYSTERY SERIES

JACK CARTWRIGHT

CHESTNUT PRESS

ONE DEADLY NIGHT

JACK CARTWRIGHT

PROLOGUE

The cool evening breeze stirred a carpet of pimples across her bare shoulders and a glaze of tears in her unblinking eyes. The fire burned there briefly, then it vanished in a blink. She pulled her sweater around her, clutching it with her arms crossed over her chest as she made her way towards the little bonfire and sat down amongst the only people in this world she could call friends.

Beyond the field, Horncastle twinkled in the late summer night. In a few hours, the darkness would shroud the entire town, but for the time being at least, the west-facing rooftops shone with the dying, distant sun, like seedlings craning towards the light.

Years before, they had called a little den in the forest not far from the field their own. But with their adolescence came the desire for space, for freedom, and the field, being just a half mile from town, offered just that.

It was Pete who spoke first, while Jake and Tony listened from where they lay in the grass.

"You okay?" he asked, to which she had no reply. None that would make sense anyway. It was all she could do to meet his gaze, smile weakly, and then look away into the fire, that endless source of distraction.

"Rosie?" he said softly, as he slid a friendly arm around her. "Rosie, talk to me. What's happened?"

Tony and Jake both looked up from their stupors, intrigued by his concerned tone.

She said nothing again and felt nothing but the numbness of a hatred so pure she questioned her own sanity from the scenarios her imagination conjured.

A log in the fire cracked and popped. She stared at it, feeling the heat of the flames on her face.

"The wood's wet," she said, then met his stare.

"It's been raining," he replied. "Of course it's wet."

"Michael says you shouldn't burn wet wood."

"Well, he's an idiot, then," Pete said, removing his arm from her waist. "All the wood is wet. It rained last night."

She stretched her legs out from beneath her, then flexed her feet against the flames.

"I have something to tell you," she said, changing the subject and gesturing for Jake to pass the bottle of beer he was sipping. She took a long swig and then handed it back, wiping her mouth with the back of her hand.

"Have you finally signed up to that Russian brides website?" Tony asked, laying his head back on the dewy grass and smiling at his own joke.

"That's not even funny," she replied. "You do realise there are people suffering from that kind of thing every day?"

"Yeah, the men they marry," he replied, to which only he laughed.

"Shut up, Tony," Pete said, and he lobbed his cigarette butt at him, causing a sudden disturbance in the vibe. The cigarette whizzed past Tony's face like a rogue firework and he glared at Pete.

"You bloody idiot. You could have burned my eye out," he

said, getting to his knees to pat out the embers. But Pete ignored him and focused on Rosie.

"I'm leaving," she said, and those three faces she adored saddened.

"Where are you going to go?" Pete said, always the first to voice his opinion.

"I don't know. London maybe. I have a cousin down there in Essex."

"What happened?" he asked. "Is it your mum?"

"No," she said, avoiding his concerned stare, finding solace in the mesmerising coals.

She knew the field like she knew her mother's house. She could find her way around it with her eyes closed. Under that tree, with the little forest behind them and the views out to the Wolds before them, she might as well have been at home. The tree had been a hideout, a camp, and a den when they had been young. It had been a refuge, and place to smoke their first cigarettes when they hit their teens. And it had been the place where, on separate occasions, she had shared intimate moments with all three of them, not through lust or desire, but adolescent curiosity. They were equals, the three of them. Best friends.

"It's him, isn't it?" Tony said, and the breeze that had raised tears in her eyes lulled. "It's Michael. I bloody know it is."

"Tony—"

"Right," Pete said. "I'm not having this."

"Pete, no—"

But it was too late. He was the largest of the three boys, across his shoulders and in height. He jumped to his feet, snatching his bottle of stolen beer from the grass.

"Where is he?"

"Pete, just leave it, will you?" she said.

But Jake and Tony were also standing now, and the three of them in the firelight, the three boys she had grown up beside, were now men.

"It's Friday night," Tony said. "He'll be in the boozer."

"Boys, don't," Rosie pleaded. "I'll deal with it. I'll tell my mum. I just need some time—"

"And then what?" Tony said. "He'll knock her about again when you're gone?"

"Don't say that."

"That bloke needs a good hiding," Tony said.

"And I suppose you're the one to give him it, are you?" she said, and in the firelight, his face hardened. "This isn't about you, Tony."

He stared back at her, his throat rising and falling as he swallowed.

"I know," he said finally. "But I still think he needs a lesson in manners."

"I say we walk in there and tell the entire pub what he's done," Jake said quietly, and a disgusted sneer spread across his pimpled face. "Tell everyone how he can't keep his hands to himself. We wouldn't even have to touch him. The older lot would do it for us—"

"You can't—"

"No," Pete said, silencing them all. "No, we take care of this ourselves. There's three of us."

"Pete, don't be stupid. He's a grown man—"

"And what? We're not?"

"No," she said, scrambling her feet. "No, you're not. We're bloody kids, Pete. We haven't even finished school."

"I have," Tony said.

"Only because there aren't any left that will have you," Jake said, but whatever amusement the comment had stirred faded as fast as it had come.

"You'd do it for me, wouldn't you?" Pete said to her. "If you could help me, you would, wouldn't you?"

"Of course," she replied softly. "But you can't help me here. It's something I have to deal with alone."

"No, you don't," he said. "He needs a lesson or two. I couldn't care less if he beats the crap out of me. If anybody asks, I'll tell them why he did it."

Rosie dropped to her knees, covering her face with her hands, and Pete crouched beside her, placing his hand on her shoulder.

"Please don't," she cried. "Please–"

But even she heard the weakness in her plight. The truth was that she would like nothing more than for her best friends to help her.

"Come on," Pete said, standing and ushering Jake and Tony towards the trees. "You don't have to be a part of it, Rosie. Wait here. We'll be back."

"What are you going to do?" she asked, and Pete stopped walking. He gave the other two a cursory glance, as if still conceiving a plan, then looked back at her, as defiant as ever she had seen.

"We'll wait for him to leave the pub," he said. "He'll walk home like he always does on a Friday and he'll cut through the nature reserve. We'll get him there, at the bridge or in the forest or something."

"And do what, exactly?" she asked.

"What did he do to you?"

She looked away again, unable to say the words.

"That's what I thought," Pete said. "When we're done with him, he won't be able to do it again, even if he wants to."

He waited a moment for the magnitude of what he had planned to sink in for all those present. Then, in a huff, he pushed through into the copse with Jake and Tony in his wake.

She fell back, breathless from the tension, and pictured the scene followed by the aftermath, the unknown. The fire popped again, another mini explosion as a damp log released an air pocket in a tiny shower of sparks.

"Wait," she called out, and their footsteps halted for a moment. She burst into the trees after them and found them in single file with Pete leading and Jake bringing up the rear. Their postures made it clear the delay was temporary and their decisions irreversible.

"It's time he learned to keep his hands to himself," Pete said. "You're not talking us out of this, Rosie."

"I know," she said gently, then resigned herself to what was to be. "I know, but if you're going to do this, then I'm coming with you. I want to see him hurting."

CHAPTER ONE

In the space of nearly a year, since Freya Bloom had left her cheating husband and his son in London to start a new life in rural Lincolnshire, she had lived in her motorhome and in a small farmworker's cottage on a friend's farm.

But now, as she hung the last of her few furnishings in the downstairs cloakroom – a framed, vintage advertisement for Bovril – she finally had a place she could call home. She adjusted the bottom until it was straight, then let it go to stand back and admire it, only to watch it gradually skew to one side as if it had a mind of its own.

She adjusted it again, happy it was dead centre on the wall and plumb.

Then, it slowly tilted of its own accord.

"Que sera," she muttered and collected her drink from where she had left it on the window ledge. She raised her coffee cup to the advertisement, remembering who had given it to her and the story behind the cracked glass with fondness. Then she drank.

The farmworker's cottage had come furnished, of sorts. To a single man in the early nineteen hundreds, the lonesome armchair and lumpy mattress would have seemed exquisite, and Freya had been grateful for them. Even the old dining table, which had weighed as much as an old oak and was probably just as ancient, had been instrumental in her easing into rural life.

But now, with a place of her own, it was time to go shopping. There would be no tattered, old armchairs, no lumps in her mattress, and the dining table would be a thing of beauty – the centrepiece of her world.

She had considered writing a list of all the things she would need, but a list of those things she already owned would have been far more concise. Still, the sparseness of her furnishings represented the next stage of her journey. Voids to fill, spaces to warm, and like the murder weapons she so often encountered, a place to leave her prints.

It was as she pondered that thought that she heard her doorbell. It was one of those plug-in types with fifty different annoying tunes to choose from that the previous owner had left behind, and whether to raise a smile or to antagonise her, they had set the device to play a rather basic and digital version of the William Tell Overture.

She would have to change that, she thought, as she stepped out into the open-plan living room and saw two figures through the frosted glass in the front door.

She set her cup down, thinking that if her new neighbours had come to welcome her to Dunston, then it may be best to at least encourage a positive first impression.

But it wasn't her new neighbours. It was her old neighbour and his new girlfriend bearing a cheap bottle of wine with a picture of a little sailing boat on the label.

"Ben?" she said, taken aback. "How lovely."

"We thought we'd help you stock your fridge with the essentials," he said, holding the bottle out for her to take. There was a joke in there somewhere that only Ben could find amusing. The little bottle with the sailing boat had been the butt of many jokes since they had met, and she accepted it with grace, then invited them inside her new home.

"I did tell him to pick something else," Michaela said, as Ben held his hand out for her to enter before him. She gave Freya a little peck on the cheek, which was a new way of greeting for them, then set about the gratuitous exclamations that accompany the first official visit to somebody's new home. "Oh, how lovely, and the view of the green is heavenly."

The pair had, of course, been to the house before, but the visit had been brief, unexpected, and they had left her in the capable, and surprisingly delicate, hands of Michaela's brother.

Leaving the exclamations to Michaela, Ben stepped inside, took a quick look around, and then stared at her.

"Where's your furniture?"

"I don't have any, remember?"

"No sofa?"

"Nope."

"Bed?"

"Nothing," she said. "I have carpet, and I have blankets, and I have a roof over my head. It's all part of my journey, Ben."

"What? Sleeping on the floor?" he replied. "And eating? Don't you have anything?'

"Sleeping, sitting, dining," she said. "You name it, I'll be doing it on the floor."

"No wonder Michaela's brother didn't hang around for long," Ben said, but the joke was ill-received. Freya gave a loud and irritated tut, while Michaela glared at him the way a mother promises her child a scolding when they get home.

"As you well know, Ben," Freya said, "Michaela's brother and I went our separate ways quite amicably."

"You could have taken the armchair from Dad's cottage," he said, poking his head into the cupboard under the stairs and peering around in the dark, searching for new ways to taunt Freya.

"I didn't want the armchair," she replied. "And what are you looking for?"

He pulled his head from the cupboard and closed the door. "Your dungeon."

"Very funny. Can I get you a coffee?" she said to Michaela, who then eyed the cheap bottle Ben had bought as a joke. "Or I have a bottle of Chablis if you'd prefer?"

"Wow, you don't have chairs or a bed, but you have Chablis?" Michaela said.

"And glasses aplenty," Freya told her.

"Sadly, it's a little early for me."

"There's coffee in the kitchen. I made a fresh pot," Freya said. "So, what do you think, anyway?"

"I think it's beautiful," Michaela said. "It's just the sort of place I would have bought. Cosy, comfortable, and ready to put your stamp on."

"That's what I thought, too," she said, calling out from the kitchen.

"And I love the village," Michaela mused, peering from the window. "What made you choose Dunston?"

"She doesn't know many other places," Ben said from the back door. "She only knows the places where somebody has been murdered in the past year. It was either here, Woodhall Spa, Bardney, Nocton, or Anderby."

"So very crass, Ben," Freya said.

"You chose well," he replied offering her a friendly wink. "And you can sleep soundly at night knowing that a man was brutally murdered half a dozen doors away, even if it is on the floor."

"We all have our histories," she countered, as she handed Michaela a cup of coffee. "Coffee, Ben?"

"I'm good thank you," he replied. "I've had too many this morning already."

"There's water in the tap. You can help yourself," she told him, enjoying his brief disappointment and returning that wink with ample gusto. "And as you're driving, you can do me a favour."

"What do you need? New chains for your dungeon? Shackles? Wall fixings?" he asked, but Freya ignored his remarks and caught Michaela's attention. She presented the empty space with a sweep of her arm.

"Shopping?" Michaela said, her eyes lighting up with glee.

"I need everything," Freya told her, the two women sharing the excitement.

"Shopping?" Ben said, and his face sagged under the weight of what was to be a truly awful day.

"Yep," Freya said, as she sank the remainder of her coffee and stepped into her shoes. "Consider your company a moving in present."

"I bought you wine," he said, as she opened the front door and beckoned them out.

"You bought me a door stop," she corrected him when he passed her. "But at least that's one thing you won't have to carry while Michaela and I choose furniture."

CHAPTER TWO

Birds sang somewhere outside Rosie's window. Their morning calls had somehow grown louder without her realising it. The long and sleepless night had given way to morning while she had stared at the ceiling, listening intently for the sound of the front door slamming.

She hadn't missed it. She was sure, positive, in fact, that she hadn't slipped into sleep, however brief.

Which meant he was still out there. *He must be*.

Her mum was up and about, getting ready for work as she usually did on a Saturday but without the thrum of raised voices Rosie had grown used to. The arguments were normal – bitter and spiteful, childish at best.

But this morning, there was none.

Maybe he was still asleep, hungover and ashamed of how he must look? Maybe he couldn't face her mum with black eyes of his own, far worse than those he had given her? Maybe he was waiting for her to go to work, so he could creep into Rosie's bedroom?

Maybe he hadn't learned his lesson?

Fully dressed, Rosie lay on her bed listening. It was like one of those shows they played on Radio Four, where actors acted various parts each and used various props; somebody added the sound effects – the gravel driveway, the closing door. She had seen it once on TV. Her mother moved about the house, providing her own sound effects to add to the drama – the plates being shoved into the cupboard, the glasses being stacked, the cutlery being sorted then tossed into the drawer compartments. She could picture her mum, and she wondered if the bruises she bore would fade away, never to return.

Maybe Michael would fade away? Maybe they had hurt him enough for him to move on to wherever he had come from in the first place?

The toilet flushed downstairs, which meant one thing. Her mother would be leaving imminently. That was her routine, sort the kitchen out so it wasn't a mess when she got home, use the loo, and then leave.

The front door slammed and the little brass knocker rattled once.

The birds still chirped outside, oblivious to Rosie's dilemma, oblivious to her straining to hear movement of any sort from the room next door.

Had Michael heard her mum leave, too? Was he lying there waiting for his moment to revisit Rosie? Or worse, did he know it had been them who had followed him? She was sure they had been careful to hide their identities.

She checked her phone for messages but found none. The four of them had a group chat on WhatsApp, *The No Hopers*, they had called it, referring to themselves as social outcasts with no chance of ever achieving anything.

Morning, she typed, then watched for the little status message to signify that somebody was replying.

Pete had told her to keep the group chat open and to call it if Michael tried anything or said anything about the previous night. He had said she should act normal and, of course, surprised when she saw his injuries. Jake had even added that she could ask if somebody down the pub had hit him to add a little credibility to her innocence.

What's the weather like today? Tony messaged, and if she read it right, he was asking if she'd seen Michael yet.

I haven't opened the curtains yet. Quiet outside. No birds singing, she replied.

Wanna meet up at mine? Dad's away this weekend.

Later probz. I'm waiting for the birds. Should be singing by now, she wrote.

Too early? Tony replied, clearly following what she had meant. But then the little message below the chat name said that Jake was typing a message.

Too early for birds to sing??? It's 8am. It sounds like a Hitchcock movie outside my bedroom window.

She let her head fall back onto the pillow. Jake wasn't the sharpest of them all, and she was in no mood to explain the coded message to him.

The fact was that the birds were singing. They were in full chorus, making it hard for her to hear any movement from next door.

Anyone heard from Pete? she wrote.

I think he hurt his hand. Mine's as big as a balloon, Jake wrote back, destroying any efforts they had made at not leaving a digital trail for Michael to follow should he get his hands on Rosie's phone.

You moron, came Pete's first addition to the conversation.

What?

Tony's house. 9am, Pete wrote.

Why u call me a moron? Jake asked, to which Pete gave no reply. Instead, he directed his attention to Rosie in a private message, as she knew he would.

You okay, Rosie? I can swing by on the way past if you want? We can walk to Tony's together.

All good. I think everyone's out, she said, hoping he might read between the lines.

Already?

Mum went to work a while ago, she wrote.

What about her bloke?

I don't think he came home. Think he went to the pub. Must have been a heavy night, she wrote, happy that, should Michael get hold of her phone, as he often did, he would be dissuaded that they had anything to do with the previous night.

A moment or two passed while Pete was considering the possibilities, and then a message popped up informing her that Pete was typing.

I'll be there in 30 mins. We can cut through the forest. I want to make sure we put the fire out.

K, she replied, praying, for the first time in her life, that she might hear Michael moving about next door.

A folded piece of paper on her dressing table caught her eye. Her name was on the front in her mother's scrawled handwriting. She opened the note to read but startled by voices from outside on the street. A car door slammed, followed by another.

She froze, expecting to hear Michael grumbling his way down the stairs to berate whoever it was, then stuffed the note into her pocket.

But there was no movement, no grumbling, and no groaning from his injuries when she stepped onto the landing. She peered down to the coat hooks in the hallway below and saw only her gilet hanging there. He had been wearing his denim jacket. She was positive. Only he could think that wearing double denim was a good summer look.

His keys were missing, too. He normally tossed them onto the little hallway table and kicked off his shoes.

There were no shoes on the hallway carpet except for her flip flops.

Slowly, she bent into the stairwell to peer at the front door, hoping to see the outline of whoever the visitor was.

But nobody was there, and she cursed her own nerves.

She rose and gave a little knock on her mum's bedroom door.

"Michael," she called out, hating herself for doing it. But she had to know. She couldn't just leave not knowing if he had come home. "Michael, do you want some coffee?"

Not a sound. Not even the birds responded.

Slowly, she opened the door. Inch by inch, the old carpet was revealed, and inch by inch, she prayed to see his shoes, his keys, or his bloody denim jacket.

But she saw nothing, and eventually, the bed was in full view, made neatly, the way her mum always made it, in that immaculate way that only mums seem able to achieve.

She stepped inside to make sure he wasn't lying on the carpet or something. It wouldn't be the first time. But then something caught her eye. Movement outside. She walked to the window, vaguely aware that, since Michael had been staying with them, the room was a no-go area for her. She peered down at the road and her heart skipped a beat as a man and a woman walked up the garden path. The older of them reached inside his pocket and pulled out a wallet, then held it ready to present his ID as he rang the doorbell.

CHAPTER THREE

"Twelve weeks?" Freya said, her voice reaching the far corners of the huge furniture store where Ben witnessed a few startled heads turn, and he cringed with embarrassment. "What am I supposed to do until then, sleep on the bloody floor?"

"I'm afraid there's not a lot I can do about the timelines," the salesman explained. "They are stipulated by our processes, I'm afraid. I'll place the order today and your furniture will be on the next shipment from Europe."

"Europe?" she said. "We are in Europe."

"Actually, Freya–" Ben started, but she hushed him with a single raised hand.

"What about this one?" she asked, pointing at the showroom demo. "It's the exact bed I've ordered. I don't mind a few knocks here and there."

"I'm sure it'll be getting a few more," Ben added, which only served to irritate Freya even more.

"I'm afraid I can't do that," the salesman said, holding his own.

"I'll hire a van," she said, then tapped Ben's chest with the back of her hand. "You'll drive it for me, won't you?"

"A van?" he said, but the salesman's face said it all.

"I'm sorry," he said.

"Twelve weeks," she repeated. "Let me get this straight. I'm paying you fifteen hundred pounds for a bed with no mattress, twelve hundred pounds for a dining table with no chairs, and another two thousand on bookcases, coffee tables and side tables, not to mention the three thousand pounds for the sofa and armchairs, and I have to wait twelve bloody weeks to actually see them. I could put that money in the bank and earn interest in that time."

"Actually, Freya–" Ben began again, and once more he was silenced by her raised hand.

"It's our policy, I'm afraid," the salesman said. "We do pride ourselves on quality, and to ensure that quality, each of our pieces is handmade to order."

"In Europe?"

"Well, no, actually they're made in Asia, but they come through Europe."

"Asia?" she said, and those people at the far end of the store looked up again, shaking their heads in disgust. "I'm staring at the thing I just bought. I don't need somebody in bloody Asia to build me a new one. I want this one."

The man was clearly experienced at having the same argument with like-minded individuals, and he moved on, keen to close the deal and get her out of the store. And if Ben was honest with himself, he didn't blame him.

"We also offer a scratch repair service on the dining table for an additional one hundred and fifty pounds," he advised. "It's a one-off payment and just covers you for any mishaps."

"Scratch repair," she said, her mouth hanging open in abhorrence.

"If we can't fix the scratch, we'll replace the entire table," he said. "Free of charge, of course."

"But it's not free, is it? I'm paying one hundred and fifty pounds for it," she said, and Ben watched with mild amusement as her mind caught up with her mouth. "Hold on. If you have to replace a scratched table, do I have to—"

"Wait twelve weeks for a replacement?" he said, foreseeing where she was going. "No, we keep a small amount of stock for such occasions. It helps avoid any unnecessary disappointment."

"Disappointment?"

"I'll take that as a no," the salesman said, ignoring Freya's reddening face. "Now, last thing before I let you go. Delivery."

"Delivery?" she repeated, defeated and out of arguments, which in Ben's experience was a rare but wonderful sight to behold. Behind her, Michaela had to turn away to hide the smirk she had done so well to keep at bay.

"It'll be fifty pounds delivered to your doorstep, one hundred pounds to a room of your choice, or you can opt for our premium service and we'll put the furniture together for you."

"Excuse me?" she said, as if she hadn't heard a word or what he had just said, or was in utter disbelief. "Are you saying that after spending nearly nine thousand pounds on matching furniture, for fifty pounds I get to sleep on my new bed in my front garden?"

"You'd have to build it, of course," he replied. "But yes."

"Build it myself?"

"I'll put you down for the premium service," he said, clicking a few buttons with his mouse. "Okay, that's great. We're all done. You'll receive an email shortly with your invoice. Will there be anything else I can help you with?"

"No," she hissed.

"Actually, yes," Ben said. "She's also going to need some kind of wall fixings. You know the type I mean? Big iron rings, suitable for chaining somebody to for an hour or so."

"Ignore him," Freya said, refusing to look his way.

"What about jump leads?" Ben asked, milking Freya's reaction for all it was worth.

"Right, come on," Michaela interjected, reading Freya's expression and realising that Ben wasn't going to stop there.

The salesman looked between them all, expecting somebody to bring the deal to a close, then took it upon himself.

"Well, I'd like to thank you for your business," he said. "I hope you get many years of enjoyment from your furniture."

He held out his hand for Freya to shake and Ben had to guide her arm towards it, reminding her of her manners. He then turned her to face the exit and gave her a gentle nudge, thanking the man for his patience with a nod and a smile.

"I feel violated," Freya said when she climbed into the back seat of Ben's old Ford. "I feel genuinely violated."

"Oh, don't worry too much," Ben told her, as he started his car. "You've got a blanket and some carpet, remember?"

"Twelve weeks?" she said, shaking her head in disbelief. "I thought it would be a few days."

He pulled his seat belt across his chest just as his phone began to ring over the car's Bluetooth system.

"Ben Savage," he said when he answered the call.

"Ben, it's Jackie," the familiar voice of their colleague said with a gentle flavour of a faint Scottish accent. "I've got some bad news."

"Please tell me somebody has been murdered," he said, which raised a playful glare from Michaela beside him.

"No, Ben, nothing like that," Jackie said. "There's a new station near Market Rasen."

"That's right," he said. "We heard about that. They aren't closing us down too, are they?"

"No, Ben," she said, sounding genuinely upset, enough even for Freya to forget her woes and meet his concerned gaze in the rear-view mirror. "I just thought you should find out from me directly. I've put in for a transfer and it's been accepted."

"You did what?"

"It's DCI Standing. I can't help it. I hate him. I hate coming to work now. It's been awful since he took over from Granger."

"Jackie—"

"I'm sorry, Ben. I can't do it. I'm leaving," she said with a sob. "I'm leaving the team."

"Jackie, it's Freya," she said from the back seat, leaning forward between the two front seats. "Jackie, why don't we talk about this? If you feel this strongly, I might be able to do something. The team won't be the same without you, you know that?"

"That's just it," Jackie said. "The team… I'm not the only one who's leaving."

CHAPTER FOUR

"Good morning, miss…" the man said, hoping Rosie would provide her name.

"Rosie," she said, feeling the word fall from trembling lips. "Rosie Sinclair."

"Thank you. I understand a Michael Levy lives here. Is that right?"

"Michael Levy," she repeated, clinging to the front door as if her life depended on it. "Michael? Yes… Yes, sorry. Michael lives here. That's right."

"Are you okay, Rosie?" the man asked.

He wore dark trousers and a striped shirt. He could have been a schoolteacher or one of those men who drank with Michael in The King's Head during the week, with his side parting and thick glasses. The type who had nothing better to do. No wife to go home to and no future – waiting for the day they could hang their crappy clothes, don a woolly cardigan, and resort to a life in slippers.

"I'm fine," she said. "Sorry, you just caught me off guard. I was expecting somebody."

"Oh, we apologise. Well, we shan't keep you too long. If you could just go and get Michael for us, so we could have a quick word."

"Michael?" she said, again, realising how much of a fool she was making herself look.

"Michael Levy," the man said. "You just told us he lives here."

"Oh right, yeah. He does. But, um, he's not in."

"Do you know where we can find him?"

She looked along the street, hoping that Pete would come to her rescue. He would know what to say.

"He's not in," she said again, which did little but raise a couple of eyebrows. "I mean, he didn't come home. At least, I don't think he did."

"Oh?"

"His coat isn't here."

"It's summer," he said. "Perhaps he put it away?"

"His keys," she said. "And his shoes. And the bed's made. I don't think he came home."

"What was he wearing?"

"Wearing?" she said.

"You said his coat isn't here. What coat was it?"

"A denim one."

"Blue?"

"Yes. That's it. A blue denim jacket. It's his summer jacket."

"Anything else?" the man asked. "Or are we to assume he's out there somewhere naked from the waist down?"

She shook her head.

"I didn't really see him."

"But you know he's wearing the jacket."

"I mean, I didn't pay any attention to what he was wearing. You don't, do you? I see him every day, don't I?"

"Do you know where he might be?" the woman asked. "Or perhaps you could give him a call? Ask him to pop home to see us?"

She looked younger than the man and wore clothes her

mother might have worn to work – not flashy, but a trouser suit which was smart, functional, and easy to wash.

"I'm sorry, I can't."

"Can't, or won't?"

"I don't know his number. Not off by heart anyway."

"Perhaps you have it written down somewhere. He's your stepdad. Is that right?"

"No," she said, almost immediately and not without revealing a hint of disgust at the idea. "No, he's just my mum's bloke."

"Your mum's partner?"

"Yeah."

"Perhaps your mum has his number?"

"She's at work. Sorry, what's this about? I mean, if I see him, what should I say?"

"You should tell him, Rosie, that I want to speak to him regarding a friend of his, and that he's expected to attend the police station to answer a few questions."

"A friend of his?" she repeated. "He doesn't have friends."

"Why don't you just tell him to pop down and see us?" the man said, and he leaned forward to give her his card, which bore the name DI Grant Burns. "Or he can call me. Whichever works best. We just want to talk to him, okay?"

"Right," Rosie said. "I'll make sure he gets it."

The man looked her up and down.

"See that he does," he said, as he turned to walk away. But then he stopped at the gate and called out to her, "Oh, and Rosie?"

"Yeah?" she said, watching his roving eye pick up every tiny detail.

"Those bruises on your wrist," he said. "Where might you have got those from? Is everything okay?"

Immediately, she folded her arms to hide her bare wrists.

"Everything's fine," she replied, seeing Pete at the far end of the road. He saw the liveried car and turned on his heels, disappearing around the corner before he was seen by either of the two officers. "I just fell, that's all."

The man peered up the street, finding it empty, and then turned back to her.

"You should take more care," he told her, gesturing for his colleague to follow. "See to it Michael gets the message, will you? I don't want to have to come knocking again."

CHAPTER FIVE

"What the bloody hell was that about?" Pete asked when Rosie caught up with him in the lane behind her house. "What did you tell them?"

"Nothing," she said, peering back out into the street. "They were looking for Michael. They said something about a friend of his. He was very cloak and dagger."

"You haven't reported him for..."

"For what, Pete?"

He looked ashamed to say the words but held her stare.

"You know... What he did to you. You haven't, have you?"

"No, of course, I didn't. What do you think I am? Stupid?"

"No, sorry. But why do they want to speak to him?"

"I don't know," she told him. "But he definitely didn't come home last night. His shoes are missing, as are his keys and jacket."

"What that denim thing with the sheepskin collar?"

"All missing," she said. "Exactly how badly did we injure him?"

"I don't know. Bad enough, I suppose," Pete said, holding up his hand with bloodied knuckles. "My foot's swollen, too. Had to throw my trainers away, they were covered in claret."

"Oh, for God's sake," Rosie muttered to herself. "Where?"

"In my neighbour's bin, don't worry. I'm also not a dummy."

She gave the situation some thought, concluding that if the police were involved, it was already getting out of control.

"He could have taken himself to hospital, in which case the police will catch up with him there, and if he does, he's bound to tell them he was jumped by four people in the dark."

"Oh, bloody hell. What if he tells them what happened? What if he saw one of us? What if he recognised one of our voices?"

"We didn't speak, and we hit from behind, remember?" she said.

"Tony hit him, you mean?"

"We all hit him, Pete. Tony just knocked him down," she said, dragging him out of the lane. "Come on, we need to go back."

"What? You're kidding?" he said, breaking her grip on his arm. "Rule number one, Rosie. Never return to the scene of the crime."

"Rule number two," she countered. "Never leave any evidence."

"We didn't, did we?"

"I don't know. I imagine you left some skin behind if your hands look like that."

"What? They wouldn't check for that, would they?"

"I don't know, Pete. I don't bloody know. But if there's a chance your DNA is on his face, then there's a chance one of us left something else behind."

"Like what?"

"Blood, Pete. Footprints. Anything. We need to go and have a look before he takes the old bill there."

"Right," he said, agreeing with her. "I'll message the others."

"No," she said. "We're going to Tony's. That's what we said we were going to do. We'll cut through the nature reserve."

"The what?" he asked, as she began crossing the quiet road heading towards the scene of the crime. He ran the few steps to catch her up. "Rosie, we need to be sure about this. We can't be seen."

She stopped at the edge of the fields where they had to climb a stile to get off the road.

"What would you rather, two friends being seen walking in their local woods, or a bunch of coppers knocking on all our doors?"

He gave it some thought, then nodded a reluctant agreement and jumped the stile in a single bound, holding his hand out to help her down.

"Pete," she said when she had planted her feet firmly in the soil and he was about to stomp off towards the trees in the distance. He turned back to her, his eyes wide and alert.

"What?"

"I just wanted to say thanks," she told him. "I shouldn't have got you all into this."

He softened, and for a brief moment, it was like they were just two friends going for a walk on a nice summer morning.

"You don't need to thank me," he said. "You don't need to thank any of us. He deserved everything he got last night. And if we do get caught, I'll tell them exactly what he did."

"No," she said. "No, please. I don't want that. I don't want people to know."

"There's nothing to be ashamed of, Rosie," she said. "It's him who should be ashamed, not you."

"But still. I don't want anyone to know. Especially not my mum."

He shook his head in disbelief and sighed. "Well, let's hope it doesn't come to that then," he said. "Because if we get caught, we're going to have a lot of explaining to do."

CHAPTER SIX

Between Ben and Freya, they carried nine coffees in cardboard trays up the fire escape stairs, along the corridor, and into the incident room, where DC Gabby Cruz was waiting with his feet up on a chair, engrossed in his phone.

"Morning, Cruz," Freya said, setting the drinks down on the centre table. He startled and quickly whipped his feet from the chair.

"Morning, boss."

She studied him for a moment, eyeing the gleaming white trainers, socks pulled halfway up his ankles, the little, white gym shorts, and the thin sweater he had draped around his shoulders with the arms crossed over his chest.

Ben set his drinks down and followed Freya's line of sight, giving her a shake of his head to suggest that making a joke of Cruz's attire probably wasn't the best idea, all things considered.

"Here you go, fella," he said to Cruz, handing him a sickly hazelnut latte topped with cream and chocolate powder.

"For me?" he said, accepting the drink. Originally from London, Cruz was the youngest member of the team, and very often the butt of the jokes, which to his credit, he handled well, Freya thought. "Cheers. Nice one. What's all this about, then?"

"The fact that you felt compelled to ask, Cruz," Freya began, "tells me I don't need to worry about you."

"Eh?"

"How are you?"

"Me?" he said, suddenly concerned. "I'm alright, I suppose."

"Have we disrupted your morning workout?"

"My workout?"

Freya nodded at his choice of clothing then sipped at her coffee. Thank God they had decided to get some real coffee in.

"Oh, these? No, I was just doing some housework. Hermione is working, so while the place is empty, you know?"

"Oh," Freya replied, rather surprised. She looked across at Ben who simply shook his head, telling her to drop it. "Well, I'm sorry to have disturbed your day then. It's an emergency meeting. We've called the whole team in."

"Not another body?" he asked.

"No. No bodies today, thankfully. When we're done here, we can all go back to whatever it was we were doing before."

"Right," he said, as the doors burst open in a flurry of activity. "What were you doing?"

Gillespie marched into the room, his long hair pointing in every direction but down, bags under his eyes large enough for a fortnight's holiday, and wearing what appeared to be the previous night's clothes. He plopped down into his chair, laid his hands on his desk as a pillow, and then let his head drop with a thud.

"Shopping," Freya said, by way of answering Cruz. She collected Gillespie's coffee and made her way towards him, setting it down on the desk beside him. "Morning, Gillespie."

A single hand rose from the mass of hair, then flopped back down.

"Good night, was it?" Ben asked.

The hand rose again, this time with an upturned thumb. Then it flopped down again.

"Well, good," Freya said. "It's nice to see everybody making an effort."

A hum of female voices carried along the corridor outside and Ben glanced through the window, opening the door as the rest of the team approached.

"Morning, ladies," he said, to which they chirped various greetings in reply. "Grab a coffee and take a seat."

Jackie collected her drink then sat down beside DC Chapman, meek and mild-mannered, and wearing a guilty expression. DC Anderson, another London-born member of the team, looked worried but knew not to ask any questions just yet. DS Anna Nillson, arguably the team's toughest member, sat with her arms folded and one leg crossed over the other. To the untrained eye, it was a defensive posture. But Freya knew better. That was just how she sat.

"Thanks for coming," Freya began when the team had settled and the hum had died down. "I appreciate it's the weekend, so I'll keep this as brief as I can. I've had some alarming news. News which, dare I say it, affects us all in one way or another."

Gillespie raised his head, saw his coffee, and then took a sip, which seemed to provide enough energy for him to maintain eye contact with Freya for the next few minutes. But then something else caught his eye.

"Are you entering Wimbledon?" he asked Cruz, which raised a few soft laughs from around the room.

"Eh?" Cruz said.

"What is it? Women's doubles today?" Gillespie asked him, to which Cruz shook his head and his face reddened.

"Alright, come on," Freya said, keen not to let the momentum fade. "The fact is that since DCI Standing was promoted, at least one of you has put in for a transfer, and now I'm told there are more of you. Now, you don't have to tell us if you don't wish to, but I'd like to make it clear that I will not let this team fall apart without a fight."

"But what can you do about it?" Gold asked, then, rather surprisingly, she made her announcement. "I might as well tell you all. I'm leaving."

"You what?" Gillespie said, sweeping his hair from his face.

"I'm leaving," Gold repeated. "I've put in for a transfer at the new HQ in the Wolds, and it's been accepted."

"But *I've* put in for a transfer," he said, then glanced sheepishly at Freya. "Sorry, boss."

"That's okay," she replied, not altogether surprised that he was one of the others to have expressed an interest in leaving.

"It's just, well, Standing was my DI, and now he's in charge of us, I think he feels like I'm his spy or something. It puts me in a pretty uncomfortable position if I'm honest."

"I imagine it would," Freya said. "And thank you for being honest."

"Aye, no bother. I was going to tell you once I had it confirmed. I'm waiting for some fella called DI Larson to give me the green light."

"Larson?" Freya said. "George Larson?"

"Aye, that's him. Seems nice enough. Bit long in the tooth, but anything has to be better than this place right now."

"He's a good man," Freya agreed. "Anybody else?"

She studied the faces in the room and felt the tug on her stomach when Chapman slowly raised her hand and bit down on the corner of her lip.

"Sorry, ma'am," she said.

"Chapman, no."

"I just can't bear it," she explained. "It's toxic in here. We can't laugh anymore, everything we do is scrutinised, and we never know what mood he's going to be in. It's just not what it used to be."

"I understand," Freya told her. "Anybody else?"

A few heads scanned the room in case anybody else had decided enough was enough, but thankfully nobody else raised a hand.

"Well, three out of eight," she said. "That's a forty per cent hit rate."

"Just to be clear, I haven't actually agreed to move yet," Gillespie said, with his head propped up by the palm of his hand the way a tired schoolboy might get through a boring maths lesson. "We're still just talking about it."

"The fact is, Gillespie, that you are talking about it. That's bad enough."

"We're sorry," Gold said. "If the others feel like me, we don't want to go. It's just—"

"Become unbearable?" Freya said.

"Aye," Gillespie growled in agreement.

"And it's affecting your mental health?"

Gold nodded, and when Freya turned to Chapman, she too gave a slight nod.

"That's what I thought. What can I do?" she asked. "What can I do that might help you change your mind?"

One by one, the individuals stared at each other in turn, hoping that somebody might have a solution.

"Come on," Freya said. "Think. We're all smart people. What can we do that might make life more bearable?"

"Have him sacked?" Gillespie mumbled.

"He's a DCI," Freya said. "We'd need to enlist the help of Granger for that, and as far as I'm aware, Will Granger is happy to let him run the team how he sees fit."

"He won't if three of us have left," Gillespie said. "That might be enough for Granger to step in."

"That's the point," Ben added, "when you've already left, by which time it will be too late. The words horse bolting and closing the gate spring to mind."

"We could always off him?" Cruz suggested, which silenced

the room. There was something quite sinister about a small man with his sweater draped around his shoulders like some kind of Oxbridge schoolboy making such a suggestion.

"I beg your pardon?" Freya said.

"We could off him," Cruz said as if he'd suggested nothing more than the team head out for lunch. "I mean, it's not like we don't know how to get away with it, is it?"

Nillson laughed out loud, which was a rare occurrence.

"With any luck, we'd be assigned the investigation," she said.

"Do we have any credible suggestions?" Freya said, and the mood fell like a morning fog, silent and foreboding. "Gold, do you have a date?"

"Two weeks," she said. "The office isn't ready yet."

"Chapman?"

"Same," she said. "I'm expecting the paperwork in next week sometime."

"Well, don't sign anything," Freya said. "The way I see it, I've got a week to change your minds."

"What are you going to do?" Gillespie asked.

The question was direct and innocent, and she stared at the faces before her. Never before had she worked with such an array of personalities. But she loved them in her own way, and allowing any one of them to leave would be like cutting a limb from the team.

"I don't know," she said honestly. "But let's just hope we aren't called into play this week. I'm going to need every spare moment available if I'm going to get rid of Standing."

CHAPTER SEVEN

It might have been the clammy morning air, or it could have been the fact that Rosie hadn't washed that morning, but when she entered the forest in the nature reserve, she felt the damp beneath her arms and her t-shirt clinging to her sweaty back.

The silence was deafening. It was as if the birds and creatures that usually filled the place with life had witnessed what they had done the previous night and were now hushed, watching them from the safety of a thousand nooks and crannies.

"I feel sick," Rosie said. "What if we're too late? What if he's already told them and they've been here? What if they're here and see us? The police, I mean."

He turned and hushed her with a finger to his lips, making a show of listening for voices or some kind of sign they weren't alone.

He leaned in close to her and she stiffened, very aware of her hygiene.

"We're just two friends walking to another friend's house," he whispered. "We're cutting through the forest like we've done for years. Like most people around here do."

He waited a moment for her to nod and calm down a little,

and then he moved on, holding a long, leafy branch from the path so she could pass.

They walked in silence from there, but Rosie's mind housed a chorus of whispered voices, questions, and wonderings, and her heart was the beating drum that kept time.

Pete held his hand up for her to stop, and pointed to an area in the lee of a large tree.

"That's where we hid," he said, treading carefully around the area, studying it from every angle until something caught his eye, and he stepped in, crouched, and then produced a cigarette butt. "Jake's."

He pocketed the butt then, happy there were no more, snapped a leafy branch from a low-hanging bush, and used it as a rake to spread the debris around, making it appear as natural as he could. When he was done, he tossed the branch beneath the bush, kicked some dirt onto it, and then moved on into the clearing, beyond which was the small footbridge where they had surprised her mother's boyfriend.

"Keep your eye out for more fag butts," he said softly, as they moved towards the few trees that concealed the bridge.

High up in the treetops, a bird screeched, startling Rosie but not Pete. He remained impassive and stoic, as dependable as they come.

"We're just going to walk through, cross the bridge, and go to Tony's," he said. "Remember?"

She nodded and he pushed on through the trees, and just as she was about to follow, he backed up, letting the branch he held swing back into place.

The calm and stoic young boy she had trusted since they were knee-high had paled.

"What's wrong?" she said, vying for a view through the overgrown bushes. "Are the police there?"

He shook his head and took a breath, then held onto the branch again, pulling it back for them both to take another look.

They were face to face, cheek to cheek, two clammy and breathless teenagers staring down the barrel of a huge problem.

The narrow footbridge was blocked by the still slumbering mass of Michael Levy, the man who had made Rosie's life a misery.

"He's still a-bloody-sleep," she hissed.

"I'm not surprised. He was hammered. You saw him. He could barely stand up even before we…" Pete replied quietly, stopping before he verbalised what didn't need to be said. "We need to get past him."

"I'm not climbing over him."

"What else are we going to do?"

"Go back and go the long way round," she suggested.

"No. We're just two people walking to a mate's house, remember?"

"We could always call the police?" Rosie suggested. "Tell them there's a man who looks like he's been beaten up sleeping rough in the nature reserve."

"Absolutely not," he hissed. "We need to wake him up."

"What?"

"Think about it. If we wake him up, pretending like we've just found him there, he'll never think it was us who did it. If he goes to the police, then so what? We didn't do it. We just found him there on our way to Tony's place. We've even got WhatsApp messages to prove what we were doing."

"I'm not waking that bastard up. He can sleep there all day for all I care. With any luck, he'll get piles from the cold ground."

Ordinarily, the comment would have made them both laugh, but neither of them was in the mood.

"At least we know he hasn't gone to the police yet," Pete said hopefully, as Rosie edged past him to get a better look. The footbridge crossed the old River Bain and was just a few metres from the trees where they whispered like the schoolchildren they were.

"Bloody hell, Pete," she said, dragging him forward to where she now stood. "He's a mess."

She turned to face her friend, who offered her a solemn look.

"He deserved it though, right?" he said, and she nodded.

"I didn't know we did that much, though. It was pitch black."

"He'll have a headache when he does come round, that's for sure," Pete said. "Did you see Tony going at him?"

"Stop it," Rosie said, feeling nauseous at the sight of what they had done.

"Jake too," Pete said. "He was out of breath from hitting him."

Rosie shook her head and, for a moment, felt pity for the man before them.

"Okay, keep your eyes peeled," he said. "We won't wake him up, we'll step over him and go to Tony's. Then later, we can come back to make sure we haven't left anything behind."

"I can't," she told him, suddenly afraid to step out into the open.

"Rosie?"

"I can't," she said, louder but still hushed. "I can't step over him, like he's a lump of dog poo."

"Well, he kind of is, isn't he? In fact, that's exactly what he is. Dog crap. The shit on our shoes."

"I can't do it," she said. "I can't bear to go near him. Not because of what we did to him..."

"Because of what he did to you?" Pete finished for her, saving her the ordeal of annunciating her thoughts.

She nodded.

"What if he wakes up and sees us?"

"Well, what do you suppose we do?" he said. "How about we go back and go the long way round, like you suggested?"

"No. No, you're right," she said, taking a deep breath. "We'll go this way. Maybe I can scoot along the edge of the bridge on the outside?"

"It's not exactly London Bridge, is it?"

"Right," she said, zipping up her hoodie. "Let's do it. We're going to get past him and leg it, right?"

"Right," he confirmed and led them out into the open, where suddenly a chilly wind found her sweaty back. Together, they edged closer to Michael, and with each step, more of his injuries became evident. He lay on the ground with his legs facing them and his arms and head rested on the bridge itself, as if he'd hauled his broken body into a semi-seated position, then fallen unconscious, blocking the way.

His face was swollen on one side, as were his lips. His hands gripped the bridge posts on either side as best they could with at least two of his broken fingers facing the wrong direction. A large, dark patch had formed on the front of his denim jacket where his head had fallen forward and blood had been dripping from his wounds all night. The sheepskin collar was dotted with drops of blood and mud, and at least one of his bodily functions had given way, staining his light blue jeans the colour of a midnight sky.

But it was as Rosie edged past him, reaching for the handrail to keep herself steady, that she noticed something. A trail of blood had leaked across his face, which she traced up his flattened nose, all the way to his open eyes.

She felt Pete watching her, as if he'd read the last chapter of a terrifying book and was waiting for her to finish so they could share their horrors.

She cast her eyes to Michael's chest, expecting, hoping, praying to see it rise and fall, even gently.

But there was no movement. None at all. He didn't blink. He didn't move. He didn't groan or moan, or sneer, though she wished he would do any of those things. She wished he would just stop ruining her life; all he was doing by not moving was making it worse.

"Shit," she said, aloud, and she looked up at Pete, who was white with fear, edging away from the bridge, his eyes wide. "He's bloody dead, Pete. We've bloody killed him."

CHAPTER EIGHT

"This is impossible," Freya spurted as she slumped into one of Ben's armchairs. The old house was cool, a pleasant relief from the muggy heat outside.

"How did it go?" Michaela said as she descended the stairs. She poked her head into the lounge. "I heard you come in."

"Were you napping?" Ben asked her.

"I might have closed my eyes for a few moments," she replied. "It's too hot to do much else."

"Jackie, Chapman, and Gillespie," Freya said, answering her original question. "Bloody three of them."

"That's a significant chunk of your team," Michaela said.

"Forty per cent," Ben told her.

"Well, thirty-seven point five, to be precise," Freya spat.

"Are they all going to Kirkby?"

"Apparently," she said. "And who can blame them? A nice, shiny, new office. No DCI Standing looming over them like a great big bloody thundercloud with bad breath and a penchant for bad clothes. Why would they stay?"

"And the others?" Michaela asked.

"I'd be naive if I thought the others would turn the opportunity down given the chance," Freya said. "Cruz might not, seeing as Hermione is a local uniformed officer, but Nillson? She'd go in a heartbeat. If she stays here, she won't make DI until Ben moves on or up. But over there? Who knows? In a bigger station, she'll be promoted in under three years."

"Have you spoken to this Larson chap about this?" Michaela said. "Surely he can't pull your team apart?"

"Oh, I don't blame him," Freya told her. "Good luck to him. No, my beef is with the beast from the East Midlands. He's been nothing but trouble ever since he's been back in the station. You know, while Ben and I were in Saltfleet, he had Gillespie trawl through my old investigations looking for evidence against me."

"Evidence? Evidence of what?"

"Of my mistakes," she said. "It's like being in the Met all over again. One black mark against you and they'll dig up everything you ever did to get you out."

"Do you really think he'd do that?" Michaela asked. "I worked with him a few times as lead CSI on some of his cases, and sure, he might have said a few inappropriate things and his eye wandered a few times, but surely he wouldn't..."

"I know he would," Freya replied. "I'm his biggest threat. No offence, Ben, but I'm the only one experienced enough to be close to competition. With me out of the way, he knows he can do what he likes with the team. Sure, some of them will leave—"

"Like Gold, Chapman, and Gillespie," Ben added.

"Right, but whoever remains will be moulded to his work ethic, and God help them if that happens."

"Well, then surely the answer is simple," Michaela said.

"Really?" Freya replied. "And please don't suggest we throw his body in the river, Michaela. We've already had that one."

"I wasn't going to," she said and looked at Ben quizzically.

"Don't ask," he said.

"I was just going to suggest you fight fire with fire."

"Fight fire with fire?" Freya said, letting her head fall into her hands. "I need a bloody volcano to fight this fire. He has destroyed my team."

"Not yet he hasn't," Ben said.

"I need a drink," she said, and shoved herself out of the seat and edged past them both into the kitchen.

"You don't have to give up on them just yet," Michaela called out.

Freya opened a few cupboards and was surprised to see that in the short space of time that Ben and Michaela had been an item, she had managed to stock his cupboards with more than the usual Crunchy Nut Cornflakes and coffee.

"There's wine in the fridge," Ben called out from the lounge, and Freya poured herself a glass from a bottle with a little sailing boat on the label.

She took a large mouthful, topped up the glass, and then stepped back into the doorway.

"What are you suggesting?" she said, more able to focus now she had a glass in her hand.

"I'm suggesting that if DCI Standing has invested resources into digging up your old dirt, surely you can dig up some of his old dirt?"

Freya watched her lips move and heard the words, but the two were out of sync. She felt a little giddy at the idea, and angry that she hadn't thought of it herself.

"Who would we get to do it?" she said, looking at Ben.

"Can't one of the team do it?" Michaela asked. "They do still report in to you, don't they?"

"He's micromanaging them. He wants to know what each of them is working on at any given time. Besides, if any of them request files from the archives, he'll want to know why."

"Is he that bad?"

"As far as I can tell. Even Cruz has had his toilet breaks limited to ten minutes."

"*Limited* to ten minutes?" Michaela said, bemused at the idea of anybody spending longer than five at the very most.

"He has a weak constitution," Ben explained.

"Well, then one of you will have to do it," Michaela said. "It might mean working into the night, but if it's as serious as you're saying it is—"

"Unless," Freya said, cutting her off, then leaving them hanging as the idea germinated, sprouted, and came to fruit all in the space of a few seconds.

"Unless what?" Michaela asked as Freya stared hard into her eyes.

"Unless we had a friend with access to old forensic reports," Freya said. "Somebody who could request the complete investigations from the archives."

Michaela's eyes widened as she realised what Freya was saying.

"Oh, no. Not me. I only have access to forensic reports, not police files. I can't get statements."

"You can from the archives," Freya said, sipping at the cheap wine. "What do you think, Ben?"

"Me?" he said, holding his hands up in defence. "Don't get me involved."

"But you agree that Michaela is perfectly placed to help us?" Freya said. "She can access Standing's old cases."

"You're talking about hundreds of files," Ben said. "That could take weeks."

"Well then," Freya said, "we'd better get started, hadn't we?"

CHAPTER NINE

"What do you mean he's dead?" Tony said, as he slammed the front door behind them and followed them into the lounge where Jake, who had already arrived, was lying with his feet up on the sofa, nursing a swollen hand.

The house was open-plan and resembled those fashionable houses of the seventies. Some of the internal walls were of exposed stone and the archway through to the kitchen was purposefully uneven, or quirky, as she had heard Tony's father call it once, many years ago.

"I mean not breathing. Dead. No-pulse dead. Eyes wide open with blood pouring from every orifice dead, Tony," Rosie replied. "We've bloody killed him."

Jake twisted his body around to sit up. He stared at her, and then at Pete, to see if it was some kind of joke.

"You checked him though, right?" he said, and for a moment Rosie saw him as he'd been five or more years ago; a pale-faced and immature boy who scared easily.

"What do you mean we checked him? He's dead."

"You felt for a pulse?" he said, and his voice seemed to rise in pitch.

"No, I didn't bloody feel for a pulse."

"So, he might still be alive."

"Jake, he's dead, mate," Pete said, shaking his head, and the light beard that had begun to emerge this past year seemed to enhance his age, so that Rosie saw him as the man he might become. "I saw him. We took it too far."

"We?" Jake shouted. "*We* took it too far? I barely touched him."

"Oh, come off it. You were out of breath from hitting him. Look at your bloody hand, it's like a football."

"Yeah, well, if you think I'm getting involved in this, you've got another thing coming."

"You are involved," Rosie said. "Don't try and squirm out of this. We're all involved. We all waited for him."

"Yeah, but you didn't hit him, did you?" Pete said to her. "You might have been there, but you didn't exactly deliver any blows, did you?"

"I did actually," she began. "At least one."

"I'm not saying you didn't try, Rosie. But the fact is, if anybody is going to get done for this, it'll be us three."

"No, no way. I won't have it. I'm just as much a part of this as all of you. It's my bloody fault you did it in the first place."

"Don't say that," Pete said quietly. "It's not your fault. It's his fault. It's not your fault he couldn't keep his hands to himself, is it? Dirty bastard deserved it, as far as I'm concerned."

"Is that what you'll tell the police?" Tony asked, his tone flat and devoid of anything but the harsh reality. He may not have been as tall or broad as Pete, but his long limbs gave him an ape-like look. Although he hadn't the need to shave just yet, the acne scars that adorned his cheeks aged him beyond his fifteen years, which suited his mess of reddish hair. He'd tried to style it once, but the three of them had teased him so much that nowadays he barely even had it cut.

He moved to the fireplace, where his mother could be remembered in a line of framed photographs. His mother's death was something they never spoke of yet respected the way only true friends can.

Pete stared back at him in a brief moment of conflict.

"There won't be any police," Pete said quietly, and he glanced across at Rosie for support.

"There...what?" Tony said. "Of course there'll be police. There's a dead man in the nature reserve, Pete. Pervert or not, he's still a dead man. They don't not investigate a murder just because the dead man happens to be a nonce."

"I mean, there won't be any police because there won't be a body," Pete said, then watched both Jake's and Tony's faces come to the same conclusion.

"You what?" Jake said. "You're not going to–"

"Bury him," Pete said. "We're going to bury him. All of us."

"You've got to be bloody kidding me–"

"What's the alternative, Jake, eh? Wait until someone finds him? Maybe if we wait long enough, the birds will peck his eyes out and the badgers will eat his remains."

"Yeah, but burying him? Isn't that worse than just coming clean?" he said. "Shouldn't we just go to the police and tell them what he did?"

"Jake, have you any idea what it's like in a young offenders institution?"

"Not really, no."

"Well, you know all those movies you like? The prison movies? It's not like them, it's worse, mate. Young offenders units are not like an adult prison. They're not like Porridge or any of the stuff you see on TV. Young offenders are notorious for being bloody dangerous. And if I'm honest, you wouldn't last a day, let alone until you're eighteen and transferred to an adult prison." Pete paused, waiting for what he had said to sink in. "Nobody is going to the police. Nobody is going to tell anybody about this. Not a soul. Do I make myself clear?"

Tony walked away a few steps, kicked the door, and then turned and rejoined them.

"What's your plan then, Pete?" he asked. "I'm guessing you two have come up with an idea?"

"We have," Rosie said calmly. "We'll wait until this evening. When the sun is low. Then, we'll go down there with spades and shovels and whatever, and we'll move him."

"Where are you getting the tools from?"

"Your old man's shed," Pete told him.

"No, you are bleeding not–"

"Where else are we going to get them from?" Pete said, raising his voice again. "You said yourself your dad is away for a few days. I can't go to my house, it's on the other side of Horncastle. I can't have every man and their dog see me carting a bloody spade and shovel through the streets. At least from here, we can get into the nature reserve without anybody seeing us. We can go out the back gate."

"For God's sake," Tony said, turning to kick the door again but regaining his composure en route. He began to pace, thinking the idea through, just as Rosie and Pete had already done. He'd be considering the consequences of every option they had. And then he'd come up with the one idea they hadn't voiced. "We could just leave him."

"Yeah," Jake said, his light voice contrasting with Pete and Tony's. "We could just leave him there. Deny all knowledge, like."

"Oh right," Pete replied. "Tell me, Tony. When were you last arrested?"

He shrugged. "Last year. That bakery thing. You remember?"

"Right," Pete said. "Swab you, did they?"

"Swab me?"

"Did they take your DNA?"

"Well, yeah, it's standard practice now, isn't it?"

"And how certain are you that not a shred of your DNA is on that body?" Pete said, his eyebrows raised in question but already knowing the answer. Tony said nothing and Jake slumped back on the sofa. "They'll be checking every inch of Michael's body for blood. They'll test every bit they find, and when they do, they'll run it through their machine, or whatever it is they do, and do you know what will happen? A little bell will ring. A little bloody chirpy bell to signal the machine has found a match, Tony. A DNA sample belonging to a dopey little kid in the arse end of nowhere with three mates who were all too frightened to do what was right. The next thing you know, about thirty coppers will be tearing through Horncastle at four a.m., kicking down our doors. And when they do, Tony, when they drag you out of this house in your underpants, just do me a favour, will you?"

"What's that?" Tony said quietly, unable to meet his stare.

"Look up," Pete said. "Look up at the sky. Because I promise you this, if we leave that body there for somebody else to find, that will be the last time you see it for a very, very long time."

"What do we do until then?" Jake asked.

"We stay here," Rosie said. "We get the tools ready. We need gloves, plastic bags, a saw–"

"A what?" Jake said.

"A saw, Jake," she replied, holding his stare for as long as it needed to drill the point home. "Just hope we don't need it."

"For crying out loud–"

"And we also need rope, spades, and shovels. Have you got all that, Tony?"

He waited a moment, doing his best not to emulate Jake's reaction, and then nodded.

"I can't believe I'm actually agreeing to this, but yes. I think my dad's got all that in the shed."

"We'll also need some old clothes," Pete said. "Anything will do. We'll come straight back here afterwards and burn them."

"Here?" Tony blurted out, then relented, seeing it was the best option they had. "My old man's got an incinerator bin. We can use that."

"Bloody hell," Jake said. He leaned forward, and as Rosie had expected, he was the first to break into tears. His breathing was heavy and his hands visibly shook with fear. "What if somebody finds him during the day? A dog walker or something?"

"They won't," Pete said when Rosie looked to him to respond. He held his bloodied hands up. "We rolled him into the ditch and dragged him under the bridge. If we don't move him tonight, he'll start to smell. Then we're well and truly stuffed."

"Tonight it is then," Rosie said and looked to the other two for their agreement.

"Tonight," Tony mumbled, and all eyes fell on Jake, who wiped away his tears with the back of his hand and stood to join them.

"Alright then," he said finally. "Tonight."

CHAPTER TEN

Michaela slapped a pile of blue folders onto Ben's dining table with enough gusto to rouse Ben from his slumber in the armchair.

"You're back," he said, moments before Freya poked her head into the lounge, eyed the pile of folders, and then took a moment to read Michaela's mood. It had been a big ask, but the risk was worth it if they could actually make it work.

"Did you have any trouble?" Freya asked.

"No, not really. I had to tell them I was looking to analyse historical data."

"Not really a lie then," Ben added, hoping to bring a little cheer into the chat.

But he failed.

"It was a lie, Ben," she said. "Because, of course, it won't be me doing the analysing. That will be the pair of you."

"That's fine," Freya said. "And listen, Michaela, thanks for doing this for me."

"Just make it work," Michaela replied, and she gave Freya one of those tired gazes Ben had learned to watch out for. "Just make it worthwhile."

Freya stepped forward and flipped through the files.

"They're all there," Michaela told her. "Every investigation you asked for. The hit and run in Woodhall Spa, the old man who helped his wife die, the couple with the creepy basement, and more."

"This is perfect," Freya said. "I can't believe you got them all."

"He was actually quite helpful," she said. "I had to do a little flirting, of course. Sorry, Ben."

"You probably made his day," Ben replied.

"He was able to run a search for any investigations for which Standing was SIO. Took him all of ten minutes to locate the files."

"But won't he wonder why you only wanted Standing's investigations?"

"I told him it was less about the SIO and more about the dates of the investigations," she said. "You see, Standing transferred to Lincoln HQ what, eight months ago?"

"Give or take, yes," Ben said.

"We've had a new centrifuge since then. I told him I wanted to see the difference in separation rate between the old and the new. I said it was a budgeting exercise."

"Separation rate?" Ben said.

"It's a calculation from the average separation factor of a particular centrifuge minus the angular velocity of the centrifuge rotor, minus—"

"Alright," Ben said, holding his hands up. "It's complicated then. I get it."

"That's funny," she replied. "He had almost the same reaction."

Freya smiled and ran her hand over the pile of folders.

"Well, I for one don't care what you had to tell him. I'm just glad you did. Drink?"

"I need one," Michaela said.

Freya disappeared into the kitchen, from where she called out, "I'm also doing dinner, Michaela. Are you okay with scallops?"

"Scallops?" she muttered quietly and peered quizzically at Ben.

He smiled apologetically and lowered his voice.

"I said she could stay for a few days."

"A few days?"

"She doesn't have any furniture," Ben said.

"She's your bloody ex—"

"Are scallops okay for you, Michaela?" Freya said again. "We're having it with baby spinach and a spiced pomegranate glaze."

"Sounds posh," Michaela said.

"I thought I'd better use up what I had in the fridge," she replied. "We popped back to mine while you were gone."

"Well, then I suppose Ben should go and get some more wine." She eyed Ben angrily then smiled through the kitchen door at Freya.

"Oh, it's okay. I brought plenty. I usually keep a good cellar." Freya walked into the lounge and held out a glass for Michaela, who accepted it gracefully and then smelled it with caution. "Chardonnay. It pairs wonderfully with scallops."

"Right," Michaela said. "Of course it does."

"No allergies? Seafood okay?"

"Perfect," Michaela said. "Looking forward to it."

Freya gave Ben a knowing smile behind Michaela's back then sauntered off into the kitchen.

"She's my what?"

"Your ex. You bloody well slept with her," Michaela hissed. "Now forgive me for sounding a little highly strung, but I've been more than accommodating so far. You disappeared off to Saltfleet with her, stayed in a caravan with her, and you spend every minute of every day either with her or under her influence somehow. Now I come home after doing her a favour, which was incredibly risky, I might add, only to find you've bloody well invited her to stay for a few days."

"She doesn't have any furniture, Michaela. What was I supposed to do?" She stared down at him and her glare somehow softened. "She's a mate. That's all. This is what mates do, right?"

"Come and get it," Freya said from the doorway. She burst into the room holding three plates just as a waiter in a restaurant might then set them down on the table.

Eventually, Michaela relented, succumbing to Ben's good nature.

"I hear you're to be our guest for a few days," she said, turning to greet Freya with a welcoming smile. "How lovely."

"I did protest," Freya replied. "But where would any of us be without good friendship?"

"My thoughts precisely," Michaela said, then eyed the food and any good-natured pretence was lost to genuine awe. "Wow. This looks incredible."

"Oh, it's just a little something," Freya said modestly. She eyed the three seats but remained standing. "It'll keep the wolves at bay, as they say. Now, where should I sit? I'd hate to get in the way."

"Anywhere you like," Ben said, as he plopped down into one of the old, wooden dining chairs and dragged a plate closer. Michaela took the seat beside him, leaving Freya no alternative but to sit opposite, beside the stack of files which she had opened before she'd even picked up her cutlery. He jabbed his fork into what looked to him like an internal organ of some kind. "What the hell is this?"

"That's a scallop, Ben," Freya replied without looking up.

"A scallop? I thought scallops were like chips?"

"No, Ben, you're thinking of potato scallops. Different food group, I'm afraid."

"So what's a scallop?"

"Seafood," Freya replied. "A mollusc."

"Fish?"

"No, it's a mollusc, Ben. Different again."

"Do they come from the sea?" he asked, holding his laden fork up for inspection.

Freya looked mortified. She looked up from the file and across at him as if she was daring him to try and eat the entire thing in one bite.

"Yes, Ben," she said slowly. "But it's not a fish. It's a scallop."

He took a large bite and then placed the fork down to wash the mouthful down with a swig of wine.

"I see what you mean," he said, still chewing the weird, buttery texture. He swallowed and ran his tongue across his teeth. "The wine goes well with it. Good choice."

He caught Michaela's amusement in the corner of his eye, and, as he'd hoped, he witnessed Freya's despair opposite him.

Michaela peered over the table to see which investigation Freya was perusing.

"The weird couple with the basement?" she asked, to which Freya nodded and gave her a questioning look. "I had a quick read while I was waiting for him to bring more."

"And here's me thinking that Ben and I were to do the analysing."

"Oh, you are," Michaela said. "I have no interest in whether or not a police procedure has been carried out to the letter or not."

"No, I don't suppose you do."

Michaela cut a small portion off of a scallop and slipped it into her mouth along with a few leaves of baby spinach. She chewed, swallowed, then drank, savouring the taste. All the while, Ben watched her with fascination.

"I do have a vested interest in scientific protocol, however," she added, which caught Freya's attention. "You might want to read the transcript from the interview with their landlord. John Spencer, I believe his name was."

Freya flipped through the mass of pages, finding the statement after a few short moments, but then discovered it was quite lengthy, too lengthy to read through with scallops on her plate.

"Do you want to give me the highlights?" Freya said, clearly astonished at Michaela's intuition.

"Don't be surprised. I've read hundreds of them," Michaela

said, maintaining that glorious and victorious smile. "If a suspect or a witness declines to provide a DNA sample, the interviewing officer usually mentions it at the beginning of the interview."

"And this is significant because?" Ben asked.

"Because the evidence Standing submitted to CPS includes a DNA sample from John Spencer," Michaela said. "But if he declined to provide a voluntary sample, how did Standing obtain it?" She took another bite and set her fork down to collect her glass. "Delicious, Freya," she said. "Absolutely delicious."

Freya laughed loud and carefree, louder than Ben had heard her laugh for a long time.

"You're missing one thing," Freya said, as she slipped a delicate slice between her white teeth, rolled the morsel around, then chewed and swallowed with all the practised etiquette of royalty.

"What's that?" Michaela asked, and Freya turned the file around for them both to read.

"Standing is smarter than he looks. He wouldn't submit flawed evidence to CPS. At least, not while he had minions to take the fall for him."

"He didn't submit it himself?" Michaela said, and Freya leaned across to jab a well-manicured fingernail at the signature box.

"DS Gillespie," she said. "If we flagged that little faux pas to an independent committee, we'd be sure to break the team up and one of our friends would probably be up on a charge."

"The sneaky–"

"No vulgarities at the table, Ben, please," Freya said before she returned her attention to the files. "One thing is for certain, this is going to be one hell of a minefield to navigate."

"And we have just one week to find something?" Ben said.

She winced at the comment and grinned. "It's going to be a long week," she said. "Let's just hope we don't get any distractions."

CHAPTER ELEVEN

From the raised decking in Tony's garden, they watched the sun sink lower and lower, seeming to pull the pit of Rosie's stomach down as if the two were connected somehow.

"Are you sure we won't be seen?" Rosie said, and Tony pushed himself out of one of the rattan seats and came to stand beside her, staring at the sunset with equal dread.

"We should be fine," he replied. "We just need to act normal."

"Act normal?" Jake said, the smallest of the three boys. He held his arms up to show the lengthy sleeves covering his hands. "I look like a bloody puppet."

Ignoring Jake's emotional outburst, Rosie stepped over to inspect the tools they had collated, and Pete joined her.

"I'll take the spade and the shovel," he began. "You take the bag with the rope and the gloves, Tony takes the bag with the saw and hand tools, and Jake can take the bag with the tarp. That way, it's only me who looks suspicious. You three just look like you're going somewhere carrying bags."

"Oh right," Jake said. "A bloody puppet with a bag of rope. If anyone asks, I'll tell them I'm looking for someone to reconnect my strings."

"Using humour to mask your fears is not an attractive trait," Rosie told him. "We're all scared, Jake. None of us wants to be doing this."

He lowered his head in embarrassment and mumbled something to himself.

"Why don't we just put it all in one bag?" Tony asked. "Why do we all need bags?"

Pete stepped forward, his expression grave.

"Imagine if whoever is carrying the bag gets stopped by the police, Tony," he said. "What's in the bag, sir? Oh, you know, just my body-burying kit, officer. Some rope so I can drag the body somewhere nice and quiet, a tarp to wrap him up in, and a nice, sharp saw, in case I have to cut him up into bits."

Tony said nothing. If anything, Pete's sarcasm had not only delivered the message but had also accentuated the gravitas of what they were about to do.

Tony looked away, finding some kind of solace in the sunset.

"Alright," he said. "I get your point."

"This way if one of us gets stopped, we'll have a much easier time explaining things."

"Some rope?" Jake said. "How am I going to explain that?"

"I don't know. I can't think for you, can I?" Pete said. "Make something up. You found it, or you borrowed it for something."

"It's time," Rosie announced, her voice cutting the spitting head off of what could have escalated into an emotional argument. She picked up one of the bags and made her way down the garden to the gate that opened onto the nature reserve. She waited for them to follow – Pete, then Tony, and Jake at the end, whose complexion was a shiny pale grey. "Ready?"

Nobody replied, which she took to be her cue to open the gate and peer out, searching for signs of life.

"Can you see anyone?" Pete whispered.

"It's clear," she replied, and with a final look at them all, she stepped out into the open. "Just four friends walking through the nature reserve like we've been doing for years. That's all we are, right?"

She would have expected Jake to offer some kind of humorous comment, but he was quiet, and rightly so, Rosie thought. What they were about to do deserved to be a solemn affair. They were robbing a man of his life, robbing his family of memory, and leaving in his wake a whole host of questions they would never know the answers to.

And it was that thought that stuck with her during the five-minute walk to the bridge. It wasn't the memories of his visits to her room. It wasn't the smell of alcohol on his breath or his pressing weight on top of her. Those things she would deal with in time. She would never get over them, but maybe she could learn to live with them. What she would never learn to live with, however, was the guilt of what they were about to do.

They walked in silence. Not like four friends cutting through the nature reserve, not like four friends on their way out on a Saturday evening, but like four friends who had made a grave mistake, and when faced with the opportunity to make amends were choosing the easy way out.

"This is it," Pete said, as they neared the bridge. He spoke as they walked, quietly but with an authority that Rosie had grown to admire. "We're going to walk over the bridge and into the forest."

"I thought you said you dragged him under the bridge?" Jake said, his whiny voice in stark contrast to Pete's pubescent grumble.

"We did," he said. "But before we dive under there and drag him back out, we need to make sure there's nobody in the forest, and we need to dig a bloody hole, don't we? Unless you think we should dig the hole with him lying beside us?"

"Alright, alright," Jake said. "I get it. You only had to say."

They crossed the bridge and, for Rosie, the tale of the three goats and the old troll sprang to mind. But in this instance, the troll would not call out to question who dare trip-trap across his bridge.

Only when they were in the safety of the trees on the far side of the bridge did she relax a little, and once more, it was Pete who took charge.

"Right, we need somewhere out of the way," he said, scanning the darkening forest in search of the ideal spot.

"What about under that tree?" Jake said, pointing to a tree so laden with thick, bushy branches that it was almost impossible to get near. "If we cut a path in, we'd be out of sight and nobody would go in there."

"We can't dig under a tree, Jake," Pete said.

"Why not? It's perfect."

"Because trees have roots, mate."

"So?"

Pete stared at him in disbelief.

"Have you ever dug a hole, Jake?"

"Yeah, course I have."

"Was it next to a tree?"

"I don't know. It was ages ago now."

"Well, trust me. If we dig there, we'll hit tree roots. We need somewhere covered. Maybe the ditch over there?" he said, pointing to a covered space concealed by bushes, where, as children they had built a den. He ran to the spot and tossed the spade and shovel to the ground. "This is it. We'll do it here."

"This is where we used to play as kids," Tony said, sounding a little unnerved at the idea.

"And why did we play here?" Pete said. "Why did we build our den here?"

"Because nobody comes here. Because it gave us privacy," Rosie said, stepping forward to stand beside him. "It's perfect."

He stared at her knowingly, and she remembered a time when it had been just the two of them in the den. Two teenagers exploring each other, not with lust, or with love, but with curiosity. It had been a few brief moments of wandering hands, inquisitive minds, and virgin sensations that would forever more be marked by a shallow grave.

He dug the spade into the ground, levered it back, and then tossed the earth to one side. The others looked on with dread in their eyes. This would be the easy part. The grotesque memories would be formed from dragging the putrid carcass from under the bridge and across the forest to the hole.

She suspected, exactly as she had done many times during the day, that each of them had imagined the rolling of his limp body. Or perhaps they had imagined rigor mortis to have set in, in which case, there would be no rolling or lolling of limp limbs, just a stiff, awkward pose to make the task even more arduous.

"Your turn," Pete said, breathless from the exertion. He held the spade out for her to take, then collected the shovel to excavate the pile of earth he had created.

She set to work, and although her efforts were far less impactful than his, she was determined not to sit back and watch. She discovered that if she broke away the sides of the hole and loosened the soil beneath, Pete could come in with his shovel and scoop the debris away.

Before long, they were at least a foot deep – the length of a school ruler – and the hole was large enough for Jake to lay in if he curled into a ball.

They dug for another twenty minutes until the hole was so deep that she had to step down into it to make more of a difference. The sides were as high as her thighs.

"That's deep enough," Pete said, at last, taking the spade from Rosie. He threw the tools to one side and wiped the sweat from his brow, leaving a brown smear across his forehead. He collected one of the bags and pulled out a coil of blue rope Tony had found in his dad's shed. All eyes were on him until he tossed it to Tony. "We've done our bit. Now it's your turn."

"You what?"

"You two go and get him. You haven't done anything yet."

"That's not fair. You didn't even give us a chance to dig."

"I didn't see you trying to get the spade off of me," Pete said. "You were quite happy to stand there and watch us work so it's your turn now. He's under the bridge. You can't miss him."

The stalemate lasted seconds. It wasn't swayed by bravado or by masculinity, but by Tony's sheer willpower to get the job done and get out of there. So, he caved, and with it, he took Jake's hopes.

"Come on, Jake," he grumbled, as he made his way back towards the bridge. Jake followed with his head hanging low and his hands in his pockets. He kicked a piece of tree bark across the forest, then stumbled on a tree root, only just managing to stay on his feet.

He didn't look back. Neither of them did. They just walked out into the open, ready to do what had to be done.

"Get the tarp ready," Pete told Rosie when they were alone. "We'll wrap him in it before he goes in the hole. It might keep the smell in for a few days."

"Might?" Rosie said.

"I haven't done this before either," he reminded her. "This is a collection of things I've learned from watching the bloody telly."

"And the saw?" she asked, at which he sighed.

"I'm hoping we don't have to use it."

He stared down at the hole, which, judging by its size, could accommodate a full-grown man, so long as they could bend his limbs a little.

They stretched the tarp out over the hole and Rosie leaned against a nearby tree.

"Do you think they need help?" she asked. "It's quite a steep bank."

But no sooner had she asked the question than somebody came running into the forest. They prepared to make a run for it, and Pete nudged Rosie back to put himself between the dark figure sprinting through the dark forest and the two of them.

"It's Tony," he said at last, and she felt his grip on her arm wane.

Tony, however, was less relaxed. He ran all the way up to them, eyes wide, his mouth hanging open in panic.

"He's not there," he said finally, grabbing onto his scraggly hair with both hands in desperation. "Oh God, oh God–"

"Who isn't?" Pete asked, although it was clear who Tony was referring to. Rosie eyed him and watched as her friend's usually calm manner gave way to something else altogether.

"Who do you think? Michael. The body," he said, and his usual low voice had elevated by at least two octaves. "It's not bloody there."

CHAPTER TWELVE

The trouble with sharing a ride to work with Ben Savage was, Freya thought, that she dare not moan about being stuck behind a tractor on a Monday morning, seeing as his family had farmed the land for generations. Just about everyone and their dogs either farmed themselves or knew somebody who did.

They had slowed to twenty-two miles per hour and the lane was too narrow and winding to attempt a pass, so she settled back and took a deep breath, before breaking what had become an uncomfortable silence.

"I'll be out of your hair in a few days," she told him. "I was looking at the used marketplace online last night, and I think I've found a decent couch that will serve me as a bed until my furniture arrives."

"You don't need to hurry," he said.

"Yes, I do. I heard what Michaela had to say, and for once I think she's right."

"The part about you being a spoiled cow?" he said.

"No, the part about you and I having a history, and how accommodating she's been so far," she said. "Did she really call me a spoiled cow—"

"No," he replied. "I was kidding. I'm just trying to lighten the mood a little. Listen, you can stay as long as you like. It's my house, after all."

"But she lives there too."

"She stays with me, that's all," Ben said. "She still has her own place. Hang on, why don't I ask her if you can use her place until your furniture arrives? I'm sure she won't mind."

"Because, Ben, I've just spent most of my savings and a large part of my pension on a pretty, little cottage in a pretty, little village, and I want to be in it, with furniture or not. If I have to slum it on a couch for a few weeks, then I will."

"Don't say I didn't ask," he replied, as the tractor eventually pulled into a lay-by to let the traffic pass. She accelerated past it, checked her speed, and then slowed to thirty as they passed through one of the many tiny hamlets that dotted the rural landscape.

"She could be useful though," Freya said.

"Useful? As in making dinner useful, or, like, Swiss Army knife useful?"

"As in, she has an eye for details. She could help us go through the files."

"I think you'll find she's made her position on that quite clear," Ben told her. "And if you don't mind, I don't really want my girlfriend involved in my career."

"You didn't say that when she helped us with the Saltfleet job."

"I didn't have much choice, did I? Neither did she, come to think of it. By the time you'd waved your magic wand, we'd been corralled into a threesome and she spent her days off scanning through forensics reports."

"Play to people's strengths, Ben," she said. "That's the key to great leadership."

They turned into the station car park and she had a feeling he had more to say but was refraining. It was Monday morning, and they had a monumental task ahead of them, so she gave him that little bit of freedom, to stay quiet.

They parked and strode towards the fire escape door side by side but in silence, which Freya was enjoying. It gave her mind room to stretch its legs, to unpick ideas and imagine what the future might look like should they actually manage to get Standing off their backs one way or another.

"Inspector Bloom?" a voice said when they were just halfway up the staircase to the first floor. They both stopped and found Sergeant Priest, a burly Yorkshireman who took pride in being the longest-serving officer in the station and rejecting any career path more advanced than custody sergeant.

"Sergeant Priest, good morning," she replied, then left him room to speak.

"Got a fellow down here wants to speak to somebody," he said.

"Can't uniform deal with it?"

"He wants a detective."

The smell of cheap coffee that wafted down from the first floor was not an alluring one, but it was far more appealing than having to deal with whiny customers at seven forty-five in the morning.

"Do we know what he wants?"

"Wants to report a missing person," Priest said.

"Well, then surely that's a job for uniform? CID at best."

"Says there's been foul play. He's adamant, in fact."

"What's all this?" another voice said, this time from above them on the first-floor landing, and Freya recognised the Birmingham accent; a little part of her died inside.

"Missing person, guv," Priest said. "Fellow reckons his colleague is in trouble, or something. Been missing since Friday night."

"Bloom?" Standing said, leaning over the handrail.

"I have explained that a missing person is most likely suited to uniform or CID," she said, then added a reluctant, "guv."

"CID has a lot on this week," Standing said, musing aloud. "You? What do you have?"

"Reports, reports, and more reports," she said, seeing where he was leading her.

"Good. Reports can be done anytime," he said. "Go with Sergeant Priest and take a statement. We don't want the community waiting on cheap, plastic seats while we play hot potato, do we?"

"Guv," she said, by way of a confirmation.

"You can get a coffee afterwards if that's what you're worried about."

"Coffee?" she said, as she descended the stairs she had just climbed. "Is that what you call it?"

They pushed through from the fire escape stairwell into the ground floor corridor that linked the custody suite at the back of the building to the front desk.

"Sorry, Freya," Priest began. "If I'd known he was up there listening, I'd have kept my voice down."

"No need to apologise," she told him. "It's not your fault we're now under the influence of a class A moron, is it?"

He smiled an apology, then buzzed through to the waiting room with his access card.

"Mr Barker?" he said, and a man in a pair of brown coveralls and a tweed flat cap stood from one of the cheap, blue, plastic seats and sauntered over to them. "This is Inspector Bloom and Sergeant Savage. They'll take your statement from you."

"Right," he said, eyeing Freya and Ben. Then, as if he had just remembered his manners, he snatched his flat cap from his head to reveal a mass of dark, curly hair that on a more confident man might have swayed her attraction. He held his hat in both hands before him, fumbling with it nervously. His fingers were grubby and his nails unkempt and he carried the distinct, but pleasant, aroma of a man who works with wood.

"I'll just leave you to it, then shall I?" Priest said, and he slipped off back to the comfort of his custody desk.

"Mr Barker, follow me," Freya said, leading him along the corridor and into a vacant interview room. "Have you had a coffee this morning?"

"Um, no," he said, as he took the seat Freya proffered.

She sat down opposite him, pulled in her chair, and prepared herself for what was sure to be a mundane account of a paranoid man.

"Good, neither have I," she told him, and she gestured for Ben to take notes. "How can we help?"

"Well, as the man said, I'd like to report a missing–"

"A missing man, yes," Freya said, hurrying him along. "What makes you think he's missing?"

The question seemed to stump him. It was a simple question that should have elicited the simplest of responses.

However...

"Well, I haven't seen him for a few days."

"Do you live with this man?" she asked, to which he pulled a face.

"No."

"And had you arranged to meet him at any point over the course of the weekend?"

"Not meet him exactly."

"Have you tried to call him, at least?" Freya asked, which sparked a little more enthusiasm from him.

"Yes," he said. "Yes, I have. Several times, in fact."

"Well, that is often the best place to start," she said. "Okay, let's take some details, shall we? Name?"

"Um, will that be my name or his?"

She stared at him, and, for a split second debated whether or not this man was a plant from Standing to test her patience. Maybe the Beast from the East Midlands was watching them on the camera, smiling to himself at Freya's reactions.

He probably had a coffee, too.

"Are you missing, Mr Barker?"

"Eh?"

"Are you missing?" she said again, which raised a wry smile on Ben's face, which she caught from the corner of her eye.

"No," he said, a little confused.

"Well, then let's start with the name of the missing person, shall we?"

"Oh, right," he said, then leaned forward towards Ben who waited with his pen poised. "His name is Michael Levy."

CHAPTER THIRTEEN

"Right, listen up," Freya said, and she clapped her hands three times to get everybody's attention. "As of ten minutes ago, we're busy. So, please close your laptops, get a coffee if you need one, use the washroom if you need to, and cancel any plans you have for lunch."

"Can I ask, boss," Gillespie started, "should we do those things in that order?"

He smiled at her, having clearly recovered from yesterday's hangover.

"In your case, no," she said. "Your laptop is rarely open and, if I know you like I think I do, there is already more caffeine inside you than a Brazilian rainforest. Everybody else has full autonomy."

"I haven't got any plans for lunch," Cruz said, scratching his head.

"Well, good. I'll be sure to assign you a suitable task that takes you as far away from the station as possible. In fact, you can start by getting the coffees in. Proper coffee from the bakery, not the muck in the kitchen. Standing might have bought a new coffee machine, but the coffee is still cheap and nasty," Freya said. She pulled a twenty-pound note from her purse and held it out for him. "Eight coffees. You should know what we all drink by now."

"Eight coffees?" he repeated.

"That's right," she said. "Make mine strong and black. The type that gives you heart palpitations and breath like a geography teacher."

Puzzled, but not daring to question her remark, he turned on his heels and made his way towards the door.

Freya set her bag down on her desk and addressed the room. "Five minutes to use the washroom, everyone. Cruz is getting the coffees in."

A scrape of chairs followed, and then a little voice called out from the doors.

"Boss?"

"Cruz? That was quick."

"Oh, I haven't been yet," he said, stating the obvious and missing Freya's acerbity. "I was just wondering…"

"You were wondering if, by doing a coffee run, you would still be entitled to five minutes to use the washroom," Freya finished for him, without looking up from where she hunted for a whiteboard marker that actually worked.

"Well, yeah."

"No," she told him, then checked her watch. "Four minutes."

"But I might miss something," he said.

"Oh, I imagine that your colleagues will fill you in on any details," she said. "Besides, it doesn't take a rocket scientist to know what part you'll be playing in our little investigation, does it?"

"Not door to door," he said with a whine. "Not again."

"Bingo," she replied, with as much enthusiasm as she could muster. Then her amusement faded. "Coffees, please, Cruz. And don't worry, I can assure you there will be plenty of opportunities for everyone on this one."

"What are you doing?" Ben asked when the room had cleared.

She began where she always did, at the whiteboard with a single name in the centre. "It's a bloody missing person case, not the Yorkshire Ripper. We can't put all our resources onto it."

"Au contraire, Ben. DCI Standing said we were to investigate a missing person, so we're going to investigate a missing person."

"I don't get it," he replied. "What are we all going to do? It's not like we have a body. All we have is the word of a—"

"Of a what?" Freya said, seeing Ben about to use a less-than-politically-correct description.

"Of Drew Barker," he said. "For all we know, Michael Levy is at home with his feet up watching the news."

"Well, then it'll be a quick investigation, won't it?" she said, then relaxed a little and sat back on the edge of her desk. "Listen, DCI Standing has requested – no – instructed us to work on a missing person investigation. Now, I don't know if that's because he genuinely has CID tied up with more mundane tasks or if he's doing this to belittle me, but either way, I'm going to do exactly as instructed. I'm not having him pull me up on an insubordination charge. So if he wants a major crimes team to investigate the musings of a paranoid lunatic, then that's exactly what we'll do, and we'll throw everything we have at it."

"Right," Ben said. "As long as you know what you're doing."

"Oh, Ben," she replied, as the team began to file back into the room. "I know what I'm doing. But the fun part is that Standing doesn't have a clue what I'm capable of. He won't know what hit him."

"I hope you're right," Ben replied. "If not, this is going to be the most resource-intensive manhunt in history."

"Michael Levy," Freya called out before the team settled back at their desks and found distractions. "Last seen on Friday morning at his workplace, which is a furniture restoration workshop in Horncastle."

"Sorry, what?" Gillespie said.

"Is something I've said not clear?" Freya asked.

"Aye, well, only the part about a man who hasn't been seen since Friday morning, boss."

"No, I'd say that was a fairly accurate understanding."

"You mean, he's a missing person, boss?"

"That's right," she said. "Problem?"

"Aye, well, not really. It's just that we normally deal with major crimes, boss," he said. "The clue's in the name of the team. Major investigations."

"And this isn't a major investigation?" she asked. "A missing man?"

"Aye, well, it could be construed as major, I grant you, boss," he said, digging himself a hole deep enough to park his ego in. "It's just that we normally deal with dead people. Bodies and the like, you know?"

"Yes," she said. "Yes, we do, don't we?"

"Aye," he said, to which Freya said nothing.

"Well, I'm glad that's cleared up," she said, readdressing the room. "Does anybody else have any questions so far? We do have a lot to cover, so if we're going to stop every couple of minutes for Q and A sessions, then I'll need to call Cruz to order some more coffees."

"I'm good," Nillson said.

"I'm okay so far," Anderson added.

Freya glanced at everybody else who appeared ready to move on.

"Good. So, as DS Gillespie has rightfully and rather intuitively noticed, this is, in fact, a missing person investigation, and before anybody asks, we're just doing this because our illustrious leader has asked us to do so."

"What about CID?" Gold asked.

"Busy, apparently," she replied. "Probably doing what you've all been doing for the past few weeks."

"What, paperwork?"

"It's very likely," she said. "But we are where we are, and we've been given a job to do, so we'll do it to the very best of our abilities. Michael Levy owns a furniture restoration business in Horncastle. He lives in Horncastle with his girlfriend and her daughter. His dear friend and colleague, Drew Barker, reports that he was acting very strangely on Friday morning and hasn't been seen since."

"Did he describe strangely?" Nillson asked.

"Not really, but he did mention that they had a particularly large consignment due yesterday afternoon and he didn't show. Which resulted in the lorry being turned away as Michael Levy is the only one with keys to the workshop."

"Is that it?" Nillson asked.

"Nope, there's more. Mr Barker has tried to call him and has even been round to his house. All to no avail."

"Car?" Gillespie said.

"He has a company van which is still parked outside the workshop," she replied. "Next?"

"Phone," Gold said. "Maybe Chapman can ask her contact at the network provider to see where and when his phone last communicated with a mast?"

"Nice idea," Freya said, and she gestured for Ben to hand the number to Chapman. "Any other ideas?"

"The pub?" Gillespie said.

"The what?"

"The pub," he said sincerely. "If ever I'm reported missing, that's the first place you should look for me."

"Barker mentioned a pub," Freya said. "He said he's often in there. I suggest we visit all the pubs in Horncastle to see if anybody knows him, and if they do, when did they last see him?"

"All the pubs?" Gillespie said with a grin.

"All the pubs," Freya replied. "That should keep the pair of you occupied."

"Aye," he replied with a laugh. "I'll see you next week sometime."

"Of course, I'd expect you not to drink on the job, Gillespie," she replied. "Do you think you can manage that?"

His smile faded.

"You want us to visit every pub in Horncastle and not have a drink in any of them?"

"It makes sense to start with those pubs closest to his home," she said. "That should make the task a little less arduous."

"Aye," he said, with far less enthusiasm than he had shown only seconds before. "I suppose we do have his address, do we?"

"I'm typing up Ben's notes," Chapman said. "I'll send everyone a copy. The address is on there."

"Thank you, Chapman," Freya said.

"What about me, ma'am?" Gold said, her delicate voice innocent in contrast to Gillespie's gruff Glaswegian grumblings.

"I want you to visit the girlfriend," Freya replied. "Find out when he was last home, where he went, his mood, you know? The usual. I'd be keen to understand why it wasn't her who reported him missing."

"Right," Gold replied.

"Chapman, Mr Barker suggested that our missing person was not himself. He said he had something on his mind," Freya said. "Check his bank records. Check for previous, too, while you're at it. Let's see if we can understand who exactly we are looking for. If you need a warrant for his bank details, let me know."

"No problem, ma'am," Chapman replied, like an ever-faithful Border Collie.

"Which leaves DS Nillson and DC Anderson," Freya said. "I want you to visit his workshop. You'll need to go with Gold to his house to get the keys from his girlfriend. Failing that, employ uniform to help you gain entry. He might have locked himself inside if he's as unstable as Barker suggested."

"Sounds good, boss," Nillson said.

"Have a look around. Check any recent paperwork. If you can

access his emails without breaking protocol, do so. Find me something."

"I have a question, boss," Anderson said, and she shifted uncomfortably in her seat.

"Go on, Jenny," Freya replied.

"Isn't this a bit overkill?" she said. "I mean, it's a missing person. Won't Granger have something to say about eight of us working on it?"

"I'm sure he will," Freya replied. "But DCI Standing has given us an instruction and we are going to obey his orders to the tee. If he wants us to waste time with a missing person, then that's what we'll do, and when Detective Superintendent Granger questions me on why his resources have been applied in such a manner, I shall tell him exactly that. We'll have evidence of our investigation, including statements, a family liaison officer, a search of the property and workplace, the works."

Anderson smiled, as did Nillson, who thankfully saw the ingenuity of Freya's plan.

"I like it," Nillson said, and Freya winked at her.

"Any questions?" Freya asked, snapping the lid back on the marker. "No? Good. Let's get to it. Let's find Michael Levy."

The silence that followed spoke volumes.

"Right, get to it," she said. "Let's show DCI Standing exactly how capable we are."

The door opened and Cruz stumbled through carrying two cardboard trays with eight coffees.

"What did I miss?" he said, slightly breathless.

"I'll fill you in on the way," Gillespie told him, as he pulled the cup marked with a large Jim in felt tip from the tray.

"On the way where?" Cruz asked.

At this, Gillespie called out from the corridor, "Down the pub, Gabby. You and me, pal, are going on a wee pub crawl."

CHAPTER FOURTEEN

The house was average looking, much like her own, Jackie thought. It would be a two bedroom, three at the most, with a single bathroom upstairs, and maybe a cloakroom downstairs. She'd heard her mum tell her they were thrown up after the Second World War to accommodate growth, and to replace those that were demolished during the bombings.

The path was of solid concrete with a few steps at the door and a steel tube handrail with barely a scrap of green paint left on it.

In her rearview mirror, she saw Nillson's car turn into the road, and she climbed out ready to meet them.

It was a quiet area with a forest that ran the length of one side of the road, plunging the houses into a cool shadow.

Nillson left the engine running and climbed from the car, leaving Anderson alone.

"I don't want to go in too heavy-handed," she said, as she led Jackie up the garden path. She rang the doorbell once, listening for the ring inside, then knocked hard three times.

"It all seems a little bit silly," Jackie said. "All this. He might not even be, you know, missing, like."

"I think that, given the circumstances," Nillson replied, "the boss is making the right call. Standing is looking for something to pull her up on."

"I know, but—"

The door opened and a face peered out, tired and worried looking.

"Hello?" Jackie said, holding her warrant card up for her to see. "Are you Alexandra Sinclair?"

The woman nodded, still peering around the door as a child might spy a stranger from behind her mother's skirt.

"I'm Detective Constable Gold," Jackie said. "We wondered if we could have a quick word."

"What about?" the woman replied.

"It's about a Michael Levy. We've had a report he's missing."

"A report?"

"Somebody is worried about him, Alexandra. Can you tell us when you saw him last?"

"I don't know. Friday, I suppose."

"Friday morning?"

"Yeah. Before I went to work. He was here. Sorry, what's all this about? Who's reported him missing?"

"A friend," Jackie explained. "We're just following up, that's all. Have you heard from him at all?"

"No. No, I haven't. I've been at work mostly."

"Do you know if he's been home? It's quite important, Alexandra."

"I don't know. I suppose I could check."

"It might be best if we came inside," Jackie suggested.

"Oh, I don't think that's a good idea," Alexandra began, and she pulled back to close the door, which banged against Nillson's boot. She saw the blockage then understood the tenacity in Nillson's stare, before reluctantly letting the door swing open.

"You've got five minutes," she said.

By the time Jackie and Nillson were inside, Alexandra was in the kitchen filling the kettle.

"We're just trying to help," Jackie said, as she moved through the hallway, making a mental note of everything she saw. "Do you have any idea at all where he might be?"

Alexandra clicked the kettle on, then turned to face them, leaning back on the kitchen counter and folding her arms.

It was only then that Jackie saw the deep bruising around her left eye and the swollen lower lip.

"Do I look like I care where he is?" she said. "With any luck, he'll be lying in a ditch somewhere."

"I'm sorry," Jackie said. "We didn't know—"

"Nobody does, do they?" she replied. "It's much easier to turn a blind eye."

It was Nillson who spoke next, driving the conversation on before they became entangled in a domestic abuse case.

"We need to access Michael's workshop," she said. "Would you happen to know where he keeps the keys?"

Alexandra peered at her, seemingly impressed that she hadn't questioned the bruise.

"He must have them with him."

"Are there any spares?" she asked, looking around the kitchen for a dish or a basket where a man might drop his keys. She opened an old metal biscuit tin on top of the microwave and flicked through a stack of opened envelopes, each marked only with Alexandra's name. No address and no stamp. "It's important that we get inside."

"Not that I know of. You can snoop all you like, but I can tell you now you won't find his keys here," Alexandra said, reaching across to close the biscuit tin lid. Then she spoke directly to Jackie, "He has trust issues."

"Even with his partner?"

"What do you think?" she said, letting her injuries speak for themselves. She took a breath, then, spying a box of cigarettes, took one and lit it. "I don't know who reported him missing, but the last time I saw him was Friday evening before I went to work. He wasn't here when I got home, and neither was he here on Saturday when I got home, and as far as I can tell, he hasn't been home since Friday."

"How can you be sure?" Nillson asked.

"There aren't any skiddy boxers in the laundry," she replied. "As for where he might have been, not a Friday goes by without him going down the pub."

"Which one?"

"The local. Across the way there," she said. "The White Horse."

"Alright," Nillson said. "You're sure his keys aren't here?"

"Positive. They'll be in the inside pocket of his jacket."

"What type of jacket is he wearing? Do you remember the colour, maybe?"

"Denim," she replied. "One of those with a sheepskin collar. God knows why he had it on, though. Not exactly arctic conditions out there, is it?"

"Right then," Nillson said. "Thanks for your help, Alexandra."

She turned to make her way towards the front door.

"Is that it, then?" Alexandra asked.

"From me, yes," she said. "DC Gold will stay with you for the time being. Just to make sure you're okay."

"Stay with me?"

Nillson opened the front door, glanced at Gold to make sure she was okay, and then once Jackie had given her a slight nod, she left and closed the front door behind her, leaving Jackie and Alexandra in an awkward moment of unease.

"I suppose you'll want tea," she said.

"I can make it if you like. Why don't you sit down and let me do it?"

"Because it's my house, and while I've got two hands and two feet, I'll make the tea, if it's alright with you."

The tone was abrupt, but it could have been far worse.

"As you wish," Jackie said. "Listen, I'm not here to make life difficult for you."

"No?"

"Quite the opposite, in fact. I'm here to talk to you. I'm your family liaison officer."

"My what?"

"It's a role designed to help victims of crime," Jackie explained.

"And what crime would that be?" Alexandra asked, to which Jackie said nothing. She took a seat on one of the kitchen stools and linked her fingers, a posture designed to put the other party at ease, to show she meant no harm.

"I think we both know the answer to that," Jackie said. "Do you want to tell me what happened?"

Alexandra poured the water into two mugs, then lost herself in the mashing of the tea bags, so much so that Jackie thought they might split. But eventually, she rescued the beaten bags from the cups, stepped over to the bin, and flicked them inside with a teaspoon.

"Milk?" she said, to which Jackie nodded.

"Please."

She watched the charade play out, wondering if Alexandra was taking the time to develop a story that might conceal the true cause of her injuries, or if she was just plain old avoiding the question.

But instead, she slid one of the mugs across the worktop and resumed her defensive position, leaning against the side with her arms folded.

"He's having a hard time," she said. "Michael, that is. His work. It's up and down."

"He's frustrated, then?"

"Frustrated, angry, depressed," Alexandra replied. "It all depends on the day."

"Has he done this before? To you, I mean."

"Listen, I don't want to make a fuss of it—"

"I'm not asking you to make a fuss, Alexandra," Jackie told her. "I'm just trying to understand who it is we're looking for. If you want to report a crime to me, then I'm all ears, but if not, then I'll understand. There's no pressure here. I want to be clear on that, but I do know what it's like. I do understand how it feels to—"

"To what?" she asked, as if she was daring her to voice her assumptions.

"To go through something like this."

"I'm sorry, but you don't understand anything. Nobody does. How could they? They don't see him when he's like it, do they?" She shook her head, disregarding everything Jackie had said. "You're just a copper trying to nose her way into our lives."

It was a sad position to be in, Jackie thought, in a violent relationship but finding reasons to defend a man who vents his frustration on the one person who stands by his side.

"I used to say things like that," Jackie said eventually. She took a sip of tea to show her resolve more than anything else.

"What do you mean?"

"I used to defend him."

"Who?"

"The man who used to beat me. The man who used to come home drunk and lash out. The best part of my day, Alexandra, was when I had to drag him off the floor onto the bed and undress him. The worst part of the day was when he was out, knowing he could walk through that door at any moment in any number of moods. No, the best time was when I knew he was home and asleep. That was when I could truly relax. That was when I could live my life."

Alexandra let her arms fall to her sides. She was quiet, like she was processing what Jackie had said and studying her face for signs of a lie.

But there had been no lies on Jackie's part.

"Do you have kids?" Alexandra asked.

"A boy," Jackie replied. "Charlie."

Alexandra gave a weak smile.

"You'll know then," she said. "You'll know what it's like, and I suppose you'll be wondering why I don't just take Rosie and leave."

"Because you have no place to go," Jackie told her, then met her teary stare. "Because you think that of the few options you have, this is the best for her. For Rosie."

Slowly, Alexandra nodded, seeming surprised at Jackie's insight. That somebody might actually have been through it and lived to tell the tale.

"Talk to me, Alexandra," Jackie said. "Get it off your chest. Even if we leave it there, it's good to tell somebody. You're not alone, you know?"

Tentatively, Alexandra made her way around the kitchen worktop and dropped onto the stool beside Jackie.

"I haven't seen him since Friday," she said. "I didn't report him missing, because–"

"It's okay–"

"No. No, you should know why."

Jackie saw something shift in her eyes; they narrowed and her pupils dilated.

"I think deep down I was hoping something had happened to him. In fact, I know I was," she said.

"Statistically, he'll come home in a day or so," Jackie said. "You should be aware of that."

"I know," she replied, gently and thoughtfully. She took a sip of her tea and then stared at the front door at the end of the hallway. "But a girl can hope, can't she?"

CHAPTER FIFTEEN

"Shame it's not open," Gillespie muttered aloud.

"Eh?"

"I said it's a shame it's not open. The pub, I mean."

"It's nine-thirty in the morning," Cruz said, peering at him from the passenger seat like he was some kind of animal.

"Aye. I was thinking, we could drag the first couple out. If we time it right, we'll be in The King's Head for opening. Had a few in there last year. Nice pub."

"The King's Head? It's not exactly within spitting distance of the bloke's house, is it? What's his name?" Cruz said, checking the printout Chapman had provided. "That's it, Michael Levy."

"Aye, but they do a fine pint. Food's good, too. Nice pies, if I remember rightly."

"Jim, we're supposed to be looking for someone."

"Aye, I know."

"So, we can't base our search on what pub serves the best food."

"Aye, I know that, too," he said. "I'm just a wee bit hungry, that's all. Tell you what, why don't you go and give the landlord of this place a knock? See if he remembers this Levy fellow being in on Friday."

"While you sit here in the pub car park and do what, exactly?"

Just then, both of their phones pinged.

"Ah," Gillespie said. "Would you look at that? An email."

"You're a piece of work, you know that?"

"Aye," he replied. "So I'm told, Gabby. So I'm told."

Cruz pulled his phone from his pocket to read the email as he climbed out of the car, then leaned back inside.

"Did you get this message from Gold?" he asked, holding his phone up for Gillespie to see.

"Aye. Looks like the game is on," he replied. "We'd better get a move on. Do you have any idea how many pubs there are in Horncastle?"

"No," Cruz said. "But, as the resident alcoholic, I'm sure you'll be able to provide some kind of list."

"Lots, that's how many," Gillespie replied. "Close the door, will you? You're letting the cold air out."

Cruz closed the door and walked across the pub car park to the rear entrance. It felt odd knocking on a pub door; normally, he'd just push it open and go inside.

It took a few minutes and two knocks on the door, which seemed to upset a dog somewhere inside, but eventually, bolts were pulled back, the door creaked open, and a middle-aged man with an earring and a t-shirt that was damp with sweat stared at him while barely holding onto the collar of a large German Shepherd.

"Help you?" he said.

"Ah, yes," Cruz said, finding his most professional and authoritative voice. He flashed his warrant card for the man to see. "I wonder if you can help me. My name is Detective Constable Cruz. I'm investigating a report of a missing person."

"Right," the man said, struggling with the German Shepherd.

"I was wondering if he'd been here at all."

"Who?" the man said, clearly growing more impatient with every passing second.

"Oh sorry. His name is Michael Levy. A local man, apparently–"

"I know him," the landlord said, then shook his head. "Haven't seen him for a while, though."

"Do you know where we might find–" Cruz said, but the door closed before he could finish, and he heard the metallic clicks of the bolts being engaged from the inside. "Thanks for your help."

Back at the car, Gillespie had reclined the driver's seat and was scrolling through Gold's email. Cruz climbed in, fastened his seat belt, and stared at him.

"How do you spell reluctant?" Gillespie asked, reading his phone as if he was doing the crossword.

"What?"

"Reluctant," he said again. "How do you spell it?"

"R-e-l-u-c-t-a-n-t," Cruz said. "Why?"

"Just wondered," he replied. "I thought it had another E in it."

Cruz shook his head in despair. "No E, Jim. Definitely only one E."

"Right. How did you get on?"

"About as well as expected."

"Not seen him then?"

"He knew the name but doesn't remember seeing him recently."

"Ah well," Gillespie replied, making no effort to adjust his seat so they could move on to the next pub. "Apparently our man is a bit of a wee bastard."

"A what? As in small?" Cruz asked. "You mean he's a small man?"

"No, Gabby. You are a *wee* bastard. Our man, however, is a wee *bastard*."

Cruz puffed out his cheeks and stared through the windscreen.

"I often wonder what I've done to deserve this," he said. "I'm a good bloke. I mean, I try to help people. I try to do the right thing. So, why have I ended up being paired with a man who has the vocabulary of a guttersnipe?"

"He beats her," Gillespie said distastefully. "I can't stand men like that. Gives us all a bad name. Do you know what I mean?"

"Who beats who?" Cruz asked. "If you're going to make a statement such as that, at least provide some context."

"Levy," Gillespie said in a huff. He sat up and pulled the lever for the seat to pop back into the upright position. "Beats his girlfriend. According to Gold's email, she has a black eye and a fat lip. That really gets my goat. It's no wonder women don't feel safe walking the streets. How can they be safe walking the bloody streets if they can't be safe at home? Should be strung up if you ask me."

"Agreed," Cruz said, familiar with Gillespie's rants and well-versed in the practice of acknowledging the topic without feeding the outbursts or obscenities.

"Well, I suppose in your case it'd be the other way around, wouldn't it?" Gillespie said.

"What does that mean?"

"Aye, well, I just meant that Hermione is a wee bit larger than you, eh? Tougher too, probably."

"Tougher?"

"Aye. I'll bet she wouldn't take any lip from you."

"Jim, domestic abuse has nothing to do with being tough."

"Aye, well, you know what I mean, though."

"No. No, I don't. The people that resort to domestic violence aren't tough. In fact, they're the opposite."

"I know, I just meant that it's not always the men who incite the violence, is it? Sometimes, it's the woman who lashes out. Sometimes the man is the passive one. Know what I mean?"

"I'm sorry," Cruz said, turning in his seat to face him. "Have we travelled back in time? Is Queen Victoria still the monarch?"

"Ah, come on–"

"No, hold on, Jim," Cruz said. "You can't go mouthing off about domestic violence. Not everyone shares your opinions. All it would take is one person to make a complaint and that would be your career finished."

"I'm not condoning it–"

"No, but you're insinuating that it's the victim's fault by not being as physically large or tough as their assailant."

"That's what's wrong with your generation," Gillespie said. "You're too busy being offended by words. You can't cope with the reality of life."

"The reality of life? Have you lost your mind?"

"Aye, the reality of life, Gabby. Whatever happened to free speech?"

"We still have free speech, Jim. It's just frowned upon to give your Victorian opinion on domestic violence."

"I'm not excusing it."

"I know you're not excusing it, but what if somebody heard you? What if somebody was living that nightmare right now, as thousands of people are, and they heard you?"

"We're in a pub car park, Gabby. It's nearly ten a.m. Who's going to hear us?"

"That's besides the point–"

"I just said that people who incite domestic violence should be strung up. I'm not exactly defending them, am I?"

"Will you keep your voice down?" Cruz said.

"There's nobody to hear us, you halfwit," Gillespie said, his voice growing louder with every sentence he spoke. He pointed around the car park. "Look, white van, empty. Red Mercedes, absolutely stunning, but empty. Grey BMW, empty."

"Hold on," Cruz said, and he unfolded the piece of paper Chapman had provided. He found the details of Michael Levy's car and checked the number plate. "It's bloody it. The red Mercedes. That's his bloody car."

"The boss said he didn't have one," Gillespie said, to which Cruz jabbed his slender index finger at the printed paper.

"Drew Barker said he drives a work van which was left at the workshop," Cruz said. "The DVLA however, doesn't lie."

CHAPTER SIXTEEN

The address Chapman had provided led Nillson and Anderson to a small unit off Holmes Way, a business park of sorts with a variety of buildings to offer local entrepreneurs and global powerhouses alike.

"It's quiet," Anderson said, stating the obvious. "No sign of a disturbance."

"There are also cameras on the neighbouring unit. When we're done here, let's pay them a visit. With any luck, one of their cameras might cover this forecourt."

As requested, a liveried car with two uniforms inside cruised slowly along the road toward them. Nillson flashed her lights and they rolled into the space beside her car. The driver lowered his window.

"Now then," he said, eyeing the unit in question. "Sarge says you might need a hand getting inside."

"We do," Nillson replied.

"Warrant?"

"No need," she said. "We have reason to believe the owner might be inside and may be a danger to himself."

"Righto," he said with a loud exhale, the way men do when

they reach a certain age. He hauled himself from the car, opened the boot, and removed a ram, generally used for gaining access to the houses of criminals, not the properties of missing persons. In many circles, Nillson knew the ram to be aptly named 'the enforcer'. "You sure about this?"

"As sure as I can be," she replied, as the pair of them followed the mature uniform and his younger colleague to the front door.

"Have a quick look around, will you?" the man said to the younger officer. "Check the back door before we go making a mess."

He set one end of the ram down by his feet and leaned on it.

"He's keen," he said. "I like to keep him busy."

"Well, let's hope our man isn't inside bleeding to death," Nillson replied, as cheerfully as she could. "Or I'll expect the young PCSO won't be very busy for a very long time."

A serious expression drained the officer's face, so much so that when the PCSO had completed a circuit of the building and returned, calling out that it was all locked up, the elder of the two began to berate him, telling him to hurry up and knock the door in.

Anderson and Nillson shared an amused look as the two men took care of the door, and as an added courtesy, and most likely to win favour with Nillson, the senior officer stepped inside to have a quick look around, returning a moment later with a curt, "All clear for you. It's all yours."

"Thank you," Nillson said, as she stepped past him and into the small warehouse. "That'll be all. I don't want to take up too much of your valuable time."

"We're done?" he said. "You don't need us for anything?"

"You could ask your duty sergeant to send somebody to fix the door when we're done. That would save us a lot of time. Thank you."

A little bewildered, the officer tapped his younger colleague on the arm and steered him back towards their car, after handing him the enforcer to carry, of course.

"That was probably the highlight of their day," Anderson said.

"What, breaking into a warehouse and finding nothing but old wardrobes and dressing tables?"

"No, getting to break a door down for two female officers. No doubt they'll be talking about it for months."

"I don't doubt it," Nillson replied, as she snapped on a pair of blue, latex gloves. "Plus, I'm sure there'll be a few indecent references added into the mix."

"To be a fly on the wall," Anderson mused, as she nosed her way into a small side office.

A heavy smell of turpentine or cleaner of some sort hung in the air, the way a pub smells of alcohol and a butchers smells of meat. It was a smell that would cling to the building for eternity now, she thought. Paperwork was scattered across what appeared to be a fine, mahogany partner's desk, so much so that the green, leather inlay was barely visible. There was no computer, no screen, and no digital device of any kind, except for an old solar-powered calculator. The paperwork appeared to be mostly invoices and delivery notes, some paired, some singular.

"I wonder how much all this is worth," Nillson called out from the workshop. Anderson peered out of the office and found her strolling with her hands behind her back, among the various items like she was walking through Hyde Park enjoying the ducks and the swans on a blissful Sunday afternoon. "A load of old toot if you ask me."

"Valuable toot," Anderson said, and she nodded at a piece close to her. "See that dressing table?"

"This one?" Nillson asked, stopping to study the piece in question.

"How much do you think it's worth?"

Nillson pulled a face as she attempted a valuation and Anderson collected the pile of invoices from the desk.

"Fifty quid?" she said.

"Close," Anderson replied, finding the right piece of paper. "Add another zero."

"Five hundred quid? Who pays five hundred quid for something that gets covered in makeup and sits in your bedroom?"

"How about the chest of drawers?" Anderson asked, and Nillson smiled as what had started as a reality check for them both had now become a game.

"It's walnut, isn't it?" she said, and Anderson nodded. "Seven hundred?"

"Two grand," Anderson replied.

"Two grand for something you keep your socks in? This is ridiculous."

"Last one?" Anderson said, and Nillson agreed. "The chairs. The matching pair."

Nillson sucked in a breath and gave them the once over, as Anderson would expect somebody who actually knew what they were looking at to do.

"Fifteen hundred quid?"

"Three grand," Anderson said. "I win."

"Three thousand pounds for two chairs?"

"Matching."

"But three grand? That's a month's salary and all you get to do is sit on your backside."

"I doubt it's a month's salary for the individual who buys them," Anderson said, trying to match the delivery notes with the invoices but finding far more of the former than the latter. "That's odd."

"What is?" Nillson asked.

But Anderson was already back in the office, scouring through the remaining paperwork. Nillson came to the doorway.

"Is everything alright?" she asked.

"No," Anderson said. "In fact, it seems to me that our friend Mr Levy has a cashflow problem."

"So? Isn't that usual for businesses? Especially one that deals in big-ticket items like these."

"I have delivery notes for a Mr J Graham totalling more than twenty thousand pounds," Anderson said. "Along with a pile of unpaid invoices."

"He's in debt," Nillson said. "Who else does he owe?"

"You're missing the point, Anna," Anderson said. "Somebody owes him. One man in particular to be precise."

"J Graham?"

"Yes," Anderson said. "Some of these invoices date back to over a year ago."

"A year?"

"I think we need to pay this J Graham a visit," Anderson said, and she turned an invoice around for Nillson to see. "And as luck would have it, he has a shop right around the corner."

"Good. We've been summoned to a briefing," Nillson replied. "We can pay him a visit afterwards."

"A briefing? Where?"

"Well, Gillespie is involved," Nillson said. "So I'll give you one guess."

CHAPTER SEVENTEEN

Just like Gillespie, Nillson and Anderson, the focus of Cruz's attention was a bright red, nineteen eighty-seven Mercedes SL. The interior was a fine, tan leather, and the chrome bumpers shone like mirrors. It shared the car park with a beaten-up, old Ford Transit, and a grey BMW, overshadowing them all with its sheer magnificence.

"Bloody hell," Cruz muttered.

"Aye," Gillespie murmured, refraining from running his hand along the door.

"What a pile of old rubbish," Cruz said.

Three heads turned to look at the young DC, each of them as astonished as the next.

"You what?" Gillespie said.

"It's a pile of rubbish," Cruz said again. "It doesn't even have air conditioning, it's still got a tape player, and the speedo takes up most of the dashboard. You might as well be driving around in Big Ben. Who listens to tapes anymore? I don't think I've even got any. Chucked them all away when CDs came out."

"Gabby, this is a nineteen eighty-seven Mercedes SL hardtop. It is the most coveted car of all time," Gillespie said.

"No, it's not."

"It is in my book," Gillespie replied. "The point is, it is not a pile of old rubbish."

"Ah," Cruz said, turning his back on the old vehicle, "I can think of better ways to spend my money."

"Like a new tennis outfit?" Nillson said, raising a laugh from Anderson.

"Very funny," Cruz said. "What are you doing here, anyway? I thought you two were going to the workshop?"

"Been there," Nillson said.

"Done that," Anderson added. "The boss asked us to meet her here. She's on her way with Ben."

"Did you find much?" Gillespie asked, peering through the car window. It was almost as if he was trying to find a flaw on the bodywork or the interior.

"Not sure," Nillson said. "We'll see what the boss says."

Gillespie tore himself from the old car and joined the others standing near Nillson's hatchback.

"I'd be happy to give you my opinion," he told her.

"I'll wait, thanks. I'm not in the habit of telling the same story twice."

"You didn't find him though?"

"If we found him, do you think we'd be standing here talking to you?" Nillson said. "The answer is no. We'd be back at the station where sweat doesn't run down my backside like the Colorado River."

It was enough of a statement to silence Gillespie, and Cruz felt his brow furrow trying not to think of it.

A heavy engine sounded at the far end of the street, then grew louder as it accelerated towards them.

"That's them," Nillson said, and the four of them watched as Freya steered the big Range Rover into the pub car park and came to a stop beside Gillespie's old banger.

"Alright, boss," Cruz called out when Freya stepped down

from the car. She took a swig from a bottle of water, then slipped it into the door pocket, before being joined by Ben.

"Oh my God, look at that," Ben said, staring at the shiny, red Mercedes. "Somebody is doing okay for themselves, aren't they?"

"Somebody is clearly compensating for something else," Freya said, and Cruz did little to stifle the grin that he proudly presented to Gillespie safe in the knowledge that the boss agreed with him.

"See?"

"See what?" he said. "Ben agrees with me. It's gorgeous."

"It's a death trap," Freya corrected him, and then her head cocked that way it did when an idea struck her. "Is this why you called us here?"

"Aye, well–"

"Hang on. Red Mercedes," Freya said. "Is that–"

"Michael Levy's," Cruz said. "Apparently he still listens to cassettes."

Ben strolled over to the car, admiring it from various angles.

"She's a beauty, eh?" Gillespie said, and Ben dropped to his knees to peer under the front. "Four-point-two litre V-eight. I'm surprised he can afford to put petrol in it if I'm honest. Must be quite a thirsty girl."

"I'm surprised it even got here," Ben said, as he stood and dusted his trousers down with his hands.

"Eh?" Gillespie said. "She's been going since nineteen eighty-seven. She's not giving up just yet, eh?"

"Well, with an oil leak like that, I don't think she'll be going much further," Ben said, and Gillespie dropped to his knees.

Cruz couldn't help but smile at the big Scotsman's disappointment. The entire team craned their necks to peer under the car at what Ben had spotted.

"That's a lot of oil," Cruz said.

"And the leak is slow," Ben said. "Which means it wasn't parked there this morning."

"Last night?"

"Maybe," he said. "Maybe longer."

"Friday night?"

"More than likely," Ben said. "Which tells us a lot."

"It means he didn't drive home," Freya said.

"Well, we already know he didn't drive home," Gillespie said. "Or he'd have been there in the morning."

"No, we know he didn't leave here in his car," she said. "What we don't know is where he went."

"The landlord said he hadn't seen him," Cruz said. "He could have got into another car."

"He could have," Freya said. "But, tell me, Gillespie, if you owned his car, would you leave it here unless you really had to?"

"Here? Not on your nellie, boss."

"Precisely. Which tells me he was over the drink driving limit. Probably by a considerable amount, too."

It amused Cruz that, with all the strong personalities on the team, nobody said a word when the boss was mid-thought. She had a way of staring into space, and he could almost see the cogs turning.

But then she snapped out of her trancelike state with an infectious energy.

"Right then," she said. "Not an ideal place for a meeting, but I've dealt with worse. What do we have? Nillson, tell me about the workshop."

"Pretty standard," Nillson said. "Antique furniture restoration. Looks like he brings it in from auction houses around the country, shines it up, and flogs it to the local antique shops. Horncastle is full of them."

"Anything nice?" she asked.

"That depends on your version of nice," Nillson replied. "Personally, I think only an idiot would spend five hundred quid on a dressing table, or thousands on a chair or two."

"Really?" Freya said, and for a moment, Cruz thought he

caught Ben suppressing a grin. "I suppose it all depends on the buyer, doesn't it? What else?"

"Anderson matched the delivery notes to the paid invoices. There are quite a few unpaid invoices dating back over a year, in the name of a Mr J Graham."

"Our missing man is in debt?" Freya remarked, with more emphasis on the old car. "Now that is a surprise."

"No, boss," Anderson said. "This Graham fellow owes him."

"He's owed money? How much are we talking about here? A few thousand?"

"Twenty-odd," Anderson said. "That's an estimate. I've sent the paperwork back to the station with the uniformed officers."

Freya paced around the old car with her hands behind her back. She came to stop on the far side of it, peered in though the window, then straightened and looked at each of them in turn.

"So we know from Gold's report that Michael Levy was at home on Friday morning, and he usually visited The White Horse after work. However, the landlord says he didn't see him, which doesn't mean he wasn't here."

"Eh?" Cruz said, and he looked over his shoulder at the old building. "You can't exactly get lost in there. It's tiny."

"The fact that the landlord didn't see him doesn't mean Michael Levy wasn't here," Freya explained. "It just means that the landlord, or whoever it was you spoke to, wasn't working the bar on Friday night. It was the landlord, wasn't it? I mean, I presume you checked such a significant detail?"

"The landlord?" Cruz said, feeling his face begin to redden and his armpits heat up like two furnaces. "He had a dog, you see? A German Shepherd."

"You didn't check to see if he was the landlord?" Freya said.

"Well, who else could it have been? He was all sweaty. He was working."

"Aye, could have been the bloody cleaner, Gabby," Gillespie said, shaking his head in a show of disappointment.

"Either way," Freya said, "we have good reason to believe Michael Levy was here, and we have good reason to believe he left here inebriated."

"Aye," Gillespie said, in his most agreeable tone.

"Ben, how far is Levy's house from here?"

"On foot?"

"Yes."

"Twenty minutes," he said. "If he cut across the nature reserve, that is."

"The nature reserve?"

Ben nodded at the expanse of green on the far side of the road.

"It's protected," he said. "But if I'm right, there are paths. There's even a bridge over the old river course."

Freya folded her arms, closed her eyes, and then relaxed.

"Right then, Anderson and Nillson, can you please locate this Mr J Graham, and see what he has to say about the debt?"

"Will do, boss," Nillson said, and she tapped Anderson on the arm to coax her into action. But Anderson raised a hand, keen to hear the end of the meeting.

"Gillespie," Freya continued, "I presume you have actually run the plates by Chapman and the DVLA?"

"The plates, boss?" he replied, and Cruz savoured the reddening of the great brute's face. "Well, aye. We were going to do that just before you arrived."

"Do you mean to tell me you haven't confirmed this car belongs to Michael Levy?" Freya said.

"Well, how many nineteen eighty-seven Mercedes can there be in Horncastle?" he said, his voice high in defence.

"I don't know, I haven't checked," she said, then turned to Ben. "Can you, please?"

He nodded, smiled at Gillespie's faux pa, and then walked away dialling Chapman's number.

Meanwhile, Freya came to stand before Gillespie and Cruz.

"This is an easy job," she began, her voice low and quiet, forcing them to listen hard. "Do you know what will happen if we make even the tiniest of mistakes?"

"Standing?" Cruz said, to which she nodded, her expression a solemn grimace.

"So, the next time I ask you to do something, I want you both to imagine it's you who is running the team. I want to you imagine that it's you who will be dragged up in front of Standing or Granger to pay the price. I've let you have it easy, and that's my fault. But there's no room for that now. We're one week away from losing three good detectives, and yes, Gillespie, I include you in that number. Have the good grace to at least put up a fight, or else what the bloody hell are any of us doing here?"

She let the silence fill the void, and her stare added the weight that drove the message home.

"Aye, boss," Gillespie said. "Won't happen again, eh?"

"Cruz?" she said.

"I'll try harder," he said. "Sorry, boss."

"Good," she replied sincerely, and that weight dispersed, somehow bringing them back into the team in high spirits.

"It's Michael Levy's, alright," Ben called out, approaching them as he pocketed his phone.

"Thank God for that," Gillespie muttered.

"At least it has been for the past few days."

"Eh?"

"Ownership was transferred last Thursday," he said. "From a Mr Jeremiah Graham."

Freya turned on her heels to face Nillson.

"J Graham," she said. "If that isn't enough to bring him in for some casual questioning, I don't know what is."

"We're on it, boss," Nillson said.

"As for you two," Freya said, returning her attention to Gillespie and Cruz, "I want you to walk to Michael Levy's house, and I want every ditch checked along the way."

"Walk?" Cruz said. "I've got absolutely no idea where it is. Has anyone got a local map in their car?"

"You won't need a map," Ben said, and he pointed to the thick line of trees less than a mile away. "It's on the other side of those trees."

"Shouldn't be too difficult, should it?" Freya asked, and she gave them both that look she saved for when she dared them to argue.

"A breeze," Cruz said.

"Aye," Gillespie said. "It'll be a breeze."

CHAPTER EIGHTEEN

"Right then, Gabby," Gillespie said, as Ben and Freya knocked on the pub door and Nillson's car disappeared around the corner. "It's just you and me, laddie."

"I can't believe you didn't check the number plate," Cruz told him. "I mean, surely that's the first thing you do when you find a suspect's car."

"How many times do I have to tell you? It's a nineteen eighty-seven Mercedes SL, one of less than one hundred left in Britain."

"Is that an actual fact, or did you just guess that?"

"Aye, well, one can assume, you know?"

"Yeah, well, you made us look like a right pair of berks," Cruz said.

"*I* made us look like berks?" Gillespie said. "*Me?* I'm not the one who questioned somebody without even finding out who he was. I mean, did you even get his name?"

"I told you, he had a dog. It was difficult."

"Difficult?"

"Yes, difficult. I had just a few moments to ask him if he'd seen Michael Levy last Friday, and he said no."

"So you just walked away?"

"Well, no. He kind of just closed the door on me."

"Ah, now I see. So some bloke answers the pub door, could have been anyone, and you believe everything he says," Gillespie said.

"Gillespie? Cruz?" a voice called out from the other side of the road. Gillespie turned and smiled as best he could.

"Yes, boss?" he said.

"Are you actually going to do as I asked, or will you be using some kind of sixth sense to ascertain if Michael Levy walked through there?"

"Aye, boss, we're just going in now. Just planning a route, you know?"

"Well, might I suggest you start with the only footpath there is? We'll be heading back to the station soon for a debrief."

Thankfully, the pub door opened and a man in a white t-shirt appeared, holding a large, barking dog by his collar.

"Is that the dog?" Gillespie asked.

"Yep," Cruz answered.

"And the man?"

"Yep," Cruz said again.

Gillespie studied him from the far side of the road.

"Looks like a landlord to me," he said. "Come on, let's get this over with."

He stepped onto the grass, following a path that wasn't quite purpose-made; rather, it had been developed from years of people trampling over the same route. The first few hundred yards were easy going. The path followed the edge of a field with a ditch on one side and some kind of crops on the other. Despite living in Lincolnshire for most of his adult life, Gillespie was yet to grasp the difference between wheat and barley, or any other crops for that matter. The only crop he could identify was rape, and that was only because of its yellow flowers, and even then he'd heard somewhere there was another crop with yellow flowers, which he also couldn't remember the name of.

But it wasn't the field he occupied his mind with. The ditch to his left was a far more likely place for a drunk man to stumble into. Thick brambles concealed parts of the ditch, but the growth was dense and the surrounding nettles so abundant that, should somebody have stepped into them, they would surely have left a flattened patch in their wake.

"This is nice," Cruz said from behind him, and Gillespie peered over his shoulder to find him with his sweater draped over his shoulders again, walking with the aid of a long stick he'd found. "A gentle stroll through the fields on a Monday afternoon. The glorious sun overhead and fresh air all around."

Gillespie stopped and turned to face his colleague wearing his best expression of utter incredulity.

"Are you mental?" he said.

"Eh?"

"Are you off your head? We're supposed to be looking for someone, not sniffing the air and admiring the bloody wildflowers."

"I am looking," Cruz said. "I can still appreciate my surroundings while I work, can't I?"

"Where are you looking?"

"In the ditch," he said. "I'm checking the ditch on the left, you're checking the field on the right."

"Who said that?" Gillespie said. "Who assigned you the ditch and me the field?"

"Well, nobody. I just thought—"

"You just thought?"

"Well, back there you were looking at the barley. I just figured I'd take the other side."

"For crying out loud, Gabby. I'm checking the ditch, you're checking the field."

"What difference does it make?" Cruz said, and he waved his

arm at the short distance they had covered. "I'm sure if Michael Levy had fallen over between here and there, we'd see him. It's not exactly the Rocky Mountains, is it? It's five hundred yards of flat farmland with some barley in it."

"Aye, lucky for you, too."

"Why is it lucky for me?"

"Because, Gabby, you're going to go back to the start and check the bloody field."

"Me?"

"What if we missed something?" Gillespie said. "What if we missed something that is later found? Eh? We'd look like a right pair of plums, wouldn't we?"

"But why is it me who has to go back? You were checking the fields."

"Because, Gabby, I'm checking the ditch," Gillespie said, and he waved him away as if he was shooing a rabid dog.

"Bloody hell," Cruz muttered to himself as he started back along the makeshift path.

"Oh, and Gabby?" Gillespie called to him.

He turned to face him, jabbed his stick into the earth, and put his other hand on his hip.

"You do realise you look like the love child of John McEnroe and the wizard from Lord of the Rings, don't you?"

"Oh, shut up. It's called style," Cruz said, affectionately touching the crossed arms of the sweater around his neck.

"You also realise that's a flicking stick, don't you?"

"A what?" he said.

"A flicking stick," Gillespie explained. "It's a stick a dog walker has used to flick dog poo from the foot path. They probably ran out of poo bags or forgot them or something. Either way, it's a flicking stick, sometimes referred to as a shit stick, but not to be confused with a pooh stick."

Cruz studied the stick from bottom to top, where he saw the

remains of the offensive faeces and immediately tossed the stick away like it was ready to bite him.

Gillespie laughed to himself.

"What an eighteen-carat dunce, he is."

While Cruz backtracked, Gillespie, with his arms behind his back, took a gentle stroll along the path, peering into the ditch when a flash of colour caught his eye, which on two occasions turned out to be discarded beer bottles, and on one occasion was an off-cut of old, blue rope, which had probably been tossed there by the farmer.

He reached the end of the field and saw a little footbridge over to his right. Cruz was still one hundred yards behind, so he strolled over to the bridge and took the weight off his feet.

Cruz had been right. It was damn sight nicer to be out in the fields than dealing with some irate landlord and his rabid dog. The breeze was gentle and cool, much nicer than it had been a few weeks before when temperatures had hit forty degrees.

He rested his head against the bridge's handrail and studied the growth around him; the green of the long grass, the lush density of the bushes, whatever they were, and the gentle trickling of water in the ditch beneath the bridge.

If only his companion had been somebody else. Anderson, Gillespie thought, it would be nice to spend a day in the fields with her. Not Nillson, she was far too aggressive and would go against his only dating rule: never date a girl who could beat him in an arm wrestle.

Chapman was too timid and boring. She'd probably bring her laptop and make a spreadsheet to arrange the flowers she'd spotted. And as for Gold, she was too into Ben for anybody else to get a look in, though she'd never admit it.

Finally, his mind drifted to the boss, Freya. He smiled to himself, imagining her as a dominatrix. She had the personality. She reminded him of one of those classy, rich women depicted in films, who, from the safety of her mansion, dresses in leather and has man slaves to tend to her every sordid need.

"What the bloody hell are you doing?" Cruz said, startling Gillespie and rousing him from his daydream.

"You what?" he said, jumping to his feet and fighting the urge to stretch.

"Were you napping?"

"No, I was just–"

"Just what? Checking the insides of your eyelids?"

"No, I was thinking."

"Thinking?" Cruz said. "Your eyes were closed. That's called dreaming."

"I wasn't napping."

"I heard you snore from over there," Cruz said, jabbing his thumb over his shoulder.

"Well, I might have had a wee doze, but it's a nice day, and if I'm honest, Gabby, working with you is bloody hard work, mate. I feel like I've done a full day's graft already."

Cruz shook his head and Gillespie succumbed to the stretch his body was calling for. He yawned and rubbed his face with a sigh.

"Right, then," he said. "Looks like the path crosses the bridge and heads into the forest."

"Hold on," Cruz said, retying the arms of his sweater and dropping to a crouch. He peered at the wood from various angles, then studied the handrail from top to bottom.

"What?" Gillespie asked.

"It's blood," Cruz said. "You were sitting on dried blood."

"Dried blood?"

"Look, there's loads of it," Cruz said, as he tracked a dark, brown stain across the handrail post.

"That's not blood," Gillespie told him, leaning in for a better look and becoming doubtful of his own premature analysis. "Is it?"

Cruz pointed into the ditch below. "Look," he said, then ran across the bridge to the far side and peered into an area of flattened undergrowth. "Someone has been here. Recently, too."

"Ah come on, it's probably just a badger or something."

"Do badgers wear Nikes?" Cruz said, and for a moment they set aside their differences to focus on the job at hand. "I think we need to call this in. Something happened here, Jim. Something terrible."

CHAPTER NINETEEN

"Are you able to control your dog?" Freya asked as the man in the sweaty, white t-shirt fought for a grip on the German Shepherd's collar. "Or do I need to call in a canine unit?"

"Who are you?" he said, and his expression was one of absolute disgust. Presumably, he wasn't used to being spoken to so directly.

Freya held out her warrant card for him to see.

"Detective Inspector Bloom," she said. "I'd like to ask you a few questions concerning one of your patrons."

The dog lunged forward, forcing the man to grip the collar with two hands.

"Can we do this another time?" he said. "Can't you see I've got my hands full?"

"Unfortunately not," Freya said "Might I suggest you lock your dog in another room so we can talk? Or perhaps you'd care to step outside, leaving that thing inside, of course."

"Alright, alright," the man said, and then took a few moments to edge out of the door while keeping the powerful dog inside with one hand and closing the door with the other. He appeared relieved when the door finally closed, and aside from a forty-kilo dog launching itself at the door from the inside, the mood calmed somewhat. "Police, you say?"

"That's right," Freya said, and she pointed at one of the benches in the beer garden where a Carlsberg parasol provided ample shade. "Perhaps we can sit?"

They all moved over to the bench, Ben taking a place beside Freya, and the landlord sitting opposite. Eventually, the frantic dog calmed down and issued a loud cry, presumably as it settled into a lying position beside the door, waiting for its master.

"Before we start, may I just take your name, please?" Freya asked.

"I thought you lot would have it already."

"Well, if I had it, I wouldn't need to ask, would I?" Freya said.

"John," he replied. "John Glover."

"And you are the registered landlord?"

"I am," he replied. "Have been for more than a decade."

"For more than a decade? I can see why. It's a beautiful spot," Freya told him.

"Well, I'm glad you approve. Listen, what's all this about? I've got barrels to change, pipes to clean, and floors to mop, and that's before I've even started on the lunch."

"This won't take long," Freya said. "I believe you spoke to my colleague earlier this morning."

"Your colleague? Oh, you mean the little fellow? Looks like ballboy at Wimbledon?"

"That's him," Ben said. "He's actually a fine detective."

"I'm sure he is," Glover replied. "His parents must be proud."

"He asked if you remember seeing Michael Levy last Friday night, and he claims you told him you hadn't."

"That's right."

"Yet his car is parked here, and by all accounts, it's been there for several days, at least," Freya said, and she pointed at the red Mercedes.

"That's not Mike's car," Glover said with a laugh.

"Mike?"

"Michael," he corrected himself. "His mates call him Mike."

"So the DVLA database is wrong, is it?" Ben asked.

"The DVLA?"

"Its records indicate the ownership of that car was transferred on Thursday," he said. "Can you tell me how long it's been there?"

He puffed out his cheeks and stared at the car as if the answer to Ben's question might lie somehow in the shiny bodywork.

"A few days, tops," Glover said.

"Yet you don't remember seeing Michael Levy, or Mike, as you call him, during that period?"

"I haven't seen Mike since the Friday before last," Glover told them. "He drinks in The King's Head during the week. Only comes here on Fridays so he can walk home."

"Sorry, I don't understand," Freya said.

"Why? Isn't it obvious?" he said. "He can get himself into a right old mess then cut through the fields to get home. Can't do that from The King's Head, can he?"

"I suppose not."

"But you specifically remember seeing him the Friday before last?" Ben asked.

"I do, yes."

"What makes that Friday so significant? Why do you remember seeing him, I mean?"

"Why? Have you ever met Michael?"

"No, Mr Glover, we have not."

"Right, well, if you ever do get to meet him, you'll understand. He's not a man you're likely to forget in a long time."

"In what way?"

"Listen, what is this about? What's he done? Maybe you should start by asking the right questions."

"Were you working on Friday night, Mr Glover?" Freya asked, to which he smiled.

"No, I wasn't. I've got bar staff. Fridays are my nights off."

"Good, now we're getting somewhere," she said. "So presumably the Friday before last, when you do remember seeing Michael Levy in your pub, you were downstairs socialising?"

"You're good at this," he said with a crooked smile.

"And presumably, last Friday, on your day off, you were not in your pub."

"I was down the social club," he replied. "Met a few old mates of mine."

"Right," Freya said. "Which explains why you saw Michael Levy on one Friday but not on the Friday in question."

"Anything else?" he asked.

"Would any of your bar staff remember seeing Michael Levy in your pub on Friday night?"

"Probably," he replied.

"You can be sure of that, can you?"

"Quite sure," he said, and Freya stared hard at him, eyebrows raised. "His bar tab. He owes me."

"And seeing as he drinks in The King's Head during the week, the tab could only have been accrued last Friday night," Freya said.

"You are good," he replied.

"I must warn you, Mr Glover, I am in no mood to be messed around," she said. "So I do feel duty bound to inform you that wasting police time is an offence punishable by up to six months in prison, and a fine."

"Prison?" he said, the grin slipping from his face like ice cream from a cone on a hot day.

"Now then," Freya said, keen to make the most of his attention. "Michael Levy has been reported missing."

"Reported missing," he said with a scoff. "Mike? Who reported him? Not that dopey old mare, Alexandra?"

"No, Mr Glover. In fact, it was one of his friends."

This statement incited a roar of laughter from Glover, who then reverted to the grimace he had worn moments before.

"Mike doesn't have friends," he said.

"I thought you said his friends call him Mike?" Freya said.

"Yeah, well, I wouldn't exactly call him anybody's friend. Acquaintance, maybe? But friend? No. No, he's a loose cannon is Michael Levy."

"Is he an acquaintance of Jeremiah Graham?" Freya asked. "Is that name familiar?"

"Jerry? Of course. Everyone knows Jerry," he said and glanced at the shiny, red car parked a short distance away. "That's Jerry's car. Or at least, it was Jerry's car. You could almost call it his trademark. He loves it, he does."

"I can see why," Ben mused aloud. "I bet there aren't many left in that condition."

"There aren't," Glover replied. "You say he sold it to Michael?"

"No," Freya said, "I mentioned it had been transferred."

Glover shook his head.

"Jerry would never part with that. It's his pride and joy."

"Does he usually leave his pride and joy parked outside your pub for a few days?" Freya asked. "I think if I cared so much for something so valuable, I'd take a little more care over it, wouldn't you?"

"Come to think of it," Glover replied. "I did wonder what it was doing there."

"Mr Glover, I'm torn," Freya explained. "First of all, you made it very difficult for us to ascertain if Michael Levy was here on Friday night or not, and now you seem to be offering information freely. If I'm honest, that makes me a little suspicious."

"Suspicious? Look, lady, I don't like having the police come knocking on my door," he said, holding his hands up. "And I especially don't appreciate my customers driving past and seeing me talking to them. It doesn't bode well for business if you know what I mean?"

"Which suggests your customers aren't all law-abiding citizens," Freya said.

"No, it suggests my customers value having somewhere to come and have a drink and to talk freely," he said. "Now, I've answered all your questions about Michael Levy, so if you don't mind..."

He stood from his seat and stepped over the bench.

"Actually, I do mind," Freya said, which stopped him in his tracks. "And if you're worried about what your customers might think about you talking to two plain-clothes police officers, then I suggest you sit back down because I can assure you, they will think a lot less when I send a dozen uniforms into your pub to turn it over."

"You what?" he said.

"I said, sit down, Mr Glover," Freya said. "We're investigating a missing person who was last seen in your pub on Friday night. His car is parked outside your pub and has been since he disappeared, so forgive me if I'm adding two and two and getting five, but on the strength of those facts, I suggest you think long and hard about how much more you can tell me and your tone of voice because I am not in the mood to be led up the garden path. Do I make myself clear?"

He stared at Ben, who shrugged, maintaining an impassive expression, then he sat back down, checked nobody was listening, and took a deep breath.

"You didn't hear this from me," he said. "I'll not make a statement."

"I'm not asking you to make a statement, Mr Glover, I'm asking you to be honest with me."

"Right," he said, then sighed. "There was an argument. Between them two. Mike and Jerry."

"Do you know what the argument was about?"

"I wasn't there, remember?" he said, again holding his hands up. "One of my bar staff overheard. She thought there was going to be trouble."

"This was Friday night, was it?"

He nodded.

"They left, in the end," he explained. "So whatever happened between them happened somewhere else."

Freya studied Ben's face for a sign of what he was thinking and saw only the doubt that mirrored her own opinion.

"Thank you, Mr Glover. That's been a great help," Freya said.

"So, you don't need to send anybody to search the place. They argued and they left, that's the end of it."

"I hope you're right," Freya said, as she stood and stepped away from the bench towards her car. "For your sake, Mr Glover, I hope you're right."

CHAPTER TWENTY

Aside from the street lights, the modern cars, and a few individuals with mobile phones, they could have been walking through Horncastle market square a hundred years ago or more.

The buildings were straight out of a period drama with doors that opened onto the pavement, archways that would have led to stables, and even an old farmers club, with its sign still clinging to the better times that a few locals would still remember fondly.

"This is it," Anderson said, as they approached an antique store. The sign bore the name of the proprietor, J. Graham and Son, in gold copperplate writing on a dark green background. "Did you leave your credit card in the car?"

Nillson laughed a little.

"I'm more of an Ikea girl," she said. "When my bookshelf breaks, I'll buy a new one."

"I'm with you there," Anderson said, as Nillson peered through the large window at a glossy desk set, complete with chair, ink pot, quill, and even a brass letter opener. Or maybe it was gold? "My family has a habit of leaving ring marks on coffee tables. I'm afraid I'd be quite upset if they ruined a five-hundred-pound table."

Nillson shoved through the door to the tune of an old-fashioned bell that announced their arrival, and a man in a three-piece suit stepped through a doorway at the back of the main room.

"Good morning," he called out. "Feel free to have a look around. I'll just be here should you have any questions."

He had the build of a broom handle and was tall with it, giving him a looming appearance. When he took a step, his entire body seemed to bend as if he was made from rubber.

"I have a question," Nillson said before he slipped back into the room, and he smiled his salesman's smile, unconsciously adjusted his tie and his waistcoat buttons, then approached them, sizing them up as he did. It was as if he was identifying their class as he approached and growing less than impressed with his assumptions.

"Is there a particular piece that caught your eye?" he asked.

"Several actually," Nillson replied. "I was wondering if I could discuss something rather urgent with the owner. Jeremiah, is it?"

"Father or son?" he asked.

"Father, please."

"Then I'd like to direct you to St Mary's church," he replied, and he moved across to the window pointing down the High Street. "It's a short walk from here. You'll find him close to the gate, the third grave in from the footpath."

"Which makes you the son," Nillson said.

"For my sins."

"Do you work alone?" Nillson asked, which seemed to throw him a little.

"I don't have much call for an assistant, why do you ask?"

Nillson caught Anderson's attention and gestured at the door, then watched her flip the sign to Closed, then slide the bolt across the door.

Nillson presented her warrant card.

"I think we need to talk, Mr Graham," she said.

"You can't do that—"

"We could always do this at the station," she replied. "Your choice."

He stared at them both then plunged his hands in his pockets.

"What's this about?" he asked.

"Shall we sit somewhere?" Nillson said.

"I prefer to stand," he replied. "At least until you tell me what all this is about, and why you've locked my shop."

"We were wondering where you were on Friday evening, Mr Graham."

"Friday evening?" he said and pulled a face that suggested he thought the question mundane and rather tedious. "I spent most of the night here."

"Oh, is the shop open late?"

"Not open. I was out the back," he said. "You wouldn't believe the amount of polishing some of these items require."

"So you didn't leave at all?"

"Not that I remember," he replied. "Oh, hang on. I did have to pop out around eight if I remember rightly, but I was back by nine; ten at the latest."

"Oh really? Where did you go?"

"I had some errands to run."

"You drove then?" Nillson asked, and his face paled. "You do drive, don't you?"

His Adam's apple sank and rose as he swallowed his thoughts, and he turned away, which Nillson translated into an effort to conceal his true expression.

"Mr Graham?" she said, digging into the chink in his armour. "We noticed you recently transferred ownership of a nineteen eighty-seven Mercedes to a man named Michael Levy."

"I didn't realise that was a crime," he replied, and he turned to face her, his fists clenched in his pockets.

"May I ask how much you sold it for? A car like that must be worth..." Nillson said and glanced at Anderson. "What do you think, Jenny? Ten thousand?"

"More like twenty," Anderson said. "Oh, easily. A car like that, in that condition. There must be plenty of people out there willing to shell out for it."

"Twenty thousand?" Nillson said, and she stared at Graham. "What did you get for it?"

"We came to an arrangement," he said. "I don't see the need to divulge–"

"It's been parked in a pub car park for three days now, Mr Graham," Nillson said, and his fists tensed at the thought of it. "And Michael Levy has been missing since Friday evening, too."

His fists unclenched and his grimace slipped into a look of bewilderment.

"Missing?"

"Since Friday evening."

"Michael Levy?" he said, clearly thinking she must have made some kind of mistake. "Missing?"

"Nobody has seen him since Friday night, Mr Graham. So you can see why we're keen to talk to you," Nillson said. "You see, we have somebody on our team. A researcher, to be precise. She's good, Mr Graham. The best, actually, and as you can imagine, part of the process of finding people reported as missing is to check their bank accounts. It's just a cursory check to make sure no money has been withdrawn from an ATM somewhere."

"Okay," he said, unsure where she was going with the conversation.

"No money in or out," Nillson said. "Not even twenty pounds, let alone twenty thousand."

"Just to add to that, Mr Graham," Anderson said, "our boss has just messaged me. She's found somebody who says they saw you and Mr Levy arguing on Friday night."

"Friday night? Arguing? Where was this?"

"The same pub where the Mercedes is parked, Mr Graham. The White Horse," Nillson said, taking back control of the conversation. "So, maybe we should start again? What do you think?"

"I think I need to talk to my solicitor," he said.

"Fine by me," Nillson replied. "But I can't see why, personally. Unless, of course, there's something you're not telling us."

A silence ensued, during which time Nillson paced the room, running her hand along the polished surface of an ancient-looking dresser that wouldn't have looked out of place in Downton Abbey.

But it was her phone that broke the silence, and Ben's name flashed up on the screen. She eyed Graham as she answered the call, watching his every move.

"Ben," she said. "Is everything okay? We're just having a little chat with Mr Graham."

"Not good, Anna," he replied. "Gillespie and Cruz have found something."

"Levy?" she said, aware that Graham was listening to her end of the conversation.

"Maybe," he replied. "Blood on a bridge and some kind of activity underneath it. The CSI team are on their way to confirm it, but Freya and I have both been to have a look. We're fairly certain it's blood, and we're positive it's fresh."

"Anything else?" she asked.

"As it happens, yes. It looks like somebody dug a hole nearby. The whole thing stinks. We could be dealing with a murder after all. Abduction at best."

"Well, that escalated," she said.

"What do you think about this Graham bloke? Suspect?"

"I think you can decide that for yourself, Ben," she said. "I'll see you back at the station this afternoon."

She ended the call and pocketed her phone, giving Anderson a look that she hoped conveyed the escalation in complexity and seriousness.

"Well, Mr Graham?" she said. "Do you have anything else to say? Now's your chance."

He looked at her, trying to read her expression but failing miserably. He said nothing.

"You leave me no option, then," she said. "Jeremiah Graham—"

"Hold on, hold on," he said. "You're not arresting me, are you?"

"Unless you'd care to join us at the station for a voluntary interview."

"How can you arrest me? I haven't done anything."

"I'd probably start with conspiracy to abduct and see where we go from there."

"Abduction? Is this some kind of a joke?"

"Do I look like I'm joking? I'm giving you a chance to talk, Mr Graham," she replied.

"Abduction?" he said again, utterly appalled at the idea. "Me?"

"Would you prefer the alternative?" she said, then nodded for Anderson to open the door before answering his unspoken question. "Now, are you going to join us of your own free will?"

CHAPTER TWENTY-ONE

"Right then," Freya said, clapping her hands together to get everybody's attention. She dropped her bag onto her chair, snatched a whiteboard marker from her desk, and faced the room, waiting patiently for them all to finish what they were doing and pay attention. As usual, there was one particular individual who was taking the longest. Freya gave a polite cough, which caught his attention, and he snapped his laptop closed.

"Sorry, boss," Gillespie said. "Just finishing some wee research."

"Thank you," Freya said, not wishing to create any further delays. She sat back on the edge of her desk and was about to deliver her opening statement when the doors opened and DCI Standing entered.

"Don't mind me," he said, selecting the chair closest to the door.

He sat and crossed one leg over the other, laying his hands flat on his lap. Freya stared hard at him. It was one thing to micromanage the team but to oversee a briefing was just wrong. He'd be looking for the slightest of flaws in her approach, and the look in his eye told her he knew exactly what she was thinking, which he confirmed with a friendly, "Carry on. Just pretend I'm not here."

The whole scene reminded Freya of her first day in the incident room when Ben had been leading the team following the death of DI Foster. It had been Detective Superintendent Harper who had joined his briefing on that day, but the result had been the same; an unnerving presence and a pair of scrutinising eyes.

"So, what do we have?" she asked softly, the wind well and truly gone from her sails. But there was no way she was going to let the Beast from the East Midlands get the better of her, so she dug deep and shoved off the desk to tap the name she had written on the whiteboard. "Michael Levy. Reported missing by a colleague, Drew Barker."

She added the name Drew Barker to the board.

"Let's check Barker's background," she said. "Chapman?"

"No problem, ma'am," Chapman replied, who Freya noticed that, even in the warm weather, was still wearing a knitted cardigan.

"I assume you haven't found him, then?" Standing said. "Levy, I mean."

"No, guv. But we do have reason to believe he's involved in something."

"Involved in something?" he said, just as Freya was about to continue. He looked horrified as he searched each of their faces, clearly hoping it had been a joke. "Like what?"

She ignored him, choosing instead to let him learn of their findings through her narrative. He was like a child who skips to the end of a book to learn what happens then doesn't understand how it came to be.

"Gold," she said. "Your report suggests Levy's girlfriend is a victim of domestic abuse at Levy's hands. Is that correct?"

"Yes, ma'am," she said. "I'm not sure if she'll testify to that, but there's no doubt he lashes out."

"That's okay. Stick with her for me. See if you can get her to open up a little more. I'd like to know the names of her friends. Who does she talk to? Who does she confide in? Also, we'll need some kind of DNA sample for Levy. His toothbrush or hairbrush should suffice. We can pass it on to CSI to identify a match."

"Hold on, hold on. You're not suggesting any harm has come to Levy, are you?" Standing said, which, again, Freya ignored.

"Nillson, Anderson, tell me about this Jeremiah Graham character."

"He's a bit of an oddball, boss," Nillson said. "It looks like he did transfer the car to Levy on Thursday but clammed up when I mentioned it."

"Was it a fair sale?" Freya asked.

"From what I can gather, no money changed hands. Chapman checked Levy's bank details. No money in or out since Friday evening in the pub, and certainly not any transactions of significant value anytime recently."

"He clammed up when you spoke about the car, did he?"

"He did boss, yes. The whole car thing is suspect, but when you put it side by side with the outstanding invoices, and the fact that the two were seen arguing in the pub on Friday night, it does suggest some kind of deal was done," Nillson said. "I was going to suggest we check Graham's finances. I'd like to see if he's in any kind of trouble."

"Just stop a second, will you?" Standing said, this time shoving himself from his seat. "You're talking like this is a murder enquiry. We can't go checking the bank accounts of people just because they had an argument with some bloke in a pub. You'd need warrants for a start."

"Thank you, Nillson," Freya said. "I think you're right. There's more to the transfer of that car than meets the eye."

"Is anybody actually listening to me?" Standing called out.

"Gillespie?" said Freya. "Why don't you give us a rundown of what you found? And for heaven's sake, please keep it brief."

Gillespie started, "Aye, well–"

"DI Bloom," Standing said, this time his voice raised to new levels. "Do I need to have you up on an insubordination charge?"

"Guv?" she said, as innocently as she could.

"Don't push me, Freya. When I ask a question, I demand an answer."

"You said to pretend you're not here, guv," she said. "As far as I can see, I was following your instruction to the letter."

"You're pushing your luck, Bloom," he growled.

They locked stares, neither of them willing to be the first to look away.

"Gillespie?" Freya said, daring Standing to take that final step.

"Oh, aye, boss," Gillespie began, a little unnerved at the duel taking place in the room. "Well, we think you might have been right when you suggested Levy left the pub and cut through the nature reserve. We found–"

"I found," Cruz added.

"We found traces of blood on a wee footbridge over an old river course."

"Blood?" Standing said, still holding Freya's stare, but his resolve had waned and his intrigue was piqued.

"Aye, guv. Fresh too. I mean, we'll have to wait to see what CSI say but–"

"You have CSI at the scene?"

"Aye, guv. As I was saying, it looks like somebody lost a lot of blood there. There's spatter on the handrail, and then there's the disturbance beneath the bridge with the fresh footprints."

"Don't forget the hole that somebody dug," Cruz said, and Standing broke from Freya's gaze to stare at him. "I found that. Deep enough to bury an adult male."

"Aye, if the adult male in question is Gabby Cruz," Gillespie muttered. "Anybody else would just about have their ankles covered."

"Blood, footprints, and a freshly dug hole?" Standing said. "But no body?"

"No, guv. No body. Not yet anyway," Gillespie said.

"Which is why we deem this serious enough to warrant a financial background check on Jeremiah Graham, guv," Freya said.

"Jeremiah Graham?" Standing said as if he knew the name. He turned from the team and paced a few steps, deep in thought, then he stared at the whiteboard. "Alexandra Sinclair?"

"She's Levy's girlfriend," Freya explained, and he seemed to pause, deep in thought before replying.

"She's a victim of domestic abuse, you say?"

"That's right, guv."

"And Jeremiah Graham is involved in some kind of dodgy business deal? Is that all you have? It seems to me you're looking for a murder. Is a missing person investigation not enough for your ego, Bloom?"

"I didn't think that was too bad considering we're less than twenty-four hours into what was supposed to be a simple investigation," Freya said.

"You're making a mountain out of a molehill," he replied. "All I asked you to do was find a man, not investigate bank accounts, get involved in a domestic abuse case, or call CSI out to look at what? Dried blood, you say?"

"With all due respect—"

"With all due respect, nothing," he said. "What the bloody hell do you think you're doing, DI Bloom?"

"Perhaps we should discuss this in private—"

"Perhaps we should discuss it here," he snapped. "What are you trying to do? Make a mockery of me?"

"I'm carrying out your orders, guv, to the letter. If you remember, I told you to pass this onto CID, but no. No, you had to push us, didn't you? Now, if we had approached this with any less diligence than we have done, we'd never have uncovered these anomalies, and you'd be standing here right now, telling us, no, telling me that I'm not doing my job properly. You can't argue that we haven't thrown everything we've got at this, and if you feel it's too much, then I suggest you take it up with Detective Superintendent Granger. I'd be happy to have this conversation with him."

"I just asked you to look into a missing man," he said. "I asked you to appease a troubled man who was worried about his friend, not create a bloody manhunt."

"You asked me to investigate a missing person, guv. I'm investigating it," she said, and the two locked heads with the team in full view, which Freya deemed as highly unprofessional, but it would be a string to her bow should the matter be escalated. "Do you want us to stop? I can call CSI now if that's what you want."

"No," he said. "No, you're in it now. You'd just better pray this bloody circus doesn't come back to bite you in the backside, DI Bloom, because believe me, I will take great pleasure in instigating an inquiry into your performance if it does."

She tore her eyes from his and met her team's sorry stares. One by one, they each shied away, unable to watch her be treated in such a way.

"Ditto," she said finally, and he shoved through the doors in a huff, barging the doors into somebody, to whom he offered no apology.

Ben gave her a nod, silently questioning if she was okay, and she replied by turning back to the board to study the names and develop the plan further.

"DI Bloom?" a voice said from the doorway, and Freya turned to find a mature man peering around the team, unsure if he was in the right place.

"Yes?" she said.

He was what her father would have called well turned out. He wasn't dressed to impress in a tailored suit, but rather he carried himself in a professional manner and cared for his appearance as a mature man might.

"I've been told you're looking into a missing person?" he said. "Michael Levy?"

"That's right," she said. "Who are you?"

"DI Grant Burns. CID."

"Okay," she said. "And how can I help you, Grant?"

"It's not how you can help me," he replied. "It's more about how I can help you. I've been looking for Michael Levy since Thursday."

"Oh, really? Have you had any luck?"

"No," he said. "Haven't heard a peep from him, which is unusual. He's the type of man that people tend to remember seeing if you know what I mean. And if they don't see him, they hear him. He suffers from docker's mouth, especially when he's had a drink."

"I see," Freya said. "And what is it you want with him?"

"I'm just following up on a money laundering case," he explained. "Levy is a potential witness. I just needed him to corroborate a suspect's story."

"And how does this help me?" Freya asked, sensing he had far more to say than was offering forthright.

"I went to his house on Saturday morning. Tried to catch him before he woke up."

"And did you?"

"No. No, I didn't," he said. "But I did meet his partner's daughter. A Rosie Sinclair. Young girl, she is. Fifteen or sixteen. You might want to have a word with her if you can. There's something not quite right about that house, and I doubt they're the type of people to ask for help."

"They're not," Freya agreed. "Might I have some kind of clue? What is it that has piqued your interest?"

"Her demeanour," he replied. "She was either hiding something, or she was nervous. I don't know which. Couldn't put my finger on it, if I'm honest. I just had that feeling, and over the years, I've come to trust that feeling quite well. I've been moved off the investigation," he said and nodded along the corridor towards Standing's office. "Some rubbish about a lack of resources. Anyway, I thought I'd just pass my findings on."

"Just her demeanour?" Freya said, noticing a reluctance to verbalise his thoughts in their entirety, an inability to look her in the eye as he spoke. "Or was there something else?"

He hesitated, then eventually he looked her way.

"Bruises," he replied flatly, and he pulled open the door.

"Bruises? Could you be more specific?"

He paused, holding the door open with one hand.

"On her wrists. Seemed like an odd place to have bruises, and I for one can only think of one reason why a young girl might develop bruising on both her wrists," Burns replied. "I'll leave that little chestnut for your own imagination to decipher. Let me know how you get on, eh?"

"The plot thickens," Gillespie said, adopting a playful, mysterious tone that his Glaswegian accent only added to.

"It does indeed," she replied thoughtfully and then caught Ben waving his phone at her to get to her attention.

"What is it?" she asked.

"A message from Michaela," he replied.

"I'm not a barn owl, Ben. I can't read it from here."

"It's definitely blood," he replied, amused by her retort. "We don't know whose blood it is, but it's definitely blood."

CHAPTER TWENTY-TWO

The sky outside was bright and blue, but the mood in the room suggested a storm was due. It would have been too easy to slip into a more passive role and let Standing walk over her for the sake of her job, but knowing what she knew about the transfers and seeing the look on their faces while he had berated had only fuelled her tenacity.

He had been right; they were in the investigation now, and to pull out would have dire consequences. But just as she had both feet in a can of worms, she had also gone too far in her battle with Standing to withdraw.

One way or another, the missing person investigation would be the last the team as she knew it collaborated on.

They all stared at her, and she was sure they had questions but were too polite to ask. That is, except for one individual, who demonstrated having the social skills of a grizzly bear.

"It's a bit of a situation we find ourselves in, eh, boss?" Gillespie said.

"You could say that," she replied, noting his use of we, not singling her out. She had to admit it, regardless of his thoughts, he was on her side. He was a team player. "Sod it, I'm going all in."

The statement caught the attention of every person in the room.

"Michael Levy has either been abducted or worse. He's out there, and we're going to find him, dead or alive. Moreover, whatever else we might uncover in the process of finding Michael Levy will all be a bonus."

"When you say you're going all in…" Ben started.

"I mean I'm throwing everything at the investigation. To hell with Standing. To hell with what other people think. This could be our last investigation. It could even be my last investigation. Let's do it on our terms."

"What do you have in mind, boss?" Gillespie asked.

"I want you and Cruz to lead a detailed search of the nature reserve. Contact Horncastle station. Get a team of uniforms to help you."

"You might need to get some of ours on board," Ben said. "Horncastle is tiny. The station is basically an old converted house."

"Talk to Priest," Freya said. "He'll allocate you all the resources you need. I want the entire area gone over with a fine-tooth comb. If it hasn't grown there, I want it bagged and tagged."

"Aye, boss," he replied. "Leave that with me."

"Thank you," she replied, fighting the urge to add some kind of warning for him and Cruz not to let her down. "Nillson, Anderson, do you mind if Ben and I interview Jeremiah Graham?"

"Not at all, boss," Nillson said.

"Good. I want you to pay a visit to Drew Barker," she told them. "Chapman, what do we have on him?"

"Not a lot, if I'm honest," Chapman replied, reading from the notes she'd made in the last twenty minutes. "He was involved in a fraud case a few years ago but was never charged. He lives with his son in Horncastle, works in furniture restoration with Michael Levy, and from what I can see, he might be in some kind of financial difficulties. Payments from Levy's business account to Barker's personal account seem to have stopped a few months ago. It looks like Barker has been transferring money from a savings account to cover his bills, and there's not enough in there for him to do that for much longer."

"Anything else?"

"Yep, he has an alibi for the weekend," Chapman said. "Sorry to disappoint, but there's a payment here to the Petwood Hotel in Woodhall Spa for three hundred and fifty-eight pounds, paid yesterday morning at ten a.m."

"That's plenty to go on," Freya said to Nillson. "Drew Barker is a nervous man but not aggressive, so just make enquiries for now. What was he doing at the Petwood and what time did he get there? And what does his relationship with Levy look like? See if he can tell you anything about Jeremiah Graham, too. If they work together, he might know more about Levy's business than his girlfriend does. People talk."

"He reported Levy missing though, boss," Gillespie said. "I mean, he's hardly likely to have anything to do with him going missing if he reported the fellow missing."

"I disagree," Cruz said. "In fact, statistics show that individuals involved in abductions and murders have a tendency to be overly helpful. Take Ian Huntley, for example. He was even filmed by news teams helping with the searches for his victims. They often do it to stay one step ahead of the investigation. Stephen Port, too, the Grindr killer. He was another one. He called the police to report a dead body he'd found outside his flat and it was him who put it there."

"Cruz is right," Freya said. "We can't disregard Barker. Personally, I don't think he's capable, but let's cover ourselves here."

"We'll pay him a visit," Nillson said.

"Gold, I'm sorry, but I need to add to your list. Don't ask any direct questions, but please bear in mind what DI Burns said about the daughter's wrists. If Levy is beating his girlfriend, maybe he's beating her too," Freya said. "I also want the details of her employer so we can corroborate her shifts."

"No problem, ma'am," she replied.

"The aim, ladies and gentlemen," Freya called out, "is to map the movements of every one of the suspects, friends, and relatives during Friday night. I want to know exactly where each of these individuals were, and I want it all corroborated. Anything that cannot be proved should be highlighted."

"Aye, boss," Gillespie said, the only one to verbalise his confirmation.

"Lastly, let's not forget what we're trying to do here. We're looking for Michael Levy. We're not solving a murder, we're not trying to catch people out, we're looking for somebody, and we're going to find him," she said. "Dead or alive, we're going to find Michael Levy."

CHAPTER TWENTY-THREE

Jeremiah Graham was more than well turned out. His three-piece suit was genuine Harris tweed, his Oxfords, Freya recognised as being from Crockett and Jones, and no doubt the pocket watch that hung from a gold chain attached to his breast pocket was genuine and most likely of significant value.

It came as no surprise, then, that the solicitor who introduced himself as Thomas Barnett-Mills QC oozed confidence and charm, and bore a smug, irrepressible grin.

Ben began the recording, introducing the date and the time, then handed it over to Freya to introduce the attendees.

"The purpose of this meeting," she began, once the formalities were out of the way, "is to establish a timeline of your whereabouts since last Friday, Mr Graham, and I should note that whilst you are not under arrest, anything you say may be given in evidence. At this stage, we are yet to locate Mr Levy, and we hope the information you provide us will help us find him."

"And the reasons for suspecting my client of being involved are?" Barnett-Mills asked, his Mont Blanc fountain pen poised ready above expensive and headed notepaper.

"Mr Graham has been identified as the last person to see

Michael Levy, during which time a witness claims to have seen them in an argument. Then there is the transfer of a nineteen eighty-seven Mercedes for which we can establish no transfer of money, which by itself doesn't mean a lot, but when you couple that with the significant amount of money your client owes Michael Levy, it does raise a few rather poignant questions."

"I don't see how that leads you to suspect my client of being involved in an abduction. That's absurd."

"I agree," Freya said. "And I thought the same if I'm honest. That is until we discovered a trail of blood close to the pub in which your client and the victim were last seen."

"So you don't actually know that this Levy character has been abducted?" he said.

"Not yet, but as is often the case with abductions, we don't know they have taken place until either A, the victim's body is found, or B, the victim is found alive, the latter being rarer than the former. So you can see why we're keen to push on to find Mr Levy."

"And you claim to have a witness? Has this statement been submitted?" he asked.

"No," she replied, aware that all she had to go on was hearsay and that John Glover's barmaid was unlikely to be coerced into giving a formal statement. "But I'll be collating the evidence and forwarding it to your office as soon as I can."

"Might I suggest we clarify a few facts before we progress?" the solicitor asked. "Firstly, I would like to see the witness statement you mentioned, and secondly, we need some evidence of a crime being committed before we proceed with any discussion around abduction charges."

"I clearly haven't made our position clear," Freya said. "Your client is not under arrest. I have not mentioned any charges. He is here of his own free will. However, we believe your client to be involved in some kind of business deal with Mr Levy, legal or not. He was seen arguing with a man who hasn't been seen since and is indebted to Mr Levy to the tune of over twenty thousand pounds. I'm not looking to press charges right now. I'm not looking for a quick win. I'm giving your client the opportunity to eliminate himself from our enquiries. Should he fail to do that, and should our delay result in the death of Mr Levy, then I will have no option other than to press charges."

She expected him to take a few moments to digest her statement then formulate a response, but he came back at her before she'd even drawn a breath.

"Then I suggest you prepare yourself for an inquiry, Inspector Bloom—"

"It's okay," Graham said, clearly tiring of the debate between the two. He stared at Freya. "You want me to clear my name?"

"That's all I'm asking you to do, Mr Graham."

"And then you'll leave me alone?"

"What I want, Mr Graham, is to understand your exact movements since Friday evening. I want to know when and where you left Mr Levy, and where you've been since. I also want to know about the transfer of the Mercedes and the history of debt," she said. "Do that, and you can go home right now."

He glanced across at his solicitor.

"You're under no obligation," Barnett-Mills said. "Another solicitor might not recognise their underhand tactics, but I do. That's what you pay me for."

"I know," Graham replied, and he smiled gratefully as if the two were old friends. "But I have nothing to hide."

"Shall we start with Friday evening?" Freya said. "Specifically, when you arrived at The White Horse to meet Michael Levy."

Graham's nostrils flared as he exhaled, and he collated his thoughts, putting them into some semblance of order.

"The car is collateral," he said finally. "It was my way of keeping him off my back."

"Because of the money you owe him?" Freya asked, to which he nodded.

"It shouldn't have come to this, but since the whole pandemic thing, and what with Brexit, it's been challenging to make ends meet."

"So the car was to pay off a debt?"

"No, it's just collateral. It was never a permanent arrangement."

"So what was the argument about?" Freya asked.

"Money," he replied. "What else do people argue about?"

"He wasn't entirely sold on the arrangement then?"

"Oh, he was sold on it. He'd already agreed to the deal on Thursday. But what he didn't appreciate was my request for additional credit."

"And by that, I presume you mean the items you ordered from him that are yet to be delivered?"

"And more," he said "I mean, I do need a supply chain to generate revenue, and if he chooses to stop supplying me, then he'll never get his money back. That's basic business."

"I don't understand," Freya said. "You owe the man twenty thousand pounds, and you have done for what? A year?"

"Longer. More like two years," he said quietly.

"And instead of taking out a loan to pay him back, you gave him an old car."

"That car is a classic. It's worth a small fortune."

"But then how do you expect him to run his business? He can't very well pay his suppliers or wherever it is he gets his pieces of furniture from—"

"Auctions," he added.

"Right, you can't expect him to keep his business running if his customers can't pay their bills."

"He isn't short of a few quid," Graham said.

"Mr Graham, Michael Levy lives in an old council house with a girlfriend and her daughter to provide for. You're wearing eight hundred pound shoes, your suit must have cost more than a thousand pounds, probably closer to two, and as for that watch, I dread to think. He's in debt up to his eyeballs. Is it any wonder the man is a little highly strung?"

"Inspector Bloom, I have many shortcomings, I'll admit. But I will not be held responsible for another man's financial affairs, nor shall I be held accountable for how he chooses to run his business. Michael Levy, like me, has access to services designed to reclaim money owed. If he chooses not to pursue those services, then on his head be it."

"That's a rather callous approach, Mr Graham."

"It's business," he replied. "And times like these tend to weed out the weak."

"How did you leave it with Michael?" Freya asked, feeling her blood pressure rising. "When you left him. Did you leave amicably?"

"When you say amicably, are you asking if any threats were issued? If you are, then no, they weren't," he said. "As it happens, we agreed on some new terms. He gave me a further six months to repay the money I owe him and he honoured any deals previously made."

"That's very generous of him, given the circumstances."

"It is," he said. "But then we do go way back. I could tell you a few stories about him that might cast him in a different light."

"I'm all ears," Freya said, leaning forward in her seat.

"I'll save those for another time," he said. "Over a drink, perhaps? When he's been found, maybe? It'll be a nice opportunity for you to apologise to me."

"We're just trying to find your friend, Mr Graham."

"And I'm just eliminating myself from your enquiries," he said. "I left my car with him, gave him the keys, and I walked back to my shop to finish a few bits and pieces I'd started during the day."

"Did anybody see you?"

"I called into The King's Head on my way, as it happens. Geoff Summers will tell you."

"Is he the landlord?" Freya said, and she checked Ben had made a note of the name.

"No, he runs the pool team. But I spoke to him. He'll remember me."

"And from there, you went back to your shop?"

"That's right. I was there until the early hours, after which I walked up the stairs to my flat, poured myself a glass of whiskey, and went to bed."

"And you live alone, do you?" Freya asked.

"I do. I'm not really cut out for relationships if you know what I mean," he said with a wry wink. "Do you want to know about Saturday?"

"No," Freya said. "Not right now, at least."

"Do you have any further questions for my client?" Barnett-Mills asked.

She stared up at the solicitor, then across at Graham, and she was reminded of how those members of the upper middle class her father had rubbed shoulders with seemed somehow to exist in a society with different laws. It was all a game to them, and with only coincidence and suspicion behind her, she knew she was beat.

"No," she said. "No, Mr Graham, you are free to go."

"Well, under different circumstances, perhaps it would have been a pleasure," he said, pushing his chair back and sharing a winning smile with his solicitor.

"One last thing," she said, not looking his way, instead choosing to stare at his empty chair. "If you are as innocent as you say you are, you won't mind providing a sample of your DNA."

"Excuse me?"

"It's purely so we can officially eliminate you from our enquiries, Mr Graham. You see, as we speak, our crime scene investigators are collecting samples of blood found close to where you last saw Michael Levy. We'll know if the blood belongs to Mr Levy very shortly."

He glanced at his solicitor, then back at Freya, who met his stare with a winning smile of her own.

"So, why do you need my DNA?" he asked.

"Because quite often our analysts find more than one blood sample, especially in cases of brutal violence, of which this is one."

"Okay," he said, folding his arms defensively. "Okay, I'll provide a sample. I have nothing to hide."

"So you keep telling me."

"And then you'll leave me alone?"

"If we have your DNA on file, Mr Graham, it'll save us having to contact you again," she said. "That is if you are as innocent as you claim to be."

CHAPTER TWENTY-FOUR

Drew Barker's house was a modest, single-storey property with two palms in the front garden and a few other spiky tropical plants dotted around various gravel beds. It was as if the house had been lifted from warmer climes and deposited in the heart of rural Lincolnshire.

"He has a nicer house than his boss," Anderson mused as Nillson pulled the car up to the kerb.

"And by all accounts, he's a nicer person," Nillson said.

The warm weather suited the tropical garden, which, judging by the lack of weeds and the broad spectrum of flowers, most of which Nillson had never seen before, was Barker's pride and joy.

She knocked on the door then stepped back, catching Anderson gazing at the plants in awe.

"I'd love to have the time," she said. "Not that I have a clue what to do in a garden, but still, the time to do it would be nice."

"I can think of better ways to spend my time," Nillson said. "Lying in a garden, now that I can do. On my hands and knees digging up weeds, no thank you."

The door opened and a teenage boy peered out.

Nillson let her warrant card fall open for him to see.

"We're looking for Drew Barker," she said. "Is he home?"

"Sorry?" he said.

"Drew Barker?"

"My dad?"

"If your dad is Drew, then yes, please."

"Yeah, he is," he replied. "He's just out the back."

He took a step back to call out to his father through the house.

"Can we come in?" Nillson asked, and she placed a boot on the threshold.

"No," he said, stepping back to hold the door tight. "No, I'll go get him. Wait here."

The boy left the door ajar and walked back through the house, leaving Nillson and Anderson waiting on the doorstep, a little bemused by his reaction.

"He seemed a bit nervous," Nillson said.

"He's a teenage boy," Anderson said. "He was probably in his room having some alone time. You know what they're like."

"Oh, for God's sake," Nillson said, stifling a laugh just as Drew Barker came to the door.

"Yes?" he said. "Can I help you?"

The boy lingered a few steps behind him, clinging to the kitchen door and listening in.

Nillson flashed her warrant card again, making sure the father had a chance to read it.

"Might we have a word?" she said, and she flicked her eyes at the boy and back to him. "In private?"

He glanced back at his son, who seemed to get the message and disappeared into his bedroom.

"Come through to the garden," Barker said, opening the door for them. "Do you mind if I work while we talk? There's so much to do at this time of the year."

"Not at all," Nillson said and followed him through the open-plan living space into the kitchen, which consisted of a flagstone floor, granite worktops, and a wooden cupboard door. It wasn't quite the quintessential country kitchen but would have been stylish in the eighties. There was no ceiling above, only the old roof trusses, which somehow made the space feel even larger.

Outside, a small area of decking provided the patio, while the rest of the long garden gently banked down to a fence with a small gate, beyond which was the nature reserve and fields. But it was the view from the decking that held Nillson's attention. The sprawling fields and the treetops in the late afternoon sun were quite spectacular.

"Wow," she said "That's a view to wake up to every morning."

"Lovely, isn't it?" he said, as he descended the few steps to a small lawned area, beyond which was what looked like a small allotment. He stopped to share the view for a moment, smiling gratefully. "It's one of the reasons we bought this place."

"Are you married, Mr Barker?"

"Widower," he replied sadly. Then he gestured at the house with a flick of his head. "Anthony is all I need, and more than enough for me to handle, if I'm honest."

"It must be hard for him," Anna said. "Were they close?"

Barker shook his head.

"He was young when it happened," he replied. "But he's a good lad. He still goes to see her."

"Sorry?"

"Her grave," Barker said. "He still visits, as do I. Between the two of us we keep it nice. That's how she would have liked it."

"He sounds like a good lad."

"Do you have children?" Barker asked.

"No," she replied, making a show of following him down the steps to brush over the topic. "I'd like to start by thanking you for bringing Michael Levy to our attention. Have you heard from him at all?"

"Not a peep," he replied. "It's so unlike him. He's normally such a hard worker. He wouldn't miss a courier, not for the world, and as for not answering his phone, I've never known it. Every call could be a sale, he would say. He'd make a point of answering within three rings."

"It must have taken a lot to report it, though," Nillson said, watching as he collected a garden fork and began turning the earth with smooth, practised movements. "I mean, he'd only been missing for a couple of days."

He stopped digging and leaned on his fork.

"Listen, if you know him like I do, you'll understand. Michael Levy does not miss a day's work."

"Understood," she said, and he returned to the task at hand. "What about his relationship with Jeremiah Graham? Can you tell me anything about that?"

He gave a brief laugh.

"Jerry Graham and Mike go way back. Jerry has been a customer since before I started working for him."

"How long ago was that?"

"Must be fifteen years now," he said, shaking his head. "Fifteen years. Where did that go?"

"And have you always restored furniture?"

"Me? No. I was a chippie. A carpenter, if you will. Had a break when the missus died and never really had the motivation to go back to it. Site work, hard graft that is. No, I'm happy doing what I'm doing. Same place every day, the same faces, and the same mug for my tea. Can't beat it."

"What will you do if Michael isn't found?" Anderson asked, and he stopped working to stare at her.

"What do you mean, if he's not found? Do you know something?"

"No, Mr Barker. No, we're still making enquiries. But surely the thought has crossed your mind?"

"Aye, it's crossed my mind," he said. "As for what I'll do. I'll do what I've always done. Find somewhere to work hard. Start again, maybe?"

"I hope you don't mind me saying, Mr Barker, but we have taken a look at the company accounts."

"You what?"

"You haven't been paid for three months now. Why is that?"

"The company accounts?"

"It's standard procedure in an investigation like this," she explained. "If the missing person was a young girl, as they often are, then we wouldn't have the need. But when a mature male goes missing, we often find there are financial reasons behind it."

"Well, if you've seen the company accounts, then you'll know," he said. "We've not got a lot. Not since all this Brexit lark, anyway. I don't know what it is, but the world seems to have gone mad these past few years, what with Brexit, all these immigrants, and whatnot. Do you know what I think? I think that everyone should just stop arguing over what they want to be called, or who did what during lockdown, so we can get on with fixing the country."

"You're surviving on savings, Mr Barker," Nillson said, not wishing to pursue a debate on current affairs. "That's not a good position to be in."

He stared up at her, his expression one of utter contempt.

"You've been snooping around my bank accounts?"

"We had to get a warrant, Mr Barker. We're trying to find your friend, remember."

"Well, you won't find him in there. You won't find much at all, come to think of it."

"We also noticed you stayed at the Petwood Hotel last weekend," Nillson said, to which he shook his head in dismay. "May I ask why?"

"It was a golf weekend," he said, clearly a little upset at their research. "I play golf at Woodhall. I thought you would have known that. You bloody well seem to know everything else."

"Why book a hotel? It's only a short drive from here."

"Because it tends to get messy," he said. "You know? The nineteenth. The longest hole."

"But still, a taxi would have been cheaper."

"Listen, I don't have much," he said, jabbing his fork into the ground and resting his boot on it. "I have two pleasures in life. One of them is my boy and the other is golf. So when there's a tournament, a few days where like-minded folk like me can relax a little, enjoy a few rounds of golf, and a catch-up, I tend to make the most of it. Is that a crime? You've seen my bank account. You'll see I did the same last year and the year before that."

"No, it's not a crime," Nillson said. "We're just trying to build a timeline of where Michael Levy's acquaintances were on Friday night, that's all. It's just a process we use to eliminate anybody close to him from the investigation."

"I was at the Petwood. I got there on Friday evening and I came home on Sunday morning."

"But if you were at the Petwood, who took care of your boy?" Anderson asked, peering into the garden shed.

"He can take care of himself," Barker said. "And you won't find him in there, neither."

Anderson took the hint and strolled towards the back gate.

"Listen," Barker said, sounding tired, "I've got a lot to do. I've answered all your questions, and I even bloody well reported him missing. I'm just an honest bloke trying to get by. I had nothing to do with it."

"To do with what?" Nillson asked, and he stopped again, thinking about what he might say next.

"To do with him going missing," he replied. "Now, if you don't mind–"

"One last question," Anderson said from where she stood at the rear gate, which she had opened; she was peering out over the nature reserve. "Do you always leave this gate unlocked?"

CHAPTER TWENTY-FIVE

The day was nearing an end when Jackie pulled up outside the Sinclair house for the last time that day. She checked her makeup in the rear-view mirror, then collected her bag and locked the car. Standing on the doorstep waiting for the door to be opened, she noted the peace and quiet of the street. A few kids played further along the road and birds sang in the trees opposite the row of terraced houses.

Alexandra snatched the door open, then looked disappointed when she saw Jackie standing there.

"Sorry, me again," Jackie said, waiting to be welcomed into the house. But instead of welcoming her, Alexandra turned her back and strode into the kitchen, from where the smell of home-cooking emanated. Jackie closed the door behind her and followed her in. "I just popped by to give you an update. You haven't heard from him, I suppose?"

Alexandra shook her head, seeming disinterested in anything Jackie had to say and barely even acknowledging her presence.

"The truth is, Alexandra, most missing persons are young females, not mature males. Quite often when men like Michael go missing, we find it's of their own doing."

"Depression, you mean?" she replied, reading between the lines.

"Sometimes," Jackie said, unwilling to skirt around the topic. "It's a possibility we have to face. We have to be ready, just in case."

"You talk like you know him," Alexandra said. "Like you're affected."

"Alexandra, he was last seen nearly seventy-two hours ago. Whatever it is you're going through, you have to know I'm here to help you. It's my job. I hope nothing has happened to him, I really do. But there's a chance he's out there, hurt or…"

"Or?" she said.

"Or worse," Jackie said flatly. "And that's something we need to prepare for. We can't just sit back and hope he comes back. We have to investigate every possibility."

"There are possibilities?"

"Maybe?" Jackie said. "We have to know if he argued with anybody recently, for example."

"Well, don't look at me," Alexandra replied, fingering her bruised eye. "I learned a long time ago not to argue back."

"I didn't mean you," Jackie said. "I meant his friends, his business partners, customers, suppliers, you name it. We have to look into them."

"Everyone?" she asked.

"Of course. Look, we could wait a week in case Michael turns up, and I have to say, a large number of adult males reported missing do usually come back of their own accord."

"But you have to plan for the worst," Alexandra finished.

"The problem we face is that if we wait for a week hoping he comes back and he doesn't, any evidence might be destroyed. We have to go through the process, we have to log the evidence, we have to investigate everyone he had dealings with so that if the time comes when we need to escalate the investigation—"

"You mean, if he's dead somewhere in a ditch?"

"Frankly, yes," Jackie said. "If that happens, and I hope it doesn't, but if it does, then we'll have something to work with. We're just doing our jobs."

"And what exactly does that entail?" she asked. "You'll forgive me for not having one hundred per cent faith in the police."

"Jeremiah Graham," Jackie said. "There's clearly some kind of financial dispute between them."

"There's been a financial dispute of one sort or another between those two since dinosaurs roamed the earth."

"To the tune of twenty thousand pounds?" Jackie said, hoping to see a reaction of some kind, and she did. But it was fleeting as the wind and came as no real surprise.

"Is it really that much? Do you think Jerry could have done something?"

"There's a chance somebody has done something," Jackie said. "I'm sorry to have to tell you this, Alexandra, but we found traces of blood–"

"Blood? Where?"

"In the nature reserve. You said he usually walked home from The White Horse on Friday nights. He would have cut through the nature reserve. Is that right?"

"It takes about fifteen minutes off of the walk," she replied. "Everybody cuts through there."

"We've got analysts running some checks. We could do with some help," Jackie said. "We need to identify who the blood belongs to."

"And how would you do that?"

"DNA is the simplest option," Jackie replied. "Is there any chance we could take something to benchmark his DNA with?"

"Like what? He doesn't have a hairbrush if that's what you mean."

"A toothbrush," Jackie said. "I'm sorry to ask. But if we can just see if the blood belongs to him, it might give us an idea of where he is or if something has happened to him."

"But what if the blood is his? What does that mean?"

"It means there's a strong possibility he was involved in some kind of accident or altercation, Alexandra. If it is his blood, he might be nearby. He could have crawled off somewhere."

"Crawled off?"

"He could be hurt," Jackie said. "We've got a team lined up to search the entire nature reserve at first light. Having Michael's DNA could really help us."

"I see," Alexandra muttered, and she leaned on the kitchen worktop, staring at the window into the garden.

"Are you okay, Alexandra? I know this is difficult–"

"It's not," she replied and actually laughed – a genuine laugh. "It's really not. I'm sorry, but I'm finding it extremely difficult to feel sorry for him. Is that the wrong thing to say to a police officer?"

"I'm here to help you through the process," Jackie said. "Trust me, I've seen enough to empathise with you. You're not obliged to feel anything. You can't force these things."

"He put me through hell," Alexandra said, then softened. "I just can't bring myself to feel any kind of sorrow. Does that make me a bad person?"

"No, Alexandra–"

"I want it to be his," she said, and then seemed to hear what she had said, and that by verbalising her thoughts, they were somehow set in stone. "I want him gone."

"Alexandra–"

"No, don't say anything," she said, swallowing hard. "A toothbrush, you say?"

"That's all we need."

"I'll get it for you," Alexandra said, wiping a tear from her eye. She shoved off the worktop and left the room, leaving Jackie alone.

She waited for Alexandra to climb the stairs, then sauntered over to the microwave, finding the biscuit tin where it has been before. She opened the lid, and found the stack of empty envelopes she had seen before, along with a few other personal items that somebody might not want to be kept on show but would want close to hand; a handful of pound coins, some tablets, and a few hair bobbles. Finding nothing more of interest, she closed the lid and positioned the tin as she had found it.

Jackie took a breath and leaned on the counter, just as Alexandra had. She found herself studying the photos on the fridge. The majority of them showed Alexandra with what had to be her daughter during various stages of childhood. There were the images Jackie had expected to see; Rosie blowing out candles at her tenth birthday party, theme parks, and relaxed beach holidays. Dotted amongst these were images of Michael Levy and the family, which were cold and almost staged, and Jackie could almost hear the photographer asking them to smile.

And then, above the family snaps, Jackie noticed some images which, in stark contrast to the forced smiles below, showed Rosie in a whole new light. Four friends; three boys and Rosie, their childhoods documented like a photographic tapestry, from what looked like six-or-seven-year-olds to the teenagers they were now, coming to the end of their school lives.

The photos made Jackie think of her own boy, Charlie, and she wondered if he would ever have friends like those. She hoped so.

"They're inseparable," a voice said from the doorway, and she turned to find Alexandra standing there. "Those boys have been my saving grace. After all we've been through, I always know she's looked after."

"I can see they're close," Jackie said.

"Those boys would do anything for her," Alexandra replied, and she held out a toothbrush by the handle.

Jackie had come prepared. She fished a plastic evidence bag from her pocket, held it open for Alexandra to drop the brush into, then sealed it and dropped it into her pocket.

"I'm sorry about before," Alexandra said. "I guess it'll catch up with me sooner or later. The emotions, that is."

Jackie smiled. "If it is Michael's blood—"

"Then I want to know," she said with defiance in her eyes. "Although I can't promise not to be relieved."

CHAPTER TWENTY-SIX

"It's a crying shame," Gillespie muttered aloud, as the lorry's HIAB crane took the weight of the Mercedes. The old car swung a little on its straps then settled, and amidst a few creaks and groans from the hydraulic rams, it lifted into the air.

"That's one less piece of junk on the roads," Cruz said, clearly satisfied by the spectacle. "Do you know how bad the emissions are on a car like that?"

"Just don't," Gillespie said, silencing him with a raised hand. "There'll be a time, you know, when cars like this are all gone, save for a few in museums that just sit there, sad and pathetic like those dogs you see in cages waiting for a new home."

"Jim, you cannot honestly compare a car to a dog."

"No, a car is better, this one, at least. It's far more useful, and as for the feeling you get when you drive it, ah, sheer bliss, Gabby. Sheer bliss."

"It's a bunch of metal and plastic, and from the looks of it, half a dozen cows. It has no power steering, no ABS, and as for the radio, it might as well have a gramophone embedded into the dashboard. Driving that would be like going to the gym."

"Driving it would be an experience," Gillespie said. "You don't get those sensations from modern cars. You don't get to feel the car responding to the road, to feel the weight shifting as you round a corner, and to run your hand across a dashboard that was built with love, by an actual pair of hands, not some robot cranking them out by the thousand. That's the problem with you lot—"

"You lot?"

"Aye, you lot. Snowflakes, or whatever it is you call yourselves. You've no appreciation for better times."

The lorry driver eased the car down onto the back of the lorry, and the old Mercedes' suspension sank under its weight once more.

It almost looked sad.

"Snowflakes?" Cruz said. "We don't call ourselves snowflakes. You lot call us it."

"Aye, well, whatever you are, you've no appreciation," Gillespie said. "I'd give my right arm to drive a car like that."

"Eh? And how exactly would you drive it with one arm?"

"Oh, shut up. It's a figure of speech," Gillespie said, as the driver approached them bearing a clipboard and a pen. He was a burly man who had probably spent too many days behind the wheel and not enough on his feet, but he was cheerful, which in Gillespie's view, spoke volumes for the merits of a nice bacon sandwich.

"Now then," he said. "Which one of you knows how to sign your name?"

It was one of those jokes that Gillespie presumed the man used with every new face he saw, and most likely even those he had seen before, who had heard the joke a dozen times.

"Eh?" Cruz said. "Both of us can sign our names."

Gillespie shook his head and took the clipboard from the driver. He signed his name and handed it back.

"I was just telling the lad how modern cars just don't compare," he said.

"Aye, you're right there," he replied and then turned to join Gillespie in appreciating the old motor. "My dad had a boss once, way back. He had one of these. I remember he parked it outside the office for everyone to see. Immaculate it was, too. Silver with red seats."

"Did you get to drive it?" Cruz asked.

"Me? No. Nobody got to drive it," the man said.

"I'll bet the boss was quite protective, eh?" Gillespie said.

"Aye, he was that. But not only that. Even if he had been a little more generous and let my old man have a go, he couldn't have."

"Why's that?" Cruz asked.

"It used to break down every other week," he replied, winking at Gillespie. "If there's one thing these motors did for Britain, it's finance our mechanic's businesses. Kept them busy, I can tell you."

"Thank you," Gillespie said, ignoring Cruz's beaming smile. "Come on, snowflake. Let's go."

"Go where? It's home time."

"How many times do I have to tell you, Gabby? Home time is what you call it at school. We're not at school now."

"So what do we call the time when we get to go home?"

"Pub time," Gillespie said. "Come on, it'd be rude not to."

"I need to get back."

"Well, I need a drink, so you can either take Shanks's pony, or you can join me for a drink, and I'll drop you back at the station after."

"Oh, for God's sake," he said. "Hermione will go nuts if she smells beer on me."

Gillespie held the door open and gave the Mercedes one more loving glance as Cruz walked into the pub.

"You'd better have a lemonade then," Gillespie said. "Maybe I'll buy you a bag of crisps and you can sit outside. That's what used to happen, you know? Kids weren't allowed in pubs back way back when I was a wee lad."

"Oh, God, here we go. Another lecture on days gone by," Cruz muttered. "I suppose they were better times, were they?"

"Aye, they were," he replied. "Unless you were the kid, of course, then it was just bloody boring."

"I'm surprised they even let you out to go down the pub."

"Out of where?"

"The workhouse," Cruz said. "Did you ever ask for more gruel?"

"Ah, I'm wasting my breath," Gillespie said, and he caught the attention of the bar girl. "I'll have a pint of the blonde ale, please, lassie. I don't suppose you've a packet of crisps and coke for the wee lad?"

"Oy," Cruz said. "I'll have a Corona, please. No crisps."

She was a pretty girl with eyes that belied her age, like she had seen enough of life to understand people well enough for her reservations to set in. She let the ale settle for a moment while she grabbed a bottle of Corona from the fridge, popped the lid, and stuck a slice of lemon in the top.

"You want a straw with that?" Gillespie asked, which raised a smile on the girl's face.

"I'm perfectly capable of drinking without a straw," he said quietly to Gillespie as he reached for the bottle, but, being intent on stopping Gillespie from embarrassing him and less focused on the task at hand, he knocked the bottle over. It fell onto its side, rolled, and then before the bar girl could stop pouring Gillespie's ale, it fell to the floor and smashed.

"Are you sure about that?" Gillespie said, as he took the beer from the frustrated bar girl, winked, and then took a long sip. "Seems to me you might need to sit outside after all."

"Oh, shut up," he replied, his face as red as the old Mercedes had been. He leaned over the bar to speak to the girl as she cleaned up the mess. "I suppose that happens all the time, doesn't it?"

"No, not really," she said, as she brushed the broken glass into a dustpan.

"Yeah, but, I mean, it's a pub, right? Glasses break all the time."

"No, not as often as you might think," she said, then stood and emptied the pan into a bin. "It's usually only when the punter has had a few too many, or if he or she just isn't really switched on. We should give people like that plastic cups, to be honest. Safer for them, cheaper for us."

"Hear, hear," Gillespie said.

"Alright, no need to encourage her," Cruz said, then his posture changed, and he leaned on the bar. "I don't suppose I could have another, could I?"

She looked Gillespie's way, signalling that the pub would not be footing the bill.

"Aye, go on. He doesn't get out much, poor lad," he said. "Might as well give him a wee bit of fun. He'll be beaten by his girlfriend when he gets home, forced to eat his dinner from a bowl on the floor, and then he'll have to start his daily cleaning schedule, lest he face the sharp end of a bamboo cane."

The girl smiled again, and Cruz huffed the embarrassment away.

"Just ignore him," he told her. "Thinks he's funny."

"You're the two coppers, aren't you?" she said, as she took the money for the three beers. "Aren't you supposed to be looking for Michael?"

"Aye, we are looking for him. Are you the lass that heard him arguing with Jeremiah Graham?"

"I'm the person who heard a heated conversation," she said, politely discouraging him from referring to her as a lass. She leaned on the bar, providing Gillespie with a view he had to fight not to see, else he would lose credibility. He turned away, and as the pub was virtually empty, he strode over to the window and pointed out to the far side of the road.

"He walked through the nature reserve. Is that right?"

"I don't know," she replied, and he glanced back, grateful that she was no longer leaning on the bar and was instead wiping it down with a rag that looked as if it had been used since the year the old Mercedes had been built. "I didn't see him leave."

"Shame," he said. "I mean, from what I hear, he's a bit of a character."

"That's one way of describing him," she said, as he re-approached the bar for another mouthful of his beer. She waited for him to come close, then beckoned him closer. "I did see something, though."

"See something?"

"I don't know if I should say anything, but..." she began and then checked to make sure nobody else was listening. "I locked up that night. Always do on a Friday. The boss is usually too hammered by closing time. Anyway, I saw something in the car park."

"Not a nineteen eighty-seven Mercedes SL by any chance?" Gillespie said, which failed to raise a smile.

She shook her head.

"It must have been about midnight, half past at the latest, by the time I'd cleaned up. John was upstairs, and I heard Griffin barking at something."

"Griffin?"

"His dog," she said. "The German Shepherd."

"Aye, I remember," Gillespie said. "He was barking, you say?"

She nodded and kept her voice low.

"I hate leaving here on a Friday night. I usually get my mum to pick me up, but she was out, so I had to walk home."

"Right," Gillespie said. "At midnight?"

"Thereabouts," she replied. "Anyway, I closed the door and

locked it, and just as I was putting the keys in my bag, I heard footsteps."

"You heard somebody? In the car park, you mean?"

"Not in the car park. The nature reserve. They ran off before I got the chance to see them."

"Ran off where?"

Gillespie took a long swig of his pint, noting that Cruz had barely touched his.

"Down the road," she said. "It was pitch black so I wasn't going to go after them. It was just weird, that's all. I didn't really think anything of it. In fact, I'd forgotten all about it until now."

"Until now?"

"Yeah," she said with a smile. "It's not often I get someone like you in the bar on a Monday night."

"Someone like me?"

"Yeah, you know? You're easy to talk to and you seem like fun."

"Ah, right," he said, and he swirled his near-empty glass, then jabbed his thumb over his shoulder at Cruz. "Go on then, Gabby."

"What do you mean, go on?"

"I mean, you might want to call a taxi. I'm going to stay a wee while."

"You said you'd drop me off."

"Aye, I know. But what with what the lass saw and all that, I thought I'd stay a while longer."

"You're unbelievable," Cruz said, leaving his drink and walking towards the wall where a bunch of calling cards for local businesses had been pinned.

"Aye, don't you forget it," Gillespie replied, offering the girl a wink. He downed his pint, stifled a belch, then slid the glass towards the girl. "I'll have the same again, love, and take one for yourself, eh?"

CHAPTER TWENTY-SEVEN

By the time Freya had completed the process to release Jeremiah Graham, most of the team had left. They made their way back to Ben's house and while Ben was shutting the front door and kicking off his shoes, Freya flopped sideways into an armchair so that her legs hung over one of the arms. Ben followed in time to see her kick off her shoes and let them fall to the floor.

"My bloody feet," she said. "You know it's times like this I envy Inspector Gadget."

"Inspector Gadget? Why, because he had a daughter and her dog to solve all his investigations, or because he could reach the fridge from the living room?"

"You've heard that one before," she said.

"From you, but only about five times," he said, loosening his collar.

"So?" she said.

"So what?"

"I don't suppose you could be my extending arm, could you?" she said.

"Let me have a think about that," he replied, and he left the room. But instead of heading into the kitchen, he climbed the stairs, threw off his shirt and trousers, and found the comfiest shorts he owned. He grabbed a loose t-shirt to go with them, pulled it on, and then raised it to spray some deodorant, questioning why he didn't do the deodorant first.

He descended the stairs in time to hear the sound of glass on glass coming from the kitchen.

"How are those extending arms?" he asked, stopping in the kitchen doorway to find Freya pouring a single glass of wine.

"Broken," she replied, and then she headed out to the garden, where Michaela had set up a bistro table and chairs. "They used to work once upon a time. But as with everything else, it looks like I'll have to find a replacement."

The analogy, as usual, had become quite weird, and Ben was unsure if the message he had understood was the actual message, or if she was just kidding about having extending arms. From his perspective, the matter was finished, and if she felt it wasn't, then she was sure to voice that opinion.

"We should talk to the others," he said. "I'd like to know how Nillson got on with Barker."

She took a sip of her wine, savoured it, and then exhaled, long and loud.

"Why don't you get an update from Gillespie and Cruz while I get changed, and we can call Nillson when I'm back."

"Don't you want to hear what they have to say?"

She stopped in the doorway with one foot in the house.

"No," she said. "No, I really don't. My day has been bad enough, I'd rather finish on a positive."

Ben dialled Gillespie's number then stepped inside to pour himself a wine.

"Ben?" Gillespie said, but there was something different about his voice. There was background noise; glasses chinking together and men's distant voices.

"Are you in the pub already?"

"Duty calls, Benjamin. Duty calls," the Scot replied, and Ben imagined the big man smiling to himself as he spoke.

"What's the latest, mate? Freya's looking for an update."

"It's six o'clock, Ben. What's a man got to do around here to get a little me-time?"

"When you work that one out, could you let me know?" Ben replied, to which Gillespie laughed.

"Ah, I'm just playing," he said, and it was then Ben knew that more than one pint had passed his lips already. In fact, if Ben knew him as he thought he did, he would be on his third or fourth. He was still coherent enough to hold a conversation and make the odd joke without being offensive, but the sober Jim Gillespie was gone for the day. "As it happens, a little birdie told me something."

"A little birdie?" Ben repeated. "Don't tell me you're hitting on a suspect?"

"Ah, come on, Ben," he replied, and the background noise shifted to a bird song and the breeze Ben felt on his skin washed across the microphone. "You know me better than that."

"You're outside," Ben said. "You've moved out of earshot of somebody."

"Warmer," Gillespie said.

"You went to have the Mercedes picked up. You're in the pub. You're in The White Horse."

"Warmer still."

"Not the barmaid," Ben said. "Are you hitting on the barmaid?"

"And he falls at the last hurdle. Sorry, Ben. No cigar. Better luck next time, eh?"

"So who then?"

"Ah, well if I'm honest, you were getting close, hot, in fact. Except for one tiny fact."

"Jim, it's been a long day, mate."

"She hit on me."

"You are kidding?"

"Nope. I tell you, I've bled my local pubs dry. I was only thinking the other day I need to look further afield, and what do you know, bullseye. First throw of the dart."

Ben took a sip of his wine and sank back into one of the teak chairs, lifting his feet onto the other.

"Mate, I didn't call you to get the lowdown on your sex life. I need an update."

"And I'm giving it to you, along with a wee bit of gloating, but it's coming. There's a point to all this."

"Go on."

"She did hear them argue but didn't listen to the topic. Loud pub, Friday night, she must have been busy."

"Fair enough."

"She also didn't see him leave, or which way he went."

"Oh, brilliant. She's turning out to be a right old Mystic Meg, isn't she? She's plied you with drinks and told you two things we already know."

"And one we didn't," Gillespie said teasingly. "She locked up that night. She locks up every Friday night, as the landlord is usually too wasted."

"Sounds like a fun place to work."

"He was upstairs," Gillespie said. "Anyway, when she locked up, she heard that dog of his barking."

"So?"

"So, it startled her a bit. Apparently it doesn't normally bark at night. She's a pretty girl on her own at night, and let's face it, Ben, it's as dark as it bloody well gets out here."

"Okay, so she's on edge."

"She hears something," he said. "Footsteps."

"It's a pub."

"It was gone midnight," Gillespie said. "They were in the nature reserve. Who the bloody hell was out here at that time of night?"

"What are you saying?"

"I'm saying that…" Gillespie started, then paused. "I don't know what I'm saying but it's odd, isn't it? Maybe she caught whoever had a wee ruck with Levy coming out of the nature reserve?"

"According to your new girlfriend, she heard them arguing around nine p.m. That's a three-hour window."

"Aye, well. I mean, it's just a theory."

"I thought you were going to rock my world with some kind of game-changing information, Jim," Ben said.

"There's only one world being rocked tonight, Benjamin, and it isn't yours, sunshine."

"Don't tell me you're actually going to wait for her to finish work?"

"Aye," he replied. "You've got to put the effort in. You can't expect a woman to fall at your feet, Ben. You have to treat them well. Show them some kindness."

"What time does she finish?"

"I don't know. Kicking out time, most likely."

"That's five hours, Jim. You're going to drink solid for the next five hours in the hope that A, you're still standing, and B, you haven't insulted her or been thrown out of the pub?"

"Aye, Ben. We're not all playing happy families here. Some of us are still looking for Mrs Right."

"And a barmaid you just met while working an investigation might be her, yeah?" Ben said, and the background noise shifted again as Gillespie re-entered the pub. "And as for happy families, Michaela and I are still getting to know each other. We're taking it slow."

"I wasn't talking about Michaela, Ben," Gillespie said. "Night night. Don't let the bed bugs bite."

"You've got that search in the morning," he said, but Gillespie had ended the call. Ben tossed his phone onto the table and took a large drink from the glass just as Freya emerged from the house wearing a little summer dress, shades, and flip flops.

"How did it go?" she asked.

"Ah, you know Gillespie. He's full of the joys of spring."

"He's drunk?"

"He's following up on something," Ben said, spinning the yarn into something a little more palatable. "He's managed to track down the witness who saw Levy and Graham arguing."

"The barmaid? Gillespie has tracked down the barmaid?" Freya said. "And I suppose he's going to be following up on her until she gives in and goes home with him?"

Ben searched for a reply that would shine a more favourable light on his old mate but couldn't find one.

"That's about the size of it," he said, and she scooted his feet from the chair to sit down.

"And what is this revelation he's following up on?"

"That's the funny thing," Ben said. "It might be nothing, but when she, the barmaid, locked up that night, she said she heard the dog barking."

"The German Shepherd?"

"Yeah, that. And then she saw somebody run from the nature reserve."

"So?"

"It was gone midnight, and they ran off when they heard her locking up."

"That's odd," Freya said, sipping her wine, thoughtfully.

"That's what I thought."

"So, Gillespie's revelation is that somebody of unknown sex, height, with no description of any kind, was in the nature reserve at midnight on Friday night."

"That's about the size of it," Ben said.

Freya took a large mouthful of her wine then set the glass down.

"Well, we'd better start recruiting for some new blood," she said. "Because if that's the level of input we have to work with, then we're pretty much done for."

CHAPTER TWENTY-EIGHT

They shared a moment of peace and quiet as each of them processed their own theories on their futures.

For Freya, the peace was joyous and needed after a long day of not only investigating a missing person but also going head-to-head with Standing who, without a shred of doubt, would be plotting some kind of action against her.

Ben was staring at a new flowerbed that Michaela must have planted out because Freya hadn't seen it before.

"We have a lot to do," she told him, hoping he'd pick up on the cue. "It could be a long night."

Just then, they heard the front door slam closed, followed shortly afterwards by Michaela stepping out into the evening sun; her blonde hair almost glowing in the warm light.

"Still at it?" she said, bending to kiss Ben. "All work and no play makes Ben a dull boy."

"No work and all play makes Ben unemployed," Freya countered, enjoying Ben's look of horror at the potential argument between her and Michaela. But she followed it up with a warm smile to soften the blow. "Grab a glass, Michaela. Join us out here in the sunshine."

"I'll just get changed," she replied, then caught Ben's attention. "Can I have a quick word?"

"We were actually just about to make a call," he said. "You're home late. Is everything okay?"

"I had to stay and wait for your colleague Jackie. She called and said she was dropping something off for a fast-track analysis."

"Hairbrush?" Freya asked.

"Toothbrush, actually. It's being processed overnight so I'll be able to analyse it against the blood in the morning."

"Is there anything else to report from Horncastle?" Freya asked, turning in her chair to look up at the bombshell who had clearly won Ben's heart.

Michaela made a show of re-joining them and dropped to perch on Ben's knee, taking a sip of his wine. The whole charade could easily have been a mark of territory designed to keep Freya at bay.

"There was a significant amount of blood on the bridge, including spatter which looked to me like the result of heavy blows to the victim's face, and pools which probably occurred post-attack. It's likely he or she was knocked unconscious, hence the pools from an open mouth."

"Brutal," Ben said.

"Quite," she agreed, then continued. "We pieced together what we think happened from the blood spatter, blood pools, drag marks, and footprints."

"Drag marks?"

She nodded.

"Yes, across the bridge. That bridge has been there for years. The dirt on the boards is quite consistent except for a track that runs the length of the bridge."

"Made by the victim dragging himself along or somebody dragging him."

"I think so," she said. "Which then correspond to the area of flattened nettles and grass leading down beneath the bridge."

"The killer dragged him out of sight?" Freya said.

"Yes, but not immediately," Michaela said. "It's a strange one, and one we'll need to put more time into it. But it looks as if the victim lay on the bridge for some time before he was moved."

"Which is where the pools of blood came from?'

"Yes, and we've identified where the victim was lying beneath the bridge but can find only tiny traces of blood and a partial foot print. Nike, size ten."

"Which suggests he or she had stopped bleeding when they were moved," Freya finished, more to convey her understanding than to belittle Michaela's theory.

"And then we have the largest puzzle of them all," Michaela said. "Where is the victim now?"

"Chapman has checked all the hospitals and medical centres," Ben said. "How much blood was lost?"

"Not enough to cause a death," Michaela said. "He or she could be out there right now, but with injuries that somebody couldn't fail to notice."

"Unless he's crawled off somewhere to die," Freya added.

"Unlikely," Michaela replied. "Ben did you want to speak to me?"

Freya looked up at him, waiting for him to answer, but he said nothing.

"You messaged me earlier, Ben," Michaela said. "You said you needed to speak to me."

"Oh, it can wait," he replied, dismissively. "We're just about to make a call."

Trying to stay out of their personal lives, Freya wasn't watching Michaela, but she could tell there were a few silent expressions and gestures being thrown around behind her back by the uncomfortable silences.

"Don't worry about it, then," she said with more than a threatening undertone, and then she disappeared into the house.

Distracted, Ben picked up his phone, browsed to his recent

calls, and hit the button to initiate a call. He directed the call to loudspeaker and set it down on the table, then sighed and got his head into the game as soon as the call was answered.

"Ben?" Nillson said, her masculine voice clearly recognisable. "Are you still working?"

He rolled his eyes and leaned forward closer to the phone.

"We're just looking for updates, Anna," he said heavily. "We'll be putting a plan together for the morning and wondered how you got on with Drew Barker. Did he have much else to say?"

"Not really," Nillson said. "He seems to have a mixed opinion on Levy. On one hand, he said he's a hard worker and would never miss an opportunity to make money. On the other hand, he seems to have a fairly low opinion of the man. Hard to say, really."

"What about his wages? Surely he's got a grudge to bear?" Freya asked.

"Yeah, I'm not sure if I'd be so understanding if the Chief Constable told me he couldn't afford to pay me for a few months, but I suppose it's a different industry."

"And the money Jeremiah Graham owes him?" Ben asked.

"According to Barker, the two have been doing business for years. A little debt here and there is to be expected."

"Twenty grand?" Ben said. "That's hardly a little debt."

"He seemed to think it was standard practice," Nillson said. "I did ask him about his stay at the Petwood. Apparently he was at a golf weekend, which are usually quite messy."

"Messy?" Freya said.

"Plenty of alcohol," Nillson said. "He stayed there so he can enjoy himself and not have to worry about getting home. Said it was one of his two pleasures in life."

"And the second one being?"

"His boy, Anthony."

"No wife to back his story up then?" Ben asked.

"He's a widow. Apparently his wife died years ago."

Freya sighed and finished her drink.

"We're getting nowhere here. We know Levy is missing. We found fresh blood in the nature reserve, not to mention the bloody hole that was dug. Why can't we move forward with this?"

"Boss, can I say something?" Nillson said.

"Of course," Freya said. "What's on your mind?"

"It's Barker. There's something about him I don't trust. Something's off."

"Oh, you mean like the feeling you had about Jeremiah Graham? Which, by the way, could easily have backfired on us. I had to let him go. His solicitor has probably won more cases than all of us put together."

"It wasn't what he said," Nillson explained. "It was something Anderson noticed. She was snooping while I spoke to him."

"Go on," Freya said.

"She found some stuff in his shed. Some rope, a spade, a shovel, an old tarpaulin."

"I probably have all that in my shed," Ben said.

"What, all together?" Nillson agued. "She said it was like all the stuff had been shoved into the shed at the same time, dumped on a potting bench, which means they were probably used together."

"Right," Freya said, processing the information and watching Ben do the same.

"The spade was covered in mud," Nillson said.

"That's hardly a revelation, Anna," Freya replied.

"It is when you consider that he was digging his vegetable patch with a fork while we spoke. The dirt was bone dry. It wouldn't stick, and as I understand it from Gillespie, the hole that somebody dug in the forest was in an old ditch, wasn't it?"

She was right, but it was so far-fetched that to make a decision based on those details alone was a blatant waste of resources, time, and had the potential to alert Barker to their suspicions.

"Let me think about it," Freya said. "I'm not jumping on this until I know more."

"There was something else in the pile of tools," Nillson said, her tone shifting to a grave grumble. "A saw."

"A saw?"

"If that's not a toolkit to bury a body, I don't know what is," Nillson said. "And to top it off, the back gate was unlocked."

"So?"

"It leads directly out onto the nature reserve," Nillson said, and Freya had the feeling the statement was designed to produce an impact. If so, then it had worked. "I want to move on him, search the house, and have Chapman do some more digging. He's up to something, I know he is."

"No," Freya replied. "Thank you, and well done. But no, not yet. You can do me a favour, though. Get me more on him. Go to the Petwood in the morning. See if his alibi checks out. Talk to housekeeping, too. Se if they found anything or if there was mud in his room. Use your initiative. You know what you're doing."

"But, boss, the longer we leave it, the longer he'll have to destroy evidence."

"Forgive me, Anna, but given the mood Standing is in and the recent debacle with Jeremiah Graham, it would be prudent of me to practice some kind of restraint," Freya said, then she heard her tone and regretted it. "I need you to trust me on this, Anna, okay? If it looks like Barker needs further investigation, then it'll be you who gets the job. In the meantime, go to the Petwood tomorrow and see what we get. Is that okay? I just need a little more."

"Will do, boss," Nillson said. "I'll pick up Anderson and go straight there. We'll see you at the station after."

"Good work, Anna," Freya said. "I'm not saying no. You know that, don't you?"

"I do, boss," she said. "You're saying you want more on Barker before we make a move, in which case I'll get it."

"Enjoy your evening, Anna," Freya said.

She ended the call, leaving Freya and Ben to mull over the news.

"I'm going to miss that girl if she goes as well," Freya said. "She'll go a long way."

"Well, let's hope it doesn't come to that," Ben replied, as Michaela emerged from the house, and it seemed that she had gone to great lengths to outshine Freya. She wore a summer dress that left little to the imagination, her legs had a sheen that suggested she had quickly shaved, and her wet hair was pulled over one shoulder, giving off a coconut aroma that followed her all the way to Ben's knee.

"Top up, anyone?" she said, producing a new bottle of Freya's wine.

Freya smiled at Ben's puppy dog eyes, then nudged her glass towards Michaela. The pouring of Freya's drink was interrupted by an incoming call. But it wasn't Ben's phone or Freya's; it was Michaela's.

She seemed surprised to be receiving a call, and Freya wondered what that must be like, to finish work with an element of certainty that your phone probably wouldn't ring until the morning.

"Hello?" she said into the phone, then her expression relaxed. "Oh, hi, Pat. How's it going over there?"

Freya finished pouring her own drink; it was her wine, after all. She sat back to interpret Michaela's body language and expressions while she spoke.

The leggy blonde stood from Ben's knee and strode down the garden onto the lawn, where she seemed to be having quite a serious conversation.

"This is nice," Freya said, raising a glass in silent toast to Ben. He laughed and did his best to appear relaxed, despite his tapping foot. "What do you make of Barker?"

"I think you made the right call," he replied. "We need more on him. I don't fancy doing another interview like Jeremiah Graham's."

"That was Pat," Michaela said when she finished her call. She came to stand before them, making no attempt to return to her perch on Ben's knee. "There's been a discovery."

"Well, that sounds rather ominous," Freya said cheerfully. "And what is it that the legendary Pat has discovered?"

"A body," she replied flatly. "In the boot of the Mercedes you lot had towed to the lab."

The next few moments were filled with images of death, and the dull thud of Freya's heart in her ears was felt rather than heard.

"Is it Michael Levy?" she asked eventually.

"We'll know in the morning, but it looks like it could be," Michaela said. "It's male, at least, wearing a denim jacket."

"Denim jacket?" Freya repeated, but then shook her head, allowing Michaela to continue.

"The body is being transferred to pathology tonight," Michaela finished.

"Should we get changed?" Ben said, to which Freya took a moment to respond.

"No," she said. "No, this changes things. This is murder. Not a missing person."

"So? What difference does that make?"

"It means that we're ahead of the curve, and it'll put Standing firmly back in whatever box it was that he came in," Freya said after a few moments of deliberation. She smiled broadly, unable to retain her composure, and then looked up at Ben. "And I for one can't wait to see his face when I tell him."

CHAPTER TWENTY-NINE

It was one of those mornings that promised neither sunshine nor rain, leaving the forecast as unpredictable as Gillespie's mood.

A dozen uniforms had gathered at the entrance to the nature reserve, sipping coffees from takeaway cups from the cafe on the High Street and catching up with colleagues they hadn't seen for a time.

Cruz glanced nervously at his watch, praying that Gillespie's beaten old car would trundle around the corner sooner rather than later.

The uniforms were growing anxious, and on more than one occasion, Cruz had caught a few of them looking his way, laughing amongst themselves.

Seven a.m. had come and gone, seven-fifteen, too. But when seven-thirty rolled around and the third uniformed officer voiced his impatience by stating that he'd need to pop home for another shave before he went back to the station, Cruz decided enough was enough.

"Right then," he said, just as he'd seen DI Bloom do a hundred times before. He clapped three times to get their attention.

But the hum of voices continued.

"Excuse me," he said. "Guys and girls."

A few of them had heard him and glanced his way, then peered up the road as if they were expecting somebody of importance to come along.

"How many of you want to go home at some point today?" he called out, raising his voice, and the hum of voices faded. "Right, then, if we want to get home, we'd better get moving, don't you think?"

A couple of men in the centre who appeared to be chummy exchanged confused looks, but stopped their conversation and began paying attention.

"We are looking for a man named Michael Levy," Cruz began, enjoying the attention, as scrutinising as it was. "Middle-aged, dark hair, lean, and he was least seen wearing a denim jacket on Friday night, leaving that pub right there."

He pointed at the pub just fifty yards away.

"We are going to be searching every inch of this nature reserve, on our hands and knees if we have to."

"How do we know he's there?" somebody asked.

"We don't," Cruz replied. "But we, well, I, actually, discovered traces of blood further along that footpath. The CSI team have since confirmed the blood is recent, which leads us to believe Michael Levy was A, here, and B, either attacked or involved in some kind of fracas." He pointed down the path again. "At the other end of this path is Mr Levy's house, and we believe he used the shortcut to get home and, for one reason or another, didn't quite make it."

"He's not still in the pub, is he?" one man asked, which raised a few laughs and caused that hum to begin again.

"Which means that we will split into two teams," Cruz said, hearing the nervousness in his own voice but pushing through it. "Those of you on my right will search the area from the far end of the path back, and the half of you on my left will start here. We will meet in the middle somewhere."

"What team are you on?" somebody asked.

"I'll be coordinating," Cruz said. "I want every find radioed in to me. When the entire path has been searched, we'll take the search wider, searching the fields and the forest as a whole. By that time, the dog teams will be here, so we'll have help."

"Sounds like we'll need it," somebody joked.

"I want everything that doesn't grow reported into me," Cruz said, cutting the stifled laughter off. "We're talking about a man's life here. Let's get switched on."

The team silenced again and seemed to have understood that Cruz meant business.

"Right, get to it," he said, marvelling at how a dozen men had actually followed his instructions. Sure, there had been a few comments, but on the whole, he was staggered. It was only when they had all set off, half of them towards the far end of the pathway, and the other half at the end nearest the path that he checked his hands and saw how badly they were trembling. He leaned back onto his car and glanced along the road, hoping that Gillespie wouldn't arrive and belittle him while the closest team was still in earshot.

But things had a way of not going right for Cruz, and the sound of an approaching engine grew louder. Even without looking, he knew it would be Gillespie.

He pulled into the pub car park and flashed a greeting to Cruz. Then a few minutes later, he emerged, staggering up the footpath like an old drunk doing the walk of shame.

"Where the bloody hell have you been?" Cruz hissed. "I've had to deal with this lot myself."

"I know, I was watching," Gillespie replied, muttering under his rank breath.

"You were what?"

"I was watching," he repeated, sorting his tie out in the reflection of Cruz's driver-side window. He gave up seconds later and stuffed it into his pocket. "I couldn't very well pull up with these lot standing there, could I? They'd be queueing up to nick me."

"Are you over the limit?"

"Shh," Gillespie said, gesturing for him to keep the noise down. "I don't bloody know, do I?"

"Jim, you're a copper."

"I know, which makes it worse, doesn't it?"

"For who? You, or the poor sod you knock down?"

"Listen, I'm probably alright, but you know what? I might be a wee tad over the limit. Now, to you and me, that wee tad is nothing. It's negligible. But to those lot, that's a nick, and a nick is a nick."

"It is not negligible, Jim. It's a bloody crime."

"Aye, well, what was I supposed to do? Not turn up at all?" Gillespie said, stifling a burp and scratching the growth on his face. "Is there any coffee floating about?"

"No, Jim. No coffee."

Gillespie searched his pockets. From one pocket he pulled out an old tissue, a crumpled-up five-pound note that looked like it was out of circulation before Cruz was out of school, and the lid from a beer bottle. And from the other pocket, he pulled out what had to be at least ten pounds' worth of pound coins.

"Must have got lucky on the old fruity," he muttered, looking fairly pleased with himself.

He tried to count a few coins out, then gave up and dumped the whole lot into Cruz's hand.

"Run down the cafe, would you, mate?"

"Run down the cafe?" Cruz said.

"Aye, coffee and a bacon roll. Get one for yourself, too."

"Jim, I am not your bloody gopher," Cruz said. "I was here on time, as was the search team."

"The team?"

"You, them lot. And I'll have you know, it was me who briefed them, me who gave them their instructions, and me they respect, not some drunk-driving, overweight hobo who looks like he slept in a ditch."

"They respect you, do they?"

"Yes, as it happens," Cruz said.

"And how did you win their respect, pray tell?"

"By being fair, polite yet authoritative, and by being concise in my instructions. I've got one team searching one end of the path and this team searching this end. They'll meet in the middle, by which time the canine units should be onsite."

"They respect you, do they?"

"Yes," Cruz said. "Yes, I think they do."

"And has anybody found anything yet?"

"Well, no, not as such. They've only really just got going–"

"Oy," Gillespie shouted, calling out to the team nearest them. "Oy, you lot?"

They stopped the search to see who was shouting at them.

"There's a tenner and a bacon roll in it for the best find," Gillespie called out. Then he lowered his voice. "There you go. That's how you win their respect, Gabby."

"By bribing them to do their jobs?"

"Aye, works for me every time," he replied. "Did you hear the news, anyway?"

"No, Jim, I've been here, leading. Remember?"

"Leading? Is that what you call it?"

"What news, Jim? And how have you received any news? You literally look like you've just climbed out of a ditch. In fact, had the team got going on time, no doubt they would have discovered you and mistaken you for Michael Levy. You look like something found in a pyramid, Jim, and if I'm honest, you smell like it, too."

"Ben called as I was leaving,' Gillespie said, ignoring his retort.

"Leaving where?"

"That lass's house."

"That lass? You mean, the barmaid? At least call her by her name, Jim. At least show the poor girl some bloody respect."

"Her name?" he said and shrugged. "I don't know it."

Cruz was speechless. There were a hundred things he could have said, but none of them would have made any difference to the man's sense of pride or dignity, nor would they have changed how he treated people.

"What?" Gillespie said. "It's not like she knows my name, is it?"

"You spent the entire evening together and didn't exchange names?"

"Yeah," Gillespie said, looking at Cruz as if he'd gone mad.

"What did you talk about?"

"Talk?" Gillespie said with a laugh. "We didn't talk, Gabby—"

"Okay, okay, what news?" he said, defeated and trying hard not to picture the big, sweaty oaf with the girl.

"Ben's girlfriend found a body in that old Mercedes, or somebody did anyway. Think it might have been that Pat person. I don't know."

Cruz knew the Pat he was referring to. It was Michaela's assistant who they had only ever seen wearing goggles and a head-to-toe, hooded, white suit, which meant that, despite several carefully constructed questions, they had never actually established if Pat was a he or a she.

"They found a body?"

"Aye. Must have been a right shocker," Gillespie said. "Opened up the boot lid, apparently, and there he was."

"So it's male then, is it?"

"The body?"

"Yes, Jim. The body."

"Oh, aye. It's a bloke," he said. "Been sent to the pathologist apparently, so we'll have a cause of death soon enough."

"Do they think it's Levy?"

"I don't know, Gabby. We'll have to wait and see, won't we?" Gillespie said. "But if it is him, we'll have our work cut out."

"What makes you say that?"

"Because this missing person case that Standing clearly gave us to trip the boss up will actually become a murder case, in which case, his nose will be well and truly put out of joint. And that, my friend, is not good for any of us."

A call came over the radio, which Cruz retrieved from his inside pocket, only for Gillespie to snatch it out of his hand before he could respond.

"Aye, go ahead," Gillespie said, breaking nearly every radio protocol the force had developed.

"We've got something," the voice said, and they turned to find one of the uniforms in the field two hundred yards away, waving his hand to mark the location. "Actually, we've got a few things, including some rope and a couple of beer bottles."

"Some rope and some beer bottles, eh?" Gillespie said. "Good work, you've earned yourself a bacon roll."

He handed the radio back to Cruz and shoved his hands into his pockets.

"Told you, Gabby, didn't I, eh?" he said, unable to restrain that smug grin that Cruz despised. "Now then, why don't you trot off and grab a couple of bacon butties? Red sauce on mine. None of that brown muck."

CHAPTER THIRTY

The previous day seemed like a blur, a foggy melee of memories in which Freya had been a mere spectator and the decisions around her not her own.

But it was a new day, and she had risen from Ben's spare bed having not slept a wink, as ready for it as ever. While Ben and Michaela had no doubt lain in the next room, whispering their arguments about her, she had stared at the ceiling as she so often did during complex investigations, processing the information, setting free her imagination as if releasing a wild dog from its chains, only to return with variation after variation of possibilities. Some of those variations had legs, others less so. Some of those variations had grown into real solutions, real answers that had caused her to reach for her notebook and flesh them out in more detail, only to hit wall after wall, time and again.

It was the only way she knew how. It was the only way she could come to understand where best to spend her limited resources.

And all avenues, all of those dreamlike possibilities, led to the morgue as if it was a gateway to a new world, a fresh blend of new possibilities.

"Just when I thought it couldn't get much worse," Ben said, as he rang the buzzer to alert the pathologist of their arrival. "We end up here, in the land of the dead."

"I have a rather different view," Freya replied, hearing the insulated doors inside heave open and then close with a hiss of fresh air. "I see this as a grounding. A confirmation, if you will. What we learn here this morning, Ben, will determine all our futures, not just those of Michael Levy's family. Think about that while you're considering throttling the good doctor."

The door opened before Ben had a chance to reply, and Lincolnshire's finest forensic pathologist greeted them with a sneer.

She was a buxom woman, who these days, at least, maintained a bob of brown hair, which was far better than the various colours she had dyed it in the past. And had it not been for the various piercings and tattoos, she might have looked like a regular member of society.

"Thought I might be seeing you, I did," she said in a thick Welsh accent. She checked her watch. "It's eight-thirty in the morning, and here you are, wondering why I haven't called to tell you how your man died, am I right?"

"I was actually wondering why you haven't invited us in," Freya said, smiling at the woman who, despite, or perhaps because of, her eccentricities, had become a friend. "We can deal with the cause of death, but leaving us to stand out here? That's just rude, Pip."

"Morning, Freya," Pip said, and she held the door open for them. The gap she left was ample for Freya, who gave her a friendly hug as she squeezed by. But for Ben, the gap proved to cause more than a little inappropriate touching.

"Alright, Ben, that's enough," Pip said. "A hug is fine, but rubbing yourself all over me—"

"I wasn't—"

"Bad enough I have to deal with dead bodies all day. The last thing I need is a horny detective trying to jump my bones before I've had my coffee."

"I didn't mean to touch you," he protested. "I was just–"

Pip winked at Freya, which Ben caught sight of, and he sucked in a deep breath, preparing for what was to be a challenging morning.

"You know where the PPE is by now," Pip said, closing the reception door. She pulled open the doors to the morgue and then blew Ben a kiss, before disappearing into the cold, leaving him with a final provocative and taunting statement. "I'll be waiting for you."

"Bloody hell," Ben said when she had closed the doors. "I'm just going to keep my mouth shut and let you do the talking."

"Yeah right," Freya replied. "She'll make you talk. She has a way about her, don't you think?"

"It's her ways that worry me," Ben said. "I prefer it when she's got her head inside a cavity. At least then she's preoccupied. It's like she's either winding me up and upset with you, or vice versa. I just wish we could come here one day and all get along without her being offended by something one of us says."

"I think it's in her nature, Ben. Some people are just offended by everything. The trick is not to play into their game. Let them be offended. I find that a far more effective means of getting by, than pandering to the needs of everyone I meet."

"Says the middle-aged divorcee with one friend," Ben muttered. "How's that working out for you?"

She finished tying her gown, slipped into the white wellington boots, and finally donned the hat and mask, ignoring his comment.

"Ready?" she asked and noticed that, despite them visiting Pip at least twice a month for the past year, Ben had still not managed to work out how to tie the strings on his gown.

"Oh, sod it," he said. "Can you?"

He turned his back and she felt him sigh.

"You're quite anxious, Ben," she said. "Is everything okay?"

"Okay?" he replied. "Oh, yes, it's just dandy, Freya. Three of my team are planning on leaving, our boss is a certified lunatic, a woman I slept with is staying at my house with my new girlfriend, and now, not only do we have an actual body to deal with, but the way through this all is blocked by a Welsh bloody nut job with a scalpel and sick sense of humour."

She pulled the strings tight and gave him a slap on the backside.

"I wouldn't worry too much about Michaela and me," she said. "In fact, I'm actually beginning to like her. I think we could be good friends when she gets to know me."

She opened the doors and waited for him to follow.

"Is that supposed to help my anxiety?" he said. "Come on, let's get this over with."

Doctor Pippa Bell was standing beside one of the half a dozen or so stainless steel benches, on which a large, flat, blue sheet had been laid over the corpse.

In a practised, sweeping movement, Pip pulled the sheet back to the victim's shoulders revealing a man with brown hair parted to one side. His skin was sallow rather than white; at least, those parts of his face that were not swollen and bruised were.

"I've cleaned him up best I can for the time being," Pip said, watching for their reactions. "Needless to say, his last few moments were not his finest."

"Are anybody's?" Ben said, and Freya saw him cringe at breaking his own stay quiet rule in under two minutes.

"Some more so than others," Pip said. "However, where there's bruising, there's life, as they say."

"Who says?" Freya asked.

"Well, nobody really. Just made that up, I did. But you get my point. Everything you see before you, the bruises, the scrapes, the scuffed skin, it all happened whilst he was alive. Even the few teeth he lost."

"Somebody really went to town on him," Ben said quietly.

"They did," Pip said. "But everything you see here is superficial."

She pulled the sheet down further, exposing the man's chest and stomach, which bore larger bruises than his face; foot-sized, grotesque bruising that Freya wouldn't wish on her worst enemy, or even Standing.

"Why do I get the feeling you're leading us towards something in particular?" Freya said, to which Pip stared at her with a solemn expression.

"Do you want to see his genitals?"

"Not really," they both replied almost in unison.

"Well, needless to say, whoever did this to him left no stone unturned as it were. Every inch of this man has been beaten black and blue. But," Pip said, holding an index finger in the air, "the beating is not the cause of death."

"It's not?" Freya said. "No internal bleeding, no haemorrhage?"

"Oh, there's very likely all of that," Pip said. "We'll open him up in a bit to have a look. But still, I'd like to draw your attention to his neck. In particular, these marks here."

She indicated the man's bruised neck with the end of her pen.

"It's hard to see, Pip. There's so much swelling."

"Well, I can see it if you can't," she said and then used the pen to bring their attention to some small pock marks on the man's face, like broken blood vessels. "This is called petechiae. This man died from asphyviation. Strangulation, to be more precise. If his eyes weren't so swollen, I think we'd see haemorrhaging. Out of all the bruising on this man's body, the only two marks I can find that are consistent with murder are these on his neck. Everything else is tertiary, almost as if it was done by somebody else."

"Somebody else?" Freya said.

"I'm not suggesting you have two killers, Freya. I'm merely indicating that the beating was not the cause of death. It's like his killer grew tired of beating him and went in for the kill."

"You're positive about that, are you?" Freya asked.

"Fairly," she said, pulling a marker from her breast pocket. She drew the standard Y-section on his chest with the arms of the letter reaching from behind his ears to the centre of his sternum, and from there a single line down his naval. "What I'm expecting to see is this man's hyoid fractured, and if that's the case, then you two are free to go."

"And if you're wrong?" Ben asked.

"Then you're not free to go," she replied. "And you, Benjamin, can help me take him apart bit by bit until we work out what killed him."

"One more thing," Freya said. "Before we begin the autopsy, is there any way of estimating a time of death?"

"All we can do is estimate, Freya," Pip replied. "It's the one area we haven't been able to improve on really. Not for a few decades anyway. You're aware of the stages of death the human body goes through, I suppose?"

"I'm aware there are more stages than rigor mortis, if that's what you're asking?"

"That's right. First, the body experiences pallor mortis due to the lack of blood circulation. That's when the skin begins to pale. The second stage is called algor mortis and refers to the body temperature no longer being controlled by the body functions but to its surroundings. This can take up to twenty hours or so."

"Is that why medical examiners take the temperature?" Ben asked, to which the doctor nodded.

"That's right. The challenge with our friend here," Pip said, nodding at the bloated corpse, "is that it's the height of summer and he was locked in the boot of a car. Basically, he was canned like soup in a thermos. Without recreating those conditions exactly, we can't use temperature to identify a time of death."

"How did I know the answer wouldn't be a simple yes or no?" Ben said.

"Then we have rigor mortis," Pip said, rolling the R across her tongue. "The one that everybody knows and nobody understands, during which time the muscles stiffen, beginning with the facial muscles, then moving through the body until it's rock hard. The process begins an hour or two after death and can take up to thirty-six hours to complete, again depending on the conditions. Now, what do you notice about our man here?"

"He's not stiff," Freya said. "He's been through the rigor mortis process."

"Ah, he's coming out of it," she corrected, placing a gloved hand on the man's face. "Here, touch it."

"No, it's fine," Freya said.

"Feel him."

"No, honestly."

"Alright, suit yourself. But I can tell you now he hasn't completed his journey," Pip said. "He's been stored in the boot of a car for, how long?"

"We don't know. He could have been put there anytime," Freya said.

"Well, that's where the last stage comes in. Livor mortis. The settling of the blood due to the earth's gravitational pull."

Carefully, she pulled the sheet further down, exposing him down to his knees.

"What do you see?"

"Without stating the obvious?" Freya said, finding it impossible not to look at the man's swollen and bruised groin.

"He was found in the boot of a car, yes?" Pip said.

"That's right."

"Curled up on his side, according to the images Pat sent through," Pip continued. "Now then, what don't you see?"

"There's no sign of...what was it again?"

"Livor mortis," Pip said. "And you're right, and that's because it's on his back."

Gently, she leaned across the body and pulled him towards

her, raising the man's back off the table enough for them to see the red and purple areas where blood had pooled.

"How long does livor mortis take to kick in?" Ben asked.

"A few hours, anything up to six, really."

"So he was lying on his back when he died, and he stayed that way for livor mortis to occur, but was moved either before rigor mortis set it, or when it had started to ease off, at least?"

"Ah, there you are, Ben. Thought you were going to sleep on me," Pip said, covering the man's lower half with the sheet. "And there you have it. This man has been dead for three to four days, but not much more, and he was moved either before rigor set in, which is up to eight hours after he died, or more recently when rigor mortis had started to ease off."

"And you're quite sure about the cause of death?" Ben asked, to which she answered by raising a scalpel in the air.

"I'd have money on it," she said, and with her free hand, she passed him a stainless steel tray to collect the organs as she removed them. "But let's find out for sure, shall we?

CHAPTER THIRTY-ONE

The Petwood Hotel was situated on several acres of gardens and forests that royalty would have approved of and probably had in the past. The building was half-timbered with a tiled roof and seemed to sprawl on and on with gable after gable peaking out over beds filled with lavender and roses.

"Remind me of this place when I eventually meet somebody," Anderson said, as they walked from the car to the reception.

"You've never been here?" Nillson asked, to which Anderson shook her head.

"I haven't really been anywhere," she replied. "Unless we've carried out an investigation there, I don't really feel like I've explored Lincolnshire. Except in the city. But I much prefer these types of places."

"Are you a country girl at heart, Jenny?"

"No, not really. London born and bred. I think that's why places like this appeal to me so much. It's so quiet, and so..."

"Don't worry about offending me," Nillson said, while Anderson thought of the most suitable word.

"Quaint," Anderson said eventually, stopping to admire the building once more before they stepped inside the reception, which, just like the exterior, oozed the charm and grandeur of a manor house.

A small reception desk was at one end of the reception, with seating for guests, and beyond that was a wooden staircase which captured Anderson's attention so much that Nillson had to remind her why they were there.

"How can I help?" a girl behind the reception desk asked as Nillson approached.

"We're actually wondering if we could speak to the manager," Nillson said, keeping her voice low. She flashed her warrant card briefly then slipped it back into her pocket so as not to cause a disturbance. "It's a matter of some importance regarding one of your customers."

The girl managed to listen to what Nillson said, view the warrant card, and make a decision, all while maintaining a pleasant and warm smile.

"I'll just be a moment," she said, then gestured at a pair of armchairs. "Please, take a seat."

She disappeared into a back room, leaving Nillson and Anderson some time to enjoy the interior.

"I don't know how people do it," Nillson said.

"Do what?"

"Smile like that," Nillson said. "She smiled from the moment she saw us to the moment she slipped out the back, and no doubt she's still smiling. It's like it's bloody painted on. I can barely raise a smile at the best of times, and even then I need an hour's notice."

"Well, don't, whatever you do, give up the force to go into hospitality," Anderson joked, as a woman in a smart trouser suit stepped out from behind the reception desk.

"Hello," she said, in a voice that was as warm as the decor, yet authoritative. "I understand you'd like to discuss something."

"Oh, hello," Nillson said, and she followed the woman's invitation to go through into one of the back rooms. Being a room designed purely for the staff, there was very little in the way of elaborate decor save for the mouldings, and pictures that must have run throughout the house.

"Please," the woman said, offering them seats at a small table.

They sat and Nillson tried to read the badge on her lapel.

"Thank you, Miss…"

"Mrs Tranton," she said, with another of those smiles Nillson had spoken of.

"Mrs Tranton, I'm afraid I can't go into too much detail, but I wonder if you can help. We're investigating a serious crime not far from here, and it seems an individual that we're looking into claims to have stayed here on Friday and Saturday night."

"I see," Mrs Tranton replied. "And you'd like us to confirm his reservation, is that correct?"

"It is," Nillson said, as Mrs Tranton slid a headed notepad and pen towards her, clicked open the pen, and then waited for the name.

"Drew Barker," Nillson said. "That's his full name."

"Not Andrew?"

"No, just Drew."

"And he claims to have stayed here last Friday and Saturday?"

"That's correct, yes."

"Well, okay, leave it with me. Can I have somebody bring you a coffee while you wait?"

"Coffee would be great, thank you," Nillson said.

Mrs Tranton pushed herself out of her seat and headed towards the door, stopping before she left.

"Perhaps you'd like to enjoy your coffee outside? Breakfast is still on too, if you're hungry, that is."

Nillson and Anderson followed her out, and she guided them in the right direction, where they found a table and sat amongst quietly speaking guests, each one as respectful as the other, and each one seeming to delight in the peaceful surroundings.

"It's a far cry from the hotel I stayed at last year," Anderson said. "No babies, no children, no drunks, and no loud music. I could get used to this."

"You could, but you'd have to move up a few pay grades," Nillson said. "This isn't Ibiza, and I very much doubt you'd find an all-inclusive deal."

"Shame," Anderson said, as a young but handsome man in a crisp, white shirt brought a tray of coffee to their table.

He asked if they required anything else, to which Nillson replied, "No, thank you. That will be all," before Anderson could remark on his boyish good looks and embarrass the lad.

Nillson had barely enjoyed a mouthful of coffee before the efficient Mrs Tranton came to join them.

"May I?" she asked, gesturing at one of the two spare chairs.

"Please do," Nillson said. "Coffee?"

"No," she replied, laying her notepad out. "Now, I did manage to find a booking for a Drew Barker. He checked in last Friday and then checked out again on Sunday morning."

"That's what he told us," Nillson said. "I don't suppose we can put some times to that, can we?"

"Well, I know for a fact he checked out at around ten a.m. on Sunday as it was me who took his key from him, and as for checking in, he didn't arrive until around eight o'clock on the Friday evening."

"How can you be certain it was him who checked out at ten a.m.?"

"Because I remember them," Mrs Tranton said.

"Them?" Anderson said. "He was with somebody?"

"Yes, sorry, I thought you knew."

"Male or female?"

"Female, but I'm sorry, we didn't get her name."

The guests at the tables around them were oblivious to the conversation being had at Nillson's table. Nobody stared or minded any business but their own, and she felt embarrassed when her vacant stare had landed on a lady as she considered who might have been with Barker. The woman frowned at her and said something to her husband, who then peered over his newspaper to see the offender.

"Was she there when he checked in?" Nillson asked, doing her best not to look in that direction again.

"I don't believe so," Tranton said. "The room was booked online for one guest. We obtain that information during the booking process so we can make sure enough towels are provided."

"Thank you," Nillson said.

"Will that be all?"

"I think so," Nillson replied.

"No, wait. One more question," Anderson said, as Mrs Tranton pushed her chair back to leave. "Does this place have CCTV?"

CHAPTER THIRTY-TWO

Gone were the days when Freya and Ben would arrive at the station and creep along the first-floor corridor listening to the team debate first-world problems, such as which was the best chocolate bar, the tomato sauce or brown sauce argument, or Ben's personal favourite, the beef, lamb, or pork roast dinner discussion.

These days, the first floor was silent like a library, and the librarian cracking the noisy whip was none other than DCI Stephen Standing.

It wasn't that anybody on the team feared the man. Ben certainly didn't. He got the impression it was more about the team losing the will to listen to his rants or be given a dressing down in front of their peers.

Ben couldn't remember who had said that Standing had the leadership skills of a carrot, but he agreed wholeheartedly. The man seemed to have forgotten that, once upon a time, he shared the incident room with them as a DI, and hadn't exactly led by example.

Even the incident room doors, which for years had screeched like an injured beast when they opened or closed, had been oiled at his request. The only good change the man had incited was the new coffee machine, but in retrospect, all Standing had done by installing it was remove the need for any of them to escape along the High Street to the bakery, which had often provided a much-needed breath of fresh air.

Whether through predatory means or by a natural flaw in his personality, Standing had gained control over the team and was driving them away.

And the misery he was causing was evident to Ben and Freya as they peered through the incident room windows and witnessed them all with their heads down, working quietly. It was only when Cruz wanted to get Gillespie's attention that he quickly checked the incident room doors to make sure it was safe to do so that he saw Ben and Freya and mouthed the words, "Thank God for that."

A few heads turned to see what he was looking at, and even through the closed doors, Ben sensed a relief wash through the room like a cold breeze through an open window.

They pushed through the quiet doors and waited for them to close behind them.

"It's very quiet in here," Freya said.

"Aye, it's like a bloody morgue," Gillespie said from his desk.

"Actually we've just been to an autopsy, and I can confirm that the atmosphere was far more enjoyable than this," Freya said, as she dumped her bag on her desk and perched on the edge. "Right, briefing in two minutes. If you need a coffee or the washroom, please do so now."

A few chairs scraped back, and Ben was about to join Gillespie on the way to the kitchen when his phone began to ring. He pulled it from his pocket and signalled to Freya he'd be back in two minutes.

"Ben Savage," he said, as he pushed through into the fire escape for some privacy.

"Is that Ben Savage the detective with the nice backside?" a woman said.

"Sorry?" he said, checking the number but not recognising it.

"Is that the handsome detective?" the woman asked. "I have a problem that needs investigating."

Ben checked behind him to make sure nobody was listening in and then lowered his voice.

"I'm sorry, I think you've got the wrong number," he said. "You should probably go through the operator–"

"Oh, Ben, it's me, you idiot."

"Sorry?"

"How many women call you up and tell you that you have a nice backside?"

He realised who it was and laughed out loud, slightly relieved and still fairly confused.

"Sorry, I didn't recognise the number. And as for women calling me up, well, you know? Only one or two," he said, then added, "per day."

"You wish," she replied. "How's it going?"

"Well, we've been to see the crazy pathologist and now we're about to have a briefing. With any luck, the others have done what Freya asked them to, and hopefully, the Beast from the East Midlands won't make an entry."

"So, if I told you I'm wearing a little white number and I'm enjoying the sunshine in a field in Horncastle?"

"Oh, sweetheart, I can't get out. We're just too busy–"

"I'm not asking you to join me," Michaela said. "I'm just telling you to make you jealous. The little white number is a disposable suit, for God's sake, Ben. What's the matter with you? You've lost your sense of humour."

"Sorry, it's just a bit tense here. You can feel it in the air."

"I'll be quick then," she said. "We ran the tests on the blood from the bridge."

"Go on," he said. "Give me some good news."

"It's not Michael Levy's."

"It's what?"

"It's not Michael Levy's, Ben," she said again. "We analysed it against the toothbrush. It's not his blood. I'm sorry."

"So who's blood is it?"

"Well, that's your job to find out, Ben. Whoever it belongs to isn't on the police database."

"Sorry, I was just thinking out loud," he said. "That doesn't make sense. We've just been to see him."

"You've been to see somebody. Has he been identified?"

"No, we'll be arranging that this morning," he said. "Are you saying we have somebody else out there potentially bleeding to death if they haven't done so already?"

"No, all I'm saying is that the blood on the bridge does not match the DNA sample provided. Sorry."

"I'd better get back inside and deliver the bad news," he said with a sigh, and he shoved himself off the handrail. "Thanks for letting me know."

"No problem," she replied. "It was nice to hear your voice."

"Likewise."

"I can't wait for Freya to move out. I know she's your friend, but—"

"I know, I know—"

"Why can't she just go back to your dad's cottage until she has some furniture of her own?"

"She gave it up, handed the keys back along with a nice bottle of Scotch for Dad, and he's already got somebody in."

"That was quick."

"Some of the labourers from Ukraine," Ben explained. "Dad wanted to help out, so he's given them a place to stay and jobs around the farm. It's not like the British people are clambering over themselves to pick vegetables, and they're bloody hard workers those Ukrainians."

"I can see where you get it from," Michaela replied.

"Get what?"

"Nothing," she said, and there was a smile in her voice. "I'll see you later."

There was a brief hesitation, and he thought she was going to say something but didn't, or couldn't.

"Are you okay?" he asked.

"Yes," she said, a little disappointed. "It's just that-."

"You don't trust her," he said.

She paused.

"No. No I don't." she replied. "But I trust you. In fact, I've seen a difference in you recently."

"You mean, you no longer think we're jumping into bed behind your back."

"Well, I wouldn't go that far," Michaela said. "But there's a distance between you. Like you're keeping her at arm's length, in a polite way, of course."

He sighed and leaned on the handrail, peering down to make sure he was alone in the stairwell.

"You might be right," he said, finally.

"Ben? Ben is there something you want to tell me?" she asked.

He sucked in a breath. Even if he could put it into words, now wasn't the time, and the stairwell wasn't the place.

"Do you remember that bloke we arrested in Saltfleet?" he asked, quietly.

"You mean the nutter in the church? How could I forget?"

"He said something," Ben said. "He said something about Freya's uncle. It was like he could read her. Like he knew her."

"What are you saying, Ben?" she asked. "Sorry, you're not making sense."

He laughed and straightened.

"I don't know," he replied. "Ignore me. I'm just tired. It's probably nothing."

"Probably," she said. "Listen, I'd better go. Don't work too hard, alright. I'll see you later."

The call ended, and Ben stared at the phone for a second before slipping it back into his pocket and turning to go back to the incident room, and he walked straight into Standing.

"Alright, Ben?" Standing said, peering down the length of his nose at him.

"Guv," Ben replied.

"What are you doing out here?"

"I just had a call with CSI."

"With CSI?" Standing said, and his expression told Ben everything. He didn't believe a word of it.

"With Michaela Fell," he said.

"Ah, the leggy blonde."

Ben stared at him, fighting the urge to say something he'd regret.

"I'm pretty sure that she'd have something to say about being described like that," he said.

"Would she prefer female IC-one, height five foot ten?" Standing replied. "With eyes that could melt concrete."

"I think she'd prefer us not to be discussing her at all, guv."

Standing laughed and seemed to take a moment to read Ben's expression, before leaning in close to whisper in his ear.

"Don't get too close to her, Ben," he said. "Keep it professional."

"I'll bear that in mind," Ben said, and he snatched open the door to the corridor and marched back to the incident room. Once seated, he took a deep breath before realising the rest of the team was watching him. Clearly, they had been waiting.

"Is everyone ready?" Freya said to the room, although Ben felt she was addressing him directly, so he sighed and gave a nod. "Good. The good news is that we're no longer working on a missing person case. The bad news is that we now have a body. First things first, I want a positive ID. Jackie, how do you feel about–"

"Actually, I have some news on that," Ben said, getting his head back into the game. "I've just spoken with Michaela."

"Oh, aye?" Gillespie said, and he sounded as if he was about to make some kind of lewd comment.

"I'm not in the mood, Jim," Ben said, cutting him off. He stared at the big Scotsman for a few moments, regretting his tone. "Sorry, mate. I've just had a run-in with Standing."

"You're alright, mate," Gillespie said, revealing the empathetic side of his personality that they all knew he had but rarely saw. "I was just playing."

"I know," Ben said and then turned his attention back to Freya. "It's not Levy. The body. It's not him."

"It's not him?" Freya said, sounding almost disappointed.

"The DNA from the blood on the bridge is different to that found on the toothbrush Jackie submitted," he said, shaking his head. "It's not a match."

"What about the body? Does that match?"

"They're still checking, but given the injuries and the amount of fresh blood on the bridge it's likely that whoever was injured on the bridge is lying on Pip's slab."

"What about the jacket?" Freya said. "The body was found with a denim jacket."

"And how many denim jackets are there in the world?" Ben said. "It doesn't matter what way you spin it, the blood on the bridge does not match the DNA found on the toothbrush."

"Which raises an even bigger problem," Freya said, thinking on her feet. "Right, new plan. If Michael Levy isn't dead, then perhaps he's responsible for whoever is in the morgue. Chapman, get back on the phone to the hospitals. I want to know the details of anyone who might have been treated or admitted with injuries caused by fighting. Broken hands, knuckles, fingers, jaws, anything. If Levy and our mystery man fought, he might be injured."

"Got it, ma'am," she said.

"Jackie, I want you back with the girlfriend. Give her the good news. She might open up a little more. You never know, she might even agree to ID the body for us. If it's one of Levy's acquaintances, then she'll likely know him."

"Hold on, boss," Nillson said, raising her hand casually.

"What is it, Anna?"

"We paid a visit to the Petwood Hotel," she said. "It looks like Drew Barker was there from Friday night to Sunday morning. The room was booked for a single occupant."

"Right, good. Are you saying we can eliminate him?"

"No, boss," she said, and Freya cocked her head. "We checked the CCTV while we were there. It looks like he left in the evening and came back with somebody an hour later. A woman."

"A woman?" Freya replied. "And does this woman have a name?"

"Levy's girlfriend," she said, with a look that said she knew the news was going to change the course of the investigation. "It was Alexandra Sinclair."

CHAPTER THIRTY-THREE

The room seemed to hold its breath while its occupants processed the information, internalising their responses until prompted. Except for Gillespie, who voiced his disgust with little regard for others.

"The dirty, cheating lowlife—"

"Oh, shut up, Jim," Gold said, and Freya watched as the usually quiet and reserved DC put her fellow Scotsman back in his box. "Do you know what Levy does to her? Have you seen her black eye?"

"Aye, well..." he grumbled

"Don't *aye well* me," she said. "He's bloody well deserves it if you ask me. The woman is scared out of her wits."

"Thank you, Gold," Freya said, calmly but with enough assertiveness to dam the stream of emotions that was sure to follow before it burst its banks. "But I am afraid that, regardless of what Levy does or has done to her, she is key to this investigation. If she agrees to ID the body, stay with her. Take her for lunch, take her to get her groceries, anything. Do whatever it takes, okay? Just don't let her out of your sight."

"Aren't we nicking her, boss?" Nillson said.

"Not right now, no," Freya said, and she tapped the whiteboard with the end of the pen. "If she and Drew Barker are having an affair behind Levy's back, then bringing them both in at the same time won't work in our favour."

"So we are bringing Barker in, then?"

"I don't see that we have any choice. He's mixed up in whatever this is," Freya said. "You mentioned the tools in the shed, the fact that his property backs onto the nature reserve, and we now have reason to believe he's in a relationship with Levy's girlfriend. And above all, it was him who reported Michael Levy missing."

"There's one problem," Ben said, leaning back in his chair. "All that would work if the body was Michael Levy's. But it's not. So what does it matter if Alexandra is sleeping with Drew Barker? We're not investigating Michael Levy's murder. Not yet, anyway."

"He's involved, and we have nothing else to go on. If anything, a little formal questioning might open a few doors for us."

"So we're nicking him then, are we?"

"We're not. Anna and Jenny are," Freya said, turning to the pair of strong women who were listening intently. "Bring him in and get photos of the shed. In fact, no. You said there was a spade covered in mud, didn't you?"

"Yes, boss," Anderson replied. "I'm sure of it."

"Bag it," she said. "That and everything else in the shed. Let's see if our brainy friends in CSI can match the soil like you said."

"But we don't have a soil sample," Gillespie said.

"Not yet we don't," Freya said. "But we will have by the time you two get back."

"Get back from where?" Cruz said, and Freya smiled at his naivety.

"From getting a soil sample," she told him.

"Ah, you're kidding? You're sending us back there?"

"The quicker you go, the quicker you'll be back," Freya said in a cheerful sing-song voice.

"Get back from where?" a familiar voice said from the doorway, and Freya's heart sank, taking with it the cheerful tone she had adopted.

"From the crime scene, guv," she replied heavily.

"Haven't they been there already today?"

"They have, yes."

"So why are you sending them back?" he asked.

"In light of new evidence."

"And the new evidence is?" he said, raising his eyebrows expectantly. "In fact, forget that. Why don't you give me a rundown of where we are with the investigation?"

"A rundown?" Freya said, as he pulled a chair from beneath a spare desk and made himself comfortable.

"A debrief, as it were," he said, seeming to enjoy adding pressure to Freya's day. "From the start."

"Sorry, guv, just to be clear, are you saying you want me to go through every single detail with you from the beginning of the investigation? That might take a while."

"I want to know your thought process behind every decision," he replied, checking his watch. "It's okay, I have an hour or so before I'm meeting an old friend for a drink."

"From the top?" Freya said.

"Like I told you, Freya. Horncastle is my stomping ground. I'd like to know we're doing all we can."

A dozen pitiful eyes stared at Freya. Every officer in the room knew he was being difficult for the sake of being difficult, yet none of them were empowered to challenge him. It was almost a test of Freya's resilience and leadership to handle him respectfully and dutifully.

"Right," she said. "While I debrief DCI Standing, Nillson and Anderson, start putting a plan together for Barker–"

"I'm sure they'll benefit from the debrief, too," Standing said, gesturing for them to remain seated with a wave of his hand.

"Right," Freya said, again, feeling her blood begin to boil. She stared at him, refusing to let her eyes wander. "Yesterday morning, a man named Drew Barker came to the station to report his friend and colleague missing. Despite my efforts to convince you this was a case for CID, you, guv, insisted that my team and I work on finding him. So, we did, and by doing so, we've discovered the body of another male in the boot of the car that belongs to the man who was reported missing in the first place. That's it. Full stop."

She tossed her whiteboard marker onto her desk, where it rolled and fell to the floor.

He said nothing, striving to maintain a calm disposition, clearly hoping to knock Freya off-balance. The only sign she had riled him was the way he stretched his neck from side to side and the involuntary flaring of his nostrils.

"So, you've found a body, have you?" he said eventually, to which Freya let her expression answer. "And it's not Michael Levy. You can prove that, can you?"

"I can't," she replied. "CSI can."

"Time of death?"

"Doctor Bell estimates sometime between last Friday and Saturday morning. The fact that the body was stored in the boot of a car in this heat makes pinning a time down even more challenging than it normally is."

"So, what course of action are you suggesting?" he asked.

"DS Nillson and DC Anderson have looked into Drew Barker's movements. It appears he spent the weekend at a golfing event in Woodhall Spa, staying in the Petwood Hotel on the Friday and Saturday nights. The room was booked for a single occupant, however, after scrutinising the CCTV, we can confirm that he had a guest; none other than Michael Levy's girlfriend, Alexandra Sinclair."

"Nillson?" Standing said. "Care to add to that?"

"Sure," she said casually. "He checked in at eight p.m., went to his room, where he received a call from Alexandra Sinclair. He finished his drink, then left the hotel for a while, returning at around midnight with Alexandra Sinclair. They went straight to his room."

"Did she have a bag?" Ben asked thoughtfully, causing Nillson and Anderson to exchange glances.

"Yes, she did," Nillson said.

"That seems like a strange question to ask," Standing said.

"Not really, guv," he replied. "Jackie has identified that Alexandra is a victim of domestic abuse. It's possible she finally had enough and did something about it."

"You're suggesting that this Sinclair girl–"

"Woman, guv," Freya corrected him.

"Right. You're suggesting she attacked Levy," Standing said. "But I thought you said the body wasn't Levy?"

"I'm suggesting she might not have attacked him herself, but had somebody else do it. A close friend, maybe?"

"But Levy got the better of him, too?" Standing said, musing on the theory. "It's a bit of a stretch, isn't it? I mean, she would have to reach out to somebody who was both capable of doing that to a man and trustworthy enough not to report the request. It's unlikely."

"I think it's worth checking her background, though," Freya said. "See if she has any known accomplices."

"No, leave it," Standing said. "I don't want to waste time looking into an affair, and as for the domestic abuse case, let's not open another can of worms here. This has already escalated beyond belief."

"But, guv–" Freya started.

"What else do we have?" he said, ignoring her. "I thought somebody else was in the frame. The Graham chap."

"There's nothing there," Freya said. "It's a business dispute. Graham owes Levy money and handed over his car as collateral until he can pay him in full."

"Seems odd," Standing said.

"Seems pretty straightforward to me," Freya replied. "Besides, he has a top lawyer. If we go after Graham without concrete evidence, we'll get ripped apart. Not great PR, if you ask me."

"I'm not asking you," Standing replied. "Look into him. Do some more digging."

"Guv, Barker and Sinclair have a full MMO, and they haven't been honest about Alexandra staying at the hotel. We'd be crazy not to follow it up."

"I want Graham investigated. I presume he was the ponce in the three-piece suit I saw downstairs yesterday?"

"If you're referring to the man whose outfit probably cost more than my monthly salary, then yes," Freya said.

"Well, I suggest you look into him a bit more. If I understand rightly, DI Burns was looking for him in another case," Standing said, rising to his feet and buttoning his cheap suit jacket across his swollen paunch. "The way I see it, Graham is involved in cases being investigated by two of my teams, and to use your own words against you, Bloom, coincidences only happen in films."

"What about Sinclair and Barker?"

"Alexandra Sinclair and her daughter are currently dealing with Levy's disappearance. Can you imagine how trying that must be for them?" he said as he made his way to the doors. He turned to face her, his expression unmoving as he jabbed his index finger at her, offering his final statement. "Leave them alone and focus on Graham. Come and see me when you've made progress."

"What about the body, guv?" Freya asked. "Should we just leave that, too?"

"Don't test me, Bloom," he replied. "Get an ID. We'll go from there."

CHAPTER THIRTY-FOUR

Standing left the room and the team watched as the double doors closed silently. A moment later, the door to Standing's office slammed closed further down the corridor.

Freya exhaled through pursed lips. The words to describe what she was thinking had failed her miserably.

Thankfully, seldom were those moments of silent contemplation ever prolonged when Gillespie was in attendance.

"Well, that was unequivocal, eh?" he said. "There's nothing like a clear set of objectives to make our lives just that little bit harder."

"Alright, Gillespie," Freya said, thinking on her feet. "We're all thinking it, but try not to be the one who voices it."

"What do we do?" Nillson asked. "Graham has an alibi I could check out. He mentioned some bloke in The King's Head he went to see after talking to Levy."

"Did you get his name?" Freya asked.

"It's in my notes," Nillson said.

"Good. Go and check it out. Let's prove Graham was elsewhere," Freya replied. "Chapman, do some background work on Alexandra Sinclair, for me, will you? A deep dive, if you will?"

"I thought Standing just said–"

"I know what he said. I'm not asking anybody to make a move on her, I just want our ducks in a row here."

"No problem," Chapman replied, setting to work immediately.

"Gold, same rules apply. Stay close to Alexandra for me," Freya said, holding her hand up to quell any protests. "He told us to ID the body, he didn't say we couldn't ask Alexandra to help us there. If the victim is an associate of Levy's, then perhaps she'll recognise him, and if Ben's theory is right and it was her who asked somebody to go after Levy, then she'll react to the request. Watch her facial expressions, watch her eyes, and watch what you say. Either she arranged for somebody to take care of Levy and it went wrong, or that body in the morgue belongs to somebody she'll recognise. When we work that out, we'll stand a greater chance of moving forward."

"Got it," Jackie said, and Freya noted the nod of encouragement Nillson sent her way.

"Anything else?" Freya asked, turning her attention to Gillespie and Cruz. "Or did we send a dozen uniforms and canine teams into the nature reserve for the hell of it?"

"Actually, boss," Gillespie said. "I thought you'd never ask."

"You found something, did you?"

"Oh, aye," he replied, checking his fingernails. "I think you'll find the search was a resounding success."

"Define resounding success," Freya said. "And please don't make me work for some answers."

"Oh, you know?" he replied. "Only a length of rope and a couple of beer bottles found in the ditch beside the footpath."

"A length of rope?" Anderson said. "Was it blue?"

"Aye, it was. Did you see it?"

"No, but the rope in Barker's shed was blue."

"It's a common colour for domestic rope," Ben said. "But it might be worth checking."

"The trouble is, we can't go after Barker until we've proved

Graham isn't involved," Freya said. "I don't mind pushing Standing's boundaries a little, but outright ignoring his instructions would be career suicide at this point."

She was right and Ben knew it.

"What did you do with the finds?" he asked Gillespie.

"Sent them to the lab, of course. What do you think? I left them in the boot of my car?"

"And they were in the ditch, were they?"

"Aye, just laying there in the dirt, they were. Tossed away for anybody to find."

"And who found them?"

"One of the uniformed officers. Jacobs, I think."

"It was Jacobs," Cruz said. "You know it was Jacobs because you bribed them all with a bacon sandwich, didn't you?"

Gillespie glared at him.

"You did what?" Freya said.

"Aye, well, I just gave them a wee bit of motivation, is all. Nothing like some healthy competition to up the performance, if you know what I mean eh, boss? How's that for thinking on your feet?"

"Thinking on your feet is one thing, Gillespie. Offering a bacon roll as a reward for doing their jobs is another."

"Eh?"

"It's not the motivational tactics that worry me, Gillespie," Freya said. "It's the reward itself. Were any of the search team Muslim or Jewish, do you know?"

He shook his head and shrugged.

"I don't know. Khan? Is he Muslim?"

"Khan is a Muslim," Gold said. "He goes to the mosque on Dixon Street. I saw him in Lidl once after prayers."

"Thank you, Gold," Freya said, turning her attention back onto Gillespie. "And how motivated do you think Khan would have been at the prospect of receiving a bloody bacon sandwich?"

"I don't know," Gillespie said quietly. "He could have given it to somebody else?"

"Do you think he might have felt a little excluded?" Freya said, talking to him like he was a five-year-old.

"Aye, maybe a little."

"You'd better hope he doesn't raise this in a report. Have you seen the news lately? Have you seen how many stations are being investigated for racism, sexism, and whatever else they can think of? We're the lucky ones. We all get along. We're a strong team. Those lot out there," she said, pointing out of the window, "those officers in the city work with new people every day, they don't have what we have. And it's what they don't have that I'm trying to protect. This."

She waved her arm around the room.

"Us," she said. "Our unit."

"Aye, boss. I get it," he said. "I should have thought more."

"That's okay," she told him. "And I'm sorry to call you out on this publicly, but things like that will only give Standing fuel, and it's not like he needs an excuse to drive us apart, is it?"

"No, boss," he said. "I'll find Khan and apologise. I'll tell him how insensitive I was and meant no harm."

"What about the rope?" she asked.

"Eh? What about it?"

"You said it was in the ditch for anybody to find."

"Aye."

"And Jacobs found it, did he?"

"Aye, boss."

"Yet you walked past it the previous day. I sent you and Cruz through there. How on earth did you miss a length of blue rope and, what was it? Beer bottles?"

Gillespie looked at Cruz.

"Aye, well. There was a wee bit of confusion over which one of us was searching the field and which on of us was searching the ditch."

"Hold on," Cruz said. "Don't bring me into this. I was searching the field. You even sent me back to start again. If anyone is to blame here, it's you."

"I'm not blaming anybody for anything," Freya said calmly, as Chapman's phone began to ring. "I'm just highlighting the mistakes before somebody else does. Somebody higher ranking than any of us and with a grudge against me, for example."

"Got it," Gillespie said.

"Ma'am, that was DCI Standing on the phone," Chapman said.

"I'm trying to save this team, Gillespie," Freya said. "Help me out, will you?"

"Aye, boss. I'm sorry, eh?"

"Thank you," she said softly, then addressed Chapman. "Did he say what he wanted?"

"He wants to see you in his office," Chapman replied. "Urgently."

She looked across at Ben, who then assessed the inquisitive stares from around the room.

"What do you want us to do?" he asked, to which she gave a few moments' thought before grabbing her bag from her desk.

"I want you all to carry on," she said. "Do exactly as I have asked until somebody tells you otherwise."

She marched from the room without looking at any of them, then pushed into Standing's office without knocking.

There was a moment when she thought that might have antagonised him, but to her surprise, he kept his cool, laid his pen down, and leaned back with his hands linked behind his head.

"We've got a problem," he said.

"Just one?"

"We, as in you and I, Freya. We have a problem that we need to work together on."

"If we need to work together, then I agree," she told him. "That is a problem."

"Are you aware that DS Savage is in some kind of relationship with Michaela Fell?" he asked, watching her the way he and every other detective she had met had been trained to spot mistruths.

"I am aware, yes," she told him. "But I wasn't aware of any rule that prohibits it."

"There isn't," he said. "However, there is such a thing as a conflict of interest, and while I assume you're going to contest that the pair are mature enough to keep their work and social lives separate, I should warn you that such a conflict of interest might cause complications later down the line."

"I don't see how, guv," she told him. "He's a detective, she's a crime scene investigator. He tells her where the murder took place, she tells him if a forensic analysis can support a charge and if not, why it can't."

"You see no problem with such a relationship?"

"None at all," she replied.

"And you're happy to take this on yourself, are you? You're happy that, should an incident occur as a result of their relationship, a portion of the blame should be directed at you?"

She laughed, refrained from smiling, and then leaned forward, placing her hands on his paperwork so her face was just inches from his.

"I see what you're doing," she said. "And it won't work. So, yes. Yes, I am happy. In fact, not just a portion of the blame, give it all to me. I'll take full responsibility for whatever might occur as a result of their relationship. Does that please you? You can go down on record flagging the relationship as a potential risk to the team, and if anything happens, you've got me."

"That's good," he said and leaned forward in his seat. "Because I've just had a call with a man named Harold Quinn."

"Who's Harold Quinn?"

"Oh, sorry, I meant Doctor Harold Quinn," he said, and he grinned. "Michaela's boss."

"Michaela's boss? Why were you talking to him?"

"Because it seems there's been some kind of misjudgement, most likely caused by the relationship between Ben and Michaela."

"Misjudgement?" she said, sensing he was holding something back.

"It turns out she's made a bit of a boo-boo," Standing said, Cleary enjoying the moment. "That body in the boot, remember it?"

"Of course, I do."

"They analysed the blood against what they found on the bridge and the denim jacket the victim was wearing. Three out of three. It's a match," he said. "However, there was some kind of mix-up with a toothbrush. I don't know. But the long and short of it is—"

"I get it," she said, unable to bear his smug tone for a moment longer. She held her hands up. "You've got me where you want me."

"Not yet, I haven't," he replied. "But I'm getting there."

CHAPTER THIRTY-FIVE

They rode in a silence Ben had become familiar with. Freya's brooding was synonymous with turmoil, and thanks to Standing, there was plenty of that to be had.

The only indication of her plan was the turns she took as she drove. Horncastle was out of the question, as was Woodhall Spa, as they were heading west. It was only when Freya turned towards Dunston that he realised what she was doing.

The reason why, however, still eluded him.

She parked beside the little village green, where an old telephone box had been repurposed as a book exchange, and a line of eight ducklings waddled happily across the grass behind mother duck, clueless as to their destination, just as Ben had been.

"Pretty, isn't it?" Freya said contemplatively as she switched off the engine. She sat back to admire the cottage she had bought, and Ben had to hand it to her, it certainly was a gorgeous, little property. The front garden was the very epitome of cottage gardens with lupins, delphiniums, and foxgloves reaching high out of the neat borders, and airy gypsophila with its tiny, white flowers filled the spaces between.

"You've done well," he told her.

"Thank you," she said, making no move to go inside.

"Shall we go in?"

"No. No, I just wanted to see it again."

"It's yours, Freya. You can go inside."

"I'm sorry I've put you in a rather difficult position with Michaela," she said, changing the topic but edging closer to the conversation Ben felt she wanted to have.

"She'll get over it. It's not for long, is it?"

"I'll make arrangements. I fear I was rather hasty in giving up your father's cottage."

"Ah, these things happen."

"The truth is, Ben, I was struggling," she said, still staring at the old cottage. "Seeing you with her–"

"Freya–"

"It's hard, you know? And I know I deserve it, but I still feel like I did the right thing. I still feel that we're better as friends than…" she said, then sighed. "We need to keep it professional."

"And I've told you, I agree," he said.

"Good, because I have some news, and it might be hard to hear."

She tore her eyes from the house and stared at him briefly, just long enough to convey that there was more bad news to follow.

"Go on," he said. "I get the feeling your meeting with Standing was more than just him asserting his authority."

"It was," she said. "He knows about you and Michaela."

"So?" Ben replied. "What on earth has my relationship got to do with–"

"He's in cahoots with Michaela's boss."

"Harold?" Ben said. "Harold Quinn? Why is Standing talking to him? He barely even goes into the lab."

"Standing is claiming a conflict of interest exists as a result of you and Michaela."

"A conflict of interest? We don't even work for the same department. She's not even police–"

"She made a mistake," Freya said. "Or at least, somebody has. The DNA from the blood on the bridge matches both the body in the morgue and blood found on the denim jacket the victim was wearing, which if you read Gold's report–"

"A denim jacket was what Levy was wearing," Ben finished.

"The toothbrush that Gold got from Alexandra Sinclair's house, is not Michael Levy's, but Michaela used it as a benchmark for his ID. School girl error, Ben."

"So, there is no second body? Well, that's good news, isn't it? That means Sinclair and Barker's MMO still stands. We can go after them."

"We can't," she said flatly. "Not yet, anyway. Standing is ready to make a big deal of this mistake. We both know that the mistake was pretty bad but had no real implications, but still, he's using it to his advantage."

"What's he going to do, discipline me for having a relationship with Michaela? It's none of his bloody business–"

"Not you, me," she said, flicking her eyes his way for a fleeting moment. "I took full responsibility for you. I said I was aware of the relationship and that I saw no negative consequences."

"Was that before or after you learned of the mix-up?"

"Before," she said, and he sat back in his seat, letting his head fall onto the head rest. The ducklings and their mother had waddled to the little beck that ran through the village, each of them taking turns to plop down into the water, much to the delight of a passing toddler and her father. The scene was calm, as was the village around them.

But the mood inside the car was tempestuous.

"So, what now?" he asked, at which Freya drew in a deep breath.

"So now, I have no lifelines," she said. "Now, we follow Standing's instructions, we don't push back, we don't answer him back–"

"You don't, you mean."

"The royal we, Ben," she said. "We play by the book. He wants us to investigate Jeremiah Graham, so that's what we'll do."

"What about Michaela?"

"He can't stop you from seeing Michaela, Ben. But he can make life difficult for you. Whether or not you opt for an easy life is entirely up to you," she told him. "I'll support you, either way. You know that, don't you?"

He nodded.

"Thanks," he said. "Is Harold Quinn going to be having words with Michaela?"

"I'd assume so. It's not like her to make a mistake or jump to a conclusion. But the fact is that had the mix-up *not* been identified and ended up being used in court as evidence, the entire case would have fallen to pieces. We all know the likelihood of that happening was slim to none, but it does arm Standing with everything he needs to close his grip around us."

"It couldn't have happened at a worse time," Ben said. "It's not even Michaela's fault. She was given the bloody toothbrush by Jackie."

"We can't pin any blame on Gold, Ben. It was up to Michaela to obtain or request some kind of secondary DNA source. I don't doubt that she would have made the discovery sooner rather than later, and I'm sure all she was trying to do was help us out because she knew how much it meant to us."

"She's not going to be happy," Ben said. "Her career is everything to her. I'm just a bystander. She'd drop me in a heartbeat if she thought her career…"

He stopped to pull his phone from his pocket, and then scanned his messages.

"She hasn't responded. Not since I spoke to her earlier."

"Give the girl a chance, Ben. She does have her hands full at the moment."

"She always responds," Ben said, and he hit the green button to call her.

"Ben, don't call her. Not now."

But he ignored Freya, listening to the ring tone over and over until it stopped, and the familiar recorded voice announced that he was welcome to leave a message.

"This is Jackie's bloody fault–"

"You can't blame her, Ben," Freya said. Then she froze and her eyes widened. "Oh, Christ."

"What?"

"Jackie," she said. "I told her to tell Alexandra Sinclair the body isn't Michael Levy's. She taking her to identify the body."

Ben found Jackie's number in his recently dialled list and hit the button to initiate another call, this time putting the phone on to loudspeaker for them both to hear.

The phone rang three times before it was answered, but the voice wasn't female, and it lacked the remnants of a soft Edinburgh accent.

"Hello?" somebody said.

"Hello? Who's this?" Freya asked.

"It's Gabby. Who's this?"

"It's us, Cruz," she replied. "Where's Gold?"

"Jackie? I don't know. She left a couple of hours ago. You told her to," he said. "Is this her phone? I wondered whose it was. I found it beside the new coffee machine. Speaking of which, have you tried the cappuccino–"

Freya reached over and stabbed her finger angrily at Ben's phone, taking four attempts to hit the red button to end the call.

"Call Pip," she said. "Tell her what's happened and not to let Alexandra see the body until she's been told it's very likely her bloody boyfriend."

"Bloody hell, Freya. This is going from bad to worse. We don't even know if Alexandra will identify the body for us. She's not even a friend or family."

"I know, which makes it even worse. If Standing finds out what we were doing, he'll hit the bloody roof."

Ben found the pathologist's number and started the third call in less than three minutes, turning to Freya to voice his thoughts while the call connected.

"So we've told a woman the body we found isn't her boyfriend, but can you help us identify it? Then she turns up and sees her boyfriend lying on the slab. That's got a bloody damages claim written all over it."

"I know, Ben. I bloody well know, alright?"

"Ah, which one is it this time?" Pip said, her Welsh accent strong over the line. "Tweedledum or Tweedledumber?"

"Pip, it's Ben," he said.

"Ah, the latter of the two."

"We need your help," he said. "Has Gold called to arrange a viewing?"

"She has indeed. She called an hour ago to arrange the visit, then she arrived with a young lady about ten minutes ago, who left in what I can only describe, Benjamin Savage, as a flood of rage-filled tears and using language I've never even heard before," she said. "I don't know what you've done, boy-oh, but you've really messed up this time."

CHAPTER THIRTY-SIX

It was one of those times when Freya felt torn. It wasn't a case of there being a right thing to do and the wrong thing to do. Rather, there were two right things to do and the idea of doing either of them was guilt-laden.

Ben was standing in his kitchen, silent and clearly hurting. He stared down at the handwritten note in his hand. He hadn't read it aloud, but Freya knew what Michaela was likely to have written: Thanks, but no thanks, with the added boot to the groin of something like, I wish you the best of luck.

The first of the correct things to do was to hug him and be there. Maybe even cook him dinner.

The second was to leave him to his own devices and go back to her own place so he could deal with the heartache however he needed to.

It hadn't been a long relationship, but it had been Ben's first relationship in years, and the change in him had been noticeable. Michaela had certainly made her mark, Freya thought, not only on his heart and mind but everywhere she looked. The bistro table and chairs on the patio, the little bed of flowers that were in full bloom, and the lawn had even been mowed. There was evidence of her stay in the kitchen, too. A long, cylindrical pot for spaghetti which Michaela had bought for him. Freya remembered fondly the moment Ben had questioned its purpose, stating that spaghetti came in tins like baked beans.

There were also the new tea towels she had bought to dry the dishes, which again, he had questioned, saying that everything he needed lived in the dishwasher. The cupboards were for food and surplus crockery, pans, and glasses.

"What do you want me to do?" Freya said eventually, after watching his eyes rove over the words for the tenth time. "I can leave if—"

"No," he said abruptly, but she'd let him have that. "No, stay. Sorry, I'll just..."

"Ben, do you need to talk?"

"About what?" he asked. "About how I'm less important than the careers of the women I keep falling in love with?"

"Oh, don't say that."

"Well, what am I supposed to say?" he said. He tossed the note onto the side and brushed past her, disappearing up the stairs, presumably to check if Michaela had taken everything or had just left for a few days.

The note on the kitchen worktop was calling to Freya. She peered up the stairs and heard him shuffling about, and she edged closer to the slip of paper. The pad Michaela had used was headed with the branding of John Deere, which Freya presumed had been given to Ben's father at some point. Michaela had used both sides of two full pages. It was the written equivalent of a suspect who keeps on babbling; a sure sign of guilt. Let them talk for long enough and they'll talk themselves into a confession.

Dear Ben, the note began, but before she could bring herself to read the first line, she set it back down and moved away, questioning the morality of the intrusion. Was it wrong to read it? Would he be upset? Would she be upset if the tables were turned?

If he had minded, he wouldn't have left it on the kitchen side, she thought, which perhaps could be construed as an invitation to read it.

And so she stepped closer to it again, peering at the first line from afar.

I'm sure by now you've heard...

No, it was wrong. She shouldn't get involved. If he wanted to tell her what the letter said, she should let him tell her in his own time.

But she might as well finish reading the first line.

I'm sure by now you've heard about the DNA mix-up. I'm also sure that by the time you read this, you have an idea of what the rest of this note says. Is it your fault? No. Is it my fault? Probably. Is my leaving fair on you? No. But there is one underlying question, Ben. Am I glad? Yes.

I think we both know I'm not the one you want...

"So, there it is," Ben said from behind her, and she just held onto enough composure to own the fact that she was reading a personal note. She tossed it onto the worktop as if it was worthless. "I feel like I'm playing one of those kids games and I just landed on a snake. Now I'm back to square one."

"I like square one," Freya told him. "Square one is clean and tidy. Square one is where nothing and nobody else matters. Square one is where you get to make plans."

"Is this some kind of motivational speech?" he asked, to which she shook her head. "I feel like I should go after her. Am I weak for not wanting to?"

"No, you're not weak. Going after somebody who walks out rarely works out well, in my experience anyway."

"What if she wants me to go after her?" he said. "What if deep down, she just wants to know if I'm serious about her?"

"If you were serious about her, Ben, you wouldn't be standing here now. You'd be in your car."

He bowed his head, and for a moment, Freya thought his emotions were going to get the better of him. But when he looked up at her, he was silent and thoughtful, as if some kind of revelation had taken place; he was unshackled.

"I'm sorry I read your note. If it helps, I didn't read it all," she said, then laughed. "I didn't actually have time. Doesn't she go on?"

"You can read it if you want," he said. "There's nothing in there you don't know about."

He moved past her, opened the fridge, and found the open bottle of wine from the previous night.

"Are you sure that's wise?" she asked, which he ignored, grabbing two glasses from the cupboard and filling them far beyond a level she might have deemed polite.

He took one, leaving the other for her, and then stepped out into the garden.

Freya collected her glass and moved to the back door, leaning on the doorframe while she watched him settle into one of the teak chairs.

"So," he said, "at least one of my problems has been solved."

"Which one?"

"The one about a woman I slept with sharing a house with my new girlfriend and me."

She stepped out onto the patio and took the other seat.

"That's not the biggest problem we have," she said.

"I know. I haven't spoken to Jackie yet. I'm not sure I can face it."

"I'll deal with her. It'll be fine."

"And if Alexandra Sinclair makes a complaint—"

"I'll deal with that, too," Freya said.

"You can't shield me, Freya. I'm a big boy, you know?"

"Who told you that?" she replied, with a wink she hoped would raise a smile. "The thing is, Ben, all the little things you deem as being separate problems are all rooted in one."

"Standing."

"Exactly. Did Michaela take the files she got from the archives?"

"I don't think so. I saw them on the table in the living room."

"Well then, what are we waiting for?" she asked.

"You want to go through them now? After all what's happened?"

"The clock is ticking, Ben. I mean, I'm happy to sit out here and drink all night, but it's not going to help us, is it? Today is Tuesday. We've got three days."

"Without sounding like Gillespie, can we do it tomorrow?" he said. "I think tonight I'd like to go over a few things. A few loose ends, as it were."

"Like what?"

"Like the toothbrush."

"Oh, Ben. Look, Gold wasn't to know—"

"No, I'm not looking to blame Jackie," he said. "But if it wasn't Michael Levy's toothbrush. Then who's toothbrush was it?"

Freya heard him say the words. They registered in her mind and replayed over and over until she'd exhausted any solutions she could think of.

"I think the owner of the toothbrush is a good question," she told him, enjoying the way he was using the investigation to forget, just as she once did. "The question I'm more interested in is—"

"Why did Alexandra Sinclair give Jackie the wrong toothbrush?" he finished for her.

"Don't do that," she said.

"Do what?"

"Finish my sentence."

"That's what you do to me, though."

"I do not," she argued, as his phone lit up on the table and a glimmer of hope washed over his face, but was doused moments later. He hit the button to answer the call.

"Chapman, are you still working?" he asked.

"I'm driving home now," she said. "I was going to call from the office, but Standing was hanging around."

"Like a bad smell?" he asked.

"Worse," she said, but adding any further insult just wasn't in the polite young woman's vocabulary. "I did some digging on Alexandra Sinclair."

"Go on," Freya said by way of a greeting. "What did you find?"

"Well, she's got a fairly clean record. Some minor offences when she was in her twenties, but nothing to write home about. But her name does crop up in an old record I found. I thought you should know."

"What type of record?" Ben asked, as Freya leaned in close so they could both listen to what she had to say. It was like old times, both of them huddled around a phone call with no worries about a girlfriend walking in and getting the wrong idea.

"It was an assault," Chapman said. "A sexual assault. She made a statement, but it didn't go anywhere. She dropped the charges and from what I can see, local police made no effort to follow up."

It hadn't been that long ago that Chapman had been attacked, and like many victims of assault, the wounds rarely heal in full.

"Do we think it was Michael Levy?" Ben suggested. "Jackie said he was abusive."

"I thought that, but this was before they were together," Chapman replied. "Jackie's report said they've been together for approximately ten years. This statement was made sixteen years ago but doesn't identify her attacker."

"That doesn't rule him out," Freya said. "They may have only been together for ten years, but who knows how long she's been under his spell? People like that have a tendency to work their way into their victims' lives."

"Especially when there's unforeseen consequences," Chapman said cryptically.

"How old is the daughter?" Freya said, making the connection in an instant.

"Fifteen, ma'am," Chapman said. "I did the maths already. If the daughter is the result of Levy raping her, then maybe he convinced her to give him a chance? Or maybe it wasn't rape at all. That happens all the time."

"What about forensics?" Freya suggested. "Surely she was examined?"

"Not a thing," Chapman said, her voice filled with empathy for the woman. "There's nothing in the archives, anyway. But put yourself in her shoes, ma'am. If the police needed your help, you wouldn't exactly go out of your way, would you?"

"Maybe not," she said. "Especially if, like you said, it wasn't rape."

"I also found something else," Chapman said. "I'm not sure if it's relevant, but she has a savings account with her bank. There are no transactions aside from a payment each month."

"A payment?"

"Five hundred pounds," Chapman said. "Every single month without fail, she pays in five hundred pound cash, and for a single mother, I can tell you there's quite a sum of money in there."

CHAPTER THIRTY-SEVEN

"Have you heard anything?" Freya asked, hoping to tease Ben from his brooding silence.

The morning had been quiet. They had shared a pot of coffee, and Ben being Ben had found trivial tasks to occupy his mind around the house, giving reason for him to move to a different room.

But now they were in her car, there was no escaping her intrigue.

"Jackie messaged me," he replied. "Alexandra isn't opening the door to her."

"Ben?"

"Gillespie and Cruz have submitted the soil sample from the hole that was dug near the bridge. They had to leave it at reception, of course."

"Ben?"

"And as far as I know, Nillson and Anderson are at the station with Chapman."

"And Michaela?"

"She doesn't report in to me," he said. "I doubt very much she would let me know her whereabouts."

"Has she messaged you?"

"Nope," he said. "No, she's digging her heels in and I can't blame her. She's had a flawless career so far. She's next in line to run the entire regional department across the East Midlands, then five minutes with me and she's being reprimanded for a stupid mistake."

"She doesn't hate you, Ben. You haven't done anything wrong."

"I know. But do you know what? I wish I had. I wish I had done something. I wish that she had caught me doing something, sleeping with you or something. At least then I'd be able to blame myself for my own stupidity. At least then I could say it didn't mean anything, and that she was the one I really wanted."

"Wow," she replied. "You know how to twist the blade, don't you?"

"You know what I mean," he said. "Don't make this about you."

"Likewise, Ben. Don't make this about you. It's about her and her career. She clearly likes you, it's just that..."

"That what?"

"That her career is important to her," Freya said, as gently as she could.

"The story of my life, then?"

"All I'm saying is that I get it. I understand where she's coming from. There was a time when I put my career before everything, too, love, family, even my health."

"Now who's twisting the blade?"

"Give her time, Ben," Freya told him as she nosed the large Range Rover into a tight spot. "Don't they say something about time being the greatest healer?"

"I suppose it all depends on what needs healing," he replied. "And I suspect I'll be healed before she even looks my way again."

"Que sera," Freya said.

"Please don't start off on some posh French rant," he said. "I'm really not in the mood."

She killed the engine, then stared through the windscreen at the row of shops ahead of them. They were parked in the old market square in Horncastle, where the past could be glimpsed proudly beside more contemporary features – the handwritten sign for a farmer's club, the old, cobbled stones, and the wrought-iron works brackets that had been fixed high on the building walls, on which lamps had hung for a hundred years or more.

"It's Spanish," she told him. "Well, Italian, to be precise—"

"Freya, can we just change the subject?"

"Okay, okay," she said as she reached for the door handle. "Perhaps a little chat with a little liar will provide you with a little distraction?"

"Very funny."

She climbed from the car and leaned back inside to whisper.

"Or perhaps you'd rather stay here and wallow in self-pity?" she said quietly. "*Comme un chiot malade d'amour.*"

"What does that mean?" he asked as she closed the door and strode over to the shop bearing the sign J. Graham and Son in gold copperplate writing on a classic, green background. She heard him approach from behind. "Well?"

"Well what?" she asked, finding the door to be open. The aroma of wood, polish, and her father's old house struck her. "God, I love that smell."

"Freya?" Ben hissed, following her inside.

"My father had a place in France," Freya told him. "It was a modest house set at the edge of a forest. We walked to the coast and back in the evenings and spent our days reading in the shade."

"What are you talking about?" Ben asked.

"That smell," she said.

"It reminds you of your father's house in France? So what?"

"Not the French house," she told him. "But when we returned. That's when I noticed it the most. In our home. You see, while we were away, the staff used to make the most of the empty house."

"That was a common thing," a voice said from the far side of the shop, and a figure in a tweed three-piece suit emerged from a back room. He checked his pocket watch, snapped it closed, and then tucked it into a little pocket in his waist coat before offering them a curt smile. "The smell of polish was considered offensive to a lady's rather delicate senses, and what with all that dust in the air. That would never do, would it?"

"Mr Graham," Freya said. "Thank you for your insight."

He ignored her greeting, choosing instead to stride boldly between the polished furniture on display throughout the shop. He folded his hands behind his back, holding his head high. "Drapes were removed and beaten, rugs too. Creaky floors and stairs were fixed, and of course, then there was the silver to be taken care of."

"You're very well-versed in the protocols of the upper class," Freya said.

"Sadly, not as well-versed as you," he replied. "Mine is a knowledge gleaned from rubbing shoulders with those more fortuitous than I. Yours is rather more first-hand. It's funny, isn't it?"

"What's funny?"

"I've never met an upper-class copper before," he said. "I've heard of working-class men who do well enough to reach middle class, and I've heard of middle-class men reaching the lofty heights of the upper class. Not often, but it does happen. But I've never heard of somebody stepping down."

"Vocation does not determine one's class, Mr Graham," she told him. "That honour is reserved for who we are, our morals if you like, our heritage, and the decisions we make. All of the things that mark our place in society."

He stared at her, glancing at Ben briefly then returning to appraise her.

"That's the type of thing the upper class would say," he said, to which she shook her head.

"You're right," Freya replied. "My father would have said

something along those lines. My grandfather too. But me? No, I was never upper class. At least I never saw myself as being so."

"Well, now that we're all firmly on the same playing field—"

"You'd like to know why we're here," Freya said, to which he appeared surprised at her interruption and relinquished control of the interaction. "Well, you should know my boss would like me to slip a pair of handcuffs onto your wrists and drag you to the station."

He stiffened at the statement but said nothing.

"You'll be pleased to know I disagree," she said. "But that's not to say you can't be made to be useful."

"Useful?"

"You're well-acquainted with Drew Barker and Michael Levy, is that right?" she said and ran a manicured finger along the grain of a rather fine-looking desk.

"That is correct," he replied, his attention consumed by her hand. "Would you mind? That's a nineteenth-century—"

"Mahogany partner's desk," Freya said. "Yes, that's right. My father had one quite similar."

"Then you'll know the value of such a piece," he said. "Upwards of fifteen thousand pounds."

The large number came as no surprise to Freya, who shrugged the comment off as if it were nineteenth-century dust.

"That's the difference," she told him, "between the middle and upper classes. One seeks to collect and harbour such items, allowing their pride to swell with every decimal point. The other merely inherits heirlooms; their monetary value is rather insignificant."

"I know them both," Graham said. "Is that what you came to find out?"

"How long have you known them?" Freya asked.

"I've known Mike for years. Drew came later, it was when he began working with Michael, I believe."

"Can you be more specific?"

He shook his head and puffed his cheeks. Then his eyes widened as an idea struck him.

"We were at The King's Head," he said. "Thatcher had just died. I remember it. Michael was spouting on about how she had ruined the country."

"Two thousand and thirteen," Freya said. "I remember somebody saying something quite similar."

"Your father?" he asked, to which she felt her face twitch in response.

"Somebody else. My father was a conservative through and through," she said. "And Drew Barker was present, was he?"

"He was," Graham said, checking his pocket watch once more. "Drowning his sorrows."

"How so?"

"Few things cause a man to drown his sorrows, Inspector Bloom."

"Money, power, masculinity," she replied. "Losing any of the above can be a hard cross to bear."

"I believe his wife had just died, or recently at least."

"So Drew Barker was newly widowed, was he? And Levy gave him a fresh start? He must have thought highly of him?"

"Actually, quite the opposite," Graham said. "They couldn't stand each other. They still can't, in fact. It wasn't the type of fresh start I'd wish on anybody."

"Sorry?" Freya said. "You're saying that Michael Levy hired Drew Barker even though they didn't get along?"

"Have you seen Drew's work?" Graham said. "The man is an artisan, one of the finest craftsmen I've ever met, and in a place like Horncastle where other businesses deals in antiques, you don't hire somebody as good as Drew for his personality. You hire them so that your competitors cannot."

"That's food for thought," Freya said after a while.

Jeremiah Graham made a show of checking the time on his pocket watch, then looked at each of them in turn.

"Will that be all?" He said. "Or should I call my solicitor?"

"That won't be necessary," Freya told him. "But if I were you I wouldn't stray too far, Mr Graham."

"I have no plans or reason to," he replied with a charming smile that might have worked on somebody else. "See yourselves out."

Freya let him get all the way to his back room before she stopped him.

"One last thing, Mr Graham," she said, and Ben held the door ajar. Graham seemed mildly amused at the disruption and smiled back as politely as he could. "I understand why Michael Levy might want a man of such talent to work for him. But why would a man with Drew Barker's skill want to work for Levy? That doesn't make sense."

"Ah, the elephant in the room," Graham said. "I'm afraid that, not having any insight into Drew's mind, I cannot comment."

"That's what I thought you might say," Freya said.

"Although, one only has to know what Michael Levy has that Drew Barker doesn't in order to understand," Graham said, finishing with a sly wink. "Good day, Inspector."

CHAPTER THIRTY-EIGHT

The old council house that faced the nature reserve was as sombre as Ben's heart. The central house in a terrace of three was like a rotten tooth, decaying and ready to fall. Somehow, the lifeless building gave off a feeling, a sadness, Ben thought. That was until Freya nudged him along the footpath.

"Come on," she said. "You didn't open your mouth with Graham. I suggest you start to pull your weight, Ben Savage."

The words were harsh when others may have offered kindness, but somehow he knew the approach was heartfelt and designed to rouse a grin at the very least, if not a smile.

"I was contemplating," he replied, as he reached up to rap on the door; his signature three raps.

"Not suicide?" she said, to which he spun around to glare at her.

"French. At least, I think it's French," he said, and he did his best to repeat the phrase Freya had offered him inside J. Graham and Sons.

"Come and clot marmalade the armour."

He felt confidently close to the original, yet Freya's smirk suggested otherwise.

"Comme un chiot malade d'amour. It means you're a lovesick puppy," she told him. "Et facile à taquiner."

"What?"

She laughed and leaned past him to give the door another knock.

"Don't laugh at me, Freya–"

"Alexandra, it's Freya Bloom. I just want a quick word with you," she called out, then leaned down to peer through the letterbox.

A rumble in Ben's pocket provided the distraction he was looking for. A message from Nillson flashed up on the screen

"Alexandra, I know you're in there," Freya called out, louder this time.

"Freya?" Ben hissed, just as she straightened. He tuned the phone for her to see. "CSI has matched Barker's DNA to a sample found on Levy's tooth. It's enough to confirm that Drew Barker was the attacker. Or one of them, at least."

She stared at the phone, processing the information as fast as she could.

"Tell Nillson to bring him in," she said curtly.

"Standing will have something to say about that."

"To hell with him," she said, just as the door opened and she turned to greet Michael Levy's girlfriend.

But it wasn't Alexandra Sinclair; it was her daughter who stood there staring up at them, her eyes shining and lower lip quivering.

"You must be Rosie," Freya said, and the girl nodded. Freya showed the girl her warrant card. "Is your mum home?"

She nodded again, her eyes never leaving the ID even as Freya folded it into her pocket. "She's in bed, I think. She hasn't been down today. Not that I know of anyway."

"Shouldn't you be at school?" Ben asked, hitting the button to reply to Nillson's message.

"It's the holidays," the girl replied, appearing terrified. She stepped backwards like she was in some kind of trouble, and tugged the sleeves of her sweater over her hands.

Freya stepped into the hallway, hesitating in case the girl offered some kind of argument. But she didn't. She was one of those girls with a boyish figure, short hair, and clothes that were neither male nor female – a pair of jogging bottoms and an oversized hoodie. But even through the girl's baggy attire, Ben could see her chest rise and fall in panic.

"Nobody is in any trouble," Ben said, as he stepped inside behind Freya. "You've nothing to worry about."

"I'm sorry, I just–"

"You just what?" Freya said.

Rosie Sinclair lowered her voice, then glanced up the stairs to make sure her mother wasn't there.

"Well, you know? What with Michael and that?"

"It's okay, sweetheart," a voice said from upstairs, and Alexandra Sinclair stepped onto the top step, drawing her dressing gown around her.

"Miss Sinclair?" Freya said. "We're sorry to disturb you."

"Save it," she replied, as she descended the stairs, of which at least four of the thirteen steps creaked loudly. She brushed past them and headed into the kitchen. "Haven't you lot caused enough damage?"

"Listen–" Freya said.

"No, you listen," Alexandra said. "Do you know what I had to go through yesterday?"

"I've been made aware–"

"Well, then why the bloody hell have you turned up on my doorstep today? Have you got any idea..." She stopped herself mid-sentence and looked at her daughter who stood open-mouthed.

"Can I go out, Mum?" she said.

"Don't go far, please," Alexandra told her.

"I'm just going to Pete's."

"Take your phone with you."

The young girl edged past Ben and through the open door, giving them a fearful glance as she pulled the door closed behind her.

"We're well aware of what we asked of you, Alexandra, and I can only apologise for any suffering or shock you might have—"

"Might have?" she spat. "She told me it wasn't him. She said they didn't know who it was or where Michael was, but if I could only try to identify the body, you might have a chance of finding him."

"I realise—"

"But it *was* him," she said. "I should bloody sue for damages—"

"Then please do," Freya said, which seemed to quell the bitterness for a moment. "We're not here to apologise for our shortcomings, Alexandra. Those occurred in the process of investigating a murder, and we're not here to help you heal."

"Then why are you here?" she replied from the kitchen, as she filled the kettle from the tap.

"I wouldn't bother with that," Freya said, and Alexandra stopped, her head cocked to one side as if she hadn't heard Freya properly.

"Sorry?"

"I said I wouldn't bother with that," Freya told her. "In fact, if I were you, I'd get dressed into something comfortable and a little more appropriate."

"Appropriate?" she said, taking a step back. "What do you mean?"

"I mean," Freya said. "I am arresting you on suspicion of murder."

"Arresting me?"

"Get dressed, Alexandra," Freya said. "Then perhaps we can discuss your relationship with Drew Barker at the station."

"My relationship with Drew is none of your business."

"It's every bit my business, Alexandra," Freya told her. "You've done nothing but lie to us since we first knocked on your door."

She stepped closer, and Alexandra reached for the countertop to steady herself.

"I can explain."

"I know you can," Freya said. "Now get dressed before I drag you down to the station in your dressing gown, and don't think I wouldn't."

CHAPTER THIRTY-NINE

The ground floor of the station on a weekday was marginally busier than it was on a weekend, mostly due to the increased number of uniformed officers who always seemed to be heading somewhere with purpose, which was typically a play so as not to be identified as being idle for fear of receiving a task.

Sergeant Priest, a tall and portly man in his early sixties with a Yorkshire accent as thick as any Anna had heard, led Drew Barker along the corridor with a firm grip on his arm and then instructed a waiting uniform to escort him to interview room two and to stay there until told otherwise.

Barker wore the worried expression shared by many men of his kind – good-natured and, for the most part, innocent. It was only when men like that were pushed to their limits that their reactions betrayed their morals. Too many of them had passed through the ground floor corridor, of which many had been led away in a police transporter, their fates left to the whim of a future jury.

But it wasn't Sergeant Priest who Anna was waiting for. The individual she desperately needed to talk to followed shortly afterwards, her head held high leaving a cloud of expensive perfume in her wake.

"Process her," she called over her shoulder to Ben, who guided a distraught-looking Alexandra Sinclair to the custody desk. "Nillson, how did it go?"

"Room two," Anna replied, and Freya paused at the interview room door to peer inside. She gave the officer an instruction which Anna did not hear, then continued walking her way.

"Have you spoken to him yet?" Freya asked.

"His solicitor is on his way," Anna told her. "He hasn't said anything yet."

"Tell me about this DNA match," Freya said, keeping her voice low so the suspect could not hear.

"It was Pat, boss. Michaela's assistant. They've found traces of foreign DNA on Levy's body."

"What was the medium?" Freya asked.

"Skin on his teeth, most likely from a punch. Saliva in his hair, enough of it to suggest somebody spat on him, plus some more specks of saliva on his face which Pat suggested was from the exertion of the assault."

"Are you saying there was more than one attacker?" Freya said to which Anna nodded. "Barker's profile came up straight away."

"I didn't think we had his DNA on record?"

"We didn't," Nillson said. "Until Jackie submitted his toothbrush and Pat linked the fingerprints to an earlier misdemeanour."

"His toothbrush? Freya said "That was his? Why would Alexandra Sinclair give us Drew Barker's toothbrush?"

"Why would she even have it in the first place?" Nillson asked. "Unless of course, she took it from the hotel by mistake."

"Mistake my left foot. What else was said?" Freya asked. "Did you actually talk to Pat?"

"No, I had an email overnight," Anna replied. "But there was another little discovery that might be of interest."

"Go on."

"Apparently our crazy pathologist took it upon herself to swab Levy's genitals, or what was left of them, at least."

"That's standard practice," Freya said.

"Even so, I don't think any of us expected to find a third-party DNA."

"A third party?"

"Levy wasn't being one hundred per cent faithful, boss."

"Neither was Alexandra from what you discovered at the Petwood Hotel."

"Not like this, boss."

"Just say it, Anna. I don't have time to beat about the bush, I've been on the road all morning and I would like a comfort break before I interview Alexandra Sinclair."

"A partial profile, boss. This time there was enough of the source to run a full second test."

"Who was it, Anna?"

"Rosie Sinclair," she said, and suddenly felt her throat dry up like a desert. "She's fifteen years old and we know he was abusive."

"Is it confirmed? Do we know it was her?"

"We have Alexandra's DNA from the statement she made fifteen years ago."

"The sexual assault? I thought no samples were given."

"There were no suspect samples. Only the victim's, Alexandra's, which suggests she didn't undergo the full medical examination but was processed at the station. Either way, a fifty per cent profile across two tests indicates a close relative, a parent, sibling, or offspring."

"But Chapman said there was no forensics tied to the statement. She checked," Freya said.

Anna shrugged. "Sorry, boss. I just made a call and the archivist came up with this. Do you think Levy was abusing the daughter?"

"Let's not jump to conclusions," Freya said thoughtfully. "Anything else?"

"I've had the spade from Barker's garden shed dropped off at the lab. We should have results soon enough."

A disturbance at the end of the corridor in the custody suite interrupted them, and Anna saw a man in a sharp suit carrying a tan satchel being led along the corridor.

"That looks like the solicitor," she said.

"Do you still want to handle this one?" Freya asked.

"I'll be fine. Anderson is backing me up. She'll be here in a minute."

"Well, I hope for your sake Barker's lawyer isn't from the same firm as Graham's," Freya said.

"About that, boss—"

"No need to apologise. The man is guilty of something," Freya said, as she opened the fire escape door and glanced back in search of Ben. She smiled briefly at Anna with a nod of support. "It just isn't murder. Come and see me when you're done, we'll compare notes."

Freya turned to leave just as Anderson stepped off the stairs.

"Did you bring Sinclair in, boss?" she asked.

"I did. Ben and I will interview her shortly. You two can deal with Barker. I want to know exactly what he did on Friday evening. Is that clear?"

"Yes, boss," they both replied.

"Oh, and Jeremiah Graham mentioned Barker's wife dying around the same time as he began working for Levy. See what he has to say about that, if you will?"

"Yes, boss," Anna said, and she left them to it.

Anna led the way, leaving Anderson to close the interview room door behind her. She took a moment to prepare her notes, allowing time for Anderson to initiate the recording, after which Anna began announcing the date and time, then the names of those present. "DS Nillson and DC Anderson. Also present are..."

She looked across the small table at the solicitor, beckoning him to continue.

"Geoffrey Baxter, Partner at Grace and Jones LLP."

He was an intelligent-looking man with thinning hair, a straight Roman nose, and hands that looked as if he had never held a single tool save for an expensive fountain pen. He gestured for Barker to finish the introductions.

"Drew Barker," he said, his fingers interlocking on the table until Anna's eyes flicked down to them, noticing a small cut on the knuckle of his right hand.

"And for the record, Mr Barker, you are under arrest on suspicion of the murder of Michael Levy. You do not have to say anything. But it may harm your defence if you do not mention when questioned something that you later rely on in court. Anything you do say may be given in evidence. Do you understand your rights?"

"I do," he said quietly. "Although, I'm struggling to understand why I'm here."

"We'll get to that," Anna said. "What I'd like to understand is your movements last Friday evening."

"Before we begin," Baxter said. "I'm led to believe you haven't yet submitted any evidence."

"That's correct. I'll be making a full submission shortly after this interview."

"That's highly irregular—"

"Well, we can either send your client to wait in a cell while we submit evidence, which could take a few hours, or we can take a statement from your client in the meantime. Which would you prefer?"

"Let's just get on with it," Barker said. "I'd be keen to see what this evidence is, but I don't particularly relish the idea of seeing the inside of a cell."

"Are you happy for us to continue?" Anna asked Baxter, who grumbled to himself and then slowly unscrewed the lid of his

Montegrappa fountain pen. Anna turned her attention to Barker. "Can you begin by listing your movements on Friday, please, Mr Barker?"

"When would you like me to start from?" he said, showing no sign of apprehension.

"From the beginning," Anna said. "I want to know every last detail of every minute of the day."

"Wouldn't you rather just get to the nitty-gritty?" he asked, which caught Anna's attention, but not enough to sway her. "By which I mean from the time Alex called me."

"From the beginning," Anna said. "From the moment you arrived at work."

He sucked in a breath, then exhaled loudly.

"Okay then. I arrived at around ten past nine. I know this to be accurate because I left at precisely nine and it's not exactly a marathon drive to the workshop."

"Was Michael Levy there?"

"He was. He opened up, just like he did every morning. We were expecting a large delivery from an auction house down in Norfolk the following day, so the plan was for us to make some space, finish a few odd jobs off to get what we could out of the door. It's not exactly rocket science, but it does help to stay organised. It prevents mishaps if you know what I mean?"

"The workshop didn't exactly look like anybody had made space when I visited," Anna said. "In fact, I'd say it was rather crammed."

"That's because we never quite got around to it," Barker said. "Mike was busy with the paperwork. Something was troubling him, but I've no idea what it was."

"What makes you say that?"

"Because he damn near tore my head off when I told him to put a smile on his face," Barker said. "It's bloody exhausting working with somebody in a mood like that. Anyway, he never did get around to helping me, and we have a rule not to move pieces on our own. That's how accidents happen and things get damaged."

"So he stayed in his office all day?" Anna asked.

"No. No, just until morning tea break. We usually stop for a cuppa around eleven-ish. I made the tea, as normal, gave him a shout, as normal, and then he made his excuses. He disappeared and didn't come back. Not until later anyway."

"Do you have any idea where he was?"

"I would imagine he was at Jerry's place. Although, I don't know for sure. All I know is that it was me who had to finish the load for Parker's. Nine pieces nonetheless, all polished and prepared."

"Sorry, what's Parker's?" Anna asked.

"It's an outlet. J. F. Parker's in Grimsby. It's an antiques store. They've been buying from us for years."

"And do Parker's pay their bills on time?"

"They do," he said. "And that's why I was keen to get the delivery ready. That's a tidy sum coming our way. I might have even got some bloody wages."

"You said Levy returned to lock up," Anna said. "How was he?"

"Honestly? He was happy. He seemed so anyway."

"Did he say why?"

"No, but he left the van there, so I can only assume he had a few drinks whilst he was out. He wasn't one to drink and drive. For all his sins, he never did that."

"Was that the last time you saw him?" Anna asked.

"It was," he replied. "I went home, packed my things, booked a room at the Petwood and then I was off for the weekend, as I believe I have already explained to you."

"You did explain," Anna said. "Thank you. However, after we spoke before, we paid a visit to the Petwood."

"And they confirmed my stay?"

"Yes, they did. They said the room was booked for a single

occupancy," Anna said. "So, they were rather surprised when you left the hotel at nine o'clock only to return around midnight."

"It's not a crime, is it?"

"No, no it's not a crime at all," Anna said. "But it is a crime to withhold information during a murder enquiry."

He stared at her, then glanced nervously at Baxter who was as intrigued as she was to hear his response.

"I don't understand," he said. "I'm not withholding—"

"You left the hotel at around nine p.m. and returned around midnight," Anna told him. "With Alexandra Sinclair on your arm."

He licked his lips, and his Adam's apple rose and fell as he swallowed heavily.

"Now," Anna said, "let's start again, shall we? This time, from the moment Alexandra called you, and Mr Barker I should warn you-."

"Yes?" he said.

"We need the truth," she said. "I would seriously think twice about leaving any details out if I were you."

CHAPTER FORTY

"I called him," she said, guiltily rubbing one thumb with the other, while her bony fingers remained interlaced, resembling the ribcage of some famished beast. "Is that what you want to hear?"

"From work?" Freya said. "You called Drew Barker from work, did you? From the social club?"

"That's right."

"And tell me again why you called him?" Freya said. "I just want to be clear. You see, and I'm sorry to be the one to tell you this, Alexandra, but we found DNA on Michael's body."

"Is that right?"

"On his genitals, to be precise," Freya said. "Like I said, I'm sorry, but we must have this conversation. I can assure you it's not pleasant for any of us."

"DNA? On his..." She stopped and shook an image from her mind. "What does that even mean?"

"It means that Michael engaged in some kind of sexual activity shortly before he died."

Alexandra Sinclair's chest rose and fell like the tide. She fumbled with her fingers.

"Is there something you want to tell us?" Freya said. "Something you saw, maybe?"

"I didn't see anything," Alexandra replied with enough bitterness in her tone to convey an ill-deserved hatred. "I heard it. I left for work just like I told you. I called out to Rosie to have a nice evening and to be home by ten."

"And Michael?" Ben asked.

"He was in the shower. He'd come home from work in fairly high spirits, and I didn't fancy a repeat of the previous night if you get my meaning."

"Even though he was in high spirits."

"High spirits don't last long," she replied. "You get to learn the signs."

She raised a hand to her swollen eye, and the duty solicitor, a woman named Halifax, made a note of her bruising and the cause.

"You were on your way to work," Freya said, nudging the woman onwards.

"I was half way up the High Street when I realised I'd forgotten my ID card. You can't work the tills without one. It's like a way of keeping track of who took what money or something. Anyway, I turned back. I'd only been gone ten or fifteen minutes."

She fell into silence, but the look on her face conveyed the story had continued inside her head, like a horror movie, or the part of the thriller where Freya buried her face in a cushion.

"I know it's difficult, Alexandra. But we need to know what you heard."

"It's a sound you never forget," she said suddenly, her bottom lip protruding in defiance of her emotions. "Never."

Freya looked across at Ben, hoping that he'd read enough into her expression to understand a female voice was needed to coax the rest of the tale from Sinclair.

"We know about the assault, Alexandra," she said, and Sinclair's expression faded to curiosity. "You made a statement to the police sixteen years ago. We found it in the archive."

"That's old news," she said softly.

"That was what you heard though, wasn't it? You heard Michael—"

"No. No, I heard my girl. My baby girl," she said, and she sniffed hard.

"Were they in a—"

"Relationship?" Sinclair said. "No. No Rosie would never do that. She despised him and now I know why. No, this wasn't the sound of a consensual relationship."

"Alexandra, I'm sorry, but I have to understand this, and a jury will too, but what did you do next?"

"What did I do?" she repeated, buying time to formulate an answer. She shook her head and her breathing quickened, so much so that Halifax opened her mouth to call a break. But Sinclair grasped her trail of thought and spoke as if they would have guessed what she had to say. "I ran."

"You ran?"

She nodded.

"You left your daughter being assaulted—"

"It wasn't like that," she said. "I heard them, or her at least, and I froze. I don't know how long I was there. It felt like an hour, but it was probably just minutes. I heard him finish. I know what that sounds like. You do don't you? Then I heard her bedroom door open, and then I heard him whistling."

"Whistling? You mean, he'd left Rosie's room and—"

"He was getting ready. It was pub night, wasn't it? Friday night in The White Horse."

"But you left your daughter—"

"How could I go up to her with him there? How could I?" she snapped. "Besides, if Rosie is anything like me, which I am pleased to say she is, she would have denied it. She would have tried to protect me. She wouldn't want anyone to know."

"Alexandra, this could be spoken about in court—"

"This," she said, jabbing an index finger at the table. "This will not be spoken of. I'll not have my daughter go through what I had to. It's over for her now. He's dead, isn't he? She'll never have to go through it again."

"No," Freya mused. "No, let's hope she doesn't. What happened when you got to work?"

"I don't really know," Sinclair said. "It's all a blur, really. I served drinks, cleaned tables, and God knows what else. I thought I was hiding it pretty well, but Marian, she runs the bar, she told me to go and have a smoke."

"And that's when you called Drew, is it?" Freya said, to which she nodded.

"I didn't know who else to talk to. I didn't know who else could–"

She paused and seemed to smile at the word that she had stopped herself from saying.

"Could what?" Freya said, but Sinclair shook her head, and she smiled away the comment as if it was an old memory she had been fond of, but had let go.

"Nothing," she said.

Ben raised his eyebrows and inhaled loud enough for everyone in the room to hear, which sparked Sinclair back into action.

"He's a friend. A good friend," she said, defending her reasoning. "I know I can rely on him."

"Rely him to do what?"

"To help me," she said, her tone more than a little indignant. "To listen to me, to hear me, not to judge."

"And what time was this?" Freya asked. "What time did you call Mr Barker?"

"I don't know. Nine-ish, I suppose, maybe earlier. The bar was just getting going. I remember because I felt bad about leaving the others to cover for me."

"And where was Mr Barker when you spoke to him?"

Sinclair interlaced her fingers again and began to pick at a chipped thumbnail.

"He'd just checked into his hotel. He was at a golf weekend."

"A golf weekend?"

"In Woodhall Spa. It was the Petwood. He always goes, every year. Some competition or something."

"And what did you tell him?"

"Everything," Sinclair said softly, and she shrugged. "What else could I do? Once I started, I just…"

She paused again to swallow hard, and took a deep breath.

"This is important," Freya told her, and she nodded.

"I know," she said. "I told him what I told you. What I'd heard, how I felt, how it reminded me of what happened years ago."

"Alexandra, I don't wish to drag up the past. But what happened to you? May I ask–"

"It wasn't Michael," she said. "It wasn't him. I know that's what you're thinking, but it wasn't him. I didn't know him then."

"May I ask–"

"No," she said. "No, I've long since found a way to live my life, and, like you said, I don't wish to drag up the past."

"That's okay," Freya said. "It was more of a professional curiosity."

"Is that what you call it?" Sinclair said. "I would have said it was just plain old being nosey."

"Why don't you tell us what happened next?" Freya said. "Once you'd called Mr Barker?"

"He came and got me, of course. Marian was disappointed, but she said she'd cover for me. She's good like that. Drew pulled up into the car park about thirty minutes later."

"And then what happened?" Freya said, and Sinclair's eyes darted from her to Ben and back in the flash of an eye.

"He took me home. He said I should stay with him at the hotel. He'd be playing golf all day, so I'd have the room to myself."

"And you went straight to Woodhall Spa, did you?"

"No. No, I wanted a bag," she said. Then she lowered her

voice. "I also needed to leave a note. For Rosie, you know?"

"A note?"

She nodded. "To tell her where I was, and that she should join me if she wanted to. I didn't want her to know that I knew, but if she wanted to join me, then she was welcome to."

"And did she?"

Sinclair shook her head.

"No. No, it's the holidays. She'd prefer to spend it with her friends than with her tired and grumpy old mum. She'll be with them now, I imagine. That's one thing I'm grateful for. With them boys around, I know she'll be safe."

"When you packed your bag, Alexandra, did Barker join you inside, or..."

"He waited outside," Sinclair said. "In case Michael came home early. He said he'd keep watch."

"And how long were you apart?" Freya said, at which Sinclair narrowed her eyes.

"Why?"

"Just answer the question, Alexandra."

"You think he had something to do with it?"

"No," Freya said. "I think you both had something to do with it."

"Is that an accusation?" Halifax said. "Because if it is, then I'm afraid I'm going to need to see some kind of justification."

"It wasn't an accusation," Freya said. "And believe me, when I can prove it, you'll be the first to know."

"That's just it," Halifax said. "All I've heard so far is my client's account of what happened the night Michael Levy was killed. She's provided you with her whereabouts. She's even been forced to delve into what I can only describe as a past she'd rather forget. And she's given you the names of the individuals who can account for every minute of the evening."

"Your client has not been forced, Miss Halifax–"

"Mrs Halifax," she corrected.

"Well, God help Mr Halifax," Freya said.

"Excuse me—"

"Alexandra, can you please state, clearly for the recording, the reason why you provided Drew Barker's toothbrush when my colleague, DC Gold, requested Michael Levy's toothbrush?"

"Sorry?"

"You gave us the wrong toothbrush," Freya said. "Ordinarily, one might put this down to being an accident, but in a house with just three occupants, making a mix-up of something as mundane as a toothbrush seems somewhat contrived, don't you think?"

"Is that all you have?" Halifax said.

"It was an honest mistake," Sinclair said. "I must have picked up Drew's toothbrush from the hotel by mistake. I didn't realise—"

"Thank you," Freya said, cutting her off.

"For what? Thank you for what, exactly?"

"For clarifying that the toothbrush was indeed Drew Barker's. I had a hunch, but there's nothing quite like hearing it from the horse's mouth."

Alexandra opened her mouth to speak, but Halifax held up his hand, allowing Freya to continue.

"You're aware that it was that mistake that caused us to believe the body we discovered in the nature reserve just five hundred yards from your house was, in fact, not Michael Levy's."

"I wasn't, no."

"As I thought," Freya said. "Tell me, was Michael aware of your relationship with Drew Barker?"

"Relationship? I told you, we're friends. We've always been friends."

"Always?"

"Yes, always."

"I want you to cast your mind back to two thousand and seven," Freya said. "Gordon Brown had just been made Prime Minster, and Drew Barker was down on his luck, licking his wounds, as it were."

Sinclair's nostrils flared as she exhaled, and she folded her arms defensively.

"You see, Alexandra," Freya continued, "Rosie's wasn't the only DNA that was found on Michael's body."

She stared at her, her face twisting in absolute horror.

"Who?"

"Not on his genitals," Freya said. "On his face. His tooth, to be precise."

"His tooth?"

"Most likely from a punch."

"I don't understand," she said.

"It's Drew's," Freya said gently, and she leaned forward to look into Sinclair's eyes as she spoke. "Did Drew do this? If you know, Alexandra, then you're obliged to say."

"Drew?"

"You said he waited outside your house. How long was he alone?"

"What?"

"How long, Alexandra?"

"I don't know. Twenty minutes or so. I showered. I felt so dirty–"

"Twenty minutes?"

"Give or take, yes. But he would never. I mean, he couldn't, could he?"

"Alexandra, I'm going to ask you a question, and I need you to cast aside any feelings you have for Drew Barker or Michael Levy. I just need a simple yes or no," Freya said, and she waited while Sinclair questioned her own judgement and then looked at her. "Drew Barker is in love with you. He has been since the day you left him for Michael Levy in two thousand and seven. The question is, did he, in your opinion, have the opportunity to murder Michael while he waited for you?"

Her mouth opened in disgust at first, then she appeared as if she might vomit and she clutched her chest.

"Alexandra?"

She composed herself and wiped a tear from her eye.

"I suppose so," she muttered, then affirmed what she had said. "I suppose he did, yes."

A hush fell over the room, the way a winter fog descends onto the fields, shielding the way regardless of how well the path is known.

And they did know it. They all knew it. Alexandra Sinclair had just told them everything they needed to hear.

A knock at the door dispersed the fog in a heartbeat and the door opened almost immediately.

"Boss," Nillson said, clinging to the door. She appeared anxious, quite out of character. "Do you have a moment?"

Freya looked at Ben, silently gesturing for him to see what it was that Nillson felt was so urgent. He announced his temporary departure to the recording, then slipped from the room, pulling the door closed behind him. The faint rumble of their voices lacked clarity yet reminded Freya of the path they had begun to tread.

"Alexandra," she began, "you have known Drew Barker for at least fifteen years–"

"Longer," Sinclair said. "We go way back, Drew and I."

"Thank you," Freya said. "I need to ask you something, and I'm afraid it's a little subjective."

"Is this necessary?" Halifax asked. "Surely the facts are enough–"

"Like I said," Freya said, cutting the woman off before she dug her claws into Sinclair's brooding doubt. "I'm afraid my question calls upon your judgement, and I'm asking you to cast aside any allegiances you hold dear, save for that of your daughter, Rosie."

Sinclair nodded and placed her hands palm down on the table, readying herself for betrayal.

"Alexandra, you were witness to Michael Levy's injuries," Freya said softly. "Do you honestly believe that Drew Barker is capable of causing them?"

"You don't have to answer that," Halifax said, but Alexandra silenced her with an irritated wave of her hand.

She was about to open her mouth when the door opened once more, and the tension Freya summoned slipped from the room like a wraith.

Ben took his seat and busied himself with writing in his notepad.

Freya met Alexandra's stare, hoping the disruption hadn't allowed her doubt to suffocate common sense.

"No," Sinclair said with certainty, shaking her head as if to add weight to her response. "No, Drew couldn't have done that."

Asking if she was sure would be a fruitless effort such was Alexandra's adamance, and Freya's disappointment was once more interrupted by Ben, who slid a folded note in front of her.

She opened the folded note and glanced down at Ben's scrawled handwriting, releasing any of that stubborn fog into the atmosphere.

She smiled a little, making little effort to conceal her glee, and found Alexandra's inquisitive stare where the doubt she had bred frolicked in her eyes.

"Thanks for your honesty," Freya said. "But I'm afraid it appears as if your judgement is misaligned."

"What does that mean?" Alexandra said, as Freya announced the end of the interview for the benefit of the recording and rose from her seat, collecting her notes as she stood. "What's happening?"

"It means that for the time being, Alexandra, you are free to go," Freya said. "But not by a long shot do I believe you wholly innocent, so use your time well. I suggest you find your daughter and give her a hug while you can, I should imagine she'll be needing her mother right about now and God only knows how long you'll be around for."

CHAPTER FORTY-ONE

The incident room doors burst open in silence, but in lieu of the squealing hinges that would normally announce Freya's arrival, she had to make do with momentum.

"Anna?" she said. "Is it true?"

"Perfect match," Nillson replied, looking up from where she and Anderson were huddled around a laptop.

"The soil on the spade you found in Barker's shed," Freya said, by way of affirmation. "It's the same as that found in the hole that was dug near the bridge, is it?"

"Not only is it the same," Nillson said. "But it's different to the soil found on the other side of the old watercourse. Something to do with the chemicals the farmer uses."

"And the soil in his garden?" Freya asked. "It's less than a mile away."

"Barker's garden doesn't have Sycamore trees," Nillson said. "The spot where the hole was dug is surrounded by them. The sample that the team pulled from the spade contained a number of Sycamore seed pods."

Freya looked around at the team. They were all there, except for Ben who was busy releasing Alexandra Sinclair.

"Okay. Let's talk about his MMO?" Freya said. "Michael Levy was strangled, so we can assume Barker had the means to do it. The man humps furniture around all day, so he's not exactly a ten-stone weakling."

"What about a motive?" Anderson asked. "Why would he kill Michael Levy?"

"I don't think he meant to kill him," Freya replied. "I think he just got carried away. He let his emotions get the better of his judgement. He and Alexandra were in a relationship, of which I'm not entirely sure how many people are aware."

"Ah, the old disgruntled lover," Gillespie added for effect, hoisting his feet onto the chair beside him. "Classic. The guy even reported Levy missing for crying out loud. He might as well have just handed himself in and saved us all a job."

Freya stared at him until he removed his feet.

"It might be a classic motive, Gillespie, but we still need to prove it," Freya said. "Chapman, talk to your man at the network provider. I want to know how long the conversation was when Alexandra Sinclair called Barker to ask him to pick her up. If it was a matter of seconds, then it's dead in the water. But if the call was thirty seconds or more..."

"Then what?" Nillson said, not following.

"Then she would have had enough time to tell him what she heard earlier that evening, before she left for work."

"Which was?"

"Levy assaulting Alexandra's daughter," Freya said, then turned to Chapman again. "I'm sorry, I know it's a sore topic."

A slight tweak of Chapman's brow was the only reaction she gave before dialling the number on her desk phone.

"What a bastard," Anderson said.

"Aye," Gillespie agreed.

"So Alexandra Sinclair called him to tell him about what she'd heard," Anderson said. "And you think he went looking for Levy on his way."

"That's right," Freya said. "That's the theory anyway. The timeline needs some more work, but with any luck, he'll be able to help us there."

"Timeline?" Cruz said.

"Opportunity," Freya said. "We know he left the hotel in the evening to go and collect Alexandra from work. It's what he did on his way there that I want to know."

"I don't get it," Nillson said. "Why do we think he attacked Levy before he picked Alexandra up?"

"Because of livor mortis," Freya explained, remembering what Pip had told her. "Levy was moved. He was found in the old Mercedes, but he wasn't killed there. I think he was killed on the bridge, given the amount of dried blood we found there."

"Livor mortis? That's blood pooling?" Anderson said.

"Correct. He died on his back. I think Barker attacked him on the way to collect Alexandra, which gives us the blood on the bridge. Then he took Alexandra home but waited outside, giving him a twenty-minute window to consider his actions."

"He could have slipped back to the body. It's only a short walk from there," Cruz said.

"Exactly," Freya agreed. "Michaela and her team discovered a patch of disturbed grass below the bridge, along with a Nike footprint. I think he went looking for Levy, realised he'd killed him and moved the body below the bridge out of sight."

"Sorry to burst your bubble, boss," Gillespie said. "But Drew Barker doesn't look like the type of man to wear Nikes. He's more of your Hush Puppy type of guy, or Clarks maybe?"

"That's a little presumptuous, Gillespie," Freya said. "But I take your point."

Chapman placed her handset down and finished making her notes. The move was entirely silent, but they all waited for her to speak.

"Forty-seven seconds," she said. "The call was made at eight fifty-five p.m. and lasted for forty-seven seconds."

"Thank you, Chapman," Freya said. "That's plenty of time for Alexandra to tell Barker about what she'd heard. Thanks to the CCTV footage Nillson and Anderson found at the hotel, we know Barker left the hotel at nine p.m., so we can assume he took five minutes to get dressed. Chapman, can you please call the social club where Alexandra Sinclair works? We need to know what time she left on Friday night."

"Should I ask them to check the CCTV?"

"No, that could take days," Freya said. "But they do use a swipe card system on the cash register. Alexandra forgot hers and went back to get it. There should be some kind of digital record stating the time of the last transaction her card made."

"Okay," Chapman said, making a note of the rather long-winded question.

"Ben thinks it's a fifteen-minute drive from Woodhall Spa to Horncastle. Which means that the last transaction should be at around nine-fifteen," Freya said. "Any longer than that and we'll need to know where he was. My guess is that he went into the White Horse looking for him."

"If only we knew somebody who worked at The White Horse," Cruz said, in a tone that didn't quite match the statement. Gillespie glared at him in response. "What? I'm just saying that it would be great if we had access to somebody who was actually there."

"Is there something I should know?" Freya said.

"No, boss," Gillespie said. "Cruz is just thinking out loud. Isn't that right, Gabby?"

For all of Cruz's flaws and weaknesses, he had demonstrated loyalty on more than one occasion. However, when his loyalty to Gillespie was pitched against the threat of Freya's glare, there could be only one winner.

"I said," Gillespie repeated, his eyes wide, beckoning him to agree with him. "Isn't that right, Gabby?"

The young DC looked at Freya, then to the big, brutish Scotsman.

"Sorry, Jim," he said, then turned back to Freya, who waited with every morsel of her patience under trial. "Jim shagged the barmaid, boss."

"Gabby—"

"You did *what?*" Nillson said, sitting upright from the casual slouch she adopted at every given opportunity.

"Alright, alright," Gillespie said, holding his hands up. "It was only once, and I'm a red-blooded male. You can't blame me for that."

"You..." Freya began, then sought a more delicate way of articulating what she was being told. "You entered into a sexual relationship with a witness?"

"Aye, well, I wouldn't say it's a relationship, boss," he replied. "It was just a one-night thing, you know?"

Freya stood aghast at what she was hearing.

"Is she the one with the dog?" Nillson asked, and everyone looked at her with the same confused expression. "You know? Labrador, bright yellow jacket."

"She is not blind," Gillespie said. "Besides, she doesn't have a dog."

"Will you be seeing her again?" Freya asked.

"There's a reason Jim only does one-night stands, boss," Nillson said.

"Hey," he said defensively, then turned to Freya, straightening his collar. "No boss, I doubt it."

"You doubt it?"

"Aye," he said, his face reddening.

Freya stepped over to him and held out her hand.

"Phone," she said.

"Oh, come on."

"Phone."

He sighed and fished his phone from his pocket.

"Unlock it," she said.

"Boss, look—"

"I said, unlock the phone."

His head fell back as if deliberating on whether or not he should comply, but then he relented and tapped in his passcode before handing her the phone.

"Name?"

"Eh?" he said.

"What is her name?" Freya said, which raised a smirk on Cruz's face so apparent she saw it from the corner of her eye.

"Is something funny, Cruz?" Freya said. "Or do you need to use the washroom?"

"He doesn't know her name, boss," he replied, grinning from ear to ear.

She stared down at Gillespie with a look of utter contempt on her face.

"You don't remember her name, or you never knew her name in the first place?"

"She doesn't know my name either," he said. "It's not like we're getting bloody married."

"Well, that's something," Freya said. "At least when her statement is read out in court she won't be able to point the finger at you."

She navigated to the last calls Gillespie had made, finding a random name among the list of their colleagues.

"Who is XXXX?" she said.

"Aye, that's her."

"XXXX," Freya said. "Four exes."

"Aye," he said again, the words riding a long exhale.

"Why four and not three or two, or one, even?"

He stared up at her, his expression one of unbridled guilt, but he said nothing.

She stared down at the phone and navigated to his list of contacts, then searched in the exes.

"One ex, two exes, three exes, four exes—"

"Aye, that's her," he said, leaning on the desk and covering his face with his giant hands. "She's four exes."

"Who are one ex, two exes, and three exes?" Freya said. "Or shouldn't I ask?"

"I don't actually know," he replied.

"Is this some kind of rating?" she asked. "What does it mean? Is it based on looks or…"

She stopped herself from finishing the sentence, as his expression gave enough of an explanation.

"Performance?" Nillson said. "You name the women you meet according to their performance?"

"Aye well, what am I supposed to put them under?"

"You, Sergeant Gillespie," Freya said, "are a sick, sick man."

"Aye, well. She didn't know my name either. It works both ways, you know?"

"Call her," Freya said, handing him back the phone.

"Eh?"

"Call her."

"And say what, exactly?" he said, his voice rising to the pitch of a prepubescent boy.

"Tell her you want to see her again," Nillson added, who, along with Anderson and Gold, was clearly enjoying his embarrassment.

"Not likely," he replied. "Not after—"

"Nine twenty-nine," Chapman said, placing her handset down again and finishing her notes. "The last transaction made using Alexandra's swipe card."

"Thirty minutes," Freya said. "Thank you, Chapman."

"Aye, thanks, Chapman," Gillespie said.

"I haven't finished with you, Gillespie. After what?" Freya said, to which he sighed again.

"Not after what we did, boss," he said. "Should I go into the graphic details?"

"No," she said. "But call her. I want to know if she saw Drew

Barker in the pub around that time. It would have been shortly after she saw the argument between Levy and Jerry Graham."

"Ah, come on. I can't—"

"Can't what, Gillespie?" she said. "Abuse your position?"

She held his stare until he backed down, muttering something under his breath.

"I suggest you find somewhere private to call four exes, and I suggest you do it with some urgency. Unless, of course, you want to be put up on a charge?"

"Aye, boss," he said, offering Cruz one more of his glares as he shoved himself out of his seat.

Freya then readdressed the rest of the team.

"If we can place Barker in the pub looking for Levy sometime between nine and nine-thirty, then we're well placed to pursue a murder charge. His lawyer isn't stupid, so we can expect him to claim manslaughter but that's by the by."

"So how did it get to the car?" Anderson asked. "The body, I mean. If he killed him on the bridge, then went back to move him underneath it, how did the body end up in the car?"

"He went back a third time," Gold said, catching them all off guard. "In the morning. He had to have done."

It took a few moments for Freya to read the room, gauging the expressions and individual silences, and combining them to conclude there was a shared snippet of information.

"Okay," she said to Gold. "What makes you say that?"

Gold looked down at her feet, then her hands, and then finally, she stared Freya in the eye.

"Because Alexandra forgot something," she said. "Her medication. Sertraline, I think. She didn't take it on Friday. It was still in the packet. But Saturday's was gone, as was Sunday's. I don't know why I didn't think of it before. But it makes sense now. I found the tablets on the microwave."

"What's Sertraline?" Cruz asked. "Some kind of female hormone thing?"

"No, Gabby, it's an anti-depressant," Nillson said. "Why would Alexandra have hormone tablets?"

"I don't know. I was just asking," he said. "I still don't see what difference it makes if she missed a day. She could have just taken two the next day."

"If you had ever known anybody on antidepressants," Freya said. "You'd understand how big a deal missing a day is. The question is, why didn't she mention it during her interview?"

"Do you think she knows what Barker did, boss?" Cruz asked.

"I'm not altogether sure," she replied, then turned to Nillson. "Where is Barker?"

"Interview room two, boss."

"Good. Get your files together," she said. "You're going to charge Drew Barker. If Alexandra Sinclair had anything to do with the murder, then we're about to find out exactly what it was."

CHAPTER FORTY-TWO

The solicitor's face was porcelain. Not a single wrinkle could be found, not even beside his eyes, which to Freya, suggested he rarely found reason to laugh. But the lack of emotion all suggested he had very few reasons to wince, squint, or even cry. A man, she supposed, who was used to getting his own way.

The silence in the room was one of warfare, each party holding out for the other to initiate some kind of dialogue, thus showing the first of their cards. But in the end, it was a knock at the door that provided the ceasefire, followed shortly after by Gillespie, clearly hoping to make amends for his unprofessional sexual encounter.

"Boss?" he said, and Freya waited for him to speak, retaining an impartial expression. He nodded once, then flicked his eyes across to Barker and back again.

She followed him outside, closing the door behind her.

"Go on," she said.

"I spoke to her," he replied, looking as sheepish as ever. "Barker was in the pub at around nine-fifteen. He spoke to Jerry Graham, then left."

"Did she see which direction he went when he left?"

"No, boss," he replied. "But she mentioned somebody else. A bloke."

"In The White Horse?"

"Yes," he said. "He came in when Barker had left and asked after Levy."

"Another man? Do we have a description?"

He shook his head.

"Apparently she's given me all I'm getting. She hung up."

"I won't ask if there's a double entendre in that statement somewhere," Freya replied.

"I did what you asked, boss," he said. "I'm surprised she even picked up the phone if I'm honest."

"Well, she clearly thinks more of you than I do at this moment in time," Freya told him. "Thank you, Gillespie."

It was an invitation for him to leave, which he did with good grace. If Freya knew him as well as she thought she did, he would stew in his own stupidity for a while, at least until she emerged from the interview when she could thank him and give him the reassurance he needed. After all, when they had enemies like Standing watching over them, she would need every ally she could claim.

She re-entered the room, offering no apology for the delay.

Nillson initiated the recording, stating the date, time, and those present, referencing the previous interview where necessary and announcing the addition of Freya's presence.

"Mr Barker, I understand from my colleague you are maintaining your innocence with regards to the death of one Michael Levy. Is that correct?"

A quick nod from the solicitor gave Barker the confidence to enter into the conversation, although Freya guessed he would soon wish he had maintained a boring yet effective position of no comment.

"That's correct," he said, folding his arms and leaning back in his chair as a teenager might. The pose would have been suited to a schoolboy, or even a thug, but for a man who clearly valued speaking correctly, and who took care in his appearance, the posture served only to draw attention to guilt of some kind.

"Then it falls to me to inform you that we will be charging you with the murder of Michael Levy," Freya said.

"Excuse me?" the solicitor said, peering down the length of his nose at her, yet somehow maintaining that flawless complexion. "Have I missed you providing a piece of evidence?"

"No, Mr Baxter, you have not. But it does appear that your client has failed to provide us with an accurate description of his whereabouts. When you combine that with the fact that his DNA was found on Michael Levy's body, the fact that your client was in a relationship with Michael Levy's long-time partner, and the fact that the soil sample taken from a freshly-dug grave, just yards from where Michael Levy was killed, was also found on a spade in his shed, we begin to build a picture that, anybody can see, is far from ordinary. One which can only be truly understood in a court of law where the timeline may be interrogated."

"Soil sample?" Baxter said. "DNA? Why hasn't this evidence been submitted?"

Freya glanced once at Nillson, who then slid a folder across the desk.

"It's a live investigation, Mr Baxter. Evidence is still being uncovered."

He opened the folder, gave the CSI reports a cursory glance, then closed it again without so much as a ripple of surprise or emotion cracking that porcelain skin of his.

"I would imagine that before you formally charge my client, you would be decent enough to provide some kind of narrative. A theory, as it were."

"If you wish," Freya said.

"I do," he replied. "My client deserves every opportunity to provide some kind of answer to these findings."

He looked to Barker, who failed to meet him eye to eye,

instead choosing to rub the small cut on his right knuckle. He caught Freya watching him then tucked his hands below the desk.

"I suggest your client buckles up," Freya said. "Because what we have, and I'm sure you will agree, is infallible evidence that Mr Barker was involved in the death of Michael Levy."

"If we're seeking fair opportunities," Nillson said, cutting in. "Then perhaps you'd like to say a few words before we begin, Mr Barker?"

It was a demonstration of competence, experience, and, in the eyes of a jury who would no doubt hear the recording at some stage, fairness.

He shook his head, still refusing to look at his solicitor.

"Then I shall begin," Freya said. "It is my belief, Mr Barker, based on the evidence provided to me by the Lincolnshire Crime Scene Investigation team and Forensic Pathologist Doctor Pippa Bell, along with your own account of your movements and those of Alexandra Sinclair, that you were responsible for the death of Michael Levy," Freya began. "According to your previous statement, you were at the Petwood Hotel on Friday night. That much I believe is true. As is the call from Alexandra Sinclair asking you to help her. Of course, you'd do anything for her, wouldn't you? You'd do anything for your dear Alexandra."

"What's that supposed to mean?" he said.

"It means that we now understand that you are in a relationship with Alexandra," she replied. "Or rather, you would like to be in one."

"That doesn't mean anything. It certainly doesn't mean I would kill Michael."

"No, you're right," she said. "But it does give us an idea where your allegiances lie. What did she say exactly, when she called on Friday night at eight fifty-five p.m.?"

"What did she say?"

"Yes, not word for word," Freya said. "The gist will suffice."

"That she needed help."

"With?"

He paused for breath and thought, and his nostrils flared.

"She was upset," he said finally. "She asked me to come and pick her up."

"Did she say what she was upset about?"

"No," he replied.

"The call was forty-seven seconds long, Mr Barker," Freya told him. "Surely her state of mind could have been conveyed in far less time?"

"Forty-seven seconds?"

"According to the network provider," she said, then spoke to Baxter. "We will, of course, have that information formally presented."

"Naturally," he said, sounding less than enthused at the idea.

"She said she had heard something," Barker said. "Something bad. Awful, in fact."

"I can assure you that nothing you tell us will come as a shock, Mr Barker."

"You know," he said. "You know, don't you?"

"I would like to hear it from your own mouth," she told him.

"About him? About Levy and…" He turned away as if the idea of verbalising it had left a bad taste in his mouth. "She told me she had forgotten something, a card or something for work. She popped back home to get it and heard something. Them. Him and her. He was…"

"Go on, Mr Barker," Freya said, and he seemed to summon the strength to spit it out in one phlegmy gasp.

"He was raping her."

"For clarity, you're referring to Michael Levy and Rosie?"

"Of course I am. He was assaulting her."

"You can prove that, can you?"

"Prove it? Bloody well prove it? She's fifteen years old–"

"And Alexandra heard them having sex."

"I don't believe what I'm hearing. Of course he was raping her.

She wouldn't have anything to do with him. Wouldn't even give him the time of day, so I doubt very much if she'd..." He stopped himself. "Alexandra knows what she heard and that's what she told me on the phone. Does that fill your forty-seven seconds, Inspector?"

"I would imagine so," she replied. "Which takes us to eight fifty-six p.m."

"For God's sake. What do you want from me? A minute-by-minute account?"

"Ah, I'm glad you're finally beginning to understand."

"I got dressed," he said. "I was ready for bed. I'd been gearing up for my tee-off in the morning and was hoping for an early night."

"But you didn't get one," Freya said.

"No. No, I didn't get an early night because Alex needed me."

"Needed you in particular? Or would anybody have sufficed?"

"She needed me. I know her. I know her history. I know their history. And I know what he's like."

"When you mentioned Alexandra's history, were you referring to the assault she suffered some years ago?"

He stared at her, then at Nillson, and relented with a deep intake of breath.

"Listen, Alexandra has been through a lot. Hearing your daughter being..." He paused again. "It brought back memories. Painful memories."

"Memories that she's shared with you?" Freya asked.

"Yes. Memories that are not within the remit of this interview, and are certainly not my burden to disclose to you or anybody."

"That's fine," Freya said calmly. "You got dressed. Eight fifty-eight?"

"You really are a piece of work—"

"I'm investigating the death of a man you reported missing, Mr Barker. Details matter."

"I left the hotel as soon as I was dressed. Something was on the telly. I can't remember what it was as I wasn't really paying attention, but it was ending, so I imagine it was approximately eight fifty-nine."

"And where did you go from there?"

"Eh? Where do you think I went? I went to get Alex."

"Directly?" Freya said, adopting an expression that she hoped conveyed a little confusion, enough at least to sow a seed of doubt in Barker's mind.

"Yes," he said, but with far less conviction than before.

"So you left the hotel at nine p.m., give or take a minute or two, and you went straight to the social club where Alexandra Sinclair works?"

"That's correct," he said.

Freya leaned in a little closer.

"You didn't happen to stop anywhere on your way?"

He said nothing. Not at first anyway. He feigned recalling some detail by glancing up and to the left.

"Actually, I did swing by The White Horse," he said.

"Ah," Freya said. "The White Horse pub in Horncastle?"

"Is there another?"

"There are probably several hundred across the country."

"The one in Horncastle," he said.

"The one where Michael Levy drank every Friday night?"

"Yes, the same one. It's not a crime, you know?"

"No. No, it isn't, is it? At least, if you were to pop in for a quick pint, that is. However, given the urgency of the situation, Mr Barker, I can't for the life of me think of any reason why you might decide to delay collecting Alexandra from work where, as you stated earlier, she was in some distress," Freya said, then let her expression harden. "Except one."

The four of them sat in silence for what seemed like an age. The only sounds were the hum of ambient noise from elsewhere in the building and the wet noises Barker's throat made as he swallowed.

"I went looking for Michael," he said with evident reluctance. "But he wasn't there. Honestly, I didn't see him or speak to him."

"So who did you speak to?"

"Who did I speak to?" he repeated, a classic tactic to buy himself time to think.

"Are you finding the line of questioning difficult?" Freya asked. "I can arrange for an appropriate adult to be present if you suffer from learning difficulties."

It was the first time the solicitor's porcelain cracked. His eyebrows raised in surprise, furrowing his brow, and his mouth hung open as if he was about to voice an argument. But Barker beat him to it.

"I understand just fine," he said. "Jerry. I spoke to Jerry Graham."

"Do you want to provide a brief explanation of how that conversation went? Or would you prefer to let me hazard a guess?"

"I asked him if Michael had been in, that's all."

"And he said?"

"He told me he had been in, and that he'd left shortly before I arrived."

"And would Michael have driven home from The White Horse, or–"

"Okay, he walked. He always walked on a Friday night."

"He didn't take the car Jerry Graham, had given him as part payment for the money's owed?"

For the first time in a while, Freya sensed Barker's expression was genuine. He cocked his head to one side, looking as if he was working on a maths problem.

"The what?"

"The car, Mr Barker," Freya said, and she let a smile run free. "Oh, you didn't know about the car?"

"Sorry, what car?"

"The Mercedes," Freya said. "The classic car that was in The White Horse car park. It's quite unmistakable."

"No. No, Jerry wouldn't give his car away, especially not to Mike," he said, but doubt still clung to his tone. "Would he?"

"According to the DVLA, the vehicle was exchanged on Thursday evening. From what I can tell, Jerry handed it over on Friday night."

It was as if Freya had told him somebody close had died. He shook his head repeatedly, in denial of the facts, which only served to feed the confidence Freya had in her theory.

"But…" he began, then paused. "Are we talking about the same car? The Mercedes SL?"

"Is something wrong, Mr Barker?" she said, watching as his face turned red like one of those nature documentaries showing blooming flowers in double time.

"No," he said quietly. "No, there's nothing I want to say."

CHAPTER FORTY-THREE

"So here we are, Mr Barker," Freya said. "We have you arriving at the Petwood Hotel, we have you receiving a call from Alexandra Sinclair, and we have you leaving at, let's say nine-ish, shall we? We can then place you at The White Horse asking after Michael Levy before you went to collect Alexandra from work. What we don't have are details of where you went before you collected her."

"I didn't go anywhere," he replied, and for a moment Freya saw a young, scared boy in his expression. "Honest. I went from the pub to the social club to collect her."

"And from there?"

"Straight back to her place," he said. "That's how it went. I pulled up at the club, popped my head inside, and caught her attention. You know? Just to let her know I was waiting."

"But you didn't go inside?"

He shook his head.

"Not my scene," he replied.

"And The White Horse is?"

The shrug he gave provided very little explanation, but momentum was waning, so Freya pressed on.

"Did she leave immediately?" she asked.

"Pretty much. She was serving somebody. I guess she finished serving them and then came out."

"Then what?" Freya said, not letting him take a breath.

"Then we went back to her place."

"Talk me through it."

"What?"

"Did you go inside? How long did she take? Did she pack a bag? Was she upset?"

"No," he said. "No, I didn't go in. I waited outside. I suppose she was about fifteen or twenty minutes. Her hair was wet, so I suppose she must have showered, and yes, she had a bag. Just a little weekend bag."

"And what did you do while you were waiting?" Freya asked. "Did you have the radio on? If so, what was playing?"

"No," he said, almost immediately. "No radio. I just sat there."

"You see, Mr Barker, what I'm struggling to understand is how your DNA came to end up on Michael Levy's tooth of all places."

She flicked her eyes down to the graze on his hand, and again, he hid his hands away. He said nothing, so Freya turned her attention to Baxter, who had been busy making notes, looking up every so often but offering no clue as to his thoughts.

"Would you agree, Mr Baxter, that we have a method, the means, and the opportunity?" she said. "Enough to proceed with a charge."

He replaced the lid on his expensive-looking Montegrappa and set his notes face-down. Then, slowly, he removed his glasses, all the while clearly in deep thought.

"I would agree," he said. "There's certainly enough there to proceed with a charge, and I'm sure the CPS will have no problem in proceeding."

Even Nillson sensed the result had been too easy, and Freya felt the young sergeant's eyes on her, waiting for her to respond.

"However!" Freya said, to which Baxter pulled an expression much like a manager might when an individual requests a pay rise, almost as if he was loathed to articulate the inevitable disappointment.

"However," he said, and then paused to wipe his glasses with a small, paisley cloth, "there are just too many unanswered questions. Enough, I'm sure you'll agree, to cast doubt in the minds of a jury."

"Such as?" Freya said, with an idea of what he was alluding to.

"When was my client supposed to have dug the hole you spoke of? The soil sample is of course a key piece of your evidence. And when you say Mr Barker had an opportunity to murder Michael Levy, when exactly was he supposed to have done that?"

"It's a five-minute walk from Alexandra Sinclair's house to the bridge where Michael Levy is believed to have been killed," Freya said, turning to Barker. "You said Alexandra was gone for fifteen to twenty minutes. You knew Levy would be walking back through the nature reserve because you'd been into The White Horse and you had spoken to Jerry Graham."

"And the hole?" Baxter said. "Are we to believe that my client just happened to have a spade in his car, too?"

"Oh, no," Freya said, feeling her forehead crease with the smile that was emerging. "This is the part that perplexed me. But I think I have it now. You see, men like your client, Mr Baxter, are not natural-born killers. Look at him. He's weak. He's a pushover, feeble. It takes a great deal for men like your client to lose their temper, but when they do, boy-oh-boy. When they finally explode, there's very little that can stop them."

"What are you saying?" Baxter said.

"I'm saying that Mr Barker has inhibited his love for Alexandra Sinclair for years, watching from the sidelines as Michael Levy took her for granted, neglected her, even abused her, from the accounts I've read. You can see how that temper might have been brewing for all that time. But what people often fail to understand is the guilt."

"The guilt?" Barker said.

"Yes, the guilt. The sleepless nights. The lying awake in a cold sweat while visions of the dam that had restrained the temper for so long finally burst open. Visions of spending the next twenty years in a prison cell surrounded by real men, hard men, violent men," Freya said. "Let me tell you what those sleepless nights can do to a person. They can make you do things you only read about in the paper. Things that seem so far from ordinary life that they must be fiction."

"You're suggesting that whilst my client waited for Miss Sinclair to emerge from her house, he went into the nature reserve, killed Michael Levy, then returned to his car, where he was so racked with guilt that he..."

"Go on," Freya said.

"Well, that's just it. I simply can't imagine what he might have done next."

"Isn't it obvious?" she said, watching as Barker found solace in his hands below the desk. "He told Alexandra what he had done."

Barker's head shot up, his eyes wide and mouth ajar but saying nothing, waiting for Freya to continue.

"He had to tell somebody," she said. "That's what guilt does. That's what men like your client do, Mr Baxter. They have to tell somebody. Only, the person he told, Alexandra Sinclair, isn't as weak as he. She's suffered enough for two lifetimes. We're talking about a woman who heard her own daughter being raped and walked away. She didn't walk away because of the memories it had invoked. She didn't walk away because she couldn't bear to hear it. Of course not. What mother could do that? Any normal mother would have torn him limb from limb. But not Alexandra Sinclair. Oh no. Alexandra retained enough of her senses to make a plan. A plan in which she would need somebody else's help. Somebody who cared for her. Somebody she had strung along all those years like a lovesick puppy."

Barker closed his eyes. A tear broke free of his heavy eyelids and began its descent down his face, which tensed as he bit down hard, clamping his mouth closed to the emotion inside.

"And what was this plan?" Baxter asked.

"The plan?" Freya said. "Simply to have your client do her dirty work, then help dispose of the body. The original plan was, of course, to bury the body, and we all know how the soil from the hole matches that found on the spade. They dug the hole, but meanwhile, I think an idea struck your client that would remove them both from the investigation."

"An idea?" Baxter said, in a mocking tone, to which Freya responded with a confidence to counter any attempt to undermine the narrative she had formed.

"When Mr Barker entered The White Horse on his way to collect Alexandra Sinclair, who did he speak to?"

It was odd to see a man's brow lower in a frown without a sign of a forehead crease, but Baxter managed it somehow and glanced down at his notes briefly.

"Jerry Graham," he said.

"And who was Michael Levy seen arguing with before he left the pub?"

Baxter gave a moment of silence, his eyes never wavering from Freya's.

"Mr Graham," he said finally.

"And who was it who, for over a year now, has owed Michael Levy in excess of twenty thousand pounds?"

Baxter said nothing, letting his glare do the speaking on his behalf.

"Graham owes Levy a large sum of money. Graham is seen arguing with Levy. Levy is found dead in the boot of Graham's car," Freya said. "Quite simple really."

"Ah," Baxter said, flicking back through his notes. "But my client was yet to learn of the car changing hands until the beginning of this interview."

"Precisely. As far as Mr Barker here was concerned, the car

still belonged to Jerry Graham. Where better to hide a body than in the boot of the car belonging to the man you're framing?" Freya said. "I think you'll find that covers the outstanding questions. And if I'm correct, you'll have a hard time proving your client innocent."

"Thankfully it's not for me to prove Mr Barker's innocence," Baxter said. "It is for the prosecution to prove his guilt."

"I did it," Barker said, speaking up for the first time in a while. The arteries in his eyes stood out like beacons and the vein in his temple throbbed with his racing pulse. He lowered his voice as if his initial announcement had been out of turn. "It was me. I did it."

Freya glanced once at the recording to ensure it was still operating, then at Nillson, who appeared as if a great weight had been lifted from her shoulders.

"Would you care to explain?" Freya said.

For the first time, Drew Barker sat with his head held high.

"I did it," he replied. "You're right. I stopped him from getting through the nature reserve. I returned in the morning to put the body in the car. And I even used his keys to access the workshop."

"The workshop?" Freya said.

"Did you search the place yourself?" he asked, with no sign of guilt or shame on his face.

"I did," Nillson said. "It was me and another colleague."

"And how quickly did you find the financial statements?" Barker asked.

Freya watched as Nillson recalled the search, and she saw the change in her expression when his statement resonated.

"It was Anderson," Nillson explained. "She searched the office. She found them in moments, as it happens."

Barker wore an expression that said, in no uncertain terms, that he told them so.

"It was important that you lot were diverted toward Jerry," he said, then stared at Freya. "If I plead guilty now, will the judge go easy on me?"

"You shouldn't concern yourself with the judge," Freya replied. "If I were you, I'd be concerned with those visions that kept you awake on Friday night."

"Which ones?" he asked.

She collected her folder as she stood and leaned across the table until she was face to face with Barker.

"All of them. Especially the violence," she said, then turned to Nillson, ignoring Baxter completely. "Charge him."

"Should I arrange transport?" Nillson asked, as if they were discussing the weather and not the next twenty years of a man's life. "I can have him put on remand tonight."

Freya opened the door and gave Barker a final look, studying him from his shoes to his hair. He was no villain. He was a mere man in love. A man who would do anything for the girl of his dreams.

"No, talk to Sergeant Priest to see if we can hold him here until the morning," she said, then turned to Barker. "If I were you, I'd savour the peace and quiet, Mr Barker."

She tore herself away before the solicitor could interject.

"One more thing," Barker said, and something in his tone stopped Freya in her tracks. She closed the door but held fast to the handle. "You were wrong about Alexandra. She knows nothing about it. Any of it."

"Oh, I doubt that very much," Freya said. "There's nothing more pitiful than seeing a man in love."

CHAPTER FORTY-FOUR

The sun shone through the large incident room windows, which covered nearly the entire length and breadth of the room, casting three long shadows across the carpeted floor. The first of them was from Freya's whiteboard, appearing as an elongated, oblong structure on two rigid legs. The second was from the potted plant Chapman had been nurturing for a few months in an effort to brighten up the view from her desk. It was some kind of miniature fern, yet the giant shadows were reminiscent of the tropics Ben had seen in old schoolbooks about dinosaurs and their jungle-like surroundings.

The third shadow, however, was of a beast far greater and more brooding than any illustrated Tyrannosaurus Rex Ben had spent his free time poring over.

Standing with his back to the team, peering out over the village rooftops, Gillespie leaned on a mullion, his head resting against the cold, aluminium frame. His hair, which had always been on the wrong side of what the top brass deemed an appropriate length, hung freely, as did the tails of his untucked shirt. When those shadows combined, a form was created akin to that of a cannibalistic island native peering through the tropical brush.

"You know what they say, Jim," Ben said, and the large Scotsman slowly peered back at him over his shoulder.

"No, Ben," he replied. "No, if I knew what they said, maybe I wouldn't be where I am."

"A problem shared is a problem solved," Ben said. "What's happening?"

Gold, who had been watching with interest, lowered her head. But Anderson, who had shown little interest until now, was keen to hear what Gillespie had to say.

But he turned away again, silently refusing to open up, despite being visibly troubled by something.

"It's no bother, Ben," he said, which was odd, as Gillespie wasn't usually shy of speaking his mind.

"It's Freya, isn't it?" Ben said, guessing that the reason for his silence was more to do with Ben's closeness to Freya. "What has she said?"

"Ah, what hasn't she said?" he replied in that heavy Glaswegian accent of his that seemed to marry the syllables into a single word. "I can't do anything right, Ben."

"You slept with a witness, Jim," Nillson said, speaking up for the first time. "What did you want from her? A pat on the back?"

"Well, aye, I might slip up from time to time–"

"And you bribed the search team with a bacon sandwich," Cruz added, to which Gillespie glared at him, but said nothing.

"I'm not talking about the things I've done wrong," he said. "I'm talking about the things I've done right. It doesn't matter what I do, I just never seem to get the recognition. Do you know what I mean? Until now I've been in two minds as to whether or not I should go to this new team. But when all I get from her is negativity, I feel like I'm being pushed away."

"You're seriously considering the move then?" Ben asked.

"What would you do if you were me?" he said. "You've met this DI Larson bloke. What's he like?"

"A stickler for detail," Ben replied. "He doesn't suffer fools and he's a bloody good detective. Other than that, I couldn't tell you. We didn't exactly go out for drinks."

"Aye, well, I might stand a better chance of promotion if I move. It might do me good to start afresh. God knows I've been here long enough. Roots are coming out of my feet. If I leave it too long I'll be stuck here, institutionalised, as it were. Besides, a new team might take me seriously."

"I wouldn't say that, Jim," Gold said. "Chapman and I will be on the team as well, remember?"

"Ah, I'm doomed then, am I?"

"No, not at all," she said, and there was a companionship between them, evident in the faint and soft Edinburgh accent she still carried. "I wouldn't want you to change."

"I agree," Chapman said. "This place wouldn't be the same without you."

"Or any of you," a voice said, and Ben turned to find Freya bustling through the silent doors, carrying a stack of folders which she promptly dropped onto her desk. Ben watched as Gillespie turned back to the window, and then, one by one, the rest of the team lowered their heads to their work. Freya turned to sit on the edge of her desk as she so often did. "Now then, has Nillson given everyone the good news?"

All eyes fell on Anna, who remained stoic, revealing nothing.

"Has Standing been killed?" Anderson asked playfully. "Was it slow and painful?"

"We can dream," Freya replied. "No, the good news is that we have charged Drew Barker with the murder of Michael Levy. He's in a cell downstairs as we speak, and I must give a big thank you to Gillespie."

The comment roused the big man from his brooding silence.

"To me?" he said.

"Yes, to you," she replied. "Your little endeavour gave us exactly what we needed to put Barker where we needed him. Clearly, I don't encourage what you did, but you're not the first to form some kind of relationship with somebody you shouldn't. The fact remains that your input put us over the line with Barker."

"Aye, well," he said, shoving himself off the window frame and straightening his shirt. "All in a day's work and all that."

"Well, let's hope that day's work doesn't come back to bite you in the backside," she told him. "For the time being, we've got our man. All we need is to wrap it up."

"We're done?" Cruz said. "Case closed?"

"Not quite," she said. "We have some loose ends that we'll need to close off before we submit to CPS. Right now there are too many questions to be sure of a conviction. His lawyer is quite sharp, and I wouldn't be surprised if he found some kind of technicality."

"Such as?" Ben asked, to which Freya gave him a long, hard stare in response.

"Okay," she said finally. "I'll answer that by giving the order of events as I see it. Alexandra Sinclair goes to work at a social club in Horncastle on Friday night, leaving her partner, Michael Levy, and her daughter, Rosie Sinclair, at home. Levy begins his assault on Rosie, which, as I understand it, is a regular occurrence. However, Alexandra realises she forgot her card for the cash register and returns home where she hears what's happening upstairs."

"That's awful," Chapman said, shaking her head.

"It is," Freya agreed. "Many others would have intervened, but we know from Gold's reports that Alexandra is herself a victim of rape, and we have an idea that Rosie is, in fact, the result of that rape. So she reacts differently to how most women would. She doesn't intervene. She leaves the house, probably recalling her own assault. But it's not long before the weight of what she had heard gets to her. She makes a plan and calls the only friend she can trust."

"Drew Barker?" Ben said, to which Freya nodded.

"According to Jerry Graham, they were in a relationship years ago, and it seems that Barker never truly got over her."

"You think she used him?" Gillespie said.

"Possibly. That's a detail we'll need to establish as we go. But what I'm quite sure of is that she called Barker, told him what she had heard, and asked him to pick her up from work. The information Nillson and Anderson received from the hotel confirms that he left the hotel at around nine p.m. Yet he didn't arrive at the social club until nine-thirty."

"That's a fifteen-minute drive," Ben said. "Ten if you're in a hurry."

"Or angry," Cruz added.

"Exactly," Freya continued. "Which is where Gillespie's special witness comes in. She confirmed that Barker went into the pub looking for Levy shortly after he'd left. Jerry Graham told him he'd gone, and it seems that everyone and their dog knows that Levy walks home through the nature reserve on a Friday night."

"You think he attacked him before he picked Alexandra up?" Gillespie asked.

"No, the timeline doesn't work," she replied. "I think he collected Alexandra, took her back to her house so she could grab a few things and check on Rosie."

"And Barker waited outside," Ben said, nodding as the picture became clear in his mind. "That's when he did it. He could have entered the nature reserve from Alexandra's road and met Levy as he stumbled through."

"That's the idea," Freya said. "First of all, the attack was brutal, so we'll need the clothes he was wearing. Nillson, Anderson, check the hotel bins and his home. Talk to Sergeant Priest to get some uniformed officers if you need to."

"Got it," Nillson said, and she nodded at Anderson to make a note.

"So how did he get the body in the car?" Cruz asked. "I mean, that's a long way to drag a dead body. And what about the spade?"

"He had help," Freya said. "If you had just murdered somebody, Cruz, could you sleep at night?"

"No way," he said. "I'd be bloody terrified."

"Terrified of what?"

"Prison?" he said. "I mean, Levy sounds like a bastard, so my conscience would be clear, but I'd be wondering how on earth I could get away with it."

"And would you tell Hermione?" Freya asked.

He gave the question some thought for a moment.

"I wouldn't need to," he said. "She'd know something was wrong even if she hadn't noticed the blood all over my clothes."

"So the two of them lay in the hotel on Friday night planning what to do with the body," Freya said. "And they come up with a plan to bury him in the forest beside the bridge."

"They left the hotel in the morning," Anderson said. "Are we saying they went back to Barker's house to get a spade and then dug the hole?"

"That's exactly what we're saying," Freya said. "But while they were digging, Barker had an idea. Jerry Graham's car was outside the pub. The man who was responsible for Barker's lack of wages and the man who Barker knew had argued with Levy moments before he had left the pub. At that time, Barker wasn't to know that the car had been transferred. So, together with Alexandra, he hid the body in the car, returned to the hotel, and they went about life as normally as they could."

"Come Monday morning, he reports his colleague missing in an effort to throw us off the scent," Ben said.

"But we've released Alexandra Sinclair," Gold said. "Surely she's as guilty as Barker is?"

"Oh, she's guilty alright," Freya said.

"So why have we let her go?" Gold asked.

"Because I believe Alexandra Sinclair planned this all along, and I believe she has a part to play in helping us prove it."

"I don't understand," Gold said, to which Freya smiled warmly at her.

"When Alexandra heard her daughter being assaulted by Levy, you could almost forgive her for not intervening given that she had suffered a similar assault years before. But to pack a bag and go to a hotel for the weekend leaving her daughter with a rapist? I don't know about you, but no mother could do that."

"Unless she knew he wasn't coming home?" Chapman said, and a wry smile formed on her face.

Freya pointed at her.

"Bingo," she said. "Everything else in this investigation is fact-based. It's objective. But this? This is subjective. It's emotional. It's a question that the mothers on a jury will be asking, and therefore, we need to answer it."

"So should we bring her back in?" Ben asked slowly, as he tried to read Freya's expression.

"Not yet," she replied. "There are more questions. Who was the individual the barmaid saw when she was locking the pub up for the night?"

"Hey listen, I can't call her again–"

"I'm not asking you to," Freya said. "She's done enough for the time being. I don't want to exhaust that witness – and no, that is not a double entendre. But we do need to find out who it was. There's a chance it could have been Sinclair or Barker, but something tells me otherwise."

"Something?" Ben said. "Such as?"

Freya shoved herself off the desk and walked over to the window where she stared at the rooftops, just as Gillespie had.

"If you were the defence council faced with the evidence we have, what would you do, Ben?" she asked. "You can't prove that your client is innocent. So what do you do?"

Ben felt the team stare at him, but he shoved the attention to one side for a moment to think.

"I'd be looking for another potential suspect," he said. "Somebody we haven't considered."

"Somebody like who?" she said, still with her back to the team.

"Somebody who had a reason to hurt Levy," he said. "Somebody like Rosie Sinclair."

"And if the recordings from the interviews state that Rosie, a relatively weak young girl, had friends who would do anything for her?"

"I'd be looking for a reasonable doubt claim," Ben said. "Sure, there's enough there to put Barker away and probably Alexandra Sinclair, too. But there are also three young lads who could have done it as payback for what Levy had done to their friend."

"Which gives us reasonable doubt," Freya said, turning to face them all. "That's what we're up against here. It's too convoluted. Levy's body was moved at least twice. He was dragged beneath the bridge, then he was moved to the car, and Barker didn't do that alone."

"So what do we do?" Cruz asked. "Should we bring the three boys in?"

Freya bit her lower lip as she thought. But her focus was interrupted by the doors opening, and even without turning to see who it was, Ben knew it was Standing by the hatred that spilled from Freya's glare.

"No," she said. "Let's start with Rosie. After all, she's at the centre of all this."

"Priest tells me you've charged Barker," Standing said, his dulcet tones seeming almost songlike in contrast with Freya's articulate yet flat southern accent.

"That is correct, guv," she said. "We're just tying up a few loose ends."

"No need," Standing replied. "We've got Barker, that's enough."

"Guv?"

"That's an order, Freya," Standing said. "I'm not wasting any more resources on this. Besides, that girl has been through enough, don't you think?"

"It's not my job to pity victims, guv," she said. "Regardless of the crimes against them."

"No, it's your job to do what I say," he said. "Now, get your notes typed up, collate the files, and have them on my desk by close of business. I want this investigation wrapped up."

CHAPTER FORTY-FIVE

"Guv, there are holes in the investigation big enough for a family of illegal immigrants to slip through," Freya said. "You can't expect us to just drop it when there's likely more than one person involved."

"Barker confessed. Is that right?" Standing said.

"Well, yes, but–"

"Then let the trial weed out the details," Standing replied. "We've done our bit and I've already exhausted my resources. Write up your reports and have them on my desk before the end of the day."

"But, guv," Freya said as Standing pulled open the doors, "Alexandra Sinclair–"

"Are you questioning my decision, Inspector Bloom?" he said, to which Freya said nothing. He checked his watch. "I didn't think so. If Barker had assistance, which I very much doubt he did, then I'm sure it'll all come out in the wash. Now, you've got two hours to deliver your reports. If any of you cannot manage that simple task, then I'd be happy to reassess your role within this team."

The doors closed behind him, and the motivation that Freya

had built up over the past fifteen minutes or so dispersed, leaving a cloud of frustration in its wake.

Freya stared at the doors. Gold began collating the pieces of paper that were strewn across her desk, and at the press of a key on Chapman's keyboard, the printer whirred into life.

"Well, that was unequivocal," Cruz muttered.

"He just wants a quick win," Nillson said. "No wonder the public doesn't have any faith in what we do. Everything is half-arsed and limited by budget."

"Makes you wonder why we bother, doesn't it?" Gold said. "You'd think he'd want the whole package. I mean, what if Alexandra did help Barker? We'd be leaving a criminal to walk the streets."

"Aye, you're right, Jackie," Gillespie added. "Especially when it's his home town. I mean, you'd think he'd want to do a good bloody job in his own neighbourhood, wouldn't you?"

"He lives in Horncastle?" Freya said.

"Aye, boss. He told us the other day."

"No, he just said that Horncastle was his old stomping ground."

"Ah, well, he definitely lives there. Or used to, at least. I went for a beer with him a few years back."

"Don't tell me it was The White Horse?" Freya said.

"No, some other place. On the other side of town."

"The King's Head?" Gold asked.

"No, it wasn't a pub," Gillespie said. "More of a club, if I remember rightly. Wherever it was, he was well-known. Everyone knew his name. Like bloody royalty in there, he was."

"Gillespie, I need you to think hard," Freya said. "Was it the social club? As in, the same social club where Alexandra Sinclair works?"

"Aye, it might have been," he said, smiling, "I have to admit, I wasn't the best version of myself when I left that place. It was about one-fifty a pint."

"Freya?" Ben said, and it seemed everyone in the room had made a connection except for Gillespie. Each of them stared at her, waiting for some kind of response. "You don't think he's up to something, do you?"

"That's exactly what I think," Freya said.

"What?" Cruz said, lowering his voice. "You mean like covering for someone? Standing?"

"And that's exactly what I mean, Cruz," she replied.

"Well, whatever you're going to do," Ben said. "You've got two hours to do it."

"No," she replied. "No, you heard the man. Let's get these reports finished up."

Ben nodded and inwardly sighed a breath of relief.

"I'll get the transcripts from the interviews," he said. "Do you want me to talk to Michaela? We'll need her reports."

"We're not seriously going to just drop it there, are we?" Nillson said, her face a picture of absolute disgust.

The glare on Freya's face cracked, then shattered, and a familiar smile grew in its place. It was the smile a soldier might wear as he dared his enemy to bring him down.

She turned to each of them in turn, lingering on the three members of the team who were just days from joining a new team.

"You heard what he said," she said, grabbing her car keys from her desk. "I suggest you work on your reports. I'm not going to ask anybody to come with me."

She marched across the room, refusing to look Ben in the eye.

"What about you?" he asked. "Where are you going?"

She held the door open but spoke quietly.

"I'm going to do my job," she replied. "I'd happily be given the opportunity to discuss my position within this team."

She had, as Ben's father would have said, placed one foot off the bus, and it wasn't a tentative step to test the water, it was her casting down her shield and a confident stride into battle.

In the few short moments that he stared at her, enough of a

message was conveyed for him to know she wasn't pushing boundaries for the sake of it. She'd had enough.

But those few moments were broken by the slap made by a pile of papers landing on Freya's desk. The team all turned to find Chapman in her knitted cardigan and floral blouse with a face as near to thunder as the polite young woman could summon.

"What's that?" Freya asked, gesturing at the papers.

"Every piece of research I've had to make during the investigation," she replied, defiance in her eyes.

The printer kicked into life again and Gold stood to collect the printouts.

"Gold?" Freya said, and the younger of the two slapped the papers onto Freya's desk.

"My notes from my time with Alexandra Sinclair," Gold replied, and she stood beside Chapman, folding her arms.

Once more, the printer jumped into life, and this time it was Anderson who collected the papers. Hers took a few moments longer than Gold's had, but she waited patiently and placed the results neatly beside Gold's and Chapman's.

"The workshop search and my findings, plus the initial interview with Barker," she said. "And there's one or two other reports including what we found at the hotel. Basically, everything Anna and I have worked on."

She waited for Nillson to close her laptop and then stand, and the two of them joined Chapman and Gold.

All that remained was Gillespie and Cruz, neither of whom even had their laptops open.

"I just need a wee while," Gillespie said sheepishly.

"I'm sure I can gather my notes pretty fast," Cruz said.

"Leave them for me to do," Chapman said, then looked directly at Ben. "I'll type up the transcripts from the interviews, too. If I'm left alone, I can have everything done by close of play."

"Are you sure?" Ben said. "I don't feel comfortable leaving you to do our work—"

"Positive," she replied, leaving no room for an argument. "Now go, all of you. Go and do what you're bloody well good at, and I'll do what I'm good at. If Standing wants reports, then reports he shall get. And if he wants to discuss my position within this team too, then I'll happily have that conversation."

It was the first time the gentle, young researcher had demonstrated such tenacity, and Ben felt a swell of pride at how far she had come since those early days when she had been too shy to even tell them good morning.

"Alright," Freya said. "Nillson, Anderson, find me the three boys. Gold, I want you to bring back Alexandra Sinclair. She has some explaining to do. Gillespie, Cruz?"

"Aye, boss?" the big Glaswegian said.

"Do you trust me?" Freya said.

"Trust you? Aye, I suppose I do. Aye," Gillespie replied, and he glanced at Cruz who nodded his agreement as if he'd been asked if he enjoyed the taste of beer.

"Yeah," he said. "Yeah, I trust you."

"Good," she said. "I want you to bring me the barmaid."

"The what?" Gillespie said. "The barmaid?"

"I don't care how you do it, Gillespie," she said. "Just bring her here and keep her busy until I get back."

"Where are you two going?" he asked, to which Freya stared directly at Ben with an advance apology in her eyes. "Can't you bring her in?"

"Ben is going to find Rosie Sinclair. I'm sure he can handle her alone," she said, without breaking her stare. "And it's probably for the best if none of you know where I'm going."

CHAPTER FORTY-SIX

"How are we for transport?" Ben called out, as he pushed through the double doors into the custody suite, where Sergeant Priest peered over his glasses as Nillson, Anderson, and Gold all followed Ben into the room.

He eyed them all then, after a quick look at the key rack, addressed Ben's question.

"Three squad cars and two transporters," he said.

"We'll take them, along with any able bodies you can spare."

"Warrants?" Priest said, without so much as a hint of his feathers being ruffled.

"Don't need them," Ben replied. "Although we might need a doorbell."

Priest's laugh was not the belly-rolling, joyful roar it usually was, but it was enough for Ben to see he'd understood his reference to the ram they used to break into a suspect's door on occasion.

"I can give you half a dozen for the next hour or so," Priest said. "Are these Standing's orders?"

"No, they're DI Bloom's orders," Ben said, and Priest peered over his glasses again, appraising them all with those inquisitive eyes. For a moment, it looked as if he might call upstairs for clarification from Standing, but instead, as he reached for the radio on his shoulder, he spoke to Ben one last time. "They'll be ready in two minutes. I suggest you get ready to roll."

"Thanks, Michael," Ben said, and opened the door to the courtyard before anybody could argue. The team filed out before him, and he caught the tail end of Gillespie's car as it disappeared from view.

"He's a good man, that one," Nillson said. "I could have sworn he knew we were up to something."

"Of course he knows," Ben replied, joining the three women as they headed towards the cars. "I suppose thirty years on the force gives you a good sense of right and wrong."

"It's a shame the top brass didn't get that education," Gold muttered.

Behind them, the door they had just left through opened once more and six uniformed officers filed out, dressing as they walked. A few were positioning their caps on their heads, while one or two others were fastening their stab jackets, which were laden with radios, tasers, handcuffs, and everything else the force required them to carry.

The first of them, a man Ben knew as Forsythe, led his team towards the two transporters.

"Are we following you, Ben?" he called out.

"I'll ride with you," he replied, then spoke to his team. "Anna, can you take Jenny and Jackie?"

"Sure," she said. "We'll follow you."

"Have we got a plan?" Anderson asked, yelling across the car park as Ben opened the passenger door of the transporter.

"Let's hit Alexandra Sinclair's house and go from there," he replied. He climbed into the van and pulled the door closed, glancing back at the two uniformed officers in the back seats. "We're heading to Horncastle. I'll direct you when we're closer."

"I haven't worked with you for a few months, Ben," Forsythe

said. He wore a few days' growth with neatly-cropped, reddish hair. He put the van into gear and pulled out with confidence, reaching second gear as he hit the main road, and pulling out without stopping. "How's things?"

"Yeah, it's the first time in a long while," Ben began, checking the side mirror to make sure Nillson's little hatchback had pulled out after the second van. "And if this all goes wrong, it might just be the last."

CHAPTER FORTY-SEVEN

"Is it me or does this feel like we're going into battle?" Gold asked as Anna accelerated away from a set of traffic lights to catch up with the two transporters ahead.

"It always feels like that to me," Anderson said from the front passenger seat. "I love a good raid."

"I'm not talking about the raid," Gold replied. "I'm talking about the whole thing. Standing wants us to submit the case half-closed, the boss is clearly up to something, and we're the bloody infantry wandering around in the dark unsure exactly who of us will still be here next week."

"It's hardly the Somme, Jackie," Anna said over her shoulder. "Look at it. The sun is shining, the fields are beautiful, and if I'm not mistaken, the boss is on to something."

"I know what you mean," Gold said. "She's like one of those bloody wild dogs sniffing out mushrooms in the forest when she gets going."

"The what?" Anderson said, and she turned in her seat to look her in the eye. "Sniffing out what?"

"You know?" Gold said. "Those wild dogs. In France. They sniff out the mushrooms. Worth a bloody fortune, they are. I saw it on the telly. It was some documentary about food or something—"

"Truffles, Jackie," Anderson said. "They're called truffles."

"Well, whatever they are, they sniff out these mushrooms, which, by the way, are worth a fortune, and that's what the boss is like. When she gets her nose into something, she doesn't bloody stop."

"Yep, she's a bona fide truffle, Jackie," Anna said, with a glance across to Anderson, who stifled a laugh.

"What?" Jackie asked. "What are you laughing at?"

"Oh, nothing," Anna said. She caught Gold in the reflection of the rear-view mirror. "But please don't leave. I never thought I'd say this, but I think I'd miss you more than anybody."

"Even me?" Anderson asked.

"You, Chapman, Jim, Ben," Anna said. "All of them. I honestly don't think anybody could replace you."

"Yes, well, let's hope DI Larson feels the same," Gold said. "If I'm honest, I'm actually quite nervous."

"Nervous? What do you have to be nervous about?"

"It's a new team. I won't know anybody."

"You'll know Chapman," Anna said. "And Jim."

"Yes, but not the others. And what if DI Larson is anything like Standing? I'll be jumping from the frying pan into the fire."

"Well, if you go," Anderson said, sucking in a deep breath, "then you have a fifty-fifty chance of being happy. But if you stay?"

"Then I'll be miserable for the foreseeable future," Gold said. "That's exactly what I thought myself. What a conundrum."

The vans ahead turned into a side road with the nature reserve on their right and then accelerated towards the Sinclair house.

"Okay, this is it," Nillson said. "Remember, let Forsythe and his team go in before us. They're far better equipped for this."

"Why are there so many of them?" Gold asked as Nillson brought the little hatchback to a stop. "Alexandra Sinclair is hardly going to come to the door like Al Pacino, shouting, '*Say hello to my little friend.*'"

The comment cut through the tension enough to raise a muted laugh that died before it had matured.

They watched as Forsythe and his team ran to the front door, waving for others to go around the back of the house.

Gold reached for the door handle, readying herself to do battle with Alexandra. She met Nillson in the rear-view mirror again.

"I mean it, Jackie," Nillson said sadly. "You'll be missed."

Jackie smiled back at her, for the first time seeing a friend in the hardened sergeant she had always admired.

"I'll miss you, too," she replied. "All of you."

Somebody began shouting at the front door, announcing their presence and calling for Alexandra to come to the door.

"We'd better get ready," Anderson said, and she had just pushed open the door when Anna grabbed her wrist.

"Wait," she said, her eyes wide open. She glanced back at Jackie with fear in her eyes. "She might have wild truffles in there."

Anderson laughed, and the two climbed out of the car leaving Jackie slightly bemused. She followed and caught up with them on the footpath, like three friends walking to a cafe for lunch.

"Maybe we should call the Truffle Unit," Anna said.

"The what?" Jackie said, coming to a stop at Sinclair's front gate. "What are you two going on about?"

There was shouting from inside the house and before either of them could respond, four lithe and leggy teenagers leapt from the front door darted across the front garden, and bolted towards the nature reserve.

"What the..." Jackie began when Ben burst through the door in pursuit.

"Jackie, inside," he shouted without breaking stride. "Anna, you're with me."

CHAPTER FORTY-EIGHT

The noise level in the house was in total contrast to what it had been during Jackie's previous visits, when a sullen Alexandra Sinclair had leaned against the kitchen counter, bitter and resentful, recalling the past with obvious pain.

That near silence had been crushed by the sound of men's voices as the uniformed officers moved from room to room calling out when a room was clear, of drawers and cupboards being opened and slammed closed as they searched the place, and of heavy boots pounding down the stairs.

She felt a little out of place in the melee. Like she was the only one without an immediate job to do. The kitchen was empty and tidy, save for four glasses on the counter, most of which were half-filled with what looked like orange juice.

A shrill scream blasted down the stairs and Forsythe called down from the top one. Jackie ran to the hallway and peered up.

"It's Sinclair," he said. "You need to see this."

He disappeared from view, and Jackie heard Alexandra's angry shouts, cursing and spitting like a cornered cat. She pounded up the stairs and into the front bedroom where she found two of

Forsythe's officers pinning her down on the bed with her arms pulled tight behind her back, fixed with a pair of handcuffs.

Laying beside her on the bed was a box of tablets with a half-empty, foil-backed insert hanging out.

"Alexandra?" Jackie said, and she dropped to her knees and held the box up in front of the woman's face. "Alexandra, talk to me. Have you taken any of these?"

"Tell them, Jackie," she said, her voice slurred like she had just woken from a slumber. "Tell them what I've been through. You understand, don't you? I told you what he was like."

"Alexandra, I need to know if you've taken any of these."

"He got it, didn't he?" she said slowly. "He got what he deserved."

Jackie looked up at Forsythe.

"Ambulance," she said, then read the box. "It's Sertraline, an anti-depressant, and there's at least eight missing."

Forsythe received the information and began conveying it across the airwaves, leaving Jackie to deal with Alexandra.

"Get off her," she told the officer. "And get those bloody cuffs off."

The officer stared at Jackie as if he doubted her decision.

"Now," she said. "Get her on her back."

He took a few moments more to make his own decision, then looked to Forsythe, who nodded. In a few seconds, Alexandra's arms were released, and Jackie rolled her onto her side.

"Alexandra, keep talking to me, okay? I need you to talk to me. Just stay awake. Help is coming, alright? You're going to be fine."

Alexandra smiled sadly at Jackie, and for the first time, Jackie noticed she wasn't frowning. There were no lines on her forehead or around her eyes.

"Where's Rosie?" she slurred. "I need my baby."

"We're looking for her," Jackie replied. "Do you know where she might have gone?"

"She's a good girl, she is. A real good girl."

"I know, Alexandra. I know. You did a good job raising her," Jackie said, to which Alexandra gave a little laugh.

"I love that girl," she said, her voice trailing away.

"Forsythe, how long?"

"Could be fifteen minutes," he replied. "Shall we get her downstairs?"

"No," Gold replied. "No, don't move her."

"How about some water?"

"No water, no food, no anything. We just need to keep her awake and breathing until the paramedics get here," Gold said. "Alexandra, stay with me, sweetheart. Stay with me."

"I'm not going anywhere," she slurred in reply, her eyelids hanging heavily. "I just want to lay here for a while."

"You can't sleep, Alexandra. Stay awake for me, please. Come on. Talk to me about Rosie. Tell me about the day she was born. Do you remember it? Do you remember that day?"

A weak smile formed on the young woman's face.

"Of course I do. You never forget. You never forget the day your baby is born," she said softly, like a drunk in the throes of slumber. "Have you got them, Jackie?"

"Children?" she replied, pleased to be engaging with her. "Yes, I have a boy. He's eight now."

"Eight? That's a wonderful age. I never had a boy," she said. "I had a little girl."

"I know," Gold said. "She's lovely. It can't have been easy on your own, though."

"No," she said. "No, it was lovely. We don't need anything. Just each other."

Jackie made herself comfortable by sitting on the floor beside the bed, reaching up to stroke Alexandra's hair and subtly checking her pulse, which was racing.

"Do your parents help?" Jackie asked. "My mum helps me. I

don't know what I'd do without her. I couldn't do this job for a start. Do you have any help?"

"No," she slurred. "No, it's just me. Michael used to help. There was a time, years ago, when he wanted to adopt her. Imagine that? We could have been a real family. I think he loved her once."

She looked lazily at Jackie, her smile growing distant as she imagined what could have been.

"Alexandra, we need to find her," Jackie said. "We need her here with you. Do you know where she might be?"

"She's with her boys," Alexandra replied with almost no hesitation. "They'll take care of her. They always take care of my baby."

"Can you tell us where she might have gone, Alexandra?" Gold said. "I'd really like her to be here."

"I don't want her here," she said, letting her eyes close on the world. "I've said all I have to say to her. She'll be okay. She has everything she needs."

"Alexandra, stay awake for me, please," Jackie said, thumbing her eyes open. "I need you to stay awake. Help is on its way."

"You can't help me," she said. "No. No, you can't help me."

"Alexandra, open your eyes," Gold said, far more assertive than she had been before. "Don't you dare go to sleep on me."

Her eyelids parted just enough for Gold to see the red arteries that streaked across the whites of her eyes.

"I didn't want her, you know?" she mumbled. "Not until she came, anyway. I didn't want that bastard's child in me."

"It's okay, Alexandra. You don't have to think about that right now."

She sneered at Gold, and her brow creased.

"You say it like I have a choice," she said. "You say it like I can pick and choose to remember him or not."

"No, Alex–"

"There's not a day goes by I don't think of it. I can even smell him, you know? His aftershave and the beer on his breath."

"You don't need to—"

"I think of him every time I look at her. Did you know that? Can you imagine looking at your little boy and seeing a monster? Or remembering the night you were attacked? How he pressed my face to the fence, how he ripped at my clothes, and how he tossed me to the ground when he was done."

In Gold's experience, it wasn't uncommon to be shamed by other men's crimes, especially when the crimes were of a sexual nature. Forsythe stared through the window, and the officer who had cuffed Alexandra leaned against the wall, his eyes finding solace on some irrelevant part of the ceiling.

"Can you give us a minute?" Gold said, and the two were only too happy to leave. She waited for the door to close behind them, and then stroked Alexandra's face.

"How are you feeling now?" she asked, to which Alexandra simply shook her head. "We've arrested Drew. Did you know that?"

Alexandra said nothing, but something shifted in her eyes. It was as if she had donned a protective shield, burying away the dark secrets she had carried since Rosie had been conceived.

"I know," she said. "The kids know, too."

"How do they know?"

"Because I told them."

"Alexandra, if there's anything you can tell us..." said Gold. "He confessed, you know. He told us he murdered Michael while you were packing a bag for the weekend."

The news had little effect on Alexandra's expression, but she rolled onto her back with her arms by her side.

"Alexandra, if there's anything we should know—"

"I know what he did," she said, cutting Gold off. She let her head roll to one side to look her in the eye. There was no shame to what she said. No sorrow or regret. "I know because I helped him do it."

"Alexandra—"

"At least I know my baby is safe, and I can die knowing that she won't have to endure the torture of seeing his face for the rest of her life," Alexandra said, as she closed her eyes for the final time, and mumbled her last words. "Like I did."

CHAPTER FORTY-NINE

"Bloody hell, this is like returning to the scene of the crime," Gillespie muttered as he pulled the car into The White Horse car park.

"I don't know why you do it to yourself," Cruz said.

"Eh? What are you jabbering about?"

"You," Cruz said. "You couldn't help yourself, could you? You just had to go too far with her."

"What are you on about, Gabby?"

"Well, you could have just had a flirt with her and left it at that, right? You didn't have to sit in the bar waiting for her all night. Imagine if you had walked away. You wouldn't be in this position now, would you?"

"Me?" Gillespie said. "I'm not the one in a position."

Cruz digested the statement with obvious confusion, scrunching his nose up as he processed the information.

"Eh?" he said. "How did you work that out? You, Jim, have been directed by the boss to speak to your new girlfriend and to get her to the station. Her actual words were—"

"I know what her actual words were, Gabby," Gillespie said,

easing his chair back into a more comfortable reclined position. "She said that she didn't care how I did it, but I'm to get the barmaid to the station."

"Right," Cruz said. "So, surely that means you're in an uncomfortable position?"

"Nope," Gillespie replied. "In fact, I'd say I'm quite comfortable right now. Only one thing could make me more comfortable. Alas, we're not allowed to drink on the job anymore."

Gillespie stared dead ahead through the windscreen, watching Cruz from the corner of his eye as he tried to work out what Gillespie had meant.

The brief pause in conversation soon escalated to a period of silence. They watched as two builders entered the pub for midafternoon drinks, and heard the doors slam closed.

Cruz turned his head to stare at Gillespie.

"So?" he said.

"So what, Gabby?"

"Are you going in?"

"Me?" he replied with a little laugh. "Me? Go in there?"

Cruz was incredulous. "That's what I said. That's why we're here, isn't it?"

"No, Gabby," he said. "Close, but not quite."

It was only then that Cruz fell in with Gillespie's plans.

"Oh no," he said.

"Oh yes, Gabby."

"I'm not going in there," he said. "Is that what you're waiting for? Me to go in there?"

"Aye," Gillespie said, placing his hands behind his head for a makeshift pillow.

"I am not doing your dirty work, Jim."

"I've already done the dirty work," Gillespie replied. "I just need you to go in there and get her."

"DI Bloom told *you* to get her."

"Nope, we've already established what the boss said."

"I don't care how you do it," Cruz said, paraphrasing. "Which you interpret as, she doesn't care if you send *me* into the lion's den."

"It's hardly a lion's den. It's a bloody pub."

"Yeah, with your new girlfriend behind the bar. I'm not going in there. No way," he said, folding his arms to make his position clear.

"Cruz, don't make me pull rank."

"You wouldn't."

"I will if I have to," Gillespie said. "I'm happy to write a report stating that Detective Constable Cruz refused to follow orders, despite them coming from Detective Inspector Bloom."

"Oh right," Cruz said. "Nice one. And what do I say when I get questioned by Standing? That Sergeant Gillespie slept with a witness and was too scared to talk to her so he sent me. No, actually, he ordered me."

"You wouldn't," Gillespie said.

"If I have to, I will."

Gillespie stared at him, but Cruz refused to look back. Instead, he chose to peer out of the passenger window in defiance.

"What if I said please?"

"Sorry?" Cruz said. "I can't hear you."

"I said, what if I asked nicely?"

"Then maybe I will."

"Gab?" Gillespie said.

"Yes, Sergeant Gillespie? How can I help?"

"Can you go inside the pub to talk to the barmaid?"

Cruz pretended he hadn't heard. He placed his hand to his ear as a parent might when their child is developing good manners.

Gillespie sighed.

"Alright," he said. "Please."

"Please what?"

"Please can you go inside to talk to the barmaid?"

"In the pub?" Cruz said. "You want me to go in there?"

"Aye, I do."

"Why would I do that?" he said, still with his arms folded.

"Alright, alright," Gillespie said. "Do this for me and I'll treat you and Hermione to dinner somewhere nice."

"Dinner with you?" he said, looking repulsed. "I don't think she'd like that."

"Not with me. Paid for by me. Dinner on me."

"Somewhere nice?" Cruz said, considering the idea.

"Somewhere nice. The wee Chinese place in Brayford."

"No, we have Chinese all the time."

"The Plum Duck is good," Gillespie said, hoping to coax him along.

"Jim, I happen to know that you and the owner of that restaurant are friends."

"Aye, so?"

"So you'll get a discount," Cruz said. "Besides, I was thinking of somewhere much nicer."

"Much nicer?" Gillespie replied.

"Much, much nicer," Cruz said. "Maybe the Petwood Hotel?"

"That's not bad. I could shout a meal at the Petwood."

"Not a meal, Jim. I was thinking of a room for the night."

"A what?"

"Then again, I've always fancied taking Hermione to that fine dining place in town. What's it called? Jews House? I've heard the food is out of this world."

"Right," Gillespie said, shoving open his door. "I'll do it myself."

He climbed out, slammed the door, and strode toward the pub, smoothing his hair and fixing his collar as he walked. He was just about to push the doors open when a little voice called out. It was Cruz, leaning out of his open window.

"Jim?" he said.

"God help me," Gillespie muttered himself, then turned around to face him. "What?"

"I don't suppose you could get me a Diet Coke could you?" he said. "It's like an oven in here."

"No," Gillespie hissed at him. "Get it your bloody self."

He turned once more on his heels to shove through the doors, when that voice called out again.

"You're a grumpy grump, aren't you? You know, I'm looking forward to you leaving," Cruz said, leaning back in his seat and placing his hands behind his head, just as Gillespie had. "My days will be an absolute joy."

Gillespie stopped in his tracks and marched back at the wee detective constable, who leaned into the centre of the car and scrambled to close the window when he saw what was happening.

Gillespie leaned onto the window, forcing the motor to stop.

"You what?" he said.

"Nothing," Cruz replied, his voice high and panicky.

"You can't wait for me to leave, eh? You can't wait to work for somebody else, is that it?"

"I didn't mean it, Jim—"

"Well, I've got news for you, sunshine," Gillespie said, shoving off the car and bounding towards the pub in a fresh fit of rage. He stopped with his hand on the door and looked back at the little squirt squirming in his seat. "I'm not going anywhere, and I never bloody was. I just wanted to see what people would say if I did decide to leave."

"Eh?" Cruz said. "You...you're not leaving? You're staying with the team?"

"Aye, I am. And now I know exactly how you feel, I'm going to make it my sole mission to make your life an absolute misery, Gabby." He lingered for a moment, glowering at Cruz, before he shoved the doors open and stepped into the cool shade of the pub.

The few men who were quietly sipping their pints in the saloon bar all gave him a cursory glance before returning to their beverages. The barmaid, who was leaning on the bar with her phone in her hand, looked up and gave a heavy sigh, pocketing her phone.

"You," he said, jabbing his finger at her. "Get your things. You're coming with me, sweetheart."

CHAPTER FIFTY

The forest was cool with dappled light creating a mosaic on the earth beneath Ben's feet. Overhead, the thick canopy that should have been filled with bird song was in near silence.

He waited a few moments, closing his eyes to the surroundings, focusing on the noises around him. It took all of ten seconds for the birds to start their calling again, deeming the danger below to have passed.

The path through the forest forked on either side of a thick yew tree laden with heavy branches. Nillson and Anderson had taken the left fork heading directly for the bridge where Levy had been killed. But something drew Ben to the right-hand fork – an overhanging branch swung unnaturally in the still and breezeless air.

He took the right-hand path quietly, mindful of snapping twigs or scraping his sole on the loose, debris-covered ground.

On a few occasions, he had to pull overhanging branches out of his way, trying not to let them swing back noisily. He peered into every shadowy space and beneath every bush that might conceal a scared teenager.

He wondered how things might have turned out had Freya

been with him. If she would be here now, polluting nature with her expensive perfume, or scaring the birds into silence with her incessant opinions. There would have been little call for stealth had she been there. No doubt, she would be calling the names of the four youths as she marched through the forest in her heels, or cursing loud enough for the birds to not only silence but flee in terror.

He pictured the scene, and a small part of him smiled as his imagination painted an image of flocks of birds taking flight.

Soon enough, the walk shifted from an official search of the nature reserve in pursuit of four teenagers linked to the murder of a local man to a sedate stroll. How long had it been since he had enjoyed time alone? He hadn't even had time yet to reflect on what had happened with Michaela.

And that was when it dawned on him. Everything had changed. Jackie, Chapman, and even Gillespie were leaving, Michaela had left him. And he was still a detective sergeant, having made no progress since the day Freya had come into their lives. In fact, he wasn't even sure who she was anymore, if he could trust her, if he should even be associated with her.

Ahead of him, the forest thinned, breaking open to reveal a paddock, or a field for grazing livestock. The lush, green grass sloped away following the river to his right, and on the left, a line of dense brambles marked the edge of the old river course.

He wandered out into the open with his hands in his pockets, feeling the heat of the sun on his face and the burden of the unknown on his shoulders.

And that was when he saw her – a young girl sat with her legs drawn up to her chest and her face buried between her knees. A pile of rocks and a patch of scorched earth marked the spot where a fire had been, the type a group of campers might sit around with marshmallows or s'mores.

She sobbed, sniffed, and raised her head for air, spying Ben from the corner of her eye.

"Hey Rosie," he said, gently, keeping his distance so as not to scare her into a run. The last thing he needed was to be coerced into chasing a young female on his own. "It is Rosie, isn't it?"

She nodded, then rested her chin on her knees, staring out at the field beyond like she was memorising the sight for eternity.

"He had it coming, you know?" she said softly.

"Michael?" Ben said.

She nodded again.

"He deserved everything he got."

Ben took a step closer, keeping his hands in his pockets, hoping to convey that he meant no harm.

"Mind if I sit?" he asked, and she shrugged, so he slowly dropped to a cross-legged position a few feet from her. If the fire had been lit, they could have been those two campers toasting s'mores. "You know, it's not my job to judge anybody."

"Really?" she said. Her tone was typical of a teenage girl, bored and uninterested.

"I mean it," he said, stretching his legs out before him and leaning back on his hands. "I learned pretty fast that the system wasn't designed to be subjective. It's binary. I can't tell you the amount of people I wanted to let go because I know deep down that I would have behaved as they had, or similar. We're only human, right?"

"You would have killed Michael, would you?"

"I didn't say that," Ben said. "But we know what he did to you, and if it's any consolation, judges and juries are human too."

He let that thought permeate and dropped to lean on an elbow, picking a handful of grass the way he used to when he was her age. He smelled it, savouring nature's aroma, then let it slip through his fingers and watched it fall to the ground, insignificant.

"Mum told me about Drew," she said, and she looked across at him without fear. "Will he go to prison?"

"He confessed, Rosie," Ben said.

"So why were you at our house? Why were all those people there?"

"Because we believe he had help," Ben told her, then waited for her to understand exactly what he had meant.

"Mum?" she said, looking horrified. "You think my mum helped him?"

"We think your mum might know more than she's been letting on."

"She didn't," Rosie said. "She wouldn't have. She's not like that—"

"That's not for us to decide, is it?" Ben said, and he picked another handful of grass, letting it scatter in the gentle breeze.

"Will she go to prison as well?" Rosie said, keeping surprisingly cool considering her age and the severity of the situation. "Surely the judge and the jury will listen to what she has to say? They'll know what she's been through, right? They'll take everything into consideration?"

"That's if there *is* a trial," Ben replied, and Rosie sought an explanation with a confused expression. "You only go to trial if you plead not guilty. Otherwise, there will just be a hearing for the sentencing."

"But she's innocent—"

"Then there will likely be a trial," Ben said.

"It's not fair," she said. "Why is this happening to us? Why is my mum being put through this? She works hard. She's lovely—"

"Like I said, Rosie," Ben began, "bad things happen to good people."

"And vice versa," she muttered, snatching her own handful of grass and tossing it down to the ground spitefully. "Except for Michael. He deserved it."

"Tell me why you ran, Rosie," Ben asked. "When we came to the house, why did you all run?"

She said nothing, dragging her knees up to her chest again, where she rested her chin and peered at the river in the distance.

"Is there something you want to tell me? Nobody has to know you told me if you'd prefer it that way," Ben said, and by the way her lips tightened, he sensed an imminent breakdown. "Rosie?"

"What if she is innocent?" she said. "What if I know it wasn't her?"

"Then you should say something. If you know who helped Drew Barker, then now is the time to say so."

"But what if..." She paused with a sigh, closing her eyes to the view she captured in her heart. "But what if Drew is innocent, too?"

CHAPTER FIFTY-ONE

Freya pulled into the car park and selected a space close to the only car she recognised. It was the first time she had been to that particular building, yet had been talking to the teams who had worked there since day one of her career in Lincolnshire.

But today was not the day to put names to faces. Today was make or break day, and the claws that wrenched at the very fabric of her heart dug deep and hard.

The conversation she was about to have promised to be one of the hardest in her career, to the point that when her phone began to ring, she was almost grateful for the delay. But that gratitude was short-lived when Jackie Gold spoke those first few words.

"Ma'am," she said. "It's Jackie."

"Is everything okay?" Freya asked, hearing a quiver in the young FLO's voice.

"She's dead, ma'am," Gold said. "Alexandra Sinclair. We were too late."

"How?" Freya asked, and she sat back in her seat, closing her eyes to the world outside of her car.

"Anti-depressants. She swallowed them before we could get to her. Sorry, ma'am. Truly, I am."

"Don't apologise, Gold. You didn't exactly stuff them down her throat, did you?"

"Well, no. But if I hadn't..." she began. "If we'd have got here sooner we might have been able to save her. I'm with Forsythe and the EMT now. We did everything we could, ma'am, but we were just too late."

"Okay," Freya said. "Okay, stay with her. Wait for the coroner to arrive. Can you handle that? Do you need me to send somebody to take over?"

"No," she said. "No, I'm okay, I think. I just keep thinking about that little girl, ma'am. She's got nobody now."

"We can't help them all, Jackie," Freya said. "Alexandra knew what she was doing."

"But why? What a terrible waste of a life."

"Guilt," Freya said. "And the fear of what was to come. Life sentences aren't exactly on everybody's bucket list, are they?"

"But she lived such a sad life, ma'am," Jackie said, in a gentle tone that told Freya her move to become an FLO was perfectly aligned with her personality. "All she needed was a break, something good to happen to her, that's all. Do you know what I mean? Am I making sense?"

"I think so, Jackie," Freya said. "You're saying that Michael Levy's death could have been that break."

"Well, I wouldn't say that–"

"I would," Freya said. "Can you imagine her life without him? She would have been free to spend her time with a man she actually liked. A man who would care for her and Rosie. Speaking of Rosie, please tell me she hasn't seen what happened."

"No," Gold said, with a touch of professionalism entering her voice. "No, she ran when the team entered the house."

"She ran?"

"Yeah, her and her three friends," Jackie said. "Ben and the others have gone after them. They've been gone a while now, but

I've stationed one of Forsythe's officers on the front door to stop them coming upstairs if they come back."

"Good. Well done, Jackie. I'll call Ben to see how he's getting on," Freya said. "Are you sure you're okay to stay there?"

"I'm fine, ma'am," she replied. "I'd like to stay with her. She doesn't deserve to be alone, even now."

The words came naturally to the young constable, and in a way, Freya admired her. She bore traits that Freya simply didn't possess.

"Call me if you need to," Freya said then ended the call. She navigated to Ben's phone number and hit the dial button, taking a moment to fill her lungs and exhale slowly through her nose.

"How's it going?" he said, so lazily that he could have been on a beach with a cocktail in hand.

"Well, it doesn't sound like you're in hot pursuit," Freya said.

"That's because I'm not," he replied.

"Did you find them?" Freya said. "The kids, I mean. Gold said you went after them."

"We did," he replied, and his responses were becoming noticeably brief.

"You can't talk, can you?"

"No," he said.

"Are you with them?"

"One of them, yes."

"Rosie?"

"Correct."

"Well, don't take her back to her house. Her mother just died," Freya said, and she heard him adjust his position, sitting up to pay more attention.

"Bloody hell."

"She overdosed. Gold is with her now. So I'd like you to bring Rosie in so we can get her taken care of. I think Gold should be the one to deliver the bad news. She has a nicer bedside manner than you or I."

Ben was silent, and Freya pictured him staring at the young girl, imagining her future.

"Ben?"

"Yeah, I'm here," he said. "We were coming in anyway."

"With Rosie?" she said. "What for?"

"It's complicated," he explained.

"Give me the short version," she said.

"Drew Barker is innocent," Ben said. "According to Rosie, anyway. She's prepared to make a statement."

Freya considered what he was saying, trying to find some kind of hidden message in there.

"This statement," she said. "Will it be a confession?"

"It seems so," he replied.

"In which case, are you suggesting that Rosie and her friends killed Michael Levy? And Drew Barker was covering for his son?"

"That's exactly what I'm suggesting," Ben said.

"So how do you explain Drew Barker's DNA being found on Levy's tooth?"

"I can't," he said. "Not yet anyway."

"Alright," she said, and she peered through the window at the building, sensing her procrastination was coming to an end. "Alright, bring her in. Bring them all in, especially Barker's son, Anthony."

"Already on it," Ben said, and his tone shifted. "Are you going to tell me what you're up to?"

She considered it for a moment, then decided.

"No," she said and hit the button to end the call.

Then, holding a deep breath to control herself, she climbed from the car, strode across the car park, and pushed through the double doors into a small reception that smelled like a retirement home.

"Good afternoon, how can I help?" a young girl said from behind the reception desk. She was pretty with intelligent eyes and a smile that suggested she enjoyed her job.

Freya couldn't even bring herself to force a smile, and she rested her hands flat on the reception desk, finding a calm voice from somewhere deep inside her.

"I'm here to see Doctor Fell," she said. "Doctor Michaela Fell."

CHAPTER FIFTY-TWO

It was late afternoon by the time Nillson and Anderson had scoured the nature reserve and found themselves with only one logical place left to search.

The rear gate to Drew Barker's house was ajar, and Anna peered inside the garden, then looked back at Anderson.

"The garden is empty," she said. "They must be inside the house. Do you want to cover the front or should I?"

"The front?"

"They might try to run again."

"Oh, for God's sake. I'm done running," Anderson replied. "It's too bloody warm for all this. We're not all fifteen years old. Don't they realise that?"

"I'll go, shall I?" Nillson said.

"I wonder if Barker has any cold drinks in the fridge?" Anderson mused, and Anna glared at her. "Just kidding. But it's not like he'll be needing them, is it? He'll be drinking lukewarm water from a polystyrene cup for the next fifteen years."

Anna's phone vibrated in her pocket, and Anderson quieted while she pulled it out.

"It's Ben," she said, answering the call and directing it to loudspeaker for Anderson to hear. "Ben, where are you?"

"In a field," he replied. "I'm with Rosie Sinclair. There's no sign of the others. How about you?"

"We're behind the Barker house," Anna replied. "The back gate is open. We were going to search inside."

"Do you need backup?"

"For three teenage boys?" Anna scoffed. "Come on, Ben. You know me better than that."

"Hang on a second," he said. They heard his feet swishing through long grass and his breathing grow heavier. "Still there?"

"We're here," Anna replied.

"I've just spoken to the boss," he said, keeping his voice low. "Alexandra Sinclair took her own life."

"Eh?"

"Overdosed."

"Bloody hell," Anderson said. "How did Rosie take it?"

"She doesn't know yet," Ben replied. "I'm taking her to the station to get her looked after."

"Do you need help?" Anderson asked.

"No, I'll be fine. Freya said that Jackie should be the one to deliver the news."

"I'd agree with that," Anna said. "No offence, Ben, but you're not exactly Mother Teresa, are you? Poor kid. The boss was right then. Alexandra must have had something to do with it."

"Not necessarily," Ben said. "Rosie opened up to me. It turns out that Drew Barker isn't as guilty as we thought."

"What?" Anderson said. "But—"

"Not buts, Jenny," he said. "The four of them jumped him on the way home from the pub."

"Because of what he did to Rosie?" Anna asked.

"Yeah. Apparently, they went at him hammer and tongs."

"But what about the spade and the dirt?" Anderson said, seeing the evidence she had gathered falling apart.

"Who else had access to Drew Barker's tools?" Ben said.

"Oh, for God's sake. His boy. Anthony."

"But didn't they find Barker's DNA on Levy's tooth?"

"Partial profile," Ben said. "My money is on it belonging to his son."

"So Drew Barker's confession–"

"Means nothing," Ben finished for her. "He was covering for his boy."

"But why?" Anna said. "Why did Rosie tell you all this? You didn't force her to talk, did you?"

"What would you have done if your mum and your best mate's dad were about to go to prison for a murder you committed?"

"This gets worse, Ben," Anna said. "So now we're looking for three teenage boys intending to arrest them for murder?"

A loud thud came from inside the property, followed by a metallic clang.

"Hold on, Ben," she said, handing the phone to Anderson. Anna stepped inside the garden and crept along the pathway to the shed where she had seen the pile of tools. With the toe of her boot, she pulled the door open and peered inside.

"Which ones are you then?" she said.

"Peter Davis," the larger of the two boys said, his eyes wide with both fear and guilt.

"Jake Turvey," the other said, his voice higher than the other boy's, suggesting he was slower to develop.

"So where's the other one?" she said, as Anderson joined her holding the phone out for Ben to hear what was going on. "Where's your mate, Tony?"

The smaller of the two shrugged, while the larger plunged his hands into his pockets and refused to make eye contact.

"Do you know the trouble you're in?" Anna said.

"No comment," Turvey said, which saddened Anna and clearly irritated Peter Davis, who rolled his eyes.

"We heard," Davis said, then flicked his head to gesture at the back gate. "We heard what you were saying."

"How much did you hear?" Anna asked. There was no chance of them running. They were trapped, and for the time being, vulnerable.

"Everything," he said.

"So you understand exactly how serious this is for you?"

He nodded.

"And for Tony's father?" Anna added, and again he nodded. "We need to find him. Can you tell us where he is? Is he in the house?"

"Would we be hiding in the shed if we could get in the house?" he said with a sneer.

"Don't get smart, Peter. It's not going to do you any favours."

"We don't know where he is. We split up when running."

"You had better not be lying to me," Anna said, and the look on his face told her he was being truthful. She called out to Ben, "We're just missing Anthony Barker."

Something rasped across the microphone, presumably as Ben shielded the phone to talk to Rosie. Moments later, his voice returned.

"Rosie said that Alexandra told them about Drew Barker's confession," Ben said. "She said he was upset, and that there's only one place he goes to when he's upset."

"His mother's grave," Anna said. "The cemetery."

"Can I leave that with you?" Ben asked.

"Yes," Anna said. "I'll go after him. Anderson can stay here and arrange for these two to be transported back to the station."

"I'll leave it with you then," he said, and ended the call.

Anna took the phone from Anderson and pocketed it.

"Can you handle these two?" she asked.

Anderson peered into the shed at the two boys, who despite being responsible for seriously injuring and killing a man, appeared timid and afraid.

"I don't think they'll be much trouble," she replied. "I'll see you back at the station."

Anna nodded, then spoke to the two boys one last time.

"Enjoy the fresh air, boys," she said. "While you still can."

And with that, Anna set off in a trot, running out of the back gate and along the edge of the field towards the cemetery. She stopped once to check she was heading in the right direction using the map on her phone. Then she bolted past The White Horse, flanking the few cottages that looked out over the nature reserve, and crossed the relatively busy Boston Road.

The cemetery was large and surrounded by a low fence with fierce-looking, iron spikes. The grounds were well-kept, with small trees dotted throughout which limited Anna's view and forced her to run along the fence line trying to spot the distraught teenager.

And then she saw him. He was about three hundred yards away in a far corner, sitting cross-legged before a grave.

The time for running was over, Anna guessed. He would be saying his final goodbyes to his mother, perhaps apologising for what he and his friends had done, and maybe promising to return when he was released as an older and wiser man.

Anna walked with purpose, but not so much as to appear out of place. With her hands crossed behind her back, she portrayed one of the visitors who so often sought peace, quiet, and solitude in graveyards and cemeteries. It was only when she was twenty yards from the boy that he saw her and looked up.

There was something in his look that told her he was done running. He had accepted his fate. He would meet whatever consequences were due head-on, as a proud man, not a scared child.

She gave him a moment or two more with his mother, using the time to reflect on the situation. It was easy to think of him and his friends as callous kids who had beaten a man to death. But it had been an act of love, of unity, and, despite the consequences, of solidarity. As the only girl in a family of four children, Anna knew what that protection meant. Gender had meant nothing during sibling wrestling matches, football games, and even the frequent fights when she had given as hard as she had taken. But if an outsider had threatened or bullied her, her male siblings had shielded her with vicious fury. They would have done anything to keep her safe.

Had the situation been turned on its head, then some other detective might have stared at her brother the way she was staring at Anthony Barker right now.

He shoved himself up to his feet and bowed his head to the grave, taking a final chance to carry a kiss to the old headstone and hold it there, momentarily.

When he eventually began walking towards Anna, he did so with his head held high and his shoulders back. But despite this confident appearance, understandably, his voice quivered as he spoke.

"My dad is innocent," he told her, doing everything he could to hold back the tears. "It was me. I killed Michael Levy."

"We know about the attack, Anthony," Anna said. "It's brave of you to protect your friends, but we know you were all involved."

He looked sad, as if she had blown his chances of being the man, and of taking care of his mates. He shook his head slowly.

"We might have attacked him together," he said. "But it was me who went back when everyone had gone home."

"You went back?" Anna said for clarity. "Are you telling me that you murdered Michael Levy alone? Why?"

"I had to," he said, and he glanced back over his shoulder at the grave, then smiled weakly, like a man who had finally achieved his lifetime ambition and had nothing left to fight for. "If it wasn't for Michael Levy, she'd still be alive today."

CHAPTER FIFTY-THREE

The custody suite was heaving when Ben pulled open the door to the car park and ushered a sullen and tearful Rosie through. Forsythe and three of his team were helping Sergeant Priest process the three boys. But when they saw Rosie enter, the room fell into silence.

The morose expression she had been wearing briefly gave way to a look of hope when she saw them. Then it faded like a dying candle flame when she read the look on their faces. Even Priest, an ageing and hardened Yorkshireman, offered sympathetic eyes.

Unlike Tony Barker, Peter Davis and Jake Turvey were not in handcuffs and were being held away from their friend. Forsythe's grip on Barker's arm was evident in the grimace on the boy's face when he tried to go to Rosie.

From the custody desk, Peter Davis looked up at Priest.

"May I?" he said gently, and Priest looked to Ben for an answer. Ben gave a brief nod, and the boy, who was taller and broader than the others, stepped slowly over to Rosie.

"What?" Rosie said, "What's going on?"

Peter Davis looked back at Tony, and then explained.

"It was Tony," he said.

"Tony?" she replied disbelievingly. She stared at the boy in Forsythe's grip. "You did it? You killed him?"

He said nothing, but his chest swelled with pride.

"For your mum?" she said, and he gave a loud sniff, nodding, as he fought back the tears.

"And for you," he said, the pitch of his voice belying maturity. Breathless with the effort of restraining his emotions, he gasped. "Somebody had to do it. We had the perfect chance."

Rosie took a moment to process what he had said, staring at her three friends in turn. The smallest boy, Jake Turvey, was in visible distress, unable to hold back his tears. He took a box of tissues from Priest and sank to the floor, burying his face in his arms.

She turned to Peter, who was unmoved at the sight.

"So what now?" she said, and sought the answer from Ben and the rest of the officers.

"Rosie," Peter said. "Rosie, there's something you need to know—"

The doors from the corridor burst open, killing the moment Ben had been dreading during the journey from Horncastle.

"What the bloody hell is this?" Standing said. "A mother's meeting?"

"Guv, give us a minute, will you?" Ben said.

"I'll give you no such thing. What's going on here?" he said, his cold tone emphasised by his strong accent. "I thought I told Inspector Bloom we were done. We've got Barker, so this lot can bugger off—"

"Guv, there's been a development," Ben said, raising his voice to the very brink of becoming insubordinate.

"A development? he said. "I didn't ask for a development. I asked for Drew Barker to be charged."

"He has been charged, guv," Ben said, doing his best to control his irritation.

"Then where is he?"

"Cell two, guv," Priest said.

"What's he doing here? He should be on remand right now, not taking up valuable space," Standing said, offering little regard to Priest's stature and position. "Get him out here now."

"Guv, I really think we should interview—"

"When I want your advice, DS Savage, I'll ask for it," he said, and for the first time, he took a moment to look at the individuals in the room. He stared at Anthony Barker for a few moments, noting the handcuffs and Forsythe's grip. Then he sneered at Turvey, who was still sitting on the floor. Then finally, his eyes fell on Peter Davis and Rosie, lingering on her for a few seconds more.

The moment was broken by Priest ushering a handcuffed Drew Barker into the room and handing him over to one of the uniformed offices.

"Get him loaded into the transporter," he said, and his thick Yorkshire grumble clearly conveyed his displeasure.

"Dad?" Anthony called out, and he fought against Forsythe's grip, trying to break free for one last moment with his father.

Forsythe held him fast.

"Let him go," Drew shouted. "He's done nothing. It was me. I told you it was me."

"Dad, stop," Anthony said. "You don't have to lie for me."

"We all did it," Pete said. "It wasn't just you. It was all of us."

"Stop this at once," a voice yelled from behind Ben, killing the chaos with immediate effect.

He turned to find Freya standing in the open car park doorway. She stepped into the already crowded room, somehow taking ownership of the situation with four simple words and an unrivalled presence.

"You've got some explaining to do, Inspector Bloom," Standing said, clearly seething at being publicly undermined.

"And explain I will," she said, leaving a moment for her words to take effect, letting the ensuing silence breed intrigue like a steam engine building pressure. "Everybody in this room played a part in the death of Michael Levy."

She took a few slow steps, letting her hands meet behind her back giving her the appearance of a schoolmaster pacing a detention period.

"But only one of you murdered him," she said.

"It was me," Drew said, and he forced himself in front of her. "You've charged me already. Just do what that man said and take me away."

"It's not as simple as that, Drew," she said, and Ben saw Peter Davis' hand reach down to grab Rosie's. "What is clear is that Michael Levy was a terrible individual. But did he deserve to die?"

"Yes," Peter said, with a glance at Rosie. "Yes, he bloody well did."

"And I suppose you wished it had been you who killed him?" Freya said, at which he gritted his teeth, forcing his square jaw into a look of total resolve.

"Yes," he said. "Yes, I wish it had been me."

Freya gave him a consoling look, then turned her attention to Anthony Barker.

"And you?" she said, to which he nodded.

"It *was* me," he said, unafraid of what that meant. "I went back. When everyone went home, it was me who went back."

"And you beat him some more, did you?"

He nodded slowly.

"Because Michael Levy drove your mother to her death?" she said. "Is that right?"

"If it wasn't for him, they'd still be together."

"Anthony..." Drew started, but Freya silenced him with a raised hand.

She walked up to Anthony and stopped two feet in front of him.

"Tell me what happened," she said.

He sneered, looking down at her with clear distaste, but his reasoning faltered and he tore his eyes away.

"I don't know the details," he said. "All I know is what Dad told me. That Michael Levy was to blame and that she'd still be alive if it wasn't for him."

"He's right. He doesn't know the truth," Drew said. "Nobody knows now but Alexandra and me."

"Go on," Freya said. "I think now would be a good time to let that little secret fly, don't you?"

He spoke to Freya but stared at his boy.

"It was when they were babies, Anthony and Rosie, that is. Everyone knew that Alexandra had been assaulted and Rosie was the result of a terrible rape," he said and looked at the young girl with deep sorrow in his eyes. "I'm sorry, sweetheart."

"It's okay," she said softly.

"He took care of them at first. Michael. He cared for them both, despite Rosie not being his child. But the love didn't last long. Anthony's mother and I were close, see? We were happy. But when Michael learned about me spending time with Alexandra, he grew jealous. I told him nothing was going on, but he didn't believe me. He threatened to tell my wife multiple times, but I never thought he would actually do it. Obviously, we argued as a result of it, and although we'd done nothing to be ashamed of, I just couldn't convince her that I wasn't cheating."

"She took her own life?" Freya said. "She felt betrayed?"

"You have to understand. Susan and I had been together since we were at school. We were childhood sweethearts. We didn't have secrets," he said.

"Which was?" Freya asked.

He took a deep breath and stared at Rosie.

"The first time I met Alexandra Sinclair, she was hanging from a rope in the nature reserve," he said. "Rosie and Anthony weren't even a year old, and everything she had been through had gotten to her. I cut her down in time to save her. I remember holding her, wishing I could take away her pain. Wishing there was something I could do for her. Wishing that I could find the man who had raped her and make him pay."

"And you didn't tell your wife?" Freya said. "Why?"

"Because it was my secret. Our secret. And it felt good. It was the first time in my life I felt like I had something of my own, something I didn't have to share. Something good. I didn't know how badly Susan had taken it. If I had, I would have just told her."

"Why didn't you?" Anthony said, and for the first time, Ben saw real emotion in his eyes. "Why didn't you just explain?"

"I would have," Drew said. "But I didn't get the chance. I went to confront Michael about it. I went to tell him to lay off. He told me that he'd shown Susan photos of Alexandra and me out walking together."

"He took photos?" Freya said.

"It's what we did. We walked. I became her mentor or sponsor, or whatever you want to call it, and she gave me a real sense of purpose."

"But Mum would have understood. She would have loved that, surely?" Anthony said.

"I know. I know she would have. She had a lovely heart, your mum did. But when I got home, I found you crying in your Moses basket," he said. "And I found your mum hanging from the rafters. I was too late. I couldn't save her. I'm so sorry, son—"

"It's okay, Dad," Anthony said. "Please. It's okay. You did what you could."

"We weren't lovers, you see. Alexandra and I. We weren't lovers," he said, and he looked straight at Freya. "We were friends. Nothing more. I promise you."

"Nothing more?" Freya said, to which he nodded.

"Kindred souls," he said softly. "That's all we were. Kindred souls."

CHAPTER FIFTY-FOUR

"Well, if that isn't a solid motivation, I don't know what is," Standing grumbled, and he nodded at the uniformed officer who clung to Drew Barker's arm. "Load him up. I want him on remand in His Majesty's Prison Lincoln before nightfall."

"Not so fast," a new voice said, one which Freya had been the only one to expect. The uniformed officer stopped in his tracks, looking for some kind of guidance from Standing and Freya.

"Afternoon, sir," Freya said. "Thank you for coming down."

"Never mind the gratitude, Inspector Bloom," Granger replied. "But I would rather appreciate being given a reason for being detained here."

"All will become clear, sir. In fact, the objective is to ensure that none of us are detained," she said. "Except for those we have reason to,"

"Very well," Granger said, and he stepped further into the room, coming to a stop beside Priest, behind the custody desk, where space was at less of a premium. He leaned on the desk, his spade-like hands gripping the wood, and raised his eyebrows in anticipation. "Although, you understand this is highly irregular."

"Agreed. However, given the circumstances, I felt no alternative but to use this forum to uncover the truth," she said, turning to Standing. "And after all, my job is to uncover the truth, within the remits of the law and with the resources provided to me."

An intrigued expression formed on Standing's face. He opened his mouth to speak but then seemed amused to hear what she had to say.

"I'm afraid, however, that I am unable to provide the narrative of the events that led us here, based on the evidence my team has gathered, without causing upset to some of you," she said. Then Freya took a deep breath and paced slowly to the end of the room, from where she could address her informal audience. "When Alexandra Sinclair left for work last Friday, her long-term partner, Michael Levy, took the opportunity to force himself on her daughter, Rosie, an act which forms a motive for each and every one of you, and more. Add to that the death of Susan Barker and I'm sure you'll agree that Michael Levy was not a well-liked man."

"And then there's his unorthodox business practices," Standing said, referring to the demise of Drew Barker's earnings over the past few months.

"Motives are clearly in abundance," Freya agreed. "Which leads us to opportunity. Drew, you've clearly explained your movements. You received a distress call from Alexandra whilst you were at the Petwood Hotel. CCTV shows you leaving at nine p.m. and returning two hours later. The cash register at the social club shows Alexandra's last transaction being at nine-thirty p.m. when you arrived outside to collect her. Thanks to a witness statement, we now know you paid a visit to The White Horse where you asked after Michael Levy. You were told by Jerry Graham that Levy had just left and you, of course, would have known the route he would have taken."

"The route?" Standing said. "Oh come on, we've been through all this—"

"He left on foot," Freya explained, raising her voice. "Through the nature reserve. He took the same route every week, a fact, it seems, that everyone who knew him was aware of."

"Are we going to go through every detail of your investigation, Inspector Bloom?" Standing said. "If this takes much longer, we'll miss the last induction at the prison."

"I think I'd like to hear what she has to say, Chief Inspector Standing," Granger said. "I must say, I'm more than a little intrigued."

"Thank you," Freya said, then turned back to Drew. "From The White Horse, you drove to the social club, where you collected Alexandra and took her home to collect a few belongings in a bag. You may not have been lovers, but you were close enough that she would feel safe in your room. But it was while Alexandra was inside her house that the real drama took place. You knew Michael would be emerging from that nature reserve at any moment, and you knew you had just one chance to finally do something about it – about what he'd done to Rosie, and for what he'd done to your marriage and your wife, Susan."

Drew said nothing, but his expression offered little argument.

"So you plunged into the nature reserve, Drew, in the hope that you might encounter Levy stumbling home, whereby you might give him a piece of your mind and perhaps demonstrate what he'd done to your family," she said. "To show him just how you felt about him."

"S'right," Drew said, jutting his chin out with pride. "And showed him I did."

"Except you didn't," Freya said. "Instead of finding Levy stumbling home, you chanced upon something far worse. You witnessed an attack on Michael Levy by your son and his three friends, didn't you? They beat you to it, Drew."

The four youngsters all stared at Drew, who sucked in a deep breath through his nose, but again, said nothing.

"Dad?" Anthony said.

"They beat him to within an inch of his life, Drew," she said.

"I saw his body, and I can assure you, the attack was relentless, callous, and vicious beyond words. Had Michael Levy been discovered on the bridge, the story might have ended there. But he wasn't. You see, after the attack, when the children had all run home, Michael Levy lay on that bridge, bleeding from nearly every one of his orifices. He dragged himself across the bridge in an effort to get himself home, I would imagine. You stayed a while, didn't you, Drew? You watched the children leave, and then you gave him your two pennies worth. A single punch. That's all it was, but it was something you'd been dreaming of doing for years. How did it feel?"

Only his resolve held his mouth closed, but he nodded slightly, conveying the release of that blow he had delivered, leaving a trace of his DNA on Michael's tooth.

"I can imagine how good it felt," she said. "In fact, I can picture the scene. Was Michael moving when you left him, Drew?"

Slowly, he shook his head.

"No. No, he was gone," he said, sadly. "He was still. Dead still."

She let those words permeate for a moment.

"Again, the story doesn't end there, does it?" Freya said, and this time, she turned her attention to his son. "You waited for your friends to get home, and then went back yourself, didn't you, Anthony?"

"That's what I've been telling you all. It was me. I did it. You can let him go," he said to the officer holding his father. "You can let them all go. I'm the one you want."

"Well, it's not as easy as that, Anthony," Freya told him. "Because when your father and Alexandra got back to their hotel, he explained what had happened. He explained that Michael wouldn't hurt them anymore. Naturally, he would have kept quiet about seeing the four of you there, and naturally, Alexandra would have felt mixed emotions. That's what happens, you see? Murder isn't like what you see in the movies. Real people experience guilt and fear. They don't sleep well, wondering how on earth they're going to get away with it. That's what your father did, Anthony. Along with Alexandra, he plotted to hide the body inside Jerry Graham's car, Jerry Graham being the root cause of his financial concerns. *Et voilà*," she said. "Jerry Graham becomes a suspect, and when your father reports Levy missing on Monday morning, he presumes he will therefore be eliminated from the investigation."

"Have you finished, Bloom?" Standing said. "Seems to me that all of them should be charged and we're running out of time here."

"Hold on," Granger said. "I thought I read in a report about a soil sample on a spade?"

"Ah yes, sir," Freya said. "We initially thought that Drew dug the hole, but I believe we were wrong there. You four dug the hole, didn't you?"

"How do you know that?" Peter Davis asked, realising he'd just confirmed Freya's suspicions with his question.

"Because, until now, Drew Barker has demonstrated a certain maturity, Peter. I can assure you that burying a body in a shallow grave is not as common as the movies might have you believe, and that's because it rarely works as a means to dispose of a body," she said. "I suspect that the four of you also slept poorly that night and that when Rosie told you all Michael hadn't come home, you were out as soon as you could be. I suspect you found him dead, hid him beneath the bridge, and then set out to get some tools to dig the hole. Am I right, partially, at least?"

Peter looked at Anthony apologetically for stealing his glory, then back at Freya.

"That's the gist of it, yeah," he said. "He was on the bridge when we found him, so we got some tools from Tony's house—"

"Because you knew his father was away at a golf weekend?"

He nodded, and the last piece of the puzzle clicked into place.

"During which time, Drew, you and Alexandra revisited the

scene of the crime, discovered him beneath the bridge and dragged him to Jerry Graham's car. Am I right?"

Drew squeezed his eyes closed and gained control of his breathing. Then he nodded once.

"We thought he'd crawled off of the bridge," he said and then looked at his boy. "Sorry, son."

Freya let the room enjoy a few well-deserved moments of peace to allow her narrative time to settle.

"So, there we have it," she said. "Four youths attacked Michael Levy. Drew, you thought you killed him, but you hadn't."

"He's still guilty of conspiracy to murder," Standing added, clearly unwilling to be proved wrong in front of an audience.

"Oh, I agree. Moving the body to incriminate Jerry Graham was a crime in itself, with a motive I hope a jury can empathise with."

"In fact, all of you will be charged," Freya said regretfully. "But none of you will be charged for the murder of Michael Levy."

The silence was short and sweet.

"You what?" Standing said, a sentiment mirrored by every face in the room. "One of them must have done it."

"No, I believe it was somebody else entirely," Freya said, then caught the attention of the uniformed officer at the door. "Run along to interview room two, will you? Fetch DS Gillespie and his witness."

"You're sailing close to the wind," Standing said.

"Agreed," Granger added. "Where are you going with this, Bloom?"

She smiled back at them both, hoping that her words conveyed confidence.

"Brace yourselves," she said softly. "We're heading into unchartered waters."

CHAPTER FIFTY-FIVE

Ben had watched Freya provide her account, and for the most part, he had agreed with the narrative. The seemingly complex snippets of information by themselves had appeared irrelevant and disconnected, but she had managed to sew them together to provide a united tapestry, highlighting those key moments and articulating the objective results with a poise that only she could sustain in the face of scrutiny.

The already cramped room took a breath as the door opened and Gillespie ushered a young girl in her twenties inside. Drew Barker was pulled back towards the corridor of cells, and Freya stepped over to the door to the car park, allowing others to move along.

"This is a bloody joke," Standing said. "This isn't how we do things."

"I agree with the latter," Freya said. "But I can assure you, I find no humour in the situation."

"Boss?" Gillespie said, presenting the witness with evident embarrassment.

"Ah, good," she said. "Thank you. And may I have your name, please?"

The barmaid looked at Gillespie, who coaxed her on with a nod.

"Amber," she said, which seemed to surprise even Gillespie. "Amber Pead."

"Amber will suffice for now," Freya said, adopting the tone of a prosecution lawyer interrogating a witness in the stand. "And could you please confirm what you do for a living?"

"I'm a student," she said, to which Freya seemed mildly amused.

"And in your spare time?" she said. "Do you work?"

"You know I do. At The White Horse," she said. "But only to pay my way. I'll be going legit as soon as I qualify."

"We're not here to investigate fraudulent benefit claims, Miss Pead," Freya told her. "Can you confirm where you were last Friday night?"

"Friday?"

"Is this necessary?" Standing said. "We've got five people to charge here."

"Six, actually," Freya said, and she glanced at Granger. "Bear with me, sir."

He nodded, although he appeared to be growing tired of the charade.

Freya gestured for Amber to answer her question.

"The White Horse. You know I was."

"The White Horse pub in Horncastle?"

"Aye, yeah," she said, jabbing a thumb at Gillespie. "I've told him already."

"Yes, I've spoken to my colleague. He tells me you witnessed a man coming into the pub asking after Michael Levy shortly after he had been arguing with Jerry Graham. Is that right?"

She nodded.

"Yeah, yeah, I did."

"This was around nine-fifteen in the evening?" Freya said.

"Yeah, it was, yeah."

"Is that man in this room, Amber?" Freya asked, as she folded her arms in front of her and began to pace in the little space that was left.

Amber pointed directly at Drew Barker.

"Him," she said. "It was him."

"And he left almost immediately, did he?" Freya asked, to which the girl nodded.

"Aye, he did, yeah."

"Thank you," Freya said.

"Is that it?" Standing said. "Right, I've had enough of this. Sergeant Priest, can we proceed with charging this lot–"

"That is far from all," Freya said, the pitch of her voice finding a void in the hum that ensued. She turned to Amber. "Is it, Amber? Because you said another man came in shortly after Drew Barker, didn't you?"

She nodded, although this time a little more fearfully.

"And did this man ask after Michael Levy?"

She nodded but said nothing.

Freya found a spot in the room from where the girl could see her in full, and she made sure she held her attention.

"Amber, is that second man in this room?"

The four youngsters all appeared bemused, as did Ben and Gillespie. All eyes turned to Amber Pead as she lifted her face from the floor, raised her hand, and pointed at Standing.

"Him," she said. "It was him."

"What?" Standing said, with a scoff. "Me? You must be mistaken, young lady–"

"But you were prepared to take her word that she saw Drew Barker asking after Levy," Freya said. "In fact, you wanted to charge him on the back of that fact."

"We've got all we need to charge Barker," he said. "What on earth makes you think that I had anything to do with it?"

"Horncastle is your home town, is it not?" Freya said.

"Yes, it is, but–"

"And you drink in the social club there, do you not?"

"Inspector Bloom, you had better have something to back this up with," Granger said, pulling rank and silencing them all.

"She's got nothing, sir," Standing said. "It's just the word of a bloody barmaid. All she wants to do is get herself out of the spotlight."

"Not exactly," Freya said. "I rather enjoy the spotlight. That's where all the fun takes place."

"Bloom," Granger said in a warning tone.

She held a hand up defensively and then leaned back, reaching for the door to the car park. She pushed it open and waved at somebody.

Ben watched the way the entire room craned their necks to see who might enter next, and then admired Freya in her element. The fact that Granger was there told him she had directed the entire event, surreptitiously arranging for each player to be in the right place at the right time.

The fact that Granger was there also told Ben something else, and he prayed she knew what she was doing.

He was so engrossed in analysing the scene that when he saw the long-legged, blonde crime scene investigator enter the room and stand beside Freya, he almost gasped out loud.

"For those of you who do not know Doctor Fell, she is Lincolnshire's leading forensic investigator," Freya said, then turned to a wide-eyed Michaela. "This isn't how we normally do things, but you'll understand why it had to be this way when we're done."

"I suggest we remove those we are charging and hold them in cells," Standing said. "We are at risk of unethical practices which may harm our case with the CPS."

"I disagree," Freya said. "In fact, everyone in this room deserves to be here. They deserve to hear the truth. You see, one thing that seems to have been forgotten is the cause of Michael Levy's death." She looked at Drew and Anthony Barker in turn.

"Regardless of how much you want to be held responsible, I'm afraid I can find no evidence to suggest that either of you actually killed him."

"Freya," Standing said, warning her off.

"You see, Michael Levy died from asphyxiation. Somebody strangled him. They closed off his windpipe, starving his brain and heart of oxygen. Sure, he had some internal injuries, but on closer examination of the pathology report, there was nothing to suggest they were the cause of death."

"So?" Granger said.

"So, that means we're looking for a new suspect, sir. Somebody with a motive much like the others, and with the means and opportunity," she said, and then turned finally to Standing. "May I ask where you were last Friday, guv?"

"No, you may not."

"Well, then may *I* ask?" Granger said and Standing sighed heavily.

"I was in my local."

"Which is?" Freya said, coaxing him on by rolling her hand over and over like a royal wave.

"The Sports and Social Club," he said, at which the room seemed to gasp inwardly.

"The Sports and Social Club where you have been a regular for how long?" Freya asked.

He stared at her with a hatred like no other. But she brushed it off with ease and waited with eyebrows raised.

"Since I was in uniform," he said. "More than twenty years, I've drunk there."

"More than twenty years," Freya repeated. "That's a long time. Time to see people come and go. Regulars, punters, staff even, I imagine."

"Where are you going with this?" Standing said, laughing her comments off.

"You must be familiar with the staff by now," she said. "Do

they know what you do for a living? Do they know who you really are?"

"You're in dangerous waters, Bloom," he said.

"Answer the question, Chief Inspector," Granger said.

Standing was ruffled, and Freya was basking in the moment. She almost glowed with excitement yet remained composed and professional.

"I don't need this," he said. "I've got better things to do."

He shoved his way through the crowded room to the corridor that led out to the interview rooms and the fire escape.

"I do have one more question," Freya said, and Standing stopped beside Ben, closed his eyes, and sucked in a long, deep breath. "Can you tell me why you killed Michael Levy?"

He turned slowly and his deathly stare cut through the room.

"How dare you—"

"You were drinking in the social club on Friday night. You saw Alexandra was upset and then overheard her on the phone to Drew, telling him what had happened," Freya said, turning to Drew. "When Alexandra called you, did she sound like she was inside or outside? My guess is that she stepped outside to make the call."

Drew nodded, recalling a detail he hadn't given any thought until now.

"She was outside. I couldn't hear the noisy bar."

"That's what I thought," she replied, turning her attention back to Standing. "It's not difficult to imagine you stepping outside to listen in on her conversation, is it?"

"Who the hell do you think you are—."

"You took matters into your own hands, didn't you? You heard what happened to Rosie and you saw red. Let's face it, you're hardly emotionally intelligent."

"Bloom," Granger said with a warning tone."

Freya acknowledged the warning without breaking her focus on Standing.

"The fact is that you directed me to charge Drew Barker with the murder, knowing that he'd been in The White Horse moments before you."

"You'd better have some damn good evidence to challenge me, Bloom," he growled.

"I do," she replied, and Ben heard a happy chirp in her voice. "Well, *I* don't, but Doctor Fell does."

Michaela became the centre of attention, but she handled it well, and when Freya waved her way, handing the room over, she cleared her throat then made her way to the custody desk to lay out her findings.

"I have here," she began, "the results of the DNA found on Michael Levy's body."

Standing scoffed, a stab of bitter laughter, and glared at Freya.

"And I suppose you're going to claim to have found my DNA on his body, are you?" he said.

"Not yours," Michaela replied. "But there were quite a few, of which we could only make a direct match with Drew Barker's and Anthony Barker's, due to previous offences."

"So?" Standing said.

"So, Inspector Bloom asked me to investigate the remaining samples," Michaela said. "It was a process of elimination. We found nothing on the police database, but of course, why would we? The remaining suspects hadn't provided a DNA sample."

"And that's just it," Freya said, cutting in, which Michaela allowed with grace. "The remaining suspects had provided no previous sample. But you had, Chief Inspector Standing."

"Sorry, what?"

"One of the remaining DNA samples found on Michael Levy's body was a partial match to your own DNA," Michaela said, and she turned the file around to present the results to Granger, who donned his glasses and peered down at them with interest.

"A partial match?" Granger said. "Sorry, I don't follow."

"It means, sir," Freya said, "that Chief Inspector Standing is the parent or sibling of one of the remaining suspects. I hope you don't mind but we had to go through the archives to find a record of his DNA."

Standing was struck dumb. His chest swelled and his nostrils flared, and he turned to Granger.

"Sir, this is obviously some kind of mix-up. Why would I-?"

"Not only that," Freya said, stepping forward and placing Chapman's printed research on the desk beside the DNA results. "This is Alexandra Sinclair's bank statement for the past few months. It's a savings account, so there are no other transactions. The highlighted payments of five hundred pounds each month are paid in with cash."

"So?" Granger said, sliding the statements over to peruse them. "What does that prove?"

"We found a stack of envelopes in Alexandra's house," Freya said, reaching into her pocket. She withdrew a clear evidence bag containing a single envelope. Then she turned to Standing. "I think you'll agree this is your handwriting, guv."

"It could be anyone's," he replied.

"True, but by the time Doctor Fell here has examined it for fingerprints, we'll know," Freya said, destroying the last remnants of his confidence. "And if we need any more proof, I'm sure we can match the envelopes with those found in every office in this building. But don't worry, I won't be seeking a misuse of police resources charge."

Standing said nothing. He eyed the envelope, glared at Freya, then briefly looked towards Rosie.

"I'm sorry," a little voice from the back of the room said, "but you're talking about my mum without her being here. I don't understand what's going on. What does all this mean?"

It was hard not to feel pity for the young girl, and even harder to imagine a bright future for her. But Freya typically found a way to connect to people, even those she had upset. It was a trait Ben had always admired in her.

"Do you want to tell her, or should I, Detective Chief Inspector Standing?" she asked, to which any resolve he had, crumbled.

Freya stepped away from the custody desk and placed her hand on the young girl's shoulder.

"It means, Rosie," she began, "that Chief Inspector Standing has been paying for your mother's silence."

It took a few moments for the explanation to sink in. The girl stared at Standing and a grimace of absolute hatred formed on her lips.

"But why?" she said. "Why would he give Mum money? And why didn't she tell me about it?"

"He gave her money because he felt responsible for you," Freya said. "I'm sorry to be the one to tell you this, but you are looking at a selfish and callous man who will do anything to get his own way."

"Let's keep this objective, Bloom if you will," Granger said, which Freya acknowledged with a curt nod before turning back to Rosie.

"It seems you were the one thing he truly cared about, even if it was from a distance. That's why your mother dropped the sexual assault charges all those years ago."

"I don't understand," she said. "What are you saying?"

"I'm sorry, Rosie," Freya said. "Not only did the man before you murder Michael Levy, but he also raped your mother," Freya said. "He's your biological father."

She stood motionless, staring at him with what Ben could only describe as disgust. He stared back, of course, as any father would have, feeling for his daughter as only a father can; with a combination of pride and overwhelming guilt.

Freya brought the episode to a climax by stepping up to Standing and coming to a stop before him.

"You planned all this, didn't you?" he hissed. "You could have done this in private."

"What? And miss out on my last opportunity to watch you suffer?" Freya replied, then raised her voice for the entire room to hear. "It is true that Drew Barker witnessed the four youths attacking Michael Levy. It is also true that when the attack was over, Drew took the opportunity to vent some frustration. But what we didn't know was that Detective Chief Inspector Standing witnessed Drew's attack. All you had to do was wait for him to leave and finish Levy off, didn't you? Then when Drew came in to report Levy missing, all you had to do was push us his way."

"Is that all you have?" Standing said, and he peered around the room as if he expected the other officers to provide him some kind of support. But nobody did. If anything, they backed away from him in disgust.

"Detective Chief Inspector Stephen Standing, I am arresting you on suspicion of murder and sexual assault. You do not have to say anything, but it may harm your defence if you do not mention when questioned something which you later rely on in court. Anything you do say may be given in evidence."

She looked up at Granger, who nodded his approval, and then back at Standing, who was being cuffed by a slightly stunned PCSO.

"Do you have anything to say?" Freya asked him, to which he refused to reply. Instead, he chose to speak to Rosie, who was being comforted by Peter Davis.

"I watched you grow," he said. "I watched you. I cared—"

"You disgust me," she spat, and she lunged at him, forcing Peter Davis to hold her back.

"Please," he begged. "Don't hate me for this—"

"You've hurt her enough," Freya said, then gestured for the uniformed officers to hand Standing to Ben. "Charge him and take him away. I want him on remand by nightfall."

CHAPTER FIFTY-SIX

"You should have seen her," Gillespie was saying. "He was shaking like a wet Labrador. The look on his bloody face was priceless."

Freya's hand was on the door, but she waited a moment more, listening in to what they had to say.

"So he's gone?" Nillson said. "No wonder he wanted us to drop the investigation."

"Aye, Ben marched him out to the transporter. I expect he was glad to get out alive."

"I wish I could have seen it," Chapman said softly.

"I don't doubt the boss would have got you all down there, but there was barely room as it was," Gillespie said. "What with the four kids, Barker, Standing, Granger, Priest, Ben, the boss, and me."

"Not to mention your new girlfriend," Cruz added.

"Hey, less of that. She's not my girlfriend. I had a wee chat with her before she made a statement. I don't want anything more said on the subject."

"What's going to happen now?" Gold asked. "I mean, with Standing gone, what happens to the team?"

"Well, you're leaving anyway," Gillespie said. "You too, Chapman. So what do you care?"

"Now you mention it," Chapman said. "I've withdrawn my transfer papers."

"You're staying?" Nillson said, audibly elated, and Freya bit down on her lower lip, thankful for the decision.

"Me too," Gold said. "To be honest, I haven't slept for days thinking about the move."

"You're staying, too?" Gillespie said. "Bloody hell, Jackie. I thought you were all set?"

"I was. I mean, it sounded like a good idea on paper–"

"But you couldn't bear to be away from us, could you?" he said, teasing her.

"Well, no, to be honest. I was dreading spending another five years with you, Jim," she said, which raised a few laughs.

"Ha-bloody-ha," he said. "Well, I've got news for you–"

"He's not going either," Cruz said.

"Hey?"

"You're staying?" Gold said. "How come?"

"Ah, well, it wasn't really my thing, you know? The commute would have been longer, for a start, and well, what the bloody hell would you lot do without me?"

"Enjoy myself," Cruz muttered.

"So we're all staying and Standing is going?" Gold said.

"Not only that but there's no chance of him coming back," Gillespie said. "I think this deserves a wee drink down the Red Lion tonight to celebrate."

"Did somebody say drink?" Freya said as she burst through the doors.

"Here she is. The girl of the moment," Gillespie said, clapping a few times, until he realised nobody else was joining in.

"Call me a girl one more time, Gillespie, and you'll be going house to house for the rest of your career," she said, slinging her bag onto her desk. "Right then, how are we doing for those reports? I want to get this over to CPS. Plus we can expect some kind of internal investigation on the back of what has happened. I presume Gillespie has broadcast the news to all and sundry?"

"Bloody brilliant, boss," Nillson said. "How on earth did you pull that off?"

She opened her mouth to speak, but couldn't find the right words.

"I'm not sure, if I'm honest," she replied. "Standing wasn't even a contender until Gillespie mentioned he drank in the same club. I had Chapman contact the manager this afternoon to clear a few loose ends up, and it seems that Standing drinks there every Friday night. Has done for years. It made sense that he was around when Alexandra was attacked, so you'd think he would have mentioned it. With men like him, it's all about control. He wanted us to work on the missing person investigation so he could control it. What he didn't expect, however, was for us to be so thorough. He didn't expect us to find anything, and if we did, he could steer the investigation in the direction he wanted."

"Away from him?" Nillson said.

"Precisely," Freya said. "Now, had we been fans of his, perhaps we'd have simply done as he asked."

"We've been working for a bloody rapist, boss," Gold said. "God, I feel sick."

"That's the bit I don't get. Jim mentioned some money," Anderson said. "Why was she taking money off him?"

"She wasn't," Freya said. "He was giving it to her, but she had no idea where it was coming from. At least, that's what I like to think. It's not much of a consolation, but at least Rosie has a little nest egg waiting for her. She's going to need all the help she can get."

"Speaking of which, how did she take the news?" Gold asked.

"She didn't," Freya replied. "She's in interview room two waiting for you."

"You haven't told her?"

"I'm pretty sure she suspects something, but no, that was certainly not the time to deliver such news. She needs to hear it from somebody a little more empathetic."

"Like me?" Gold said.

"If I had to hear the news," Freya said, "I'd want to be you who tells me."

"What about the others?" Nillson said as Gold pushed herself out of her chair. "What are we doing with them?"

"I thought you two could handle them," Freya replied, indicating her and Anderson. "We'll need to formally charge them, of course. But I see no reason why they can't be released on bail."

"So there is a heart in there," a voice said from the doorway. It was Granger, and he stepped into the room like an imposter. "I hope you don't mind?"

"Of course, sir," Freya said, and she perched on the edge of her desk.

"You might want to hear this," he said to the three women Freya had just issued instructions to, and one by one they returned to their seats. "I thought that, given the circumstances, we'll be needing to make some changes to the team. It hasn't been the best day, if I'm honest, but life goes on, and no doubt tomorrow we'll be moved onto a new investigation, and, well, I thought we all could do with a bit of a lift before we leave tonight."

"Never a dull moment, sir," Freya said.

"Quite right," he replied. "But we can't sail in the right direction without somebody at the helm, can we?"

"Sail?" Cruz said. "Are we going on a sailing boat?"

Gillespie spun in his seat and eyed the young constable.

"What do you think?" he said.

"Well, I don't know, do I?"

"Nobody is going sailing, Cruz," Granger said. "But I hope you'll all agree with me that if anybody is to steer the ship, then it should be you, Freya."

"What are you saying, sir?" she said. It was happening. The moment she'd been so close to so many times was actually happening. But unlike the other times, her palms remained dry and her heartbeat plodded on as if she was listening to the radio.

"Well, it's not formal yet, but I'd like to congratulate you, Acting DCI Bloom."

"Acting?" she said.

"I doubt I'll have much trouble getting the chief constable on board," he replied with a wink. "You deserve it. Well done."

"Hey, I was just saying we should go for a wee drink," Gillespie said. "Now we really should."

"Have you learned nothing?" Cruz asked him. "Look what happened the last time you had a drink."

"And what was that?" Granger said. "Or shouldn't I ask?"

Gillespie eyed Cruz from the corner of his eye, and Cruz nervously rubbed at his mop of tangled hair.

"Gillespie managed to get himself a little squiffy," Freya said, saving the big Scotsman from embarrassment and earning a favour in return. "We're trying to keep him on the straight and narrow."

"Probably for the best," Granger said. "No drinks then."

"Aye, sir," Gillespie agreed. "No drinks for me."

"Where's Ben?" Granger asked. "I thought he'd be here."

She hadn't noticed it before, but Ben was nowhere to be seen. His bag and laptop weren't even on his desk.

"I can call him?" Chapman said.

"No," he replied. "No, leave him be. I'm sure once he learns of your good news, he'll know what he has coming."

"You're making him detective inspector?" Freya asked.

"Acting," Granger said. "Same rules apply. DCI Bloom, perhaps you could be the one to let him know?"

"I'd be happy to," she said. "I'm sure he'll be delighted."

"But not over a drink, alright?" Granger said with a smile. He reached for the door but stopped and turned to appraise them all.

"Bloody good job, you lot. If I could promote you all, I wouldn't think twice."

CHAPTER FIFTY-SEVEN

With his hands on the transporter's rear doors, Ben hesitated, taking a moment to remember the scene in detail. Standing was cuffed to the security point in front of the narrow, caged seat. But the dishonoured man refused to look at him. He stared dead ahead, likely imagining his bleak future.

The driver started the engine and his accompanying guard climbed into the side door, where a seat offered a little more comfort, but not much.

"Nothing to say, Ben?" Standing said, without looking at him.

Ben thought about all the things he could say. He wondered what the individual members of the team would want to say. But words wouldn't do any of them justice.

Eventually, Standing turned his head and stared Ben in the eye, perhaps in a last-ditch attempt to win some kind of favour or sympathy.

"We're just disappointed, Steve," Ben said, with a shake of his head. "You've let the team down, the station down, and you've let the entire police force down, not to mention the lives you've ruined. But you already know that, don't you?"

Standing said nothing, but surprisingly, he continued to stare at him showing no sign of remorse.

"I imagine you'll have plenty of time to think about all those people over the next couple of decades," Ben said, and Standing opened his mouth to reply, but Ben slammed the doors, and then slammed his hand on the van's bodywork three times. The driver needed no persuasion, accelerating from the car park almost immediately.

Ben watched as the transporter came to a stop at the exit, the driver waiting for a space in the afternoon traffic. And then it was gone, taking Standing and a number of miserable episodes with it.

"I thought you'd be celebrating," somebody said. The sound tore him from his thoughts, and he blinked a few times to clear his vision, finding Michaela leaning on her car in the car park.

"Michaela," he said, giving his mind a moment to transition from one drama in his life to another. He strode over to her, then slowed, doubting himself. "You were great. In there, I mean. You did well."

"It isn't me who deserves recognition," she said. "All I did was read the data. Had Freya not pointed me at Standing, then he'd still be in there now."

"But it was you who found his DNA. Don't you see? It must have been in one of the reports you got from the archive. Don't you get it, Michaela? None of this could have happened without you."

"Well," she said, "when you put it like that. But don't go getting any ideas about making that public knowledge. I'm in enough trouble as it is."

"Your boss?" Ben said, to which she nodded.

"It's nothing I can't handle, but I'd prefer it if he didn't find out about my little visit to the archive all the same," she said. "I'm happy for Freya to take my portion of the credit, however slim that may be."

Ben's hands found his pockets and his eyes feasted on those

defining features of hers – her immaculate skin, soft, blonde hair, and gentle, vulnerable eyes that belied her outward confidence.

"She likes you, you know?" he said. "You were wrong about me and her having something."

"Still singing the same old song, Ben?"

"It's not a song. It's the truth," he told her.

"Yeah, well, I'm afraid whatever it is the pair of you have, I can't be the third wheel."

"You're not a third–"

"Don't make this hard, Ben," she said. "I could have driven off without waiting."

"So why stay? Why wait to speak to me?" he said. "Surely there's a part of you that knows we were good together? Surely you can see that?"

She leaned back on her car, fishing her keys from her bag, and with a click of the fob, the locks sprang open.

"Michaela, don't do this."

"You're right," she said, as she opened her car door. She glanced up at the building, a distraction from her thoughts. "Do you remember what you told me?"

"About what?"

"About what that man said. The man she arrested."

"What he said about Freya's uncle? Oh, come on," he said. "He was a psychopath, a nut job. He's most likely sitting in an empty room in Broadmoor as we speak."

She leaned into the car, reached for something on her passenger seat, and then emerged holding a blue, cardboard folder. She held it for a moment, glancing up at the building once more. But then, with what Ben could only describe as desperate reluctance, she handed it to him.

"What's this?" he said, opening the file. "Is this Freya's uncle's case file?"

"Don't read it now," she said. "Not here."

"How did you get it?" he said. "Are you saying he was murdered?"

She hesitated, then relented. "Let's just agree that you'll not make my visits to the archive public knowledge," she said.

She lingered for a moment, staring into his eyes one last time, and then climbed into the driver's seat and fired up the engine.

"Goodbye, Ben," she said. "It was fun while it lasted. I'll give you that much."

"It's hardly goodbye, Michaela," he said. "I'll see you on another crime scene, no doubt."

"No," she said, reaching for her door handle. "No, I've put in for a move. I'll be covering the Wolds."

"Not because of us, surely?"

"No," she replied. "Not entirely, anyway."

She closed the door and reversed out of the parking spot, pausing as she found first gear, and offering Ben one last view of her.

And then she was gone.

He watched as she turned out of the car park, closing a chapter in his life that could have, and should have, gone an entirely different way. But then, as he turned to head back to the entrance, he felt something – like he was being watched. He stopped and looked up, finding Freya staring back at him from the incident room window, her expression unreadable.

He nodded a silent greeting, to which she did nothing except smile briefly.

Standing alone in the car park, Ben took a moment to read something in her stare, in that curt nod of hers. But he found only ambiguity and mystery, such was Freya's way.

He found himself opening the file Michaela had given him and read the headings on the first page.

Surrey Police. Murder: Thomas Harold Archibald Bloom.

It wasn't the name of the victim that held Ben's attention. Nor was it the location, which was a county Ben had never even visited.

In dull, red ink, the word *unsolved* had been stamped across the front page, before being sent to the archives.

He closed the file almost immediately and let it fall to his side before looking back up to the window from which Freya had been staring down at him.

But she was gone. His eyes were drawn to the big, blue summer sky above, where clouds formed, joined, and moved on, while others roamed the sky alone for the rest of time.

Somewhere, from deep inside the station, a scream rang out. It wasn't a scream of pain or fright; it was a scream of anguish, suffering, and loss, and he knew exactly who it belonged to.

He entered the station alone and found Priest staring at him.

"I remember when the doctor told me about old Mum passing," Priest said, glancing at the corridor door briefly. "There's no easy way to break the news, is there?"

"No," Ben said, not really in the mood to engage in a conversation.

"Still, looks like you all got your wishes," Priest said. "Standing's gone. There's no reason why you lot can't get back to how you were before, is there?"

Ben could have said something then, but he didn't. Instead, he paused for thought then smiled at the big, old custody sergeant affectionately.

"Somehow, Sergeant Priest," Ben said, smiling to himself, "somehow, I very much doubt that."

The End

Click here to download Her Dying Mind, Book eleven in The Wild Fens Murder Mystery series

HER DYING MIND - CHAPTER ONE

The creaky floorboard had been on the list of things to fix before the new carpet had been put down; the list she had written that Alex hadn't even looked at. Instead he had stuffed it into his gilet pocket. It was probably still there in the wardrobe. She remembered enough of the slip of paper to see that list in her mind's eye, and at the very top was the creaky floorboard that once more groaned above her head like the bones of an old man.

But Alex had been gone for months now; forty months to be precise, or to be even more accurate, one thousand, twelve hundred and sixteen days.

There hadn't been a conscious decision to count the days. It was just one of those things that happened. One of those things the mind does of its own accord.

One of those things Alice wished she could switch off.

One day she would think of him with an uncertainty as to the number of the days he'd been gone, and she supposed that would be the day she could call herself healed.

But not today. That number was well and truly marked. Tomorrow her mind would remember today's number, and the next would automatically come to mind. And so the cycle would continue.

Grief was irrepressible, much like the creaking floorboard above her; the creaking board that caused her heart to hammer inside her chest.

Frozen to the spot, she clung to the front door, unsure if she should run out into the lane. Perhaps George was awake, two doors away. He was an early riser. He had known Alex too and wouldn't judge her for being silly.

The floor above her creaked in response.

She wasn't being silly though, was she? Floorboards don't creak of their own accord. She opened her mouth to call out, but found her throat dry and the very idea of coughing to clear her throat absolutely terrified her.

But she couldn't very well wait there. What if whoever it was found her there? She'd heard about people like her who disturb intruders or burglars, people who would do anything not to work for a living and not be caught by the police. Not that the police would do anything.

She wished she carried her telephone with her. Alex used to tell her to keep it in her bag, and to keep it switched on in case he ever needed to call her. But of course that was one of those things she hadn't done simply because he had told her to do it. The joys of marriage and the foibles that make them unique, rememberable for a number of reasons; some good, others not so much.

A thump from above was loud and clear. Not a groan our a creak. Not the noise of that board at the end of her bed, the bed they had shared for more than four decades, gently taking the weight of a person. It had been a thump. She was sure.

Alex would have gone upstairs if he'd been around. He wouldn't have been frozen to the spot like a coward. That was half his problem. He never knew when to back down. Never knew when to just shut up and walk away.

She waited. The next time she heard the floorboard creak she would go up. Or maybe she would just call out. If somebody came down the stairs at her, she could get out through the front door.

Maybe it was time to get the floorboard fixed? Maybe there was nobody even up there? Maybe Alex was trying to send her a message from the other side. She'd never believed in all that, but others did. Others swore they had seen or heard or even felt a presence, and not just one or two. Mary from Kirby Road had told them all once, she remembered now. They had been at Leslie McMillan's wake, which Alex had found to be in poor in taste. But she had told them nonetheless, how she had been sitting on the edge of her bed pulling on her slippers where she had felt a cool breath of air wash over her, despite the heating being on. Alex had said she was talking rubbish, of course. Mary never had the heating on.

"This is ridiculous," she whispered to herself, finding moisture in her throat where only moments before there had been none. Had it been moments? How long had she been standing there?

She peered up the stairs, not knowing what she might see, but she peered nonetheless.

"Hello?" She said, her heard pounding in her chest. "Is anybody there?"

It was then that she felt the cool breath of air Mary had spoken of. It breezed down the stairs, seeming to caress the fine down on her nape, not hard like a gust of wind, but gentle like somebody had passed close by her.

But nobody had.

The temperature had dropped too, of that she was certain. So much so that goosebumps rose on her arm like the Wolds she had known her entire life, seen from high above. Suddenly Mary from Kirkby Road's whimsical anecdote came to light again, and she peered up the stairs once more.

"Alex? Alex, is that you, dear?"

No answer came, and that breath of air had gone, leaving the stuffy, summer heat to take its place.

"I'm coming up," she said, albeit far quieter than previously, and she took a single tentative step onto the first stair, gripping the bannister with her right hand, and clutching her blouse together with her left. Gone were the days when she could bound up the stairs, that joy was a distant memory, rarely could she even walk up them these days. Instead, she took them one at a time, as if each one was an individual challenge. There were thirteen individual challenges, and by the time she had accomplished seven of them, her heart was just pounding with fear and trepidation. It reminded her of that man on the television, the rugby player who ran seven marathons in seven days for his friend with motor-neurones. He was a kind soul; selfless and unique. Not many people could run like that, and even less would.

Once the eleventh of her challenges was complete, she could grip the bannister and lean around to see into the back bedroom. The door was ajar. It was never ajar. It was either open or closed, but never ajar. That had been one of Alex's bugbears; one of many, but one it was, and if she put her mind to it, she could recall the hundreds, no thousands of times she had been to spend a penny during the television advertisements, and had not closed the lounge door fully on her return.

"Door," he would say without looking away from the television or up from his crossword.

She stared at the door now, adamant that she hadn't left it like that. Closing doors had been ingrained into her.

"Alex, dear?" She said, and that rush of cold washed over her once more; stronger now. "Alex? Alex, are you there?"

Twelve and thirteen were accomplished in much the same manner in which she imagined that kind soul had; on her hands and knees, trembling now, not from the cold, but from sheer terror.

She was breathless, too. Not from the exertion, but something else. It was as if somebody was crushing her chest so hard that tiny little lights danced in her eyes.

The landing was small, enough space for the tall vase of dried pampas grass Henry had bought her for a mother's day many moons before. She crawled past it, thinking not of that day, but of the door. The door that should have been fully closed, and if not fully closed, then fully open.

Not ajar. She never left it ajar.

She stopped outside the door, her eyes closed, imagining that Alex was inside; or hoping, she couldn't tell which. That was one of the things they said would happen. The doctor had said so; the Asian chap. Alex hadn't liked him, but she had. He'd had a good bedside manner and he was thorough. Not like the English ones who couldn't be bothered to get out of bed in the mornings.

Doctor Samson. That had been his name.

He had said that her imagination would run wild, and he had been right. It *was* running wild. She could see Alex now, sitting on the edge of the bed pulling his socks on the way he used to. It was a far better image the other one; the one where a burglar saw her crawl into the room and went for her. Probably a druggie. They were all druggies weren't they? Alex had said so. He said they robbed people on their own, like her. They stole whatever they could get their hands on, then sold it to pay for drugs.

Well, they were welcome to it. She had no use for anything anymore.

"Is anybody there?" She said. "I'm going to open the door. You can have whatever it is you want."

Nobody replied.

She reached out for the door. How many times had Alex painted it. A dozen or so in the thirty years they had lived there?

"I'm coming in now," she said, and she took a deep breath.

If it is a burglar, and if he does go for her, then maybe it will be blessing. Maybe then she could be with Alex again?

Maybe that was it. Maybe that was what she had felt, that cool breath. Maybe that was Alex calling her upstairs so they could be together.

She gave the door a shove, expecting to see one of them. A man probably, wearing a tracksuit like the kids do these days. They wore suits back in her day, but these days they all seemed to walk about with their hands in their underpants.

The door hit something and then shuddered back to where it had been.

Ajar.

She stared at it, trying hard to remember what it could have been. But the room was tidy. She always left it tidy. Rarely a day passed that she even ventured downstairs with making the bed, washing and dressing, and leaving the upstairs in a presentable state, and since they'd had the downstairs loo there were days when she didn't go up at all except for bedtime.

She gave the door another shove, and again it bounced back.

"Is somebody there?" She said, this time finding the strength to climb to her feet, using the door handle for support.

Maybe she should call for help? Maybe George would be awake by now?

But if it was Alex calling for her, then he wouldn't want her to go back. She had come too far. She leaned on the wood, placing her face against the twelve layers of paint and listening for a sign. Gently she pushed the door until it met with resistance.

"Is that you, dear?" She said softly. But nobody replied.

Then she shoved hard, as hard as she could, as hard as her little frame allowed and until those varicose veins on her hands seemed too bulge with the effort.

The temperature dropped once more. It was colder now. Cold like she had opened the refrigerator.

Slowly, she turned to put her back against the door, not to go and fetch George, but to catch her breath. She slid down the door until she was sitting on the carpet, blinking away those tiny dancing lights and feeling the crush on her chest.

And that was where she stayed, hugging her knees to her chest like she was fifteen years old again. Fifteen years old, she thought. Alex had been twenty and they had courted for three long years as her father had been adamant that she should be eighteen before they wed.

It was a lifetime ago, yet she could still smell him, that undeniable scent of Imperial Leather soap from where he had spent the day working under the sun and scrubbed himself clean before calling on her, cap in hand.

Those were the days, she thought before speaking aloud for the last time.

"It is you isn't it?" She said quietly, not expecting a reply. She smiled to herself and let her head rest on the wood. "It is you. I know it is."

ALSO BY JACK CARTWRIGHT

Secrets In Blood

One For Sorrow

In Cold Blood

Suffer In Silence

Dying To Tell

Never To Return

Lie Beside Me

Dance With Death

In Dead Water

One Deadly Night

Her Dying Mind

Join my VIP reader group to be among the first to hear about new release dates, discounts, and get a free Wild Fens Novella.

Visit www.jackcartwrightbooks.com for details.

VIP READER CLUB

Your FREE ebook is waiting for you now.

Get your FREE copy of the prequel story to the Wild Fens Murder Mystery series, and learn how DI Freya Bloom came to give up everything she had, to start a new life in Lincolnshire.

Visit www.jackcartwrightbooks.com to join the VIP Reader Club.

I'll see you there.

Jack Cartwright

A NOTE FROM THE AUTHOR

Locations are as important to the story as the characters are; sometimes even more so. It's for this reason that I visit the settings and places used within my stories to see with open eyes, breath in the air, and to listen to the sounds.

I have heard it said that each page should feature at least one sensory description, which in the age of the internet anybody can glean from somebody else's photos, maps, or even blog posts.

But, I disagree.

I believe that by visiting locations in person, a writer can experience a true sense of place which should then colour the language used in the story in a far more natural manner than by simply providing a banal description which can often stall the pace of the story.

However, there are times when I am compelled to create a fictional place within a real environment. For example, in the story you have just read I refer to The White Horse in Horncastle, and any resident of the town will know that no such place exists (at the time of writing), at least.

The reason for this is so I can be sure not to cast any real location, setting, business, street, or feature in a negative light;

nobody wants to see their local pub described as a scene for a murder, or any business portrayed as anything but excellent.

If any names of bonafide locations appear in my books, I ensure they bask in a positive light because I truly believe that Lincolnshire has so much to offer and that these locations should be celebrated with vehemence.

I hope you agree.

Jack Cartwright.

AFTERWORD

Because reviews are critical to an author's career, if you have enjoyed this novel, you could do me a huge favour by leaving a review on Amazon.

Reviews allow other readers to find my books. Your help in leaving one would make a big difference to this author.

Thank you for taking the time to read *One Deadly Night*.

COPYRIGHT

Copyright © 2023 by Jack Cartwright

All rights reserved.

The moral right of Jack Cartwright to be identified as the author of this work has been asserted by him in accordance with the Copyright, Designs and Patents act 1988.

All the characters in this book are fictitious, and any resemblance to actual persons living or dead is purely coincidental.

All rights reserved. No part of this publication may be reproduced, stored in a retrieval system or transmitted in any form or by any means, without the prior permission in writing of the publisher, nor to be otherwise circulated in any form of binding or cover other than that in which it is published without a similar condition, including this condition, being imposed on the subsequent purchaser.

Printed in Great Britain
by Amazon